"You must go from here," Raven whispered harshly. "There is danger now that Na-Kee rules our warriors."

"I'll go," Tess answered, coming back to his arms to kiss the point of his chin. She knew what she wanted. Maybe she had known all along. "But not yet, Raven, *not tonight.*"

He twisted his fingers in her loose auburn hair. She knew he knew what she was offering, perhaps even before she had.

"Tess—"

She touched her finger to his lips. She didn't know why she wanted to make love with Raven before she left. She just knew that no other man would ever touch her heart as he had. She knew that no man's hands would ever excite her as Raven's did.

"It . . ." He kissed the top of her head. "It would be better if we did not . . ."

She looped her arms around his neck, forcing him to look her in the eyes. "I give you myself this night as a gift," she whispered. "A Lenape can never refuse a gift. It would be an insult, would it not?"

For the longest moment Raven just stared at her with those black eyes she had lost herself to the day she escaped from the Mohawk. "Do you know what you say to this man? What you offer?" he whispered, still giving her a chance to change her mind and save face.

"I ask will you love me?" Tess begged, threading her fingers through his midnight hair. "Just tonight, Raven? Will you?"

COLLEEN FAULKNER

CAPTIVE

ZEBRA BOOKS
KENSINGTON PUBLISHING CORP.

ZEBRA BOOKS are published by

Kensington Publishing Corp.
850 Third Avenue
New York, NY 10022

Zebra and the Z logo Reg. U.S. Pat. & TM Off.

First Printing: September, 1994

Printed in the United States of America

One

Three days, and I'm still alive . . .

Tess shifted her weight on her knees and lifted the heavy paddle, thrusting it into the river again. Droplets of icy water splashed up, wetting her and the savage seated in the bow of the birchbark canoe.

The Mohawk, Broken Tooth, turned around and barked at her in his guttural tongue, raising his palm in a threat to strike her. Tess lifted her chin a notch as if to dare him, and stared straight ahead, focusing beyond him on the very tip of the painted canoe.

Bastard . . . Three days ago this Mohawk with the decayed teeth, along with a dozen others, had attacked the hired carriage in which she and her cousin Jocelyn had been traveling. The beasts had killed the driver there on the road, but they had kidnapped Tess and Jocelyn.

Tess concentrated on paddling as the canoe sliced through the water. She knew that she had to walk a delicate line between standing up to Broken Tooth and making him so angry that he slit her throat and threw her overboard into the muddy river.

Tess didn't know why the red heathens had kidnapped

her and Jocelyn, or what they intended to do with them. She didn't even want to consider the possibilities. She'd heard those whispered tales about other white women who'd been captured by Indians. Some were made slaves to hostiles up north, while others were sold to the French Canadians for whores.

All Tess knew was that she had to be brave. She had to be brave and tough. She had to want to live badly enough to survive this. That was what she had tried to tell Jocelyn.

Tess blinked back the tears that made her eye ache. She'd tried to help cousin Jocelyn. She'd tried to tell her that if she would just do what they said, Uncle Albert would come for them. He would bring soldiers and rescue them from the savages. They just had to hang on until help arrived.

But Jocelyn wouldn't listen. She wouldn't keep up. The Indians were traveling fast and they expected the women to do the same. Tess had kept her mouth shut and done as she was told. She had pretended she wasn't afraid. Jocelyn had cried. She had begged. She had laid down in the forest and refused to get up, sobbing that she was tired and hungry. Tess had tried to drag her, she'd tried to carry her, but Jocelyn had refused to cooperate. She'd told Tess she'd rather be dead than be a captive of these murderers.

The memories of Jocelyn's tortured screams echoed in Tess's mind, and gooseflesh raised on the back of her neck. She would never forget those sounds . . . not as long as she lived.

The second day after their capture, around midday, Jocelyn had sat down on a log, arranged her tattered traveling gown, and refused to get up. Broken Tooth had ordered her to rise or die. Tess had pleaded with her, but then the

Mohawk had shoved Tess and told her to get back into line behind the other men. The Indians had continued walking, leaving Broken Tooth and Jocelyn behind. Tess had screamed for her cousin to get up and run to catch up; Jocelyn hadn't budged.

Tess had heard the first shrieks just after she and the other Mohawk had disappeared from Jocelyn's sight around a bend in the road. Tess had tried to turn back, but the men had caught her and wrestled her to the ground. They'd blackened her eye in the struggle and then tied her hands together to pull her on a tether.

It had seemed that Jocelyn's screams had gone on forever. But as frightening as those sounds had been, the silence afterward had been worse.

Tess felt her lower lip tremble. She tried to think about paddling the canoe and not about Jocelyn. It was too late to help her cousin now. Broken Tooth had a hank of blood-stained blonde hair on his belt to prove it.

Tess knew that at this point she couldn't help anyone but herself. She had to stop making herself crazy thinking about Jocelyn, and concentrate on escaping. These bastards had murdered cousin Jocelyn, but they wouldn't get her. Broken Tooth would carry no red-haired scalp on his belt. But Tess knew she had to figure out a way to escape soon. The further north they got, the weaker she would become, and the harder it would be for her to find her way home to her uncle's once she was free.

Tess shifted her weight from one knee to the other and back again. The little bit of water in the bottom of the canoe had wet her worsted-wool petticoat and stockings. She was wet and cold, and her feet ached with pins and needles. She glanced over her shoulder, her mind ticking.

There were three canoes paddling in a line, thirteen Mo-

hawk in all. She was in the last canoe along with Broken
Tooth and two others. She watched her paddle dip into
the cold river water and come up again. Her arms ached
from the exertion, but she was used to hard work. Any
chambermaid in her uncle's house was used to hard work.

Tess' thoughts raced. She was a good swimmer. Why
didn't she just jump and take her chances? The river was
wide here, but they were still paddling close to shore.
With a little luck, she could cause enough commotion div-
ing overboard that it would take the Mohawk a minute or
so to come after her. If she could reach the shore, she
could quickly disappear into forest. Unbound as she was
now, she could run.

Tess studied the back of Broken Tooth's head. His head
was shaved bald save for the long scalplock of black hair
that stuck up from the top of his head like a stiff cock's
comb. God in heaven, what she wouldn't give to hang his
filthy scalp on her own belt.

Tess went on paddling. If she did this, if she dove overboard, she'd only have one chance. She'd live or die by
this one chance at freedom.

She stared at the water ahead. The river was widening.
The canoes were veering off, paddling slowly toward the
center of the river. If she waited much longer, she might
not be able to make it to the shore before they caught up
to her in their canoes.

Tess gripped the paddle, taking a deep breath.

Raven and his brother, Takooko, crept along the bank
of the great Susquehanna River, following the band of
Mohawk as they paddled close to shore in their painted
birchbark canoes.

A white-skinned woman with hair of fire rode in the

last canoe. She sat on her knees, her back ramrod straight, her paddle cutting into the water with the same rhythm as the men in the canoe.

Raven and his brother had been watching the Mohawk since dawn. They had come upon their camp and followed them, wanting to be certain the marauders were headed north to their homes and not south to attack Raven and Takooko's Lenape village.

"They cut toward the center of the mighty river, brother," Takooko whispered. "They head home. They have tired of their killing, stealing, and kidnapping, and yearn for the comfort of their lodges. They will not come our way. We must turn back."

Raven crept past his brother, his gaze fixed on the red-haired white woman in the last canoe. This morning when he and Takooko had come upon the Mohawk he'd considered trying to rescue the woman from them. Obviously she was a captive. But there were a dozen Mohawk and only two of them. Raven knew it would be suicide to enter the camp of Mohawk raiders without more men. Takooko had said it was the woman's fate to be taken by the enemy. He argued that the two of them couldn't be responsible for every captive the Mohawk took. Raven understood his logic, but still he couldn't stop thinking about her. What right did these men have to take her from her life?

The Mohawk of the Seven Nations were enemies to the Lenape. His people considered them filthy, disgusting creatures without souls.

Raven watched the redhead paddle as he crept along the shoreline. She kept glancing around her as if coming to some decision. He turned to his brother. "I think she will jump, brother," he said in the Algonquian tongue of his ancestors.

Takooko chuckled. "A white woman? They have no spines. They allow themselves to be dragged off. I would kill myself before I would let a Mohawk take me."

Raven glanced over his shoulder at his brother. Takooko was a great warrior, but he was still young—only twenty summers. He didn't understand the sanctity of life, nor the finality of death.

Raven cocked the trigger of his most prized possession, an English Brown Bess musket. He heard his brother behind him pull an arrow from his quiver and notch it in his bow.

"We shouldn't be getting involved in this, brother," Takooko warned.

"We're not involved, but should she jump, there's no reason why we cannot give her aid." Raven grinned crookedly. "Tell me you wouldn't like to see one of your arrows buried to the hilt in one of those dogs."

"Our responsibility is to return home to our village with word from the Assembly of the Clans. For a man who vies for War Chief, you forget your responsibilities to your people too easily."

Raven shook his head, walking faster as they came to a slight bend in the river. "Takooko, my brother, you—" He stopped in mid-sentence.

Just as the canoes made the turn in the river, the white woman stood up.

"I told you," Raven whispered.

The birchbark canoe rocked wildly. The Mohawk with the bad teeth was just turning around when she swung the paddle with all her might and struck him in the back of the head.

The Mohawk shrieked in pain and grabbed his head. Even from the shore, Raven could see the stain of blood.

The other two Mohawk pulled up their paddles, but when they stood to reach for her, one fell out into the river, the other fell forward. The sound of splitting wood filled the air.

The red haired woman struck the Mohawk seated in the bow of the canoe a second time and then heaved the paddle skyward. She pulled something from the Mohawk's belt and dove into the muddy water.

She entered the river with barely a splash. The other two canoes were just maneuvering turns to paddle back toward the third canoe which was slowly sinking.

It seemed an eternity before the redhead broke the surface of the water, but when she did, she was a good twenty yards from the canoe. As she came up, gasping for air, a layer of women's clothing bubbled up and drifted away. The female had taken off her skirts to swim faster.

Chuckling to himself, Raven took in the scene. This woman needed no aid, she was doing fine on her own. The Mohawk who had been struck with the paddle was wildly shouting commands as his canoe sank lower in the water. The Mohawk in the river began to swim out after the woman. The Mohawk in the bow of the sinking boat was now signalling for one of the other canoes to come for him.

Raven couldn't resist a grin. The Mohawk was slowly gaining on the woman, but she was a swift swimmer. Raven lifted his musket to his shoulder and closed one eye, beading in on the Mohawk in pursuit. He would help her out. "A little closer, Mohawk dog," Raven murmured.

Without looking back at the man pursuing her, the redhead pulled herself through the water with hard, quick strokes.

The man was almost in reach of her. He put out one hand to grab her foot.

Raven touched the trigger and his musket belched smoke and fire. The sound of the gunshot caught the attention of the Mohawk in the canoes as the musketball struck the man in the water.

He sank like a stone.

Frightened by the musket fire the white woman dove under the water.

Raven began the process of reloading. A Mohawk from one of the other canoes had jumped into the water and begun to swim toward the woman, but when he heard the musket fire, he dove beneath the surface, closer to the canoes.

The man who'd been struck by the woman's paddle shouted another command and a shower of arrows flew through the air just as she dove. But the female was smart. She veered left, instead of swimming straight for the shore.

Takooko watched over his brother's shoulder. "The girl's got bullocks and brains," he murmured with a grin.

She had almost reached the shore now. Raven slung his musket over his shoulder and ran along the treeline, taking care not to let the Mohawk see him. Takooko ran behind.

Raven waited until she reached solid ground and scrambled up the bank. Only when she had disappeared from the Mohawk's sight into the forest, did Raven step out in front of her.

"White woman—" he called in accented English.

Tess screamed. Where in Christ's name had they come from? She whipped out the knife she had taken from Broken Tooth's belt, spraying the Indian with cold water. "Get back," she threatened, brandishing the skinning knife. The hostile took another step toward her and she slashed at him with the knife. His forearm immediately stained red.

Tess stumbled backward, turned and ran.

"Wait," cried the savage in English. "We mean you no harm."

Tess was panting heavily as she dove through the briars, panicked. The two men behind her weren't Mohawk, she knew that from their dress and long braided hair, but they were Indians weren't they? Murdering savages.

"Wait," the voice called. "My brother and I, we mean you no harm."

Tess could hear his footsteps behind her as she crashed through the brush. He was gaining on her. She didn't know how much further she could run. She'd not eaten in three days and she was weaker from the hard travel than she'd realized.

Suddenly the Indian had caught up to her. He grabbed her shoulder and swung her around. Tess sliced the knife through the air, but he blocked her arm, and she struck solid flesh, knocking the knife from her own hand.

"No," Tess moaned, beating him with her fists. She'd not let them take her again. Not while there was still fight left in her bones. "Let me go! Let me go!"

"It is all right," he soothed in a strange lilting voice. "It is all right. This man will not harm you, Fire Woman."

It didn't make any sense. The Indian was speaking English. He was saying he wouldn't hurt her, but he was still fighting her. Why didn't he let her go?

Both struck the ground and rolled. Dead leaves clung to her wet hair and sodden clothing. He pushed her over on her back, pinning her wrists to the ground. Tess struggled with the last bit of strength she could muster.

Their gazes met, her frightened brown eyes, his as black as the depths of hell.

"Stop this!" he said. "I tell you I won't hurt you."

"Then let me up!" Tess snapped.

His black-eyed gaze was mesmerizing. "Stop fighting me and I will," he said softly.

Two

Tess stared into the heathen's obsidian eyes, wondering if this was where she would die. After her miraculous escape from the Mohawk, would she now lose her life here in the middle of the wilderness? Would her family ever know what had become of her? Would Abby still stand by the door of their mother's cottage waiting for word from the sister who promised she would send for her?

Tess couldn't get over the intensity of the hooded black eyes that met and held her frightened gaze. He made a sound deep in his throat, a soothing sound, as if she was some frightened animal he was trying to calm.

Despite the weight of his body pressing against hers and the grip he held on her wrists, something told her he wasn't going to hurt her. She didn't know if it was the tone of his voice, or the expression on his face, but she sensed she needn't be afraid.

In a calculated leap of faith, she relaxed beneath him. He immediately let go of her wrists.

She watched him cautiously as he climbed off her and offered one bronze hand to help her to her feet. Ignoring his hand, she jumped up, pushing down the wet skirt of her shift, now clinging to her thigh. She was still panting from the exertion of the swim and the run through the forest. Her breasts heaved beneath the filmy wet cotton of her shift's bodice. "The . . . the shot from the shore. You . . . you shot the one swimming after me, didn't you?"

He nodded. He was staring at her with a strange look on his face. He wasn't smiling, yet he seemed like he was smiling inside. He nodded. *"Kohon."*

She eyed him, still a little unsure of her own judgment. It immediately struck her that the Indian was a handsome man in an exotic way. He was barely a breath taller than Tess with a finely chiseled frame and a strikingly angular face. His hair was a sheet of ebony, his skin the color of sun-kissed red soil. Dressed scantily in a leather breech-cloth that looked like an apron and a sleeveless vest ornamented with seashells, the hides did little to cover his muscular physique. He had the broadest, most well-defined bare shoulders she'd ever seen on a man.

"Why would you . . . why would you kill one of your own?" she questioned. "They . . . they'll track you down. They'll skin you." She took a deep breath, adding softly, "I saw them do it."

The Indian's eyes narrowed, silently giving witness to his lack of fear. *"Mohawk."* He spat in the dirt as if the word was distasteful. "They are not one of my own. They are enemy to *The People.*"

The other Indian in the forest then came through the brush. Tess took a step back. Was she really standing here in her wet underclothes talking to a hostile? "Who are *The People* you speak of?"

He shifted his musket to his other hand and touched his chest with a closed fist. "We are *Lenape,* my brother and I."

She looked past him to the other red man who stood there, looking at her. There was a resemblance between the men in their aquiline noses and high, broad cheek-bones. "Brothers? You two are brothers?"

"I am called *Wee-ee-yox-qua*. My brother is *Takooko*."

His voice fascinated her. His English was so husky and foreign, yet comforting. She hadn't heard any English but her own since Jocelyn died. *"We-ox* what?" Her breath was coming more evenly now. "What does it mean?"

He laughed. "I am called the Raven to those who speak my name."

"Raven," she echoed softly. The name fit. He was dark and mysterious. His hair was as black and shiny as a raven's wing. "I . . . I'm sorry I cut you, Raven." She pointed to the bloody knife wound on his forearm. It looked deep, and might well require stitches to close it. "I . . . You scared me. I thought you were one of them," she said, still not entirely certain he wasn't.

Raven didn't even look at his bloody arm. "I think this man is lucky you did not strike at my heart or I would be dead. You are a brave woman she-whose-name-I-do-not-know." He was smiling at her now, a gentle smile meant to ease her fear.

"Tess," she answered softly. "I'm called Tess."

"Tess . . ." He said her name as no one ever had before. "Tess . . ." he repeated trying out the word on the tip of his tongue. "What does it mean—*Tess?*"

She smiled. "It doesn't mean a thing. Just a name my mum liked. She—"

The sound of movement in the direction of the river suddenly caught their attention. Tess felt a hasty rise of panic in her chest. "He'll kill me if he catches me," she said as much to herself as the two men. "He killed Jocelyn." Unconsciously she brushed her hand over her head thinking of Jocelyn's blonde scalp that hung from Broken Tooth's belt. "He'll kill me."

Raven reached out and took her trembling hand in his. It was a big hand, warm and secure. "The Mohawk will not take a life. Not today. Come, my brother and I, we disappear into the forest like the wind. We see but cannot be seen."

Tess didn't understand what he meant. Though he did speak English, some of his words were so heavily accented that she had to listen carefully to follow his meaning. *Disappear like the wind? Didn't he understand that the Mohawk were coming after her?* But when he tugged on her hand, she followed.

Back in the canoe she had prayed to God for a miracle. Was this man her miracle?

Raven and his brother led her deeper into the forest. Tess ran between them, pulling up her tattered, wet shift to run, her corset discarded days ago. This was no time for modesty. Her life was still at stake. The strange thing was that the two men didn't seem to notice that she was practically nude.

Through the forest they ran, the men making no sound as their moccasins touched the scattered leaves and soft soil at their feet. The pungent scent of rotting leaves and damp moss filled her nostrils. The ancient trees above her head formed a canopy, blocking out much of the sunlight as they went deeper into the forest.

Tess heard the Mohawk behind them. They thrashed in the brush, beating the trees violently in search of her. And then she heard the angry guttural tones that warned her of Broken Tooth's nearing presence. But as she and the brothers ran, the voices quieted, becoming more distant.

Tess was soon winded. She was breathing heavily and

despite the coolness of the forest on her damp skin, sweat
beaded above her upper lip.

The brothers made turns in the woods, left then right,
then right again. No words passed between them and yet
they seemed to know what the other was thinking. They
seemed to Tess more like two wild animals in sync with
their surroundings than two men.

Just when Tess feared she could keep up no longer, the
brothers rounded a patch of tangled green briars and sank
down into a carpet of moss. Raven brought one finger to
his lips, signaling for her to keep silent. He rested one
hand reassuringly on her arm.

For what seemed an eternity Tess sat there on the moss
between the two brothers, hearing nothing, seeing nothing
but the flitter of birds and the sway of the tree limbs
above them. Then he appeared. Out of the dense foliage
came Broken Tooth and one of the other Mohawk from
the canoe.

Tess drew in a ragged breath, her veins running icy
with fear. If he saw her, he would surely kill her. He
would torture as he had tortured Jocelyn and then he
would murder her. Tess didn't want to die. She'd fought
too hard these last three days to lose her life now. She
had to survive for Jocelyn, for Abby . . . for herself.

Raven squeezed her arm gently. Broken Tooth walked
past them not an arm's length from Tess's bare, skinned
knee. She looked at the faces of the two Lenape brothers.
They were unafraid. It was like a game to them. They
honestly thought they were invisible!

Mad savages . . . Father in heaven, she thought. *I've
been rescued by mad savages.*

Broken Tooth stopped and slowly scanned the woods
around him. Tess could feel her body trembling with fear.

Raven's arm settled on her shoulder. She didn't know how it had gotten there; it was just there.

Broken Tooth grunted something in his guttural tongue. He was so close that Tess could see the rotting flesh on the fresh scalps on his belt, and yet he apparently couldn't see her.

Were she and the brothers truly invisible?

After a moment, Broken Tooth turned around, again speaking to the other Mohawk. The two savages walked away, back in the direction of the Susquehanna.

For a long time Tess just sat there in the bed of leaves in the greenbriar thicket, following the men's lead. They remained still and silent until the sound of the Mohawk was long gone.

Tess turned her head to look at Raven. When her gaze met his, he lowered his arm from her shoulder. "Thank you," she whispered. Her gaze wandered to Takooko and back to Raven. "Thank you for helping me. I don't know why you did it, or how, but—"

Raven sliced the air with a quick movement of his hand. "For thanks there is no need." His face hardened. "Mohawk have no right to take women. Not our women, not the women of the white-hairs."

"White-hairs?"

He touched his crown of shining black hair. "White-hairs."

"The wigs." She laughed softly, a little surprised by the sound of her own voice. An hour ago she thought she would never laugh again. "You're talking about the wigs the Englishmen wear." She nodded thoughtfully. "White-hairs."

Takooko rose, slinging his bow over his shoulder. He was not as tall as Raven, but equally handsome. "Enough of your flirting, brother," he said in the Lenape tongue.

"The Mohawk have gone, but that doesn't mean they will not be back. We must take ourselves far from this land. Quickly."

Raven rose. "You worry like our old great-grandmother, Takooko. The man-eaters are long gone." He indicated Tess with a glance. "She is tired, and afraid, and hungry. Her feet are bloody from her journey. We should find a safe place to set camp and give her time to rest."

Tess stayed where she was on the ground, watching the two men as they spoke back and forth in their language. Were they arguing?

"Camp!" Takooko scoffed. "It's barely afternoon. Do you forget that we travel home to our people with news from the Clan Gathering?"

"Half a day will make no difference in the decision our village must make. The woman must rest. She's been through a great ordeal. A woman so brave deserves our attention, Takooko."

Takooko looked down at the white-skinned woman. She'd slipped off one of her English moccasins and was rubbing her bloody blistered heel. "And then what, brother? What do we do with her when she's fed and rested?"

Without answering, Raven turned to Tess. "We will rest for the night, but not here," he said in English. "Here we are too close to the great river."

"And the Mohawk," she said shakily.

He shook his head. "No. They are gone, the ones who took you. They will not harm you." He touched his bare chest with his fist. "This man has given his word to you."

Tess sat there on the mossy ground looking up at the Indian. He wanted her to go with them. Running with them away from the Mohawk was one thing. She'd had no time to consider her actions. She'd just run. But going with these Indians now, that was another thing. Could she trust them? Why would she?

"Thank . . . thank you for your help, but you can go now. You don't have to stay. I . . . I'll go on alone from here."

Raven crouched at her feet. "You cannot stay here alone, *Tess.*"

The way he spoke her name made her uncomfortable. His voice sounded so *intimate.* Like he knew her. "I'll be all right. I got myself this far, didn't I?"

"I will not hurt you. My brother will not hurt you."

"You want me to come with you." She watched the expression on his face. "Where are you going to take me? How do I know you're no different than them?"

"You know we are different because they took you from your home. This man will take you to the place you call home."

Takooko made a noise.

Tess rose up on her knees in front of Raven so that she was eye-level with him. Home? Would he really take her home to her uncle's? "You would do that?" she asked softly, feeling a lump rise in her throat. "You would take me back?"

"You were a brave woman to jump from the canoe and swim. You were a smart woman to see your chance and take it. I will take a brave, smart woman home to her people."

Tess closed her hand over her mouth to stifle a sob of what, she didn't know. Relief? Gratitude? She couldn't believe that this black-haired, red-skinned man would help her. She couldn't believe she was really going to be alright.

Raven reached out and caught a stray lock of her damp

red hair and pushed it behind her ear. It was a simple
gesture, but it moved Tess deeply. No one had ever been
gentle to her, not even her mum, not even when Tess was
little. Born the third of a dozen living children, Tess had
been dealt a harsh hand from the beginning. For years she
had toiled in her mother's tiny cottage caring for little
ones, cleaning, and working their meager garden. Then,
after her arrival in the Maryland colony she had worked
harder than any slave in her uncle's fancy house.

"I . . . I don't know where we are. The Mohawk
dragged us around in circles raiding. I don't know how
to tell you where I live, not exactly," she said softly.

"We will find your home," he promised. He rose and
offered her his hand, palm up. "Come."

She took his hand and heaved herself up off the ground.
It wasn't until she sat down that she realized how tired
she was or how badly her feet ached. She swayed a little
and he steadied her.

"I will carry you."

"No." She pushed his hand away, blinking as she struggled to get her balance. "I'll walk myself."

"You would be light in my arms."

She took one unsteady step and then another, chuckling.
"I doubt you lifted a woman with hips as ample as mine."

"Your body is attractive to this man."

She passed him, his compliment making her feel a little
uneasy. Need she fear for her virtue among these men,
too? She was convinced that the only reason the Mohawk
hadn't used her body was that they must have guessed
she was still a virgin, and so they had held more sinister
plans for her.

Tess fell in behind Takooko, following him closely. Raven walked behind her. The two brothers spoke to each

other in their tongue occasionally, but mostly they walked in silence.

As they walked south, Tess concentrated on putting one aching foot in front of the other. Her good kidskin slippers were ruined. It was true they were Jocelyn's hand-me-downs, and a size too small, but they had been the best pair of shoes she'd ever owned. The shoes she had once been so proud of were now ripped, muddied, soggy, and stained with her own blood. The too-tight slippers had rubbed open sores on her heels and on the tops of her feet.

Twice Tess stumbled and both times Raven helped her to her feet. He again offered to carry her, but when she refused a second time, he didn't ask again. He seemed to respect her need to do this on her own.

Tess didn't know how long they walked. She lost all track of time and direction. But the shadows had lengthened and a cool breeze was beginning to filter through the trees when Takooko finally came to a halt beside a slow moving stream.

"Here," Takooko declared in English.

"This man thought you would walk us home tonight," Raven chided.

Despite her exhaustion, Tess smiled. Her Indian had a sense of humor. *Her Indian?* Since when had Raven become her Indian?

Raven rested his musket against a tree and began to gather wood for a fire. Tess sank down in the leaves, propping her back against a tree trunk. Thank goodness the brothers had stopped. Tess feared she couldn't have gone much further.

With flint and steel taken from a small quilled pouch Raven wore on his hip, he started a fire. He gave her a wooden bowl of fresh cold water from the stream and then offered her a small leather bag.

"Pemmican," he told her. "Eat."

Inside the bag was a wet brown mixture. Tess grimaced.

"Eat," Raven repeated. "It is dried berries and meat."

Tess took a tiny pinch of the foul-looking concoction and hesitantly nibbled at it. The taste was odd, but not bad. She took a bigger pinch. The mixture was pungent and chewy. She was so starved that at this point she guessed she could eat anything. She crammed a handful into her mouth, then another.

Chewing, she looked up to see Raven watching her. He nodded and she turned her attention back to the pemmican. When she had eaten her fill and drank from the bowl again, she sat back against the tree trunk again and stretched out her long legs. With her eyes half-closed, she watched the two brothers across the campfire.

They spoke their own language to each other, obviously used to each other's company. As Tess watched them, listening to their strange sing-song speech, she marveled at how well the two brothers got along. Tess and her siblings had never had such a relationship. Except, of course, for Abby.

Tess smiled at the thought of her younger sister. Abby had the most beautiful straight blonde hair, so unlike Tess's unruly red waves, and her eyes, her eyes were as blue as the ocean Tess had crossed to reach the American colonies, not mud brown like her own. Abby was petite and attractive . . . she was also deaf and called dumb because she didn't speak.

Of course she spoke to Tess. The two of them over the years had developed a language of their own using hand signals. The others had refused to learn them. Even Mum said it was a waste of time. After Father had died in the mill accident, Mum said most things were a waste of time.

Tess's heart wrenched as she recalled the day she'd left the little village of Hopsbirth to sail across the sea to live with Uncle Albert. How Abby had sobbed. . . . She'd tugged at her big sister's skirts signing again and again, *Don't leave me, don't leave me.*

Tess had carefully pushed her hands away and made a vow to send for Abby as soon as she was able. "I'll marry a rich man," she'd signed as she spoke. "And you'll come across the great ocean to live with me and we'll eat gooseberry pie morning, noon, and night." Abby had always loved gooseberry.

Tears running down her cheeks, Abby had signed, *Swear, swear you won't leave me here forever.*

Tess had crossed her heart and then with a quick peck on Abby's cheek, she had run to catch the wagon that would take her to the docks.

Tess shivered. The sun had set and now she felt cold. She hugged herself for warmth, brushing her bare arms which now were covered in goose pimples.

Raven appeared at her side, offering her his sleeveless leather vest with the seashell ornaments. Tess shook her head. "No. You'll be cold without it. I'm all right."

"Take it." He draped it over her shoulders. "Get warm and then give it back," he told her.

Tess had intended to immediately lift the vest off her shoulders and give it back, but the weight of the dry leather felt so good that she kept it on. *Just a few minutes,* she told herself.

Raven nodded, the barest smile on his face. Then he looked down at her feet. Tess hadn't taken off her slippers for fear her feet would swell so much that she wouldn't be able to get them back on in the morning.

He touched one slipper. Tess tried to pull away. "No. I'm all right."

He held her ankle. "You cannot walk with feet that hurt."

"They don't hurt, r-really." She winced as he pulled off the first slipper. "Please . . ." The second slipper scraped on the raw flesh of the top of her foot and she bit down on her lower lip to keep from crying out loud.

He brushed his palm across the sole of her foot. It was a strange feeling, a man's hand touching her like that. "Please," she said again, not really knowing what she meant.

"Lay back," he said. "I carry medicine in my bag that will take away the fever of pain."

With the slippers removed and the numbness from the too-tight slippers wearing off, her feet were beginning to throb. "All right," she sighed, too tired to fight him. "A little salve would help."

He got up and walked away, going to his leather bag on the far side of the fire. His brother eyed him. Raven pulled a wooden bowl from the fringed bag and a smaller bag, but instead of coming back to her, he disappeared into the darkness. He reappeared a minute later with water sloshing from the bowl.

Tess stiffened, sitting more upright. "I . . . I can do that," she said as he knelt at her feet, embarrassed. "Really. It's all right."

He pushed her hand aside. "Lay back, this man says, and let the powers heal you, Tess."

Tess felt awkward. The thought of letting a stranger, a red man, touch her so intimately was absurd, and yet when she felt the first splash of cool water and warmth of his hand, she was powerless. She rested her head back on the tree trunk, trying not to sigh loud enough for him to hear her.

Tess lay back and let him bathe her swollen, burning feet. The cool water seemed to take away the fire of the blisters and the steady warmth of his hands as they massaged the soles of her feet relaxed her muscles. Before Tess knew what had happened, she was drifting off to sleep.

Raven massaged her calves, rubbing gently to ease her muscles. He stroked her instep and heel, relieving the tension. He sprinkled herbs from his great-grandmother's medicine bag on her open sores and then wrapped her feet in two strips of soft leather he carried for bandages.

His work complete, Raven hated to let go of her. Of course he was only practicing the healing as any Lenape would have done. It was only her feet, but he had to admit he had enjoyed the physical contact. He had enjoyed the pleasure he had seen on her face.

He yearned to touch her elsewhere.

Raven stood suddenly and walked back across the campfire, leaving the white-skinned woman to sleep.

"Done with your lovemaking, brother?" Takooko asked with a chuckle. He passed his pipe to Raven.

Raven squatted at his brother's side and took a pull. He inhaled the sweet smoke of the Maryland tobacco mixed with herbs, letting it fill his lungs and make him dizzy. "Jackass," Raven answered in English.

Takooko frowned. "If you're so infatuated with her, why not take her as your wife? Catch two fish with one net. Our mother says it's time you marry and give her grandchildren. We haven't the time to take the white woman to her home. You hear her. She doesn't even know where home is."

"Go to sleep," Raven answered, laying down on his sleeping mat. "Tomorrow, the day will be long." Raven rolled onto his side, his back to his brother, giving him no chance to respond.

Raven stared into the fire watching the orange and red flames dance and lick at the wood. What was it about this white-skinned woman with hair of fire that disturbed him so? Why had she crossed his path now? Why at this place, at this moment in time? His great-grandmother always said nothing happened by accident. Nothing. All was in the great *Manito,* the Creator's plan, a plan set in the stars before the world began.

Raven sighed, closing his eyes. Grandmother had been old and superstitious. He would take the white woman to her home or to the town of white-hairs and then he would forget her. His fate was already set, a fate with no room for a woman. He soon would be War Chief to his people, and a man with no place in his life for a woman like his Tess.

His Tess. . . . When had she become *his Tess?*

Three

Tess woke to the heavenly scent of frying fish. For a few moments she lay on her back staring up at the canopy of tree branches and green leaves that sheltered her. The sun was just beginning to break over the treetops, bathing the forest in golden light.

Freedom . . .

She closed her eyes and wiggled her hands just to prove to herself that this morning she was no longer bound hand and foot by sinew ties. *As God is my witness,* she vowed, *I'll never be a man's prisoner again.*

The Mohawk had only held her three days, but the days had seemed to stretch into a lifetime. Now she was free again. She could go home to her uncle's and go on with her plans to marry Myron. She could marry her gunsmith and live in his comfortable farmhouse and pretend none of this had ever happened. In time she would forget Broken Tooth and his band of Mohawk warriors. In time she could even forget what they did to Jocelyn. She would make herself forget the screams. She would forget it all.

"Tess," came Raven's masculine voice. "You must get up and eat. My brother is anxious to go."

Tess opened her eyes and her gaze met Raven's. *Free to forget,* she thought. *But will I ever forget these eyes?*

Tess sat up, pushing such silly notions aside. Who was

this Indian to her? No one but a man who showed her some kindness. He didn't even really save her. He admitted that himself. Tess had saved herself, and she had to remember that.

"You feel good this morning?" Raven asked, squatting to get a better look. "Your feet are better?"

Tess looked down at her bare feet wrapped in the soft leather strips. She knew her cheeks must have colored. She was embarrassed by Raven's attention. "I'm fine. I don't need to eat. Let me put on my shoes and we can go." She glanced around, but they were nowhere in sight. She ran her fingers through a pile of last fall's leaves. "They're here somewhere. I'll be ready directly."

"You cannot wear the slipper-shoes."

She got to her feet, not paying any attention to what he said. "They were here last night. Now I can't find them."

"The white *manake* shoes have hurt your feet. You can wear my brother's spare moccasins he carried in his pack. They will only be a little big."

Tess was still searching for her shoes, kicking the leaves around her. One of the leather bandages had come untied and was trailing behind her. "I want my own slippers." She didn't know why there was this sudden panic in her chest or why the shoes mattered so much. They just did. "Where are my damned shoes?"

"I buried them. I told you. This man has moccasins you can wear on your feet. They will not hurt the sores." He tried to touch her but she flinched.

"I want my slippers back," she said, her voice quivering. "They were my good shoes. J . . . Jocelyn, she gave them to me. She only wore them a little." Tess felt tears sting her eyes and she wiped at them angrily. Why was she crying over a blessed pair of slippers? She never cried. She'd not even cried when they had killed her cousin. "You had no right to take my shoes! They were mine and I want them back. Now!"

Raven reached out to her and took her arm. Tess fought him, but his grip was iron tight. He pulled her against him. "Shhh," he soothed. "All will be right, Tess."

She struck him with her fist and tried to wrench away. "Let me go. Leave me alone. I just want my bloody shoes! I want my shoes and I want to go home." Her tears no longer in check, they ran hot down her cheeks.

Raven forced her head down on his bare shoulder and stroked her hair. Tess found herself suddenly clinging to him, completely at a loss as to why she was crying or why Raven's shoulder was such a comfort. What was it about the stupid shoes that was suddenly so important to her, and how was it that this red man could so soothe her?

"They were mine," she whispered. "You . . . you didn't have a right to take them." A tiny sob escaped her lips. "They . . . they were Jocelyn's and now she's dead. They killed her, Raven. But they didn't kill me. I wouldn't give in. I wouldn't lay down and die like Jocelyn." Another sob racked her body as tears ran down her cheeks and fell to his bare shoulder. "Please, my shoes . . ."

Raven made soothing sounds in his throat as he stroked her hair. Her breasts pressed against his hard chest, Tess could feel the contours of his bare shoulders beneath her fingertips. She could hear his easy breathing in her ear. She tasted the salt of her own tears.

"Shhhh," Raven comforted. "It is not your fault that your cousin died and you lived. You tried to help her."

Tess's lower lip trembled. "I tried. I told her she had to walk. I told her she had to do what they said, whatever they said. But . . . but she wouldn't listen." She took a shuddering breath. "She just gave up. She didn't want to live badly enough."

"Some have the strength to survive and others do not, Tess. It is not right or wrong. It is the way of the Creator." He brushed her cheek with his fingertips. "Now, do not cry. I will get your shoes. You are right. This man had no right to take them."

"I don't know why I need them, I just do," she whispered.

"I will get the shoes, but you must promise this man that you will carry them. On your feet you will wear the moccasins."

Tess nodded, sniffing. She felt like such a ninny. "I'll wear the moccasins," she said, pulling away from him. She wiped at her eyes with a corner of her torn shift. "I'm sorry. I know you were just trying to help. The slippers are worthless, but—"

"They were yours." Raven went to a bare spot near the fire and began to dig with a stick. "They are proof of your will to live." He looked up at her. "We all have possessions that have meaning to us." Out of the hole he brought out the two tattered kidskin slippers. He beat them together and clouds of dust rose. "One man has no right to judge another man's possessions. What is worthless to one, can be of great worth to another."

Tess took the slippers, still feeling irrational but comforted by the weight of them in her hands. "I'd just like to keep them." She sniffed again.

Raven came to her, lifting a tiny leather bag off his chest. Tess had noticed it last night when he'd removed his leather vest and given it to her. The bag that hung on a leather tie around his neck was fringed, with a few beads sewn on it. It looked very old and well worn.

Raven opened the bag and pulled out a jagged piece of white quartz. It was an ordinary rock. He turned the stone in his fingers. "My great-grandfather brought this to me from the north country. It is of the mountains called the A-di-ron-dacks." He stared at the clear white rock. "My grandfather brought it to me as a present when I was a boy. He wanted me to make a spearpoint with it."

Tess stared at the rock trying to imagine a young boy's delight at having been brought a rock.

Raven ran his thumb and forefinger over the jagged edges. "I could not bring myself to chip away the stone and change it from what *Manito* created."

"And you saved it all these years?"

He smiled. *"Kohon.* Foolish, a man who will soon be War Chief to carry a rock an old man, long-dead, brought him."

Tess's smile matched his. "Not foolish. He loved you, your grandfather, didn't he?"

Raven dropped the quartz back into the pouch and pulled the tiny drawstring. "He was good to me. Yes, we loved."

Tess's smile turned sad. "No one ever loved me like that. You were lucky."

Raven lifted his head to look at her. For a moment it was if they were bound by some emotion Tess couldn't put her finger on. He seemed to want to say something to her. He even lifted his hand in gesture, but then let it drop. He looked away. "I fished. Come and eat. Takooko has gone scouting but he will soon return. He is impatient, my young brother. We will have to hurry." As he walked away he pointed to a pair of moccasins lying beside the smouldering coals of the campfire. "Put on the moccasins, Tess, and this man will take you home."

* * *

Takooko returned, and after a hasty breakfast of fried fish and cold water, the three set out, heading south. "My uncle's home is near Annapolis," Tess told the men. It's on the Chesapeake Bay, but I don't know where. I don't know how far the Mohawk took me. That first day and night it seemed like we walked in circles."

" 'Napolis,'" Takooko scoffed, falling into his native tongue so that the woman couldn't understand him. "A child could find the white-hair 'Napolis. I say we turn her southeast and let her find her way home, brother."

"You're getting sour in your old age," Raven returned. "We will almost pass the town of 'Napolis on our way to our village. There is no reason, but your stubbornness, why we cannot take her to the white-hairs."

"No reason! You heard the others speak at The Gathering. There are war parties in the forest. White-hairs kill for the color of a man's skin. There need be no crime against them, brother. These days the white-hairs lift scalps as easily as the Iroquois."

Raven lifted a branch and Tess ducked under it. He waited for her to pass. "Do you tell me you fear the white-hairs?" he dared.

"Fear them?" Takooko laughed. "I fear no one! I only repeat what the great fathers tell us. This land is dangerous. This is a dangerous time," he went on, becoming angrier with every word. "Why should we risk our lives for a white woman when we have duties to attend to in our own village?"

"Go on without me, then, brother. I will take her home."

Takooko didn't answer for a moment, but when he did, his agitation had subsided. "You know I cannot do that."

Raven stopped on the path, his gaze meeting his younger brother's. "And why not? Go ahead and I will meet you in our village."

Takooko shook his head. "No. You are my brother. You go, I go. We left our mother together, we will join her in our village together."

Raven glanced ahead at Tess who'd taken the opportunity to stop and lean against a tree trunk to rest. "I cannot explain myself, Takooko. I only know that I must see the white-skinned woman to safety."

"Yes, yes," Takooko groaned, once again his good-natured self. "This man can see when you are smitten even if you can't. Fiery hair, good teeth, and firm breasts, she is a fine catch even with her ugly white skin."

Raven poked his brother with the muzzle of his Brown Bess. "Shut your mouth before I shut it for you, little *nuxans.*"

Takooko laughed and hurried along the path past Tess. Raven stopped and waited for her. "Your feet, you have pain?" he asked in English.

She started walking again. "No. No, I'm fine. The moccasins, they—" she laughed "—they're the most wonderful things I've ever had on my feet." She smiled up at him hesitantly, feeling a little foolish. "I want you to know I appreciate what you've done for me. I know your brother's mad about taking me back. I don't want to cause any trouble between you two. You don't have to take me to Annapolis. I . . . I could find my own way if you'd just point me in the right direction. I know my uncle must be looking for us." She lowered her gaze, her voice softening, "For Jocelyn and me."

"I speak the truth when I say I do not mind taking you to your home. 'Napolis, it is not far. We can reach the white-haired village by dusk if we walk quickly."

"It's that close?" she asked excitedly.

He nodded.

Tess lowered her gaze to the narrow path they followed. "And then where will you go?" She didn't know why she cared. Just making conversation, she supposed.

"Takooko and I, we go to our village. We have gone to the Clan Gathering to the northwest. We bring back word to our people of what the other Shawnee and Delaware will do."

"Do? Do about what?"

He fell into step beside her, his flintlock musket resting on his shoulder. "Most of my people have moved west, far from the white-hairs and their guns and whiskey, but some of us have been stubborn. It is hard to give up the land when a man knows his grandfather's grandfather walked the same paths."

Tess nodded, drawn in by the tone of Raven's voice and the plight of the Indians he spoke of. She had never heard the red man's point of view, only the side of the English.

"Now we must decide if we will go west or stay here. If we stay, we may have to join with the white Frenchmen as many of our Lenape brothers have." He plucked a leaf from a pin oak they passed under. "Fighting is bad for the Delaware. It is bad for all men."

"You can't just stay where you are and be neutral?"

"The white-hairs do not give us that choice. If we stay and do not join their armies, they will come in the night. They will burn our wigwams, rape our women, and murder our men."

"Doesn't sound like much of a choice," Tess mused.

"Move away from your home and all you know or fight another man's war."

Raven sighed. "I do not know what is right for us. The Iroquois have been our enemy for many years. Already their war parties come further and further south, even west."

"Like the men who took me," Tess whispered.

Raven nodded. "Some Lenape join the French because they hate the English more. The French make promises to us, the English just push us off our land. I am afraid that if our village joins an army, any army, we will all die."

Tess lowered her head. "I am English," she said softly. "The French are our enemy. If you fight for the French that will make me your enemy."

Raven stared at her with clear dark eyes. "It is wrong that friends can become enemies so easily." He looked away. "But I must do what is best for my people. The French-Canadians say they will not take our land from us as the English *manake* have. They say they will protect our women and children, but they have not told the truth in the past."

"So how can you trust them now?" Tess offered softly.

"I cannot. But I cannot trust the English either. They are all liars."

Tess was silent.

Raven looked at her. "It is wrong for me to speak of your people like this."

"No." She shook her head. "They're not my people. I mean, they are, but—" She found his gaze. "The King makes the decisions, not us, not the common people."

"In my village we will decide together. We will vote, man and woman. As War Chief I will say what I think, but the people will decide."

She smiled as if he was teasing her. "The women? You said the women of your village will vote?"

"Of course."

Her laughter rose in the treetops. "Women with a vote, what a silly idea!"

"Why would a woman not have a say?" Raven asked, frowning. "It is she who will carry on the blood of the People. It is she who will raise the little boys to become warriors."

Tess chewed on her bottom lip thoughtfully. "Women voting . . ." She looked up at him. "Why not?" She laughed again . . . "Why not indeed?"

Raven smiled. He liked the sound of her voice. He liked to see her smile. Takooko said her white skin was ugly. It wasn't really ugly, just different. A Lenape woman had skin the color of red clay, while this woman, her skin was the hue of a glimmering Hunter's moon, pale and full of light. He was fascinated by the little brown markings that ran across her cheekbones and the bridge of nose. He wondered what it would be like to run his fingers through her waves of fiery hair. Was there truly magic in the flaming hair, as many said?

He wondered what it would be to kiss that mouth.

Raven looked away from Tess, disturbed by his thoughts. It was so unlike him to lust after a woman. Not that he didn't have physical desires, but he was a man with more important issues on his mind. The very survival of his race might depend on the decisions made by his people in the next year. He had no time for women.

Still, this woman tugged at his heart in a way no woman had ever done.

Minutes later the sound of a dove's call caught Raven's attention. He grabbed Tess's arm.

She spun around. "What?"

He brought his finger to his lips, still holding tightly to her arm.

She suddenly looked so fearful, and Raven wished he could do something to take that fear from her face.

He heard the sound of the dove again. This time Tess heard it, too.

"What is it?" she whispered.

"Takooko," he answered, his voice barely audible above the soft sound of the wind rustling the leaves overhead.

"Your brother?" Tess scanned the trees.

Before Raven spotted Takooko, he heard the sound of horses and men. He dipped down in a crouch, pulling Tess with him. The men were crashing through the forest, shouting. From somewhere in the distance came the sound of hounds tracking a scent.

Raven heard the sound of his brother as he approached them from behind. Tess gave a start, but Raven squeezed her arm. "Takooko," he whispered. "It is only Takooko."

She looked up to see his brother crawling toward them.

"They look for her," he whispered harshly in English. "Let us go quickly from this place, brother *Wee-ee-yox-qua.*"

"Me? They're looking for me?" Tess started to stand up, but Raven pulled her back down.

"Looking for her, how do you know?" Raven whispered in Algonquian. "They could be more evil English white-hairs."

"They call a name," Takooko answered impatiently.

"Her name?"

"A name."

Tess was trying to wriggle her wrist from Raven's grasp.

"Maybe it's my uncle," she said excitedly. "They've come for me."

"Shhh," Raven warned. He touched her chin to make her turn and look at him. "Do not give away where we hide. We do not know if these men are good or bad."

"But your brother, he said they were looking for me. They must be. They must be looking for me!"

Such an innocent, Raven thought. *Even after all she has been through with the Mohawk, she still doesn't realize what evil is in our world.* Raven held onto her wrist fast. "Listen to me, Tess. If it is you they seek, then you will go to them, but let us wait and be sure."

Takooko lifted his bow and reached for an arrow from his quiver. "They approach quickly, make up your mind, brother," he urged.

Raven glanced into the forest. It would be so easy to slip away. The white-hairs would never see the two brothers of the Bear Clan disappear in the underbrush . . . *But what if it was not Tess's family?* There were many evil men about the forest these days; renegades both red and white, slave hunters, soldiers. . . . If he left her here now, she would be unable to defend herself. She had nothing but the Mohawk skinning knife to protect herself.

"Brother . . ." Takooko bid. "A decision." He notched his arrow.

Raven suddenly stood up, waving an arm for Takooko to step off the game path and into the forest. Takooko wanted a decision? Raven had made it. He would stand beside Tess and deliver her safely into the hands of her family.

"Jocelyn!" came a voice. "Jocelyn?"

Tess's face lit up in a smile. She grabbed Raven's bare forearm just below his copper armband. "That's my

cousin, Leo. I know that voice! That's Leo's voice! I told
you they would come looking for me!" She cupped her
hands around her mouth. "Leo! Leo! I'm here!" She
jumped up and down excitedly. "Oh, God. I'm here!
Here!"

"Tess?" called a distinctively different voice. "Tess, is
that you?"

"Myron?" She turned to Raven. "That's Myron. He's
going to marry me." She turned back toward the voices,
waving her arms over her head. "I'm here Myron! It's
Tess!"

Raven could see the horses coming through the forest
now. The undergrowth was thick for horseback, so they
moved slowly. Two men had dismounted and were walking
toward them, still partially obscured by the trees.

"Raven," murmured Takooko from the cover of the forest. "Let us go, brother!"

Raven looked back toward the men appearing out of
the forest. He could go now. Tess had been returned to
her family. She was safe. He had fulfilled his duty. He
had to let her go.

Raven was just turning away when a voice broke
through the trees.

"Redskins!" cried a man in alarm. "Redskins got her!"

A musket fired in the air and Raven instinctively
dropped to his knees dragging Tess with him. Fools, they
would kill her with their own lead!

"Myron!" Tess shrieked. "Don't shoot! Don't shoot!
They haven't hurt me! They—"

More musket fire drowned out the sound of her voice
and Tess sank down beside Raven, covering her ears.
"Why are they shooting at us?"

Lead balls whistled through the air striking the trees

around them. Everything was happening so quickly that Raven had no time to think. If he didn't protect her, the white-hairs would kill Tess trying to get to him.

Raven grabbed Tess by his leather vest that she still wore, and began to drag her backward. She struggled, confused and frightened by the musket fire. "Down, Tess, keep down," he ordered.

"He's carryin' her off!" shouted a man who had dismounted and was running toward them. "Get the filthy red bastard before he gets away!"

Before Raven could react, Takooko appeared from behind a red cedar tree and released an arrow from the bow that had been a gift from Raven. The arrow flew straight and true, sinking into the chest of the man who ran toward them. As the white-hair sank to his knees, a man behind him pulled the trigger of his flintlock and it belched smoke and fire.

Raven threw himself over Tess to protect her and only out of the corner of his eye did he see his brother fall . . .

Four

"*Tuko!*" Raven shouted desperately, his voice ringing in the treetops. "*Tuko, niimut!*"

He climbed over Tess to reach Takooko who lay back in the dry leaves, a bright patch of red staining his leather quilled tunic, his eyes staring sightlessly heavenward.

"No," Tess cried wringing her hands. "No, no, please, dear God!"

Raven lay his ear to his brother's chest for a moment. When he lifted his head the kind, gentle man Tess had known was gone. The man who stared at her now was as dangerous as any Mohawk.

"He is dead," Raven hissed.

"We got one. We got one of the little red bastards!" Tess heard Myron shout from the cover of the trees. "Reload, Leo. Reload!"

Tess looked down at Takooko's ashen face and for the first time realized just how young he was. He had lived on this earth fewer years than Tess. Now he was dead. Tears formed in her eyes. "I'm sorry, Raven," she whispered, confused by her own emotions.

In the distance she could hear her fiance's voice. A part of her wanted to rise and run toward him, but a part of her longed to comfort the man who had been so kind to her when she had been in need. "I'm so sorry."

"They have killed my brother," he intoned. *"You have killed my brother."*

"No," she shook her head, suddenly frightened by the sound of his voice. He wasn't just in shock; he was angry. He actually thought she was responsible! "I didn't do it. It was an accident. I—"

"Silence!" he shouted in her face.

Tess clamped her hand over her mouth to keep from crying out. She was suddenly afraid of this man she had trusted. She was afraid and she wanted to run.

Before she could move, Raven's hand darted out and he caught her wrist.

"Raven, please . . ."

He twisted her arm viciously, silencing her. "They have killed my brother," he whispered, his upper lip turning in a sneer. "They have taken a life"—he looked toward them, then back at her—"and for that life, I will take a life."

"No!" Tess tried to pull away. She dug her heels into the soft ground and screamed. He was going to kill her! Raven was going to murder her!

Raven leaped to his feet. Myron and Leo had reloaded and were now running through the forest toward them.

"Just leave me," Tess begged, seeing a flash of Myron's brown coat in the trees. "Just leave me here."

Raven held fast to her arm, jerking her to her feet. *"Shahmalayo-kun,"* he commanded, shoving her. "Run, white woman."

Tess grabbed a tree trunk, hanging on for dear life, but he pulled on her other arm until she thought she would split. She raked her fingernails over the bark of the tree's trunk as he dragged her away.

"Run, run!" he ordered, pulling her, then shoving her.

"Run, or you will taste the bite of my knife at your throat!"

Tess couldn't believe this was happening. Raven had been so kind, so gentle only minutes before. How could he have turned into such a wild man? But as he pulled her through the thick of the forest, under branches, over fallen logs she thought of the lifeless face of Takooko. He blamed her for Takooko's death and now he would punish her. It didn't make any sense to her, but did it have to? What mattered was that in Raven's mind it made sense to him.

"Please, Raven," she cried, trying to reach his sense of reason. "I didn't do anything. I wasn't the one who fired the shot. Please let me go."

"Do not speak again!" he threatened.

Tess looked over her shoulder as they ran. Myron and Leo were still chasing them, but they were falling behind. She could hear the men cursing as they fought to make their way through the greenbriar thickets and seemingly impenetrable undergrowth. Raven, on the other hand, seemed to know instinctively the best way to go. He turned left, then right, then left again, weaving his way deeper into the woods. While Myron and the other men crashed and stumbled through the forest, Raven moved noiselessly.

"Myron!" Tess screamed, realizing she had lost sight of them. "Myron, help me!"

Raven stopped suddenly, pushing her roughly against a tree trunk. "I told you to be silent," he commanded.

Tess's lower lip trembled as she tried not to look afraid. "You have no right to take me like this. It wasn't my fault."

Raven grabbed the hem of her shift and gave a hard tug. Tess fought tears of fright as the soft cotton tore. "Please," she murmured. "Please don't hurt me, Raven.

You promised yesterday you wouldn't harm me. Don't you remember?"

He yanked the torn strip of cotton from her shift and ripped it into two pieces. Despite Tess's struggling he managed to bind her hands behind her back. With the other piece, he gagged her.

"Raven, please don't do this to me," she mumbled through the cloth that bit into the soft corners of her mouth. "Raven . . ."

He grabbed her by her arm and shoved her forward. Having wasted precious moments tying her, he ran to put more distance between him and the white men. Tess was left with no choice but to run beside him. Twice she fell, but both times he dragged her to her feet.

"I will not warn you again, white woman," he said, his eyes steely. "Hold me back and you will die here in the forest."

An hour ago no one could have convinced Tess that this man would harm her, but at this moment she had no doubt whatsoever that his words were not an idle threat. He was angry enough to kill.

Tess knew she had no choice but to run beside Raven. The voices of Myron and Leo and the other man were fading in the distance. The dogs had lost their scent. The Indian was getting away and he was taking her with him.

Not again, Tess said over and over in her mind as she raced through the forest, knowing she ran for her life. *Not again. Not kidnapped again. Not by this man who I thought was my savior.*

Tess knew she should pray, but no words came to mind. She was just angry, angry and afraid. She was angry with Myron and Leo. How could they have been so stupid as to have fired on the two men who were bringing her

home? And she was angry at Raven. How could he blame
her for his brother's death? And after all his talk of the
unfairness of the Mohawk stealing her, how could he in
good conscience do the same? Kidnapping her like this,
threatening to kill her if she didn't do what he said—it
made him no better than Broken Tooth.

Tess grew winded but still Raven ran. She knew she
was slowing him down, but he kept dragging her forward,
forcing her to try to keep up. Finally, when Tess thought
her lungs would burst, he stopped. They were in a tiny
clearing dominated by a huge fallen tree trunk. Beams of
sunlight came down through the thick overgrowth to paint
a path at her feet.

"Inside," Raven ordered, shoving her toward the fallen
tree.

"What did you say?" she mumbled in disbelief from
beneath the gag.

"The tree," he whispered harshly. "Inside."

She stared at the tree but didn't move.

He grabbed her around the waist and swept her into the
air. For a second she thought he was trying to throw her
over the monstrous log, but instead he deposited her inside
it. The tree must have fallen many years ago because it had
rotted from the inside out leaving a hollowed out center.

"Inside," he ordered again, this time pointing.

Tess crouched on her knees in the hole in the hollow
of the tree trunk looking at him. She shook her head. She
wasn't going to do it. She wasn't going to crawl into that
dark hole full of termites and only God knew what else.

But when Raven pulled his knife from his belt, Tess
made a decision. She still wanted to live. She had beaten
the Mohawk. She'd gotten away from them. She would
get away from this madman, too.

Taking a deep breath to steady her fears, Tess lowered herself until she lay flat, her cheek pressed into the soft rotting wood of the tree trunk. Then she wiggled forward into the darkness of the hollow inner tree trunk. The inside was dark and dank and confining, but not overwhelming. Tess could do this. She knew she could because she had to.

When she felt movement behind her, she realized Raven was there. She hadn't understood the purpose of the tree trunk, but now she did. He was hiding. He was hiding from the search party and he was hiding her.

When Tess could wiggle forward no further, she lay still, her cheek pressed against the bottom of the trunk. After a moment she felt Raven's hands on hers. He untied her and she pulled her arms under her, wiggling until she could get them up far enough to support her head.

"Silence," Raven said.

Then, to Tess's horror, she realized he was climbing on top of her. She started to wiggle, trying to get away from the pressure of his body, but of course there was nowhere to go. Fighting tears of frustration, she forced herself to lay still. He finally settled on his side, propped against her, his back to the outside of the tree trunk, his hand over her waist.

"I hate you," Tess murmured beneath her gag. "I hate you, I hate you, I hate you!"

Raven pinched her and Tess jumped. "Shhh!" he ordered.

She didn't try to attempt to say anything else out loud, but in her head, she was seething. *I trusted you,* she thought. *I trusted you and you betrayed that trust. You're no better than the Mohawk you supposedly saved me from. You're worse because they never tried to deceive me. I knew what they were from the first moment they came upon me . . .*

At first Tess could only hear the pounding of her own heart. Then she heard her breathing, then Raven's. Then slowly her world seemed to expand. She felt the soft, powdery wood of the rotten tree trunk and smelled its rich, dank odor. Somewhere in the distance she heard dogs barking. After a while she heard the sounds of men's voices and the sound of men and horses crashing through the underbrush.

Tess immediately tensed and Raven tightened his grip on her waist. It was so uncomfortable being in such a confined place with him, his body pressed so intimately against hers.

Please find me, Tess thought desperately. *Myron, I'm here. I'm right here.*

But of course Myron didn't find her. Myron and Leo and the horses and dogs passed the hollow tree and went on.

"Whoreson!" Tess flung. "Maggot-brained whoreson!"

Raven stooped over his campfire, adding pieces of wood. "Silence, white woman or I will put the gag to your mouth again."

"White woman! Only a few hours ago I was Tess. Now I'm white woman?" She would have gestured but her hands were still tied behind her back. "What has happened to you, Raven? You're not the man who hid me from the Mohawk."

"What has happened?" he flared. "You have killed my brother! You have taken a knife and twisted it in my heart, and you dare to ask this man what has happened?"

"I didn't kill your brother and you blessed well know

it! How was I supposed to know they were going to shoot?" She angrily jerked at her hands that were tied behind her back to the tree she leaned against. "How was I supposed to know they would think you were the one who had kidnapped me?"

"That does not matter to this man. What matters is that I must go home to my mother and tell her her son is dead." He pointed an accusing finger. "You, you do not matter."

"Then why have you taken me prisoner?" There was a desperate note in her voice. "Why have you done this to me knowing I am innocent?"

"An eye for an eye, that is what your Bible tells us, does it not, white woman?"

She hung her head. "Taking me wherever it is that you're taking me won't change anything. It won't bring Takooko back."

Raven picked up a short, broken branch the diameter of his wrist and threw it at her. The limb struck the tree trunk above her and glanced off her shoulder.

"Oh!"

"Do not speak a dead man's name! It is a bad omen."

She laughed, shaking her head. Of course there was nothing funny to laugh about. She had been captured by murderers. Her cousin had been tortured and killed. She'd managed to escape and now she was a captive again—this time the captive of a madman. "I'm sorry. I don't know your ways."

"You do not." He stood, stretching his legs. "If you knew the way of the Lenape you would know that because those men took a life from me, I have a right to take a life from them." He struck his bare chest. She still wore his sleeveless vest over her shift. "I take what is my right."

"Oh, I see. I understand," she answered, the sarcasm plain in her voice. "You're going to punish them for killing your brother by kidnapping me."

"Yes."

"But what about me? You're punishing me, Raven! Why me?"

"You do not matter to me, white woman," he answered harshly, turning toward her. The light of the campfire flickered behind him, casting an eerie light across his face. "My brother, he is who mattered to me. Now he is dead."

"Now he's dead and I might as well be," she said softly. She stared at Takooko's moccasins Raven had given her only this morning. She made herself look up at him again. "So what will you do with me? Where will you take me?"

"I go to my village and tell my mother of my brother's death. I will return with other braves to give my brother an honorable burial."

"And then what? Will you ransom me?" Tess knew she shouldn't say such things. She knew she should be quiet and not anger him any further. But she couldn't help herself. She was sick to death of being controlled by others, by men. In her mother's house it had been her eldest brother who had dictated. Then it had been her uncle and cousin, then the Mohawk, and now this man. "Tell me the truth, Raven. Will you ask for whiskey and guns in return for me?"

His black eyes narrowed dangerously. "English *manake.*" He spat into the fire. "That is all that is of worth to you. Your gold coin, your sewing needles, your muskets and powder, your fire water. White men know nothing of honor. They know nothing of tradition, of loyalty, or of honesty."

Tess's lower lip trembled. He was shouting at her, blaming her for all that was wrong in the world. "You promised me you wouldn't harm me," she whispered. "You promised and now you've broken that promise."

"What did you say?"

"Yesterday." Her voice grew stronger. She had to stand up for herself. If she didn't, who would? "Yesterday you said you wouldn't harm me."

"And I have not harmed you," he flung. "Not yet."

"You said there was no need for me to fear you." She bit down on her lower lip, her eyes transfixed on his hardened face. "I'm afraid, Raven."

For a moment he stood there staring at her. He stared so long that Tess thought surely he must be reconsidering what he had done. Maybe he was coming to the realization that he had to let her go. This was all a mistake. He was shocked by his brother's death and for a few hours he hadn't been himself. But now he would apologize. He would say he was sorry he had frightened her and he would untie her. In the morning he would help her get home.

But Raven said nothing. He turned away, presenting his muscular, bare back to her. "Do as I say and I will keep my word. This man will not harm you," he said coldly.

Tess feared she would cry. How could she have so misjudged him? How could she have trusted this Indian with her life?

Tess closed her eyes and leaned her head against the tree. She had to concentrate on keeping up her strength and escaping. She would set herself crazy thinking about her mistakes. No, she shouldn't have trusted Raven. But she had. She had trusted him and she'd been wrong. But, she'd escaped from the Mohawk. She'd get away from Raven. She'd get away because she had to. Myron was out there looking for her. Surely he wouldn't give up. She would get away. Myron would find her.

Tess smiled at the thought. Myron would hold her in his arms and kiss her cheek and tell her how sorry he was. He would marry her and she would move into the white clapboard farmhouse with him. She would plant flowers in the kitchen garden. They would send for Abby. Her sister would come from England to live with them and life would be perfect. It was what Tess wanted. It was what she would have.

She opened her eyes. Raven was seated on the ground across the campfire from her. He was cleaning his Brown Bess and scowling.

Tess closed her eyes. She was truly sorry Takooko was dead, but she refused to feel it was her fault. It was an accident, and that accident gave Raven no right to hold her against her will. She tried to relax, despite the strips of cotton that kept her bound to the tree. She'd rest tonight and in the morning she would figure out a way to escape.

The red bastard, he wasn't going to get the best of her! He made her angry and it was that anger that would keep her safe. That anger she felt toward him deep in the pit of her stomach would help her find a way to escape. Anger was what would make her tough. Anger was what would make her survive.

As for that little sliver of sorrow she felt over Raven's betrayal, pain, disappointment, she'd just ignore it. Raven was nothing but another red man like the Mohawk. He was a kidnapper like the Mohawk. He had never really cared about her. He hadn't. Had he?

$\mathcal{F}ive$

Late the next evening, after a long day of travel, Tess and Raven walked into the Lenape village. Despite her fear of Raven, she remained close to him, even more afraid of the others. In one hand, she gripped her cousin's worn shoes.

The village filled a small clearing a few hundred yards from a creek bank. The clearing was dotted with rounded hut-like structures built of saplings with woven corn husk or sheets of bark for walls. Fires flickered throughout the camp and the smell of roasted venison still hung in the air. Tess could hear the sounds of men and women talking. Shaggy ponies neighed from where they were hobbled in a grove of mountain laurel, and a hound barked from somewhere in the distance. Tess thought she heard a baby cry, but then it was silenced, by a mother's breast perhaps.

Raven spoke to the outpost guard who had escorted them into the village. As the two men walked side by side, Tess ran to keep up, wishing her hands weren't tied behind her back like she was some common criminal.

A man approached them, calling to Raven, his voice light and cheerful. Raven said something in their native tongue. Tess was certain she heard Takooko's name. The man answered, staring angrily at Tess. Though she felt like hanging her head, she glared back at him. She knew none of these Indians were going to believe Takooko's death wasn't her fault, but she refused to act guilty. She'd done nothing wrong.

Raven took Tess by the arm as they walked to one of the larger huts. He pointed to the hard-packed dirt ground near the doorway. "Sit." It was the first English words he'd spoken to her in hours. His voice was cold and void of any compassion. He took her shoes from her hand and grabbed the leather lead line and tied her to a pole in front of the dome house. A bear face was carved into the pole with feathers and animal tails attached to the top. He dropped her slippers into her lap. "Do not move. If you move this man will punish you."

Tess drew her knees up under her torn shift. The air was warm tonight, yet still she shivered. What was Raven going to do with her? He'd never answered her last night when she'd asked him if he was going to ransom her. If he was going to kill her, surely he'd have done it by now. Maybe he was going to turn her over to his people and let them kill her. What else could he do with her?

Raven pointed his finger at the ground as he told the white woman to stay there. Then he took a deep breath and walked into his mother's wigwam. His best friend, Taande, followed him inside.

"Raven, *Hokkuaa.*" Dream Woman looked up at her eldest child, smiling.

"N'gaxais."

The smile fell from her face as the light from her firepit flashed across Raven's face. "What is it, my son?" she asked in Lenape. "What sorry news do you bring me?"

"It is my brother."

Dream Woman's eyes clouded with tears. "No."

"He has gone on to the next world, Mother. He is dead."

Dream Woman crossed herself and then kissed the silver crucifix that hung between her full breasts. Hokkuaa was one of the many Lenape who had converted to Catholicism. Father Michael had been the priest who had brought Christianity to the village and taught Raven and his brother the English language as children.

"I am sorry, Mother," Raven said. He went down on one knee to take her hand and kiss it. It was as smooth as any maiden's.

"The English *manake?*" she asked softly, her lips drawn in distress. "I did not know. The flames of the fire did not tell me."

Raven nodded. "The English men, yes. But I must tell you that this is my fault, Mother. My brother and I found a woman in the forest as we crossed the great Susquehanna River north of the Chesapeake. Mohawk had taken her, but she had managed to escape. Takooko wanted to leave her; he said she was not our concern. But I said we had to take her home to her people. If I had not insisted we take her to her home, we would not have come upon her white men. My brother—"

Dream Woman held up her hand to silence Raven. Taande had come around the firepit to kneel beside her. "My son died helping a white woman find her home?"

Raven forced himself to look into his mother's eyes. "Yes. I insisted."

She shook her head, speaking softly. "The Mohawk had taken her. It was your duty, son, to help her find her way to her people. Would you not wish an English *manake* to do the same for your sister, were she to be taken by Mohawk?"

Raven released his mother's hand and Taande took it. Raven couldn't believe the words his mother had spoken. "But he's dead, Mother. My brother, your son, is dead because of a white woman."

"Did you bind my other son and force him to walk beside you?"

Raven frowned. "No."

"Did you put your white man's firestick to his head and tell him he must follow you and the white woman?"

"Of course not!"

"Then the man we loved went of his own free will, did he not?"

Raven answered slowly, confused by his mother's reaction. Takooko had been her youngest child, her baby. Raven knew that she had always held a special place in her heart for him. How could she behave so calmly knowing he had just been murdered? "Yes, yes of his own free will, but *N'gaxais—*"

She reached out and squeezed her son's hand. "Your brother made a choice. He made the right choice just as you did. That he died is sad. My heart will ache for him always, but I am comforted to know that he did the right thing. He tried to help the woman in need."

Raven stood. His mother might have it in her heart to forgive so easily, but he didn't. He was angry with the white woman called Tess, but he was more angry with himself. He had led Takooko to his death out of a silly sense of responsibility to a woman who meant nothing to him. Nothing.

Taande took Dream Woman's hand smoothing it in his. "Go to your wigwam and get some sleep, Raven," he told his friend. "You have been through much. Sleep will clear your head."

"No. I will stay here with my mother."

Dream Woman looked up from where she sat near her firepit. "Taande is right. You must get some sleep, my son. I will be all right. Taande can stay with me."

Raven looked at Taande. He had risen and was making a clay pot of herbal tea. Dream Woman had learned this tradition of tea drinking from the English priests who had passed through their village in more peaceful times. Taande knew how much she liked her tea. It was good of him to make it for her. Taande was a good friend.

Raven rubbed his eyes. He was tired, so tired that he was thinking with his emotions rather than his head. "I want to try to go back for his body, *N'gaxais*. My brother deserves a decent burial. He deserves to be buried among loved ones."

She nodded. "Tomorrow will be time enough. It is not my son, your brother, who lays in the forest now. It is only a shell of a body. My son's soul has gone on to a better place. You must remember that it is we who still remain on Mother Earth that must suffer."

Raven wasn't interested in hearing his mother's philosophical thoughts right now. He was angry, and he wanted her to be angry, too. Takooko was dead. Takooko was dead and the white men who had killed him still lived. He looked at his mother. "I want to take a war party out. I want to kill the men who killed my brother."

Dream Woman looked up from the handleless tea cup she held between her palms. Her dark eyes flashed angrily. "No!"

"Mother—"

"Think, Raven, think with your mind and not your injured heart. My dead son is but one man." She swept one delicate hand. "But this village is a hundred. These men, women, and children need you. War parties achieve nothing. War parties perpetuate the anger, the fear, the resentment," she went on in Lenape. "You want to be War Chief of this village? Then you must think of this village and not your own selfish needs."

Raven set his jaw. She was right of course. He couldn't waste the time or the braves to lead a war party. Too much was at stake here. Too many decisions had to be made in the village for him to be dwelling on revenge. Revenge was worthless.

"Tell me you will lead no war party," Dream Woman said, coming to her feet. "Tell me you will not kill in your brother's name."

Raven's dark-eyed gaze met hers. She was a fierce woman, his mother, a woman he could be proud of. "I will lead no war party. You are right." He lowered his gaze. "I loved him. He didn't always do what I thought he should do. He was lazy sometimes and self-centered. He never took life seriously, but I loved him."

Dream Woman went to her son and took his hand, resting her cheek on his muscular forearm. "I know you loved him," she said quietly. "And he knows as well." She lifted her head and rubbed his arm. "Go and sleep. Tomorrow the world will not look so dark, my Raven."

Raven glanced at Taande.

Taande nodded to say he would stay here with Dream Woman.

Raven ducked through the door of his mother's wigwam and stepped out into the night.

Tess looked up anxiously at Raven from where she sat tied to the post. The moon was beginning to rise in the sky to cast a white light in the darkness. Raven's jaw was set as he stared out over the village, his eyes unseeing.

Tess had heard the voices through the wall of the dome house. She had heard Raven's voice and the other man's, but she had also heard a softer voice, a woman. Though she hadn't been able to understand their language, she had guessed that Raven had come to tell someone of Takooko's death. Raven had shouted, but the woman, whoever she was, had been calm. Now Tess could hear the woman crying very softly. The Indian brave still inside soothed her.

Tess watched Raven. She wanted to demand he tell her what he intended to do with her, but she kept silent, feeling some strange sense of compassion for him. She could tell by the taut pull of his face that he was hurting inside. Tess imagined what it would be like for her if she had seen her sister Abby killed as Raven had seen Takooko die. If something were to happen to Abby, Tess didn't know if she could go on living. Was that how Raven felt right now?

She watched him walk away. He never said a word to her. He just left her tied there and disappeared into the darkness.

Tess leaned back against the cornhusk wall trying to make herself as comfortable as possible. If this was where he was going to leave her to spend the night, she'd just have to make the best of it. She'd sleep tonight, and in the morning she'd figure out a way to get Raven to release her. Perhaps now that he was back among his own people he'd be able to let go of the thought that she was responsible for Takooko's death. And if he wouldn't let her go, she'd just have to escape.

Tess closed her eyes. She could hear the Indian and the woman inside the hut talking softly now. The woman was no longer crying. It was odd, but as Tess drifted off to sleep she found the voices comforting.

Sometime later Tess woke. The Indian brave who had gone into the house with Raven was standing in the doorway, talking to the woman inside. He was leaving. He said something in farewell and left the Indian house, ignoring Tess as he passed.

Just as Tess let her eyes drift shut again she heard someone else step out of the wigwam. She opened her eyes.

It was the woman Tess had heard crying. She was beautiful, with long thick black hair and a voluptuous figure beneath a short deerskin skirt and open vest. Around her neck, falling between her nearly bare breasts, she wore what appeared to be a crucifix.

The woman stared at Tess, seemingly surprised by her presence. *"Auween khackvev?"*

"I . . . I'm sorry, I only speak English." Tess tried to smile a little. *"English."*

The Indian woman was frowning. "You? You are a white woman?" Her pronunciation wasn't as good as Raven's, but Tess could understand her.

"Yes." Tess could sense no hostility in the woman's voice. She sounded kind, in fact.

"How did you come to here? What man does tie you to my family's lodge pole?"

Tess lowered her gaze. "The man, Raven, he . . . he brought me here."

The Indian woman pulled a knife from the wide-beaded belt she wore and squatted beside Tess. "My son? My son Raven did this to you?"

Tess stared at the woman as she cut her away from the hut. "You are his mother?" Tess scooped up Jocelyn's shoes out of the dirt. The woman didn't look old enough to be the mother of a man Raven's age.

"I am the Raven's mother." Having cut the ties, she pulled Tess to her feet. "And for this, I have much sorry," she said with distaste, throwing the strips of leather and cloth to the ground.

Tess rubbed her raw wrists, not knowing what to say. Was this woman apologizing for Raven tying her up?

The Indian woman touched her left breast. "This woman is called *Hokkuaa.*" She seemed to search her mind for the right words. "I am sorry. I do not have the chance to speak the English much. I am called Dream Woman."

Tess smiled. "Dream Woman." Then her smile disappeared. "You're the mother of Ta—" She cut herself off, remembering what Raven had said about the custom of not speaking the name of the dead. She looked at Dream Woman. "I'm sorry about your son. I'm sorry he's dead."

Dream Woman smiled sadly. "Thank you. To share the pain with another woman, even strange woman is good." She touched Tess's arm lightly. "Come—come to this woman's home and take tea."

Tess stared at Dream Woman thinking she must have heard her wrong. Dream Woman couldn't have been inviting her into her home for tea. Tea?

When Tess made no move, Dream Woman took her hand and led her through the cut doorway. Tess had to duck to keep from hitting her head, but inside there was plenty of room to stand up. The hut seemed so much bigger from the inside.

At least ten foot from wall to wall, the hut was furnished with a platform bed against the wall and a stool. A firepit dominated the center of the room with animal hide mats spread in a circle around it. From the rafters hung baskets, dried herbs, and leather bags. Several pieces of pewter and tinware were stacked neatly near the bed. Dried flowers hung in several places from the ceiling and wall posts giving the hut a strangely feminine touch.

"In, in," Dream Woman said. "You are hungry. Tired." She led Tess to the firepit where red coals smoldered. A clay teapot sat on a flat rock near the coals.

"Tea?" Tess said, smiling at Dream Woman. She really had meant tea!

"Kehella." Dream Woman nodded. "You like tea?"

Tess sank into the soft hides on the floor. "Yes, oh, yes, thank you."

Dream Woman pushed a delicate teacup into Tess's hands and knelt beside her to lift the teapot.

Tess watched the warm tea pour into her cup, savoring the aroma. She looked at the Indian woman. Was it this woman's kindness that she had seen in Raven's eyes that first day. "My name is Tess."

"Tess?"

"Tess."

Dream Woman poured herself a cup of tea. "Tess." She nodded, sitting cross-legged across from her. "I am sorry my son has done this, Tess."

"I . . . I don't know what happened. I don't know why they shot at him, Dream Woman."

Her hostess waved a hand. "What has done, has done. You did not pull the trigger of the firestick, no?"

Tess shook her head sadly, feeling a lump rise in her throat. "No, I didn't. I tried to stop them, but they wouldn't listen. They'd have probably shot me by accident if it hadn't been for Raven." At the mention of Raven, she dropped her gaze to the pungent brown tea she drank.

"My son, he took you then?"

Tess nodded. "Mohawk took me first. Days ago. It was

me and my cousin." She took a sip of the tea, giving herself a little time before she spoke of Jocelyn. "They killed my cousin, but I got away." She exhaled. "Raven, he and . . . and his brother, they helped me get away. They hid me from the Mohawk when they chased me."

Dream Woman smiled proudly. "My sons are good men." She took a sip of her tea, gesturing. "This, I do not know why he would take you. It is not like my son. Not my Raven."

"He . . . he said he was taking me because they took his brother. He said an eye for an eye like it says in the Bible."

Dream Woman shook her head. "The Lenape, we do not take captives. No longer."

"He tied me up." She looked over the rim of the teacup. "He said he would hurt me . . . kill me if I didn't do as he said."

Dream Woman frowned. "My son spoke of a white woman, but he did not say he had claimed you."

Claimed you. . . . The words rang in Tess's head. She wondered what Dream Woman meant, but she didn't ask. Maybe she was afraid to. "I don't know what he's going to do with me," Tess went on softly. "Maybe kill me," she dared.

"No. My son would not. His words are sometimes—" she clicked her fingers, looking for the right word "—harsh, but his heart is good." She threw out her shoulders mimicking a masculine gesture. "He is brave warrior," she relaxed, "but good man. He would not kill you. He would only say the words to scare you."

Tess gave a little laugh. "Well he's done a good job of that."

Dream Woman rose and busied herself near the bed,

searching through bags and baskets. "This woman will make you corn cake and honey and then you will sleep on my mat. Tomorrow I will speak to my son. I will not have this, a woman tied to my lodge. He knows I do not approve of treating *onna* this way, any females. I will not."

Tess hugged her knees. Dream Woman would help her! She would make Raven let her go. Tess warmed her hands on the china teacup, smiling. In few days time she'd be home!

Six

Tess stepped hesitantly from Dream Woman's wigwam and into the late afternoon sunshine. Three days had passed since her arrival in the village. Raven and several Delaware braves had left two days ago to retrieve Takooko's body. They had brought him home to rest this morning.

At noon there had been a simple burial ceremony. Tess had remained within the protection of Dream Woman's lodge, but she had watched with fascination from the doorway.

The funeral was solemn, but there had been no weeping. Even Dream Woman remained dry-eyed. The Delaware had gathered in the clearing in the center of the village. The women chanted and shook hollow gourd rattles. Muffled drums pounded, and the men of the village danced intricate patterns into the soft soil.

The funeral service had been brief, but it had touched Tess. Takooko's body, curled into a fetal position, was lowered into a small pit in a sunny spot near the edge of the village where other graves were marked. Then, the villagers, one by one, passed the funeral pit in procession. Some knelt in prayer, while others placed small objects in the grave with Takooko. He had been given his bow, a hatchet, a necklace of shells, a pewter tankard, and even a basket of dripping honeycombs.

When each man, woman, and child had paid his or her respects, the villagers scattered, returning to their homes and their daily chores. Dream Woman had gone back to her wigwam and retrieved a basket. She told Tess she was going to pick strawberries. Tess was amazed by the woman's strength. Here it was the day of her son's funeral and she was going to pick berries. The young man she called Taande left with her.

Tess had not seen Raven, except at the funeral and then only from afar. It had occurred to her yesterday when he was still gone that she might be able to just walk out of the village. But when she'd wandered toward the creek, without Dream Woman at her side, a tall, slender brave had appeared from nowhere to step onto the path in front of her. He'd said nothing, but he'd pointed in the direction of the wigwams, his hand resting on the knife in his belt. His meaning was clear. She was under some sort of house arrest and whether Raven was there or not, it would be enforced.

So Tess had decided that at this point her best bet at escape was to wait. Dream Woman had promised she would speak to her son about holding her captive. Of course Tess didn't expect her to do anything about it today, but surely by tomorrow Dream Woman would see to it that Raven released her.

Tess stood in the doorway of Dream Woman's wigwam watching the activity of the village. For three days she had watched the Delaware and she had to admit she was intrigued by their way of life. These people lived in a world so different from the one she knew. There were obvious differences; the huts they lived in and the hide clothing they wore, but there were more subtle differences, too, that tapped Tess's attention. No one ever hurried in the Indian village. No one ever argued. The men and women went about their chores in an easy, carefree manner. The women talked and laughed with other women as they weeded their gardens. The men, though busy with hunting, fishing, tool making, and wigwam repairs, seemed to think nothing of stopping in the middle of a chore to sit in the grass and roll a leather ball to a toddler. Though everyone in the village—even the children—did their own fair share of the work, there was a joy about them as they set to their tasks, a joy that seemed to come from an inner peace.

Tess traced the line of a bent birch sapling in Dream Woman's doorway as she recalled life at her uncle's home. Tess had come to *MacElby's Fate* thinking she would be a sister to cousin Jocelyn, another daughter to Uncle Albert and Aunt Faith. That was the intention her aunt and uncle had implied in the letters they had sent to England beckoning Tess's mother to send her daughter to the Colonies. On the long boat journey across the ocean Tess had imagined silk gowns, tea from silver tea services, and a bed of her very own in an airy bedchamber filled with fine furniture and rich bedlinens. Tess had imagined meeting a handsome colonial prince who would fall madly in love with her. She knew she would marry her prince and live in a big brick house on the Chesapeake, a house big enough for her and her husband, and all their children, and sister Abby as well.

But reality had set in shortly after Tess's arrival in the Maryland colony. Instead of a long-lost daughter, Tess found herself a wageless servant in her aunt and uncle's tobacco plantation home. Her airy bedchamber was a cramped loft above the steaming kitchen, her bed, a hard, flat pallet shared with two other maids and too many fleas to count. Most of the time Tess wore other servants' cast-off homespun gowns which were either too tight at the bosom or billowing at the hips. She spent her days polishing silver in the front parlor and scrubbing down the staircases with sand and harsh lye.

Occasionally when visitors came to call at *MacElby's Fate,* Aunt Faith would have Tess dress in one of Jocelyn's worn gowns and serve tea to the guests in one of the twin parlors. But even then Tess had felt more like a housemaid than a niece or cousin. Aunt Faith had always spent much of the conversation telling her guests about the penniless niece she had had to take in to feed and clothe.

The only good thing that had happened in the last two years since Tess's arrival in the Colonies was Myron. Myron was a gunsmith in the nearby town of Annapolis. Tess had met him in church and after a few months he had begun to call on her. At first he'd just stood at the back fence and chatted with her while she hung wet laundry on the line, but eventually he had gained Uncle Albert's permission to take her to church each Sunday. Their relationship had developed comfortably from there.

Last Christmas Eve Myron had asked her to marry him and she'd accepted with a squeal of delight. Myron was by no means rich, not like Uncle Albert, but he was comfortable. He had a neat white clapboard farmhouse with twenty acres at the edge of town, and a pair of bond servants. He drove a small open carriage on Sundays pulled by two bays. Perhaps Myron wasn't the Colonial prince she had dreamed of, perhaps he wasn't terribly handsome, but he was a decent man. And he had promised that if she would become his wife, he would send for her sister.

Unexpected tears suddenly clouded Tess's eyes, and she wiped at them irritably. Abby needed her, and here she was stuck in the middle of the forest with a bunch of Indians. Tess set her jaw angrily, thinking of her sister. Raven had no right to keep Tess here, not when Abby needed her so much. Tess had done nothing wrong.

She scanned the village impatiently. Where was Raven? She'd seen him only a few minutes ago across the compound, talking to some men. She had hoped he might come to his mother's wigwam and speak to her, but he hadn't. He hadn't even acted like he'd seen her.

Tess' attention moved from wigwam to wigwam. There was suddenly more activity in the compound. Women were beginning to bring baskets of foodstuffs to the communal center of the village. Someone had started a fire and begun roasting a side of venison.

Ah hah! There he was. Her gaze settled on Raven's bare, broad, suntanned shoulders. He was talking to an old woman, his back to Tess. Tess gripped the birchbark doorway, mustering her courage. It was time he made up his mind, either he was going to have to let her go, or burn her at the stake, one or the other. Tess knew she had planned to wait and let Dream Woman reason with him, but she was tired of waiting.

Tess squared her shoulders and started across the compound, her moccasins, the moccasins that had been Takooko's, making imprints on the dusty ground. The fringe on the short leather skirt Dream Woman had insisted she don brushed back and forth across the backs of her legs. Dream Woman had also given Tess a sleeveless leather vest much like the one Raven had loaned her. Using one of Dream Woman's knives, Tess had cut the skirt from her shift and now wore the tattered bodice tucked into her leather skirt, with the vest over top. Tess felt vulnerable, half-naked like this, but at least her breasts were covered and not swinging in the sunshine like most of the women's in the village.

Tess passed two women carrying a large water skin on a stick; they watched her go by with interest. Tess kept walking. A husband and wife standing near their wigwam with a set of twin toddlers turned their heads to watch her with curiosity. Tess kept walking. She could hear the murmur of voices as she passed the wigwams, but she ignored them. She walked straight up to Raven. "I want to talk to you."

For a minute, she wasn't sure he'd heard her. He just stood there, his back to her.

The old woman who spoke to him stopped in mid-sentence and stared at Tess.

Tess felt her resolve waver a little. "I said I want to talk to you, Raven," she repeated. "Now."

Slowly he turned to face her.

Tess could see a smile tugging at the old woman's mouth.

"I did not give you permission to leave my mother's wigwam, did I?" Raven intoned.

Tess rested one hand on her hip. "You have to let me go." She raised her voice. "You've kept me almost a week. You can't imprison me here any longer!"

He grabbed her by her arm, just above the elbow. "Do not speak so loudly."

She tried to jerk her arm from his grip. "I'll talk as loud as I want! You can't keep me as your prisoner. I didn't do anything wrong and you know it. What happened to your brother isn't my fault!" She dared to point a finger at him with her free hand, touching his bare chest. "And you know it! You know it!"

Raven slapped her hand down and snatched her arm, nearly pulling her off her feet. He walked away, dragging her behind him.

Tess heard a ripple of voices as the villagers watched them go by.

"Let go of me," Tess demanded. "You can't do this to me! You can't keep me a prisoner when I've done nothing wrong."

Raven dragged her toward a wigwam and pushed her inside, shoving her so hard that she stumbled and fell. She slid on the hard-packed dirt floor, scraping one elbow.

He stepped into the wigwam behind her and dropped the door flap. Now that they were alone suddenly Tess didn't feel quite so brave.

"Son of a bitch," she muttered, getting up and rubbing her skinned elbow. Cursing had never been permitted in her uncle's house, but damned if cursing wasn't sometimes necessary!

Raven stared at her with his heathen black eyes. "In this village you do not speak to another like that before others. You do not speak to me in such a tone. You insult me in front of my people."

She licked her hand and rubbed it against her bloody elbow. The skin stung. "Three days! It's been three days since you brought me here, and you haven't spoken a word to me! You just left me tied to that house. If your mother hadn't cut the leather, I guess I'd still be there!"

He crossed his arms over his bare chest. "My mother, she should have left you tied to the lodgepole. Perhaps it would improve your manners."

"My manners!" Tess scoffed. "My manners! You're the one who promised you wouldn't hurt me and then dragged me through the forest! You're the one who brought me here against my will and then tied me to a post like some animal!"

He raised his upper lip in a sneer. "I could have killed you. It would be my right, a life for a life."

Tess suddenly felt her eyes stinging with tears again. She was so angry, so frustrated. But she wouldn't cry. She wouldn't give him the satisfaction of knowing how desperate she felt inside. She lowered her head, trying to get control of her emotions. "Then why didn't you?" she asked softly. Her voice grew stronger as she went on. "Why didn't you just kill me and get it over with, Raven?" Slowly she lifted her chin to meet his gaze. "Why?"

Raven stared at her for a moment. "I don't know," he answered, his hostility seeming to wane. "I do not know why. Perhaps because I have already seen enough killing to last a man's lifetime."

The tone of his voice struck a chord in Tess's heart. She hated this man, she hated him for what he'd done to her, but a part of her, a tiny part of her, wanted to comfort him. He had lost his brother, a brother he had obviously loved very much, and in a way, maybe it was her fault. If he hadn't been trying to help her get home, Takooko would never have been murdered by Myron's gun. How would Tess have felt if the tables had been turned? What if it was Abby that lay in that grave?

"Raven, I'm sorry about what happened. I'm truly sorry." She took a halting step toward him, confused by the feelings that made her chest constrict. "But I can't bring him back, and me being here, you punishing me, it can't bring him back either." She took a slow breath, hoping her words were sinking in. "You have to do something. You can't just keep me here forever, and . . . and I don't think you would really kill me, would you?"

Raven's gaze met hers and for a moment time seemed to stand still. For a moment Tess felt his pain and for a moment he seemed to feel hers. There was a strange electric charge that leaped between them, a charge that made her skin tingle.

"You have to let me go," she said softly. "Please, Raven . . ."

Raven turned away. He pulled down some sort of headdress from the birch rafters and fingered the feathers. "Tonight we feast. A tribute to the man I called brother. You will come."

"And what?" She gestured. "Be the main course?"

Raven looked back at her, his solemn face breaking into a smile. "You are funny, Tess. My brother, he was a man who liked humor."

Tess was now utterly confused by Raven's sudden change in mood. He hadn't answered her. He hadn't said what he meant to do with her, but he didn't seem to be angry anymore. He was almost laughing!

So, was he going to let her go after this feast? Is that what he was telling her?

"I didn't know your brother long, but I liked him. This feast, it's to honor him?"

Raven nodded. "When one of us dies, we must rejoice. Though our hearts are saddened for our selfish selves, we must be glad that his soul has risen into the heavens."

She nodded. "I'll come. I'll come and celebrate with you, but then you have to let me go. You can't keep me here. Your mother said you can't keep me for a slave like the Mohawk would have. She said your people don't do that."

"My mother should not speak to you of what is not her concern. Go back to her wigwam and prepare yourself. You may go to the creek to wash. But,"—he pointed— "this man warns you. The sentries watch you and will not allow you to escape. If you try, you will be punished."

Tess opened her mouth to comment, but he didn't give her a chance.

"—I will come for you when the drums call. Go and leave me so that I might make ready."

Realizing she was dismissed, Tess walked toward the doorway. She turned back to look at him before she ducked out. He was gathering clothing, paying no attention to her. She stepped out into the humid late afternoon and walked back to Dream Woman's wigwam.

Tess found Dream Woman alone in her house. The older woman was drinking tea from a porcelain teacup, staring idly. Tess hesitated in the doorway, not wanting to intrude. When Dream Woman spotted her, she waved her in.

"Come." She smiled as if today was not such a terrible day. "I found berries. Tomorrow I will teach you how to dry them for the long winter."

Her comment seemed odd to Tess, but Tess didn't say anything. A lot of the comments these people made seemed odd to her. "I . . . I don't mean to bother you, but he . . . Raven said I would go with him to the feast tonight. He said I could go to the creek and wash up." She came inside. The wigwam floor had been covered in fresh pine boughs and smelled pungent and sweet.

Dream Woman got to her feet. "My sorries. I am a poor hostess." She went to a basket woven of dry pine needles that hung above her head. "Let me give you soap to wash your hair and oils for your young skin. Clean hair brings life to woman."

"No, no that's all right." Tess touched her hair, suddenly feeling self-conscious, realizing how dirty the thick tresses must be. "I was just going to wash my hands and face. I was thinking . . . a towel maybe or a piece of old cloth?"

Dream Woman turned to look at Tess. "Tow-el?"

Tess made a motion, brushing her arms with her hand as if she was drying off. "You know, to rub off the water."

Dream Woman frowned. "It is our way to let the Mother Sunshine and wind wipe the water from our flesh." She came across the wigwam to press two small soft leather bags and a porcupine hairbrush into Tess's hand. "Go, clean yourself. Make your hair fresh and sweet for the Raven. A man likes a woman with hair that smells of the sunshine."

Tess twisted her foot in the pine boughs on the wigwam floor. "I know I shouldn't ask, but,"—she looked up at the beautiful Indian woman—"did you speak to him about me . . . to Raven?"

"I have not had the chance to talk to my son, but tonight at the feasting I will." She patted Tess's shoulder. "This woman, she promises all will be right. I am called Dream Woman for the futures I see in the flames of the fire. Go. Soon darkness will fall and the drums will call us."

Tess took the brush and little leather pouches and left Dream Woman's home. She crossed the compound, weaving her way between the other wigwams. The village was alive with activity, but no one paid her much mind. She was greeted with a few curious stares and the occasional wave.

Tess sighed. Maybe Dream Woman was right, maybe cleaning up would make her feel better. She was so confused by all that had happened in the last week and the strange mixture of emotions she felt inside. A bath might clear her head.

Tess followed a narrow path through a grove of sycamore trees toward the creek. She passed two women on her way, both of them with wet hair and bodies still dewy from bathing. Tess nodded hesitantly, after all no one in the village but Raven had been unkind. One of the Indian maids nodded and smiled at Tess. The other looked away. Tess continued her way to the creek.

At the creek bed Tess walked upstream a little to avoid several Indian women bathing naked. Tess was shocked by their lack of modesty. There they were standing in broad daylight wearing nothing but tiny triangular leather skirts over their netherparts. They were bathing barebreasted in the creek where anyone, any man, could come along and see them!

Tess glanced back over her shoulder. She was certainly shocked as any decent white woman would be but she couldn't help wondering what it would feel like to stand in the sunshine all wet and naked. Would she laugh like these women laughed now?

Around a slight bend in the creek she found a place where the shallow water turned deeper. Tess sat down on the side of the mossy bank and removed her moccasins. Setting the brush and leather pouches down, she dipped her feet in. The water was so cold she had to stifle a squeal. But after a moment her feet grew a little numb and the fresh water felt good.

Dangling her feet in the creek below, Tess opened the drawstring of one of the little bags Dream Woman had given her. A strange herbal scent rose from the doeskin pouch. Inside were fibers from some frothy weed.

Soap? Tess thought to herself. Was that what Dream Woman said this was? She opened the second pouch to find a smooth cream that smelled faintly of honeysuckle. Tess smiled to herself. Jocelyn had always had jars and pots of strong smelling perfumes on her dressing table. Once Tess had tried a little from a small blue jar. She'd only used a dab of the oily perfume and hadn't even liked the smell of it on her skin, but later Jocelyn had noticed the scent of it on Tess and had thrown a fit. After that Tess had not been permitted in Jocelyn's bedchamber, even to clean.

Tess closed the second drawstring bag and shrugged off the woman's vest Dream Woman had given her to wear. Wearing the short leather skirt and the remnant of the bodice of her shift, Tess leaped into the creek. The cold water hit her mid-section making her gasp for air. How did those women swim in this icy water?

The temperature was so cold that Tess was tempted to climb out, but she found herself so grimy that her desire to be clean overrode her discomfort. Her body slowly numbing to the cold, she grabbed the soap bag and waded out a little further. Sitting on the gravelly bottom she leaned back and wet her hair. Then, removing a bit of the frothy weed from the bag, she tossed it to the bank and began to soap her hair. The weed was surprisingly rich, forming soapy bubbles in her hair as she massaged it into her scalp.

Heavens, how long had it been since she'd been able to wash her hair? Tess groaned with delight as she leaned back in the cold water and swirled her hair to rinse it. It was then, just out of the corner of her eye that she spotted the Indian.

Tess sat up, trying to cover the transparent wet cotton of her shift bodice with her arms.

The Indian stood leaning against a tree watching her. Unlike Raven, he wore his hair shorn in the front and long in the back. From one ear dangled a silver earring and around his neck he wore necklaces of shells and acorns. He was a handsome enough man with a long aquiline nose and high cheekbones. His bare shoulders were every bit as muscular as Raven's, but this man was shorter, stockier. *Funny that I would immediately compare him to Raven,* Tess thought.

The Indian smiled, showing even white teeth as he waved a greeting. He appeared friendly enough despite the fact that he was heavily armed. Strapped over one shoulder, he carried a flintlock musket. From his beaded belt hung a feathered hatchet.

Tess just stood there looking at him for a moment, debating what to do. Should she scream? Run? Her hair hung in thick hanks, dripping down her back and shoulders. Standing out of the water like this, she shivered with cold.

"Greetings," the brave said lazily. "I am called Na-Kee."

"I . . . I'm Tess."

"I know. My village is alive with women's chatter that the Raven has flown in with a white woman beneath his black wing."

Tess rubbed her bare arms for warmth taking care to keep her breasts covered.

Na-Kee gave a wave. "Do not fear me. I will not hurt you. I am War Chief of my people and a respected man." He smiled again. "Some maids say I am even an attractive man."

Slowly Tess waded toward shore, keeping her eye on

him. At the bank, she twisted her hair in her fingers. "I . . . I was just bathing," she said. "I'm going to the feast."

"Hair the color of the flame," Na-Kee mused. His gaze met hers. "Good, I will see you, then. I will go to the feast as well."

Still feeling self-conscious of her wet bodice, she reached for the leather vest on the ground and slipped into it. When she looked up, he was standing right beside her.

"A woman so beautiful needs beauty to adorn her." He lifted a necklace of acorns from his bare chest and lowered it over her head.

Tess touched the pretty necklace. "Thank you." She offered the barest smile.

"Na-Kee. I am called Na-Kee."

"Thank you, Na-Kee," she repeated softly.

He brushed her chin with a finger. Before Tess could react he had walked away, back up the path Tess had come.

He was nice enough, Tess thought as she opened the bag of honeysuckle cream and dipped her finger into it. But come to think of it, everyone in the village had been pleasant enough. Everyone but Raven. She rubbed the cream onto her dry hands and arms, even rubbing a little at her neck. The acorn beads around her neck clicked as she moved and she liked the sound. She knew the necklace was just worthless acorns, but she'd never owned any jewelry before.

Realizing she'd probably been gone long enough, Tess gathered the leather bags and brush Dream Woman had given her and started back down the path. As she walked, she pulled the thick bristled brush through her hair. Halfway back to the village, Tess met Raven.

He stopped on the center of the path, staring at her. "Where did you get that?" he demanded.

Tess looked at him. He was angry at her again. "Where did I get what?"

He pointed. "The necklace!"

Tess touched the acorn necklace the brave in the forest had given her. *A woman so beautiful needs beauty* he had said. No one had ever called her beautiful before. "From a man in the woods. He knew you. He said his name was Na-Kee."

Raven reached out and grabbed the necklace from around her neck, snapping it with one swift, angry motion. The string broke and the acorns tumbled to the ground. "Never, ever take another thing from Na-Kee," he warned. "Never!"

Before Tess could say a word, Raven stalked off, leaving her on the path alone, acorns scattered at her feet.

Seven

At first, Tess barely recognized the sound she heard as that of a drum. The beat was pounded out slowly, so slowly that she thought surely each soft beat would be the last. But then gradually they grew closer together . . . louder. First there was just one drum, then many that beat as one. The resounding, hollow pulse drew her to the edge of the sleeping platform she sat on inside Dream Woman's wigwam. She began to breathe in anticipation of each beat, taken unaware by the control the echo of the drum held over her. The drums were calling her . . .

Wasn't that what Raven had said. *'I will come for you when the drums call?'* Hadn't Dream Woman said, *'Soon the drums will call us?'*

After her encounter with Raven, Tess had returned to Dream Woman's wigwam. Finding the older woman gone, Tess was left alone to brush out her hair and prepare herself for the feast that would celebrate Takooko's death. With Raven so angry at her over Na-Kee's gift she wondered if he would still come for her as he'd promised.

Tess could hear the villagers as they shuffled past the wigwam headed for the communal fire. She could smell the smoky aroma of the roasted venison that mixed with the pungent, unfamiliar odor of incense. And still the drums beat, calling, calling, not just the *Lenni Lenape,* but calling her.

When Raven finally walked into the wigwam, she was ready. She bounced up off the sleeping platform. "I . . . I was afraid you wouldn't come," she said, allowing her gaze to meet his, forcing him to look at her. "I'm not used to spending so much time alone. In my mother's house and then my uncle's there were always people around." She gave a nervous laugh not knowing why she felt she needed to tell him that. "No privacy."

"To be whole, a man must spend time alone with himself." He tapped his bare chest. "Only then can he truly know himself and his desires."

Was he chastising her? By the light of the tallow lamp that hung from a birch rafter Tess stared at Raven. He wore a brief leather loincloth that a week ago would have shocked her. Now it seemed almost sacrilegious to cover a body as perfectly molded by God as was his. Raven's intricately quilled moccasins nearly reached his knees. He wore a belt made of a snapping turtle's head and neck that ran diagonally across his broad bare chest from his shoulder to his slender hip. Around his waist he wore a white doeskin bag embroidered with flowers and leaves. Out of the top of the bag the stem of a clay pipe protruded. His freshly washed hair, still damp, fell in a curtain as far down his back as Tess's own hair. Woven into his tresses, as black and shiny as a crow's wing, was an ornament of feathers, shells, and white leather strips.

Self-consciously Tess smoothed her short skirt, feeling out of place beside a man so innately handsome. "I didn't have anything to dress up in," she said softly. "I'm still wearing his moccasins." She showed him one foot. "I hope that's all right."

"Where my brother has gone he will not need them, Tess," he said gently. "He would be glad you could wear them to protect your feet." Then he beckoned her with curling fingers. "Come, we must go. The drums call."

Tess followed Raven out of the wigwam and he indicated that she was to walk at his side. Had she been promoted from prisoner to something more? She couldn't tell.

Darkness was settling in on the Lenape village nestled in the fork of a creek that ran somewhere off the Potomac River. The ancient trees that surrounded the village seemed to Tess to hang protectively over it allowing the last of the day's sweet sunlight to seep through the leafy branches. The air was smokey from the large campfire in the center of the village, but not unpleasantly so, not like the kitchen back at her uncle's home. This smoke that smelled of venison, pungent herb incense, and pine boughs seemed to cloak the men and women who gathered, rather than smothering them.

The hollow leather drums still beat, but now the sounds of gourd rattles and bone sticks had been added to the rhythm. As Tess and Raven approached the campfire, she watched with fascination as men danced in circles around the blaze. Old women chanted in an ancient tempo that matched the drum beats and Tess had to suppress the urge to lift her hands and clap with the other women and children.

The circle of dancers opened as Raven drew closer. Giving her a nudge toward the women, he left her so that he could join the men. Lifting his head to sound an eery cry, Raven tapped his feet to the haunting music. Around and around he and the other men danced, Raven leading, the other men imitating him in sound and motion.

What Raven had said was true; this was no dance of mourning. That was evident in the suntanned faces of the villagers as they sang and danced in honor of Takooko who had fallen. This was a dance of celebration. Even as Tess watched the smoke from the campfire rise and curl heavenward, she could feel the villagers releasing Takooko's soul.

All too soon the men's dance came to an end and Raven came to Tess, breathless, his entire body moist with perspiration. "You think our customs are barbaric," he said, weaving his way through the crowd.

"No." She followed him. "I thought it was a beautiful tribute. I had a brother once who died. He was just barely a year old. We buried him in an open field and then we went home to make dinner. Little Harry would have liked us to have danced for him."

Raven had stopped next to a woman, her face lined with scores of years, ladling drinks with a dry gourd. He took a turtle shell cup filled to the brim and handed it to Tess. His eyes were gentle as he met her gaze. "So we have both lost, Tess."

She brought the turtle shell to her lips enjoying the sound of her name on the red man's lips. She tasted the drink to find it cool and minty. "Tell me why you were angry with me today when I accepted Na-Kee's gift," she said softly. "I don't think he meant me any harm."

As the old Indian woman pressed a turtle shell cup into Raven's hand she said something in her native tongue. Raven frowned and walked away. "That's why," he said, waiting for Tess to catch up.

Tess looked over her shoulder at the old woman. "Why? What did she say?"

"She asked me if I intended to return to my duties now that I've finally decided to return home from my wandering."

"I thought you told me you went to an important meeting for your village." She followed him to a tree where he squatted near the base and drank deeply from his cup.

"I did, but there are those of my people who felt Takooko and I should not have gone to the Gathering. There are those who say we must decide on our own whether we fight the English white-hairs."

"Who said you shouldn't have gone to the meeting?"

Raven nodded and Tess followed his gaze until she spotted Na-Kee deep in conversation with two braves on the far side of the campfire.

"Na-Kee?" Tess didn't know why she cared. But somehow this suddenly seemed important to her. For the moment her own troubles were lost. "You mean he wants to fight and you don't?"

With one hand Raven tugged back a handful of his thick black hair. "It is not that simple." He paused as if reluctant to go on. "Na-Kee wishes to become the new War Chief of our village. I must become the new War Chief. Na-Kee believes the duty of War Chief is to lead warriors into battle. I believe the duty is to use the wisdom of the village young and old to *decide* when men must fight and when they must not. Only then does a War Chief lead his warriors into a battle."

"I see," Tess breathed. "Who'll decide who will be War Chief if both of you want it?"

Raven finished the last of his drink and set the turtle shell aside. "Our people will vote."

Tess looked back in the direction of the old woman dipping drinks. "Some people don't think you should be the War Chief? Is that why she said that to you?"

"My opponent spreads falsehoods faster than a woman spreads honey. Na-Kee is a burr that works his way into men and women's moccasins, making them question what they know to be true." Raven idly drew in the dust with his finger. "While I travel to and from the Great Algonquian Gathering, Na-Kee busies himself bringing gifts to the village, bribes sent by the French Canadians. He tells our people we will be better off with the protection of the French white-hairs. He tells them he thinks only of their welfare." The expression on Raven's face hardened. "I think Na-Kee's hand itches to carry a war axe again. I do not think he cares what happens to our people. Not in his heart of hearts."

"And you do, don't you?" she murmured with understanding. After a moment of silence, she looked through the darkness to see his face. "You don't think you should fight, do you?"

He lifted his gaze to stare into the orange-yellow light of the campfire. "I do not know, but what I do know is that our decision will change the path of my people forever. The English have been driving us further from our homeland for one hundred years. It cannot go on if we as a race are to survive, but this is too important a decision to make so quickly without thought. Who is to say the English are any more our enemy than the French? It is a decision that should not be made with gifts and false words."

Tess looked through the smoke of the fire at Na-Kee. He caught sight of her and smiled a handsome smile. She looked back at Raven. "The King's army is the greatest in all the world, you know. I do not know that the French could win. My fiance says they are fools to think they can fight and win."

Raven looked up at her sitting cross-legged beside him. "You were to marry?"

She twisted her fingers in her lap. "Soon. His name is

Myron." She didn't tell him Myron was the man who had shot Takooko. What was the point?

"You love him, this My-Ron?" Raven asked bluntly.

It seemed a strange question to Tess. No one else had asked her if she loved Myron, not her uncle when he'd agreed to the union, not even Myron. "He's a good man." She thought of Abby sitting alone in her silent world waiting for her big sister to send for her. "He'll be a good provider."

Raven shook his head. "I do not know why I try to understand the white-hairs. I will never understand them."

She finished her drink and set the turtle shell cup beside his. "Why do you say that?" She sat beside him now, close enough to brush elbows.

"A man and a woman were meant to marry only when there is love between them."

Tess laughed. What an absurd thought. Women married for security, men married for legitimate heirs. Everyone knew that. "And what if love never comes?"

He stood up, stretching his long limbs. "Then you do not marry, Tess."

She wanted to ask him if that was why he had no wife, but she didn't. He offered his hand and Tess rose to find herself facing Raven, only a few inches separating their bodies. He dropped her hand, but then reached up to brush a bit of hair from her cheek. Tess was surprised by the tingle of sensation his warm fingers left behind.

"My mother tells me I cannot keep you prisoner. Already the women talk. They say I should not have brought one of the English white-hair's daughters to our village. They say a man who wants to be War Chief should not be so irresponsible."

Tess looked into his black eyes, mesmerized by the

depths. The pounding music and the nearness to Raven was making her light-headed. For a moment she seemed to be caught in some sort of spell. "And what do you say?" she heard herself whisper.

He touched her again, this time drawing the back of his fingers along her jawline. It was an intimate touch that made Tess tremble inside. She was confused. Why had Myron never made her feel like this?

"My head tells me I must let you go . . ." Raven said softly, his words meant only for her.

"But?" Tess breathed.

"But . . ." He was touching her hair again, this time twisting a bit between his fingers. "But I see you in a vision, Tess. I see your magic hair, hair that would bring good luck to any man's hearth." His black eyes were suddenly piercing. "I see you as mine, Tess."

Tess didn't know what to say. She wasn't even sure just what he meant. His? She couldn't be his! She was going to marry Myron. She was going to marry Myron and bring her deaf sister to the Colonies to live with them.

But Myron had never made her feel like this. . . . He had never made her warm in the pit of her stomach. He had never made her want to touch him like she wanted to touch Raven at this moment.

Tess didn't know whether or not she had expected his kiss. She was relatively inexperienced. Myron's kisses were few and far between, and when he did kiss her, it was often a hasty peck. But when Raven leaned toward her, when he drew her chin with his fingertips so that their gazes were locked, she couldn't help herself. She was afraid, and yet she couldn't make herself turn away. Thoughts of her capture, of Myron, even of Abby slipped from her mind. All that mattered was Raven and this intense attraction she suddenly realized she felt toward him.

His kiss was gentle, but firm, a bare brush of his mouth against hers. Tess heard herself sigh as she closed her eyes exploring the feel of his lips. This was crazy, it was mad, but she wanted the kiss to go on forever.

Raven curled his fingers at the nape of her neck, his senses reeling. He didn't know why he was kissing the white woman. He only knew that the intoxicating scent of her sweet clean hair and the hint of honeysuckle on her skin had drawn him in. For an instant he became her captive. Their lips touched, she meeting him halfway. Her eyes closed and he felt her rest her hand on his bare shoulder. How long had it been since a mere kiss had made Raven feel like this?

Never . . .

Too soon their lips parted and Raven found himself looking down into startled doe brown eyes. A part of him wanted to comfort her, to tell her there was no need to fear him, and yet a part of him wanted to warn her. *Run, Tess. Run sweet Tess. Run before it's too late for both of us.*

Tess touched her lips with her own fingertips, still seeming to be surprised by their kiss, by the intense reaction they had shared.

He reached out to touch her, wanting to tell her it would be all right, but she bolted. Like a frightened animal in the forest, she turned and ran. Raven contemplated going after her, but then he heard laughter. He turned to see Na-Kee coming toward him.

"Does this mean your captive does not appreciate your attentions?" Na-Kee asked in their native tongue.

Raven scowled. "You creep about the darkness like a rat, Na-Kee."

Na-Kee only laughed. Raven could smell the stench of the French brandy-wine on his breath. More bribes. "Better to hand her to me now, brother, and let me teach her of lovemaking."

Raven's eyes narrowed dangerously. Although it was the tradition among his people, it galled him to hear Na-Kee refer to him as brother. Raven's brother was dead. This man would never, ever be his brother. "She is mine, Na-Kee— my captive. This man warns you, stay away from her."

"They say it is odd, a man who wishes to be War Chief to his people, bringing a white-skinned woman into the village. An English woman no less. They say she will bring bad luck. They say perhaps they should not trust your judgment."

Raven knew Na-Kee was baiting him. He knew he must not bite, not here in front of so many, not on the night of his brother's funeral. "Take heed, Na-Kee. Sooner or later our people will see through your bribes and lies and know you for the man you truly are."

"Best you not be concerned with me and mine, brother, but yours." He nodded to the far right.

Raven turned to see his mother and his friend Taande in an embrace. He was utterly taken aback, but tried not to let on so. "Taande is a good friend to me and to my mother," he answered evenly, forcing himself to look away.

Na-Kee chuckled, slipping a silver flask from his pipe bag. "That does not look like the embrace of a friend, brother," he taunted. "I think your mother is infatuated with Taande's young flesh." He made a clicking sound between his teeth before raising the whiskey flask to his mouth. "It does not look right, a woman of her age with a man the age of her own son."

Raven looked back at Dream Woman and Taande. They

were now standing side by side in the shadow of a wig-wam, talking to each other. Raven's mother was laughing the laugh of a young maiden with her first buck.

When had this happened? Raven wondered. Could he have been so busy with his own pursuit of the position of War Chief that he had failed to notice that his best friend had begun courting his mother?

Raven walked away from Na-Kee without a word. First there was the situation with the village and the white-hairs, then Takooko's death and Tess's capture, and now this. How had his life suddenly become so tangled? How would he know what was right to do?

As he walked, Raven glanced overhead at the stars be-ginning to prick through the cover of darkness. *The Star Bridge of Souls,* the Algonquian tribes called the constel-lations. He prayed silently to the God above to give him strength and wisdom. He was going to need it.

Eight

"What have you done to her?" Dream Woman demanded of her son in their Algonquian tongue.

Raven looked up from where he sat outside his wigwam repairing a chipped arrow point. It was mid-day and the sun was hot on his face. He squinted, looking up at his mother. "Who, *Ngaxais?* What have I done to who?"

"You know who. The white woman. Tess."

Her. Raven returned his attention to the stone arrow point in his hands. He'd slept little last night. His head had been too alive with thoughts for sleep. But it was not Na-Kee or the position of War Chief that had kept him awake. It was not even Takooko's death. It was that pale-skinned woman. It was Tess.

He regretted kissing her. He should never have allowed himself to have become attracted to her. It was a mistake to think of a captive as anything other than property. He knew that. To think of her as anything else weakened his position as the captor. All these facts raced through his mind, yet still he had thought of the taste of her lips on his, and the smell of her honeysuckle-scented skin. Even in the midst of chastising himself for making such a mistake as kissing her, he thought of what it would be like to kiss her again, to thrust his tongue between her lips, to cup her rounded breast in his hand . . .

"I have done nothing to the white woman." Raven reached for a stone chipping-tool that had been his great-grandfather's. "Why do you ask?"

Dream Woman knelt beside her son. "Last night when I entered my lodge, she was crying. This morning she begs me to ask for her release. I think she fears for her life, Raven. You know the Mohawk tortured and murdered her cousin."

"I am not Mohawk!"

"Of course you are not. But she looks at the color of our skin and she sees red men and women. To her, to the white-hairs, there is no difference, my son."

"I will not kill her."

"I know you won't."

"She knows I will not kill her. She spoke the words herself."

Dream Woman sighed, leaning on her bare thighs. "I am concerned for you. Na-Kee tells others that bringing the white woman into the village will call the spirits of bad luck. Tell me the truth, son of my heart, why do you keep her here?"

"I am a man full grown. You have no right to ask me such questions."

"You do not have to answer me, but once a long time ago, I suckled you at my breast." She waggled her finger at him. "That gives me the right to ask."

Raven slipped with the sharp stone tool and struck his hand. Blood stained the soft inner flesh between his thumb and first finger. He sucked at his hand irritably. "Do not worry. I will deal with Na-Kee and the woman in my own time."

Dream Woman smiled a mother's smile. "You want her."

"That is ridiculous. She is white."

"And so is the future of our race. It is a mixture of red and white. Your grandmother, my mother said as much, God rest her soul." Dream Woman made the sign of the cross and lifted her crucifix to her lips.

Raven set aside his broken arrow point knowing it was useless to go on. "Just say what you came here to say. I have a great deal of work to do, *Ngaxais.*"

"I am saying free her or make her your own. At a time like this, you cannot afford to anger the elders. I see through Na-Kee's handsome smiles and his gifts of blankets and pretty baubles, but there are those who do not."

"They are fools."

"Perhaps. But they cling to the old ways. They want desperately to believe Na-Kee. They want to think they can remain here as they are, as they have been for a thousand summers." She shrugged. "So they believe Na-kee's lies."

Raven glanced sideways at his mother. "You speak of making the white woman my own? What do you mean?"

"I say marry the fire-haired woman and together you will bear sons and daughters that will withstand the upheaval of our world. They will change what you and I cannot." She clasped her hands and then separated them, showing him her palms. "Half red, half white, and perhaps a few drops of our ancestors' blood will survive the ages, Raven."

"Marry her?" Raven laughed at the absurdity of such a thought. He would marry no white woman! Most likely he would marry no woman at all. Soon he would be War Chief of his people, and then he would have no time for a wife and children. "I need no woman!" he scoffed.

"Hah! A woman is exactly what you need, my son. A wife and a papoose hanging from a cradleboard is what makes a man realize what is important in life and what is not. Only a man who has married and seen a child of his blood enter this world can truly know what life is."

"I will not marry the white woman. Do not speak to me again of such ridiculous matters."

Dream Woman gave a disgusted snort as she rose. "Stubborn like your father, you are. When will you learn, my son, that you must follow your visions?"

"I have had no vision."

Dream Woman smiled, shaking her head. "Go back to your man's weapons, Raven. You can fool yourself but never the woman who bore you."

"While you are here," Raven said, dismissing the subject of Tess, "let us speak of another matter, my *ngaxais.*" He rose.

Even when Dream Woman drew herself to her full height, her head barely reached her son's shoulders. "Yes?"

"Taande."

She lifted a feathery eyebrow. "Taande?"

Raven could tell by the twinkle in her black eyes that she knew very well what he was talking about. "I saw you last night."

"You saw me what?"

"He was touching you. You were touching him. I believe there were others who saw you kiss."

Dream Woman laughed. "You are a man full grown, you tell me. Surely you are not shocked by what a man and woman do?"

"Mother, it does not look right."

"I am a widow. I have born three children. I have buried one. I have a widow's rights to seek the attentions of any unmarried man I wish."

Raven wasn't sure what to say. He didn't want to hurt his mother's feelings, but he felt a duty to say something. "Mother, Taande was born the same summer as I."

A smile spread across Dream Woman's pretty face. "You think I'm too old for a man!"

"Not too old for a man, *Ngaxais,* only too old for Taande." He offered his hand. "What of Sleeping Bear? He's your age and a widower looking for a companion."

"And he is toothless. He doesn't want a companion, he wants a woman who will chew his food for him!"

Raven grimaced. Sleeping Bear was toothless. "He-Who-Frowns?"

"Exactly."

"Two Squirrels?"

"He wants to do nothing but sit by his fire, have his daughters and sons bring him food and tobacco, and talk of the old days when he was young and virile." She dropped her hands to her hips. "Raven, I'm too young to sit by my fire and smoke my pipe." She rested her hand on his arm. "Take care of your sleeping mat and I will take care of mine."

"Tell me you have not slept with my best friend, Mother."

Dream Woman laughed. "Do not worry yourself over me, *ngwees.*" She gave him a pat and turned away. As she walked away, she called over her shoulder to him. "Think on what I have said about Tess. You will see that I'm right."

As Raven stood watching Dream Woman depart, he wondered why he could not have had a mother like Taande's. Little Swan had always tended to her woman's duties and never concerned herself with her son's affairs.

Little Swan had never been nearly as perceptive as Dream Woman.

Myron Ellsworth chewed on a thumbnail nervously. He had been standing here in the Great Hall of *MacElby's Fate* for nearly an hour. He waited on Albert MacElby, his betrothed's uncle and guardian.

Myron had dressed carefully in his Sunday coat and breeches, and polished his boots until they shone. The truth be known, he was more comfortable in his homespun breeches and shirt and leather apron than these gentlemen's trappings. Myron didn't know why MacElby had sent for him, but it was important he look his best. He might well only be a gunsmith, but he was as good as any MacElby on this plantation.

Myron caught a bit of his thumbnail between his teeth, tore it off, and spat it on the polished hardwood floor. Cleanest hands on the Chesapeake his mother had always said, clean hands, clean soul.

To keep his hands clean of his trade's thick oils and black smudges he scrubbed them each night with lye soap. It was true the harsh chemical had burned his flesh over the years, but at least they were clean.

Impatient to get the meeting over with, Myron paced the airy hallway. Walking to and fro, he caught a glimpse of himself in a narrow mirror as he passed by. Painted gold cherubs danced at the corner of the frame.

Myron stopped and peered into the mirror. He licked his hand and smoothed what hair remained of his fast-receding hairline. He wasn't a handsome man, he knew that. He was short and thin, but with good teeth and only a few pockmarks. He would never be a handsome man, his mother had always said, but good looks were the work of the devil anyway.

Myron stared at the sad reflection of himself. He had been decent enough in appearance for dear Tess, hadn't he?

He walked away from the mirror, beginning to pace again, his boot heels clicking on the floor, his cocked hat crushed beneath his arm. The thought of Tess made Myron shudder. Poor Tess, poor, dear Tess. To have been kidnapped and ravaged by savages! It was almost too much for him to bear. The search party had found Jocelyn's tortured body, or what was left of it only a few days after they'd been taken. Myron had expected it would only have been a matter of time before they found his darling Tess, dead.

Then the search party had come upon the hostiles who still held Tess. Myron had tried his best to catch them; he'd killed one bloody beast. He'd caught a glimpse of Tess's face, frozen in stark fear. Then she'd disappeared, dragged into the forest by the wild Indian. The men in the search party had been unable to track the savage and had finally given up to start home. On the journey back toward Annapolis, the other men had tried to comfort Myron. They had said he had to give up on her. All hope was lost.

But Tess had agreed to marry him. She had agreed to sleep in his bed and give him children. Myron figured he couldn't just leave her behind, never knowing what happened to her. He owed Tess more than that.

Suddenly Myron heard a commotion from the rear of the great house. Dogs barked and ran, sliding on the hardwood floor, their nails scraping. Albert MacElby hollered for a servant to take his darlings into the kitchen for their supper. Myron heard a young man shouting at the dogs, trying to get control of them as they raced through the house.

Myron pressed his heels together as he heard MacElby come down the hall.

"Ellsworth!"

Myron heard the tall, sturdy man before he saw him. "Here, in the hallway."

"What the hell are you doing in the hallway, Ellsworth?" Albert MacElby walked by him and into a paneled library. "Misses MacElby said you've been here over an hour."

Not knowing what else to do, Myron followed. "Yes, I have." The library smelled of tobacco, musty pages, and oiled leather.

MacElby walked behind his desk and lifted a decanter from a cherry sidetable. "Why the hell didn't you have someone show you in, get you a drink?" He lifted the cut glass French decanter. "Drink?"

Myron raised his hand. "No, no drink. Not a man who partakes."

MacElby grunted in derision as he poured himself a healthy portion of the brandy-wine. He took a long drink before glancing over the rim of the pewter cup at Myron. "Just why are you here, Ellsworth?" he asked absently.

Myron shifted his weight from one foot to the other. He knew he was as good a man as MacElby, not as wealthy, but a good tradesman, a well-to-do tradesman. He knew he had nothing to fear from MacElby, but still, the man made him uncomfortable. He made Myron feel small. "I . . . I don't know. You sent word to me that you needed to see me."

"Oh, that's right. You'll have to excuse me. Since Jocelyn's death I haven't been right."

The man didn't seem to be terribly distraught to Myron. "I understand."

MacElby leaned on the back of his desk chair. "This is a delicate subject. I don't know how to broach it except to come right out and say it."

Myron tucked his hands behind his back. "Tess."

The older man nodded. "You have to forget her, son. She's gone."

"But I saw her alive."

"Don't you understand, boy? She's probably long dead now, butchered like my Jocelyn."

Myron could feel tears stinging his eyes. He was so embarrassed. He wanted Tess like he had never wanted a woman before. That thick shining crown of red hair, her soft white skin, her pink lips. At night he had laid in bed touching himself and dreaming of what it would be to touch her. Now that would never come to be. He looked up at MacElby hoping he didn't see the moisture in the corners of his eyes. "If she isn't dead—"

MacElby's gaze met Myron's, suddenly cold, his face rigid. "Are you addlepated, smithy? Don't you understand what I'm saying? Even if she isn't dead, you wouldn't want her! You *know* what those red demons have done to her, boy. You *know* how they must have soiled her again and again. I for one am glad my daughter didn't survive the ordeal."

Myron looked down, focusing on the tips of his shiny black boots. He didn't know what to say.

When MacElby spoke again, his tone was kinder. "Find another woman and forget Tess. That's my advice. I know she was my niece, and I shouldn't say this. But as I warned you when you asked my permission to marry her, the chit would never have made a good wife. Tits aren't everything, boy. She was stubborn and willful. Too much a mind of her own for a woman."

Myron continued to study the leather of his boots. He hated it when other men called him boy, or smithy. He bit down on the soft inner lining of his mouth determinedly. He didn't care what Tess's uncle said. He couldn't just forget about her, not knowing she could still be out there somewhere being tortured at the hands of those filthy heathens. She had been his betrothed. He had to do something. He had to make sure she really was dead like MacElby said. He owed her that much . . .

Nine

Dream Woman rested her head in the crook of Taande's arm, her bare legs still tangled in his. They lay on soft sleeping mats on the floor of his wigwam, still breathing heavily, their naked bodies covered in a thin sheen of perspiration.

"Ah Taande," she whispered in her native tongue, staring up at the spidery rafters. "I had forgotten what it was to feel a man's love." She brushed her fingertips over her bare breasts remembering his touch only moments ago. "It has been too long."

He pushed up on one elbow, pressing a kiss to her breast. "I am honored that you would choose me to make you a woman again."

She laughed, lifting to press her lips to his. "You make it sound like such an honorable feat. The truth is that I, Taande, was as anxious to roll in the sleeping mat as you were."

Their laughter mingled as Taande caught her hand and threaded his fingers through hers. "I was afraid I would never find a woman to love, Dream Woman, and suddenly she is in my arms."

Dream Woman lay on her back staring up at the virile brave who had become her lover today. She shook her head. "Don't feel that you have to speak of love, Taande.

To enjoy each other's company for a while, to enjoy the pleasures of the sleeping mat, is enough for me. I'm nearly twenty summers older than you. I don't expect words of love. I have had those in my lifetime."

Taande looked down at her, his face etched with concern. "I don't care about your age. I care about what I feel here." He hit his bare chest with his fist. "You bring alive a part of me I didn't know existed, Dream Woman. I think of you night and day. For longer than I can remember I have dreamed of this day when I would hold you in my arms and make love to you."

Dream Woman brushed his cheek with her fingertips. "Something tells me that the words you speak are true and not just a young man's wooing."

"Because they are true. They are what I feel in my heart."

She felt her eyes sting with sweet tears. She had loved her children's father. Their life together had been so good that she had never expected to feel this way again about another man. Was it possible that the great *Manito* was granting her such a precious gift for the second time in her life? Was this feeling she felt for Taande truly the spark of love, or was it just infatuation with the young, lusty man? Only time would tell.

Dream Woman sat up and reached for a gourd of honey water. She sat cross-legged and uncovered, unashamed of her nude body. Perhaps it was true that her breasts didn't stand as high as they once had, or her belly wasn't as flat as it had been nearly thirty years ago, but she didn't care. If this young buck was truly interested in her, he would have to take her for who she was.

She offered the container to Taande and then drank herself. The water was cool and sweet. "My son does not approve of you and I, you know." She smiled over the rim of the dried gourd.

"I was afraid he would not."

Dream Woman gathered a handful of her long black hair, only sprinkled with grey, and pushed it over her shoulders. "Do you mean you have not spoken of the matter with him?"

"How could I? What would I have said? Raven, best friend I have on this earth, I'm attracted to your mother?"

Dream Woman laughed, the tiered pewter earrings in her ears tinkling with sound. "I must admit you were coy with your attentions. For months I thought you were just looking after your friend's old mother."

"I think that is what I told myself at first. Then when I realized I cared for you, I was fearful you would reject me."

Dream Woman rose on her knees, dropping her hands on Taande's shoulders. He rose pulling her closer until her breasts touched his bare chest. He nuzzled her neck and she sighed.

"This woman is glad you risked my rejection, else I would not have known how attracted I was to my son's friend."

Their lips touched, their tongues mingled, and when they parted again, both were breathless. Taande pulled Dream Woman into his arms and together they laid on their sides so that they could touch and be touched.

"So what do we do about Raven?" Taande murmured, kissing her here and then there.

It was hard for Dream Woman to concentrate when Taande was touching her with his mouth in such delicious ways. "Do? We do nothing." She stroked his cheek, drawing in his gaze for a moment. "But let us allow my son to get used to the idea that we have become friends. He has so much on his head now, that were he to know we were lovers, it might only add to his confusion." She caught Taande's nipple between her teeth and tugged gently.

Taande moaned. "So for now we sneak about like forbidden lovers?"

Dream Woman laughed, her voice low and sensual. Already she could feel that once again familiar tingle deep in her belly and a moistening at her thighs. "It could be fun, couldn't it, lover?"

She giggled, feeling younger than she had in years as, in response, Taande rolled on top of her, covering her mouth with his and silencing her laughter.

Tess paced Dream Woman's wigwam, twisting her hands in anguish. She was angry with herself; she was angry with Raven, even with Myron.

How could Raven have kissed her like that? How could she have enjoyed it so much? Where in sweet Jesus' name was Myron? How could he know she was alive somewhere out here and not be looking for her? Surely an Indian village this large couldn't be impossible to find!

Tess touched her lips for the hundredth time. No matter how hard she tried, she just couldn't forget the feel of Raven's mouth on hers. She couldn't forget the taste of him or how her heart had hammered when he'd kissed her.

This man was the enemy. He had kidnapped her. He had tied her up. He had dragged her through the wilderness. How could she have felt such an intense . . . intense desire for him? This feeling could be nothing else but physical desire. How could her body be betraying her mind like this, even at this moment? How could she want to kiss Raven again?

All Tess could afford to think of was Abby and how carefully she and her sister had laid their plans. Tess couldn't care for this Indian. She couldn't afford to like it here among the Lenape where men and women were so gentle, so accepting. She was going to marry Myron. So what if his kisses didn't excite her? She was going to marry Myron and live in a white clapboard house. She was going to bring Abby here to the Colonies to live in that house with her. Everything was going to be perfect then. There was no room for this black-eyed man that made her tremble when their fingertips met. Her life was going to go exactly as she had planned it.

Tess stared overhead at the domed ceiling of the wigwam feeling a sense of panic rising in her chest. She squeezed her eyes shut trying to calm herself. *Of course those were her plans . . . but how was she going to get on with them stuck here in this village?* What if Raven didn't let her go? What if Myron didn't find her? What if he wasn't even looking for her? What if he'd given her up for dead?

Last night Tess had dreamed she had become Raven's wife. Last night she had dreamed of holding an infant to her breast, a little round-faced baby with almond-shaped eyes and suntanned skin. Even in a dream Tess didn't know how she could abandon her promise to Abby like that. How could she even think subconsciously of becoming Raven's wife? The man was a heathen. She was betrothed to Myron.

Tess had heard of this happening to captives before. Living among them, the captive can begin to think she is one of them. Jocelyn had once told her about a woman from across the bay who had been captured, and when she was finally rescued by her family, she'd said she didn't want to go home. She had wanted to stay with the savages. The rescue party had had to return her to her parents bound and gagged. Jocelyn said it had been the talk of the Maryland colony for months. The rumor was that the white woman had become pregnant by a redskin. Rumor was the poor woman had been sent to a home for the mentally ill somewhere in England.

Tess opened her eyes. She didn't feel mentally ill. But she was confused and frightened. She was confused by her feelings for Raven and frightened of what she might do. She stared at the closed flap on the wigwam door. She had to get out of here; she had to get out of here now while something still made sense.

Tess didn't know where Dream Woman had gone, but when she had left this afternoon she had mentioned that Raven had gone with Na-Kee to meet some scouts. Perhaps Tess could just walk out of the village. She thought of the sentry who had stopped a few days before. Surely she could outsmart one or two men.

Summoning her courage, Tess pulled back the leather flap on the door. Hidden from view, she watched the activity of the village. There had to be a way to sneak out of here undetected. Outside, there were several women hoeing tiny corn plants in the garden to her far left. Two young boys fed the shaggy ponies hobbled near the edge of the village. An old man sat on a tree stump watching two naked toddlers make mudpies in a puddle. Half a dozen wigwams away, a cluster of young women about Tess's age gathered with baskets on their arms . . . berry baskets. They were laughing and talking.

Tess glanced over her shoulder. There hanging from the birch bark rafter above the sleeping platform was Dream

Woman's berry basket. She strode across the wigwam and snatched the basket down from the eaves.

If she was going to escape, she knew she would need a few things. She took a water skin off the wall and tucked it into the basket. To that she added a handful of dried meat she had seen Dream Woman put into a large hanging basket only yesterday. From the wall near the door she took a boning knife. Tess knew it wasn't a great knife for defending one's self, but it had to be better than nothing. Lastly, from under the sleeping mat she had slept on since arriving in the village, she pulled out Jocelyn's slippers. The leather was flat and hard, barely resembling a pair of shoes any longer. But the old slippers gave Tess courage. They were solid proof that she had survived the Mohawk attack and had gotten the best of them. She would get the best of Raven, too.

Tossing a square of tanned leather over the items in the bottom of the berry basket so as not to appear suspicious, Tess ducked out of the wigwam. Outside, in the late afternoon sunshine, she walked confidently across the compound. The women had left the place where they had stood and had started toward the path that entered the woods.

Tess walked casually, as if she'd intended on going berry picking all along. Halfway down the path that led to the creek, she caught up to the other women and eased her way into the group. Most of the young women just looked at her, then ignored her.

One petite woman with her hair in a thick plait down her back smiled hesitantly. "Me am . . . am Dove's Call."

The woman's smile was contagious. "I'm Tess."

Dove's Call looked down at the ground shyly. "This

woman, she knows that. Everyone knows of the English woman the Raven has brought to our village."

Tess didn't know what to say so she didn't say anything. The group of women had reached the creek now and were veering off to the right.

Dove's Call spoke again after an awkward moment of silence. "The others . . . the other women, they have no manners. They are . . ." She snapped her delicate thumb and forefinger searching her mind for the right word. "Jealous! Yes, they are jealous of the white-skinned woman the Raven has brought to our village." Dove's Call waved a hand. "I . . . I am sor-rry. My English words are not good. I was not the good . . . good stu-dint when the Father taught us his words."

"No, no, your English is fine." She laughed. "Better than my Len . . . Lena—"

"Lenape."

"Yes. Lenape." It was strange, but Tess felt an instant camaraderie with this woman. How odd it was that Tess had never had a woman friend in her life but her sister, and in the last week she had met two women she would have liked to have become friends with.

Tess looked at Dove's Call curiously. "You said the other women were jealous of me. What did you mean? How could they possibly be jealous of me?"

The two women had fallen a few steps behind the group. Dove's Call glanced up at them. They were laughing and chattering as they followed the winding path through the forest. "They wish that the Raven . . . they wish he gave them his attentions."

Tess laughed. "Gave them his attentions? Let me tell you, they can have them. Don't those women understand that I don't want to be here? Didn't they see me walk into the village tied up? Don't they understand I have a home?" *That isn't really true. Uncle Albert's home will never be mine.* "I have a family." *Abby, Abby is my family. Abby is all I need.* "Raven has brought me here against my will!"

Dove's Call lowered her gaze. "I am sorry. I have offended you."

Tess touched the Indian woman's arm lightly. "No. No, you haven't. It's not you, it's me. It's just that I—" Tess looked out into the trees overhead feeling a lump rise in her throat. "It's just that I have to get home. I have a sister who's waiting for me. She needs me. You see, she's deaf."

Dove's Call shook her head. "I don't know this word, *deaf.*"

Tess touched her ear. "She can't hear. She had a terrible fever when she was a baby." She smiled, thinking of her sister. "But she's smart. Really smart. She can talk, but she talks with her hands. And the problem is that no one else can understand her but me. Not because they couldn't, just because they won't try. They think that because her hearing was affected by the fever her head must be too."

"My people speak to other tribes with their hands. It is not so odd."

"They do? My sister and I just made up the motions for the words. We don't have a lot of words, but enough to communicate."

"Our people have many sign words," Dove's Call said. "If you like this woman would be happy to teach you the hand signs and then when you are with your sister again, you will have more words to teach her."

Tess couldn't help smiling. Of course she wouldn't be here for Dove's Call to teach her the new words, but she couldn't know that. The offer was a touching gesture. "Thank you, I would like that." She wasn't really lying. She would have liked to have learned the Indian sign language if she was going back to the village. But of course she wasn't. Two days of good luck and she'd be back in her Uncle's home.

The two women walked side by side in comfortable silence. Soon they entered an open meadow where the ground was covered in lush green foliage and tiny red ripe strawberries.

The other Lenape women scattered, spreading out to pick. Dove's Call squatted near the path and began to pluck the sweet berries. She dropped two into her basket and popped one into her mouth. "You could pick with me if you did wish, Tess."

Tess was torn between wanting to spend a few more minutes with the friendly woman and knowing she needed to be closer to the far edge of the forest. That was northeast and that was the direction she knew she needed to go.

"Thank you, but I think I'll pick over there." She pointed.

Dove's Call nodded. Already her lips were red with berry juice. "We will walk home together my new *n'tschu.*"

Tess started to walk away, but then turned back. *"N-chu* . . . what does the word mean?"

Dove's Call licked a berry-stained finger. "In your words it is . . ."—her face suddenly brightened—"friend. You are my new friend, Tess."

Tess walked away, feeling a little sad. No one had ever called her their friend before. It didn't make any sense. She picked a place near the far side of the meadow and dropped on her knees in the strawberries to pick. How could there be good things about being here in this Indian village? How could she, knowing she was a captive, still take pleasure in some of the aspects of the life the Lenape led? She dropped a handful of tiny berries into Dream Woman's basket.

When had life become so confusing? When she and Jocelyn had been kidnapped? No, life had been crystal clear those first two days. Tess had wanted to survive and she'd done what she had to to preserve her life. No, it wasn't until she'd met Takooko and Raven there on the bank of the Susquehanna that her life had become a tangled mess.

Tess lowered her head and concentrated on picking berries while slowly moving away from the group of women. The young maids talked in their native tongue as they filled their baskets, paying no attention to Tess.

Once Tess looked back to see Dove's Call but when the Lenape woman looked up at her, Tess lowered her gaze. Tess almost felt as if she was abandoning her new friend. Of course that was ridiculous. What about Abby? To not try and escape would be like abandoning Abby.

The shadows of the late afternoon began to lengthen as Tess put more and more distance between herself and the other women picking the wild strawberries. It wasn't until she was well out of sight of them that she finally picked up her basket and ran.

Ten

Raven stepped out of his mother's wigwam and into the last sun rays of the day. "Where is she?" he demanded in English.

Dream Woman was just crossing the compound, her hair tousled, her body still tingling from Taande's lovemaking. "Do not shout at your mother," she retorted good-naturedly in the Lenape tongue. "Where is who?"

"You know who. The white woman!" Raven was trying not to sound alarmed, but he had looked everywhere; down by the creek, in his mother's wigwam, even in his own. She was no where to be found.

"You mean Tess?"

Raven brushed back a lock of thick hair irritably. This had not been a good day. He and Kolheek had met with French scouts from a Fort called Dusquesne. An English *manake* General by the name of Braddock was making plans to march north from nearby Fort Cumberland to take the French-held Fort Dusquesne. The French scouts wanted a commitment from Raven's village to help defend the fort. Other Lenape villages further north had already joined them. The Frenchmen wanted braves to serve as escorts, scouts, and fighting men.

Na-Kee was, of course, anxious to make the agreement. When Raven had attempted to question who would remain behind to protect the village the white-hairs had grown agitated. They had upped their payment of guns and whiskey. Raven had tried to press them for guarantees of the village's safety. The discussion had ended in a shoving match. One of the scouts had pulled a knife. Raven had cut off his ear. The filthy scout finally backed down before Raven had been forced to kill him.

On the return trip to the village Raven had tried to discuss the matter with Na-Kee, but he had skirted the issue of why he thought the village should join with the men at Fort Dusquesne. What he did speak of was taking the scalps of the English *manake* and of the money and arms the French would pay them for their hire. Na-Kee said nothing of the old, the ill, and the very young, the braves would have to leave behind in their own village if they went to the Fort. The discussion had done nothing but bring more bad blood to the relationship between Raven and Na-Kee.

Raven looked at his mother, forcing himself to be patient. He had to push today's incidents from his mind and deal with the matter at hand. "Yes, I mean Tess. I cannot find her."

Dream Woman ducked into her wigwam. "Look down by the creek. She has taken to our custom of daily bathing. She goes there often."

Raven followed her. "I looked there."

"The garden? This morning she helped She-Who-Sleeps weed the squash. I think your white girl enjoyed getting her hands dirty in the mother soil."

"She is not there, *Nin-gea*. It is almost dark and she is nowhere to be found." He hesitated. "I fear for her safety, mother of mine."

Dream Woman turned to her son. "Have you asked anyone? Certainly someone has seen her."

"I have asked. No one remembers seeing her since this morning when she was in the garden. *N'gaxais,* why did you not keep a watch on her? Where have you been? I have looked for you everywhere as well."

"It is not of your concern where I have been. The white girl was not my captive, Raven. She was not my responsibility."

"I could not take her with me to meet with the French scouts!"

"Then you should have asked someone to watch her. You should not have assumed I would keep an eye on her. You know I do not approve of your keeping her prisoner to begin with."

Raven frowned. "It is too late for this discussion. I am sorry I have accused you. You're right. She was my responsibility. When I left this morning my head was too full of Na-Kee and what he would say to the Frenchmen. I should not have left her untended, but I truly didn't believe she would leave the camp."

"You don't think she would try to run, do you son?" Dream Woman rested her hands on her hips, suddenly concerned. "She is an innocent. She doesn't know the forest or its dangers."

"What else could have happened to her? I would suspect Na-Kee, but he was with me all day."

"I don't know. I—" Dream Woman looked up and something caught her eye. "My basket."

"What?"

"My berry basket. It's gone." She laughed, lifting her hand with relief. "The girl has gone to pick strawberries."

"But it is dark now. She should have returned to the village."

"There were other young women who went picking today. I'll go ask them if they've seen her. Perhaps she just shares the evening hearth with another family."

Raven watched his mother leave the wigwam. He rubbed his temples hoping to ease the ache in his head. Why had he left Tess unguarded? Why hadn't he given her instructions not to pass the borders of the village? If she was harmed, it would be his fault. She was his. He had not really realized that until this very moment. She was his and he was responsible for her life now.

A moment later Dream Woman returned with a young woman in tow. It was his cousin, Dove's Call.

"My aunt tells me Tess is missing," she said hesitantly in their native tongue.

Dove's Call was an attractive young woman with a great deal of common sense. Raven liked her. In fact he liked her so well that on several occasions he'd suggested to Taande that the brave might want to court her, but his friend had never showed any interest. "Have you seen her?"

"She went berry picking with us this afternoon. Before dark when we gathered to return she was not among the other women. I thought she must have returned to the village earlier and I didn't see her."

Raven exhaled slowly. "Where did you go picking, Dove's Call?"

"I'm so sorry," she said. "I feel responsible. I should have looked for her back here at the village, but grandfather was hungry. I—"

"Do not blame yourself. The fault is mine. Just tell me where you went."

"The meadow southeast of the creek. We had not picked there all week so the berries were plentiful and sweet."

Dream Woman looked up at her son. "Do you think she wandered off and got lost, or do you think she ran away?"

Raven thought for a moment. "She came with two leather slippers. Did you see them?"

"Yes. She keeps them here." Dream Woman lifted Tess's sleep mat. There was nothing there. Dream Woman looked up, her gaze meeting her son's. "She has fled."

Dove's Call touched her cheek. "I hope she's all right. Last week Sweet Rain saw English white-hairs in the forest. They tried to attack her but her father and brothers came along before she was harmed."

Raven squeezed her arm as he passed her on his way out of the wigwam. "Don't fear, Dove, I'll find her before any harm comes to her."

"You want me to come with you, my son?" Dream Woman slapped her thigh soundly. "This old horse can still travel."

"No. You stay here in case she comes back, *N'gaxais*." On impulse, Raven kissed the top of his mother's head as he went out the door. "Don't worry. I will find her and bring her home."

Raven crossed the village in long strides. He stepped into his wigwam and grabbed his leather traveling pack, always filled with a bag of pemmican, the high energy food, a fishing line and hook, medicinal herbs, a water skin, and other necessities. On his way out the door he snatched up his Brown Bess rifle, a powder horn, and a shot bag.

How far could she have gotten in only a few hours?

Most likely she was lost within a mile of the camp. He chuckled beneath his breath as he strode through the village toward the forest. He was worrying for nothing. This was a woman who said she wasn't certain where she lived. He would walk out into the forest, find her seated on a tree stump crying, and still be back in time to share in the herbed fish he had seen Taande's mother bury in the coals at her firepit.

Tess wiped the sweat from her brow, trudging forward, the bright moon lighting her way. She was exhausted, but refused to give into her fatigue. She kept telling herself as she cut through the dense foliage and greenbriars that Myron was somewhere out here looking for her. He was looking for her and she would meet him if she just kept walking.

After leaving the strawberry patch Tess had decided to walk north and then turn east after a few hours. If she could just walk to the bay, even if she didn't find Myron, surely she could find someone to help her get to Annapolis. If she could just find a white man, any white man, she knew she could get help. She could get someone to send a message to her uncle and her uncle could come get her. Better yet, Myron could come get her and they could be married right away.

Tess swatted at a mosquito on her calf and reached into her berry basket. She popped a sweet berry into her mouth and trudged forward. The first hour of darkness had been scary. Familiar objects of the forest had suddenly become unfamiliar. Every scraping branch, every crackling leaf, every scurry of a mouse, made her jump in her skin. But then, as the first hour stretched into the second, she began to relax. By midnight she had actually begun to enjoy the forest of the night, a place so different from the forest of the daylight she knew.

Everywhere she saw the glowing eyes of the animals that appeared with the moon. There were foxes and mice, bats and owls. Twice Tess had come upon deer. The first time she had startled them and they had nearly knocked her down crossing the game path in front of her. But the second time, she saw them before they saw her and she was able to creep up and watch them. A mother and two fawns stood side by side, eating leaves from a mulberry tree. When they had finally noticed her, they had stared at her with their wide brown eyes and then returned to their feeding with disinterest. They had been the most beautiful creatures she had ever seen. How she would have liked Abby to have seen them . . .

Tess stepped over a log and reached into her basket for another strawberry. It had to be between one and two in the morning by now. She was tired, but wanted to press on, putting as much distance between her and the Lenape village as possible before daylight.

Tess wondered if Raven knew by now that she was gone. Dream Woman said he had left early in the morning to meet with French scouts. She hadn't known when he would return, but surely he was back by now. Her hope was that he'd decided just to let her go. In her heart she had known all along that he didn't really want to harm her. Perhaps he'd even allowed her to escape. This way they could both save face.

Tess smiled thinking of Raven. She touched her lips with her fingertips, remembering again the feel of his mouth on hers. She couldn't help wondering if when Myron kissed her she would remember Raven's kiss.

Heavens . . . *Myron.*

The further she got from the Lenape village the more she thought about Myron and her decision to marry him. The night he had proposed she'd been thrilled. It was what she had wanted. It was a way to get Abby to the Colonies. But the more Tess thought about it, the more she wondered if she could really make herself happy as Myron's wife. He took life so seriously and he was forever comparing himself to others. Everytime she thought of climbing into that four-poster bed with him, she remembered the feel of Raven's arms around her. Myron had never stirred such feelings in the pit of her stomach. He had never made her ache for what she'd yet to experience.

Tess shook off her thoughts, fearing she'd drive herself mad second-guessing herself. She lifted the water skin she'd filled miles back and took a long drink of the cool water. Of course she'd marry Myron. She'd marry Myron, bring Abby to the Maryland colony, and make herself content. Who ever said a husband was supposed to set a wife's blood on fire? She'd forget about Raven and the way his long inky hair had blown across his broad shoulders. She'd forget his black eyes and the way he had looked at her.

The smell of smoke suddenly tapped Tess's attention, and for the moment both Myron and Raven were forgotten. She stopped and let the wind carry the odor to her. It was definitely smoke, wood smoke, but not a forest fire. She breathed deeply. A camp fire! God in heaven, it was a camp fire!

Tess walked another hundred yards and stopped again. The smell was stronger. She could even catch the hint of the scent of roasting meat. She stood still for a long moment allowing the wind to carry the smoke and the sounds toward her. Men . . . she could hear them talking. Her heart skipped a beat. More Mohawk? But as she listened carefully, the sounds became words. English! They were speaking English!

Tess hurried down the path. Maybe it was Myron and the search party! Maybe they really were still looking for her!

Tess spotted the light of the fire as the game path took a turn. "Hallo!" she called through the darkness.

She immediately heard the ominous click of a rifle hammer cocking and froze.

"Who's there?" shouted a deep voice.

"Myron?"

"Yo! I say who's out there!"

"Sounds like a woman to me, Billy," a man said excitedly. "Sounds female!"

Tess walked a few more feet and stopped again. Neither voice was Myron's, and suddenly she was hesitant. "Could . . . could you help me? I . . . I'm lost." She knew enough not to tell the men she'd been captured by Indians, at least not right away. "I'm looking for my uncle's plantation."

The light of the fire illuminated the form of the men. Both were bearded and dressed in tattered militia uniforms. One was wearing an Indian war club on a belt at his waist. The men looked filthy . . . and rough. Could they be deserters from Fort Cumberland? Or were they men just headed home on furlough? Tess suddenly wondered if she'd made a mistake.

One of the men waved his long rifle. "Step into the light so's we can see you."

Tess could feel her heart beating in her chest. Why was she suddenly afraid? These were white men, not Indians.

They would help her get home! She forced herself to take a step. "My . . . my name is Tess. Can you help me get to Annapolis?"

"A little closer," said the bigger of the two men with a wave of his hand. "A little closer, sweet."

Tess took a step into the circle of firelight.

The smaller of the two men gave a whistle. "Tole ye she was a female, Billy." His beady black eyes devoured her bare legs. "Tole you!"

The big one called Billy sunk his elbow into the other one's side, his gaze locked on Tess. "Shut up, Joey, before I have to shut you up." He lowered his flintlock rifle and spat a stream of tobacco juice into the fire. The flames sizzled. "Say you're lost, do ye?"

Tess dropped her hands to her sides awkwardly, glad she had thought to bring Dream Woman's knife. With that tucked into the waistband of her short leather shirt, she felt a little less vulnerable. They were staring at her, at her state of undress. Why had bare skin meant nothing to the Lenape and yet was of such great interest to white men? She wished she had something to cover her legs. "Yes. Lost."

Joey pointed to her leather tunic. "Looks to me like she's been with the Injuns."

Billy's eyes narrowed. "Been with the Injuns, have ye?"

Tess lowered her gaze to the fire. The men had built a spit and were roasting three plump squirrels. Her stomach growled. "Just a few days."

Billy broke into a grin, showing black stubs where his front teeth had once been. "Hear that, brother Joey? The girlie says she's been with the Injuns."

"Heard that, brother Billy. Heard it well."

Suddenly a branch snapped in the woods and another

man, dressed in a fringed buckskin tunic and red English army-issue breeches, appeared in the circle of firelight. He was just hiking up his breeches. "What's all the fuss?" he asked.

Joey pointed toward Tess and the third man followed his line of vision. "Sweet mother of Jesus," he whispered. "Where'd you two get her?"

Joey shrugged. "She found us, Sandy."

Sandy pulled on the drawstring of his breeches and nodded. "Evenin' to you, ma'am."

Tess nodded. "Good evening. I . . . I was saying I was lost. I'm looking for my uncle's plantation. It's near Annapolis. Do you know it?"

Sandy looked to his brother, breaking into a grin. "We know it. Sure do. Want us to es-cort you there, ma'am?"

She looked at the man called Sandy. His face was shaven and he appeared cleaner than the other two men. He seemed the most approachable of the three, so she spoke directly to him. "Would you?"

"Might."

"I . . . I'm sure my uncle would pay you for your trouble."

Sandy came slowly around the campfire toward her. "My brothers and I wouldn't take anything from your uncle."

"That's kind of you."

He was still coming toward her. "Nah, wouldn't take a thing from your uncle. But me and the boys, we wouldn't mind accepting a little payment out of you, luv."

Tess took a hesitant step backward. "I . . . I don't know what you mean. I have nothing to pay you with, but my uncle—"

"You been with the Indians haven't you?"

Tess took another step back. Sandy was still coming toward her. "Yes. Yes, I told you that."

"Well then, you screwed them redmen, surely you wouldn't mind a tumble with a few good white boys."

Tess shook her head, stunned. She stumbled a step backward. "No, no it wasn't like that." Was this man saying what it sounded like he was saying? She was so frightened for an instant that she couldn't will her limbs to move. She just kept shaking her head. These men weren't going to help her. They weren't—The sudden realization of what was about to happen hit Tess like a bucket of icy creek water.

She bolted, but she was a second too late. Sandy grabbed her arm, and began to drag her toward him. Tess tried to jerk her arm free. "Let me go! Let me go or you'll regret it!"

Sandy let out a cackle, pulling her hard against his chest and forcing his mouth down on hers. With one free hand he squeezed her breast viciously. The two brothers on the far side of the firelight stomped their feet, hooting with glee.

"Go easy on her, Sandy. You got to save a piece for me!" one shouted.

"Yea! Save a piece for us," the other echoed.

Tess couldn't breathe. The man called Sandy stank of tobacco, whiskey, and urine. She struggled, but he seemed unaffected by her protests. He was a bear of a man and he knew she was no match to his brute strength. He shoved his hand under her leather skirt and touched her bare inner thigh.

Tess didn't think.

She just reacted.

Her gut feeling told her it wasn't just her virginity she

fought for, but her life. These men would never take her home to Annapolis. She would never survive their gang rape . . .

Tess pulled Dream Woman's knife from her belt, and gripping it fiercely in her palm, she sank it into her attacker's chest from the side.

The man gasped with pain as she twisted the blade and pulled it out, ready to strike again if she had to. To her shock he pitched forward and fell to the ground.

"God damn!" Joey shouted from the far side of the campfire. "God damn, she's kilt him, Billy!"

Tess looked at the knife in her hand, then up at the other two men. They were advancing toward her. The one called Billy was raising his rifle.

Sandy had fallen to the ground across Tess's foot, dead before he hit the soft earth. Throwing down the bloody knife, she leaned over his body and snatched his pistol from his rawhide belt. She raised it to eye level, beading in on Billy.

"There's two of us and one a you," Joey shouted from the far side of the campfire. "You only got one shot, bitch."

Tess glanced sideways at Joey's rifle laying a good ten feet from him. Only Billy was armed. She slowly pulled back the hammer on the pistol in her hand. "True enough, but I'm better with a pistol than a knife." Her voice barely wavered. "Whether you shoot or not, one of you's a dead man. You want to take the chance it's you, Joey?"

"She's crazy, Billy. God damned woman's crazy! Thinks she's an Injun," Joey cried, backing behind his brother. "Kill 'er! Kill 'er afore we're dead as Sandy!"

Billy's aim grew unsteady. "What . . . what do you want?"

"Shoot 'er!"

Billy threw a glance over his shoulder. "Shut the hell up, Joey! I'm the one standin' in front of the damned pistol!"

"I don't want a thing," Tess hollered. "Just take yourself and your brother and go."

"Kill 'er, Billy. Kill 'er. She'll track us down and skin us alive. I just know it!"

"Shut up, Joey."

Tess still held the pistol steady, amazed she wasn't shaking on the outside like she was shaking on the inside. "Best make up your mind. My hand's getting tired. I slip and one of you's dead."

Billy took a step backward. Joey remained well behind his brother. "You . . . you killed my brother Sandy."

"He touched what didn't belong to him."

"You going to track us if we go on peaceable?" Billy was lowering his rifle.

"Probably not."

Billy elbowed his brother. "Let's go, Joey."

"You just gonna leave poor Sandy there dead like that?"

"Like what? You don't think he'd have left you there to save himself?"

Tess watched the two men back slowly out of the firelight arguing as they went. She heard the crackle of leaves and branches, and then she heard the two turn and run.

For a long time she heard the sounds of the two soldiers retreating. It wasn't until the forest was silent again that she finally released her grip on the pistol and fell to her knees.

Eleven

By midnight Raven truly feared for Tess's life.

He had underestimated the white woman with the magical red hair. He had severely underestimated his adversary, a mistake a man couldn't afford to make often in the forest.

Tess wasn't lost in the strawberry fields. She wasn't sitting on a tree stump trembling with fright, waiting for him to rescue her. She was gone. She had escaped from the village and she had escaped from him. She was headed northeast in the direction of the Great Bay and she was traveling fast for an English *manake*.

Raven had found evidence of her here and there along the woods trails, but she was difficult to track. She was a fine adversary whether she knew it or not. She stuck to game paths where her footprints were hard to detect. Over the years the deer had beaten the narrow roads through the forest with their sharped hooves until the ground was as hardpacked as baked mud. Tess left nothing behind as most white-hairs so foolishly did. Raven wasn't even certain that he was still on her trail.

Well after midnight as he stopped to drink from his water skin and get his bearings, he wondered if he should just let her go. There would be no shame on his face to return to the village to say his captive had foolishly tried to escape and lost herself in the forest. He could say she had not been worth his trouble to track. The villagers, with the exception of his mother, would be glad to see her gone. Raven could return to his village and get on with the life he had laid out for himself before Tess had crossed his path. He could forget her . . .

Of course he could not forget her. His little brother Takooko was dead. Takooko's death forever bound Tess and Raven together. He couldn't just let her go. He couldn't forget about her, never knowing what became of her.

What if she couldn't find Annapolis? What if she became injured? There were many dangers in the forest even for an experienced brave. Takooko was proof of that. How would Tess survive long enough to reach her uncle's home? What if at this very moment she lay on the forest floor wounded by a wildcat or a mother black bear? What if she had been raped and mutilated and left for dead by one of the many bands of red and white renegades that roamed the area?

Raven didn't know why he cared. This white woman was nothing to him. She was the enemy. She had brought death to his family's lodge. But then he remembered the taste of her lips on his. He remembered his mother's foreshadowing words. He remembered the dreams that haunted him at night.

The black raven perched on his tattered nest, a nest torn and shredded by the wind and rain of time. Then the raven soars . . . he soars, searching, searching the earth . . . until at last he finds what he seeks. A single strand of magical red hair. Always the raven returns to his nest with the red strand, and always the nest is rebuilt tighter, stronger than before.

Raven lengthened his stride. The moon was drifting in the western sky. Dawn would burst forth in a few hours and Tess would have spent a night alone in the forest. Raven knew that it would do no good to worry about her. What mattered was that he find her and find her quickly. Fate had brought them together, he had to have faith in the great Creator above that fate would bring her safely into his arms again.

Raven found Tess just after dawn. First he smelled the dying coals of the campfire and the scent of burnt squirrel. He approached the encampment slowly, circling it until he was certain she was alone. He found her on her knees on the ground staring numbly at a dead English soldier at her feet. She made no reaction when Raven stepped out of the brush.

"Tess?" he said softly, approaching with care. She seemed to be in shock. Had she known this dead soldier? What had happened?

He studied the telltale signs in the soft, leafy humus. There had been a struggle. The big soldier had died from a single stab wound well placed in his chest. His gaze fell to the bloody knife lying in the leaves beside the dead man. It was a Lenape knife. He recognized the handle carved with apple blossoms. It belonged to his mother.

Raven looked at Tess. She was still staring at the dead man, her face void of any emotion. She was as pale as last night's moon. Had his Tess done this? Had she killed a man?

Raven dropped to one knee, taking her hand in his. It was so cold and lifeless that he warmed it between his larger hands. *She was safe. His woman with the magic hair was safe.* "Tess?"

Slowly she lifted her gaze. "He . . . he's dead."

"He is dead, yes." Raven rubbed her hand between his. "Did you do this, Tess?"

He saw tears form in her eyes. She nodded.

Raven couldn't resist a proud smile. She was tough, his white woman, and brave, as brave as any Lenape maiden.

"He . . ." She was having a difficult time finding her voice. "He . . . they . . ."

There were others? Raven glanced about the camp. He had been so concerned for Tess's welfare that he hadn't noticed the signs of more men. Now he saw them. Three tin army plates. Three bedrolls. Three men. He wondered if he need search the surrounding forest for more bodies. At this point nothing about this white woman would have surprised him.

"They tried to harm you, Tess?" Raven asked, trying to make it easier for her to speak.

Again, she nodded. "I thought . . . they said . . ." She looked up at him, her eyes reflecting those of a lost child's. "I thought they would take me home. Home to Annapolis." She looked down again. "But . . . he tried to . . . *he touched me . . .*" She shook her head. "He . . . they . . . they would have killed me, Raven. It wouldn't have been enough . . ."

Raven groaned, feeling her pain twist his own heart. "Ah, *ki-ti-hi,*" he murmured, running his palm over her head to smooth her hair and then pulling her against him so that her cheek rested against his shoulder. "Yes, they would have taken your life. Men like this are not satisfied to take a woman's dignity. They are wolves that devour."

A tiny sob made her shudder in his arms. She made no attempt to pull away. "I . . . I was so afraid. I didn't mean to kill him. I just wanted him to stop. I didn't want him to touch me. Not like that." Tears slipped down her pale cheeks. "My virginity, it's all I have to give of myself to a man. Don't you understand, it's all I can give freely." She shuddered. "I didn't mean to kill him," she repeated.

He smoothed her unruly hair again and again, wishing desperately that he could take the pain from her heart. Raven remembered well the pain of the first life he took. He had been only seventeen summers the morning he and his uncles had been ambushed in the forest. To this day Raven still spoke a prayer each morning to the rising sun in remembrance of the Seneca warrior who had died by his hand so many mornings ago.

Raven gripped her shoulders. "Listen to this man. If you had not killed him, Tess, he would have killed you. Do you understand?" he asked, not certain that she did. "It is the way of the forest."

Another sob shook her body. "The other two. I would have killed them, too, I think."

Again, he had to smile. No doubt she would have. "To defend yourself is never wrong. You did not provoke them, did you?"

She shook her head. Her hands now rested on his shoulders. Raven didn't know how they had gotten there, but he liked her touch. She was clinging to him, pressing her soft breasts against his chest. Her touch made him feel powerful, powerful and confident.

"I just wanted to go home," she told him. "That's all. Just home . . ."

Raven pressed a kiss to her temple. He told himself it was only impulse, but when she made no move to push him away, he kissed her again. It was just a brush of his lips against her earlobe, but he felt her soften in his arms. He was so thankful to find her safe. How good it felt to hold her in his arms and to touch her soft white skin.

Raven brushed the backs of his fingers against her cheek wiping away the damp streak of a tear. Never had he felt such a fierce tenderness toward a woman. Never had he suddenly wanted so badly to touch and be touched.

"Tess," he murmured in her ear. "I feared for your life. I feared I would not see your face again. Tess . . . My Tess . . ."

Tess tightened her grip around Raven's neck. She heard him whisper her name. No one had ever spoken her name like that, so softly, so gently, so sensually.

His strong arms felt so comforting around her waist. His touch was soothing. He brushed his fingers across her cheek; he smoothed her hair. He traced the line of her jaw with his forefinger and then the bridge of her nose. Each place his fingers touched he left behind a trail of warmth.

What had begun as a comforting touch was suddenly making Tess hot at the back of her neck. Her breathing had become irregular. The scent of Raven's skin was as heady as any strong drink. He smelled of the pine forest, of the rain, and of the strength of the oak tree. When his lips touched hers, she turned to him. There was no thought involved, only instinct. She wanted this man to kiss her. She wanted to kiss him.

"Tess . . ."

"Raven . . ." She parted her lips needing to taste him, needing him to kiss her until all thoughts of the dead man were washed clean from her mind. "You came for me," she whispered. "Myron didn't come, but you did."

"It was fate that we have found each other in the middle of such a mad world, my Tess." He was brushing his fingertips over her bare arms setting them afire with tingling sensation. "This man could not let you go."

Tess lifted her chin so that he could kiss the soft spot in the hollow of her neck. Nothing had ever made her feel so alive as his touch. *Couldn't let you go. . . .* His voice echoed in her mind. *Did she want to go?*

Raven's mouth was on hers again. As he thrust his tongue between her lips he pressed her into the soft earth. The morning sunshine poured over his shoulder as Tess stroked the hardened muscles of his back beneath his leather vest, her tongue twisting with his. His taste was foreign and utterly male. His limbs were tangled in hers, his weight heavy against her, pressing her into the leaves. But she was not afraid.

In the past, with Myron, she had never felt quite comfortable with his touch. His kisses had always been quick, stolen. His touch . . . his touch had always seemed forbidden. Tess had always assured herself that that feeling would change with marriage. Only married men and women were supposed to enjoy the intimacy of lovemaking. Tess almost laughed aloud at the foolishness of her rationalizing.

Myron had never touched her like this . . .

Tess lifted her lashes to stare up into Raven's heathen black eyes. To this point he had only touched her arms, her legs, her face. Now his hand was beneath her breast. He cupped it in his hand gently. Even through the leather of her tunic she could feel her nipple growing hard in response. He was asking her permission. She could see it in his eyes.

Tess didn't know what to do. She didn't know what to say.

"Let me touch you, sweet Tess," he whispered huskily. "Let me stroke you. Let me bring my lips to your breast."

She swallowed hard, her breath coming in short gasps. His words were as arousing as his touch.

Tess covered his hand with hers, not trusting herself to speak. This was what she wanted, wasn't it? Their gazes locked. He moved his palm in a circular motion, stimulating the silken flesh beneath the leather of her tunic that suddenly felt rough against her sensitive breasts. Tess felt her heart hammering in her chest. She couldn't believe this was happening. She was lying in the forest with a savage. She was lying in his arms letting him touch her as no man should touch another but his wife, and she was enjoying it. Never in her life had she felt such glorious sensations.

"Speak the word and I will stop," he whispered, his breath hot in her ear. His tongue darted out to tease her earlobe. "I would not force you."

"Be . . . because I'm a virgin?" she whispered.

"I would never force you or any woman. A woman's first time is to be given freely of her choice, but even if you had lain with a thousand men, I would not force you." He dropped his head to the pulse of her throat and pressed a kiss to the gentle throb. "But I must tell you, this man longs to lay his head at your heart. This man longs to touch . . ." he brushed his fingers over the leather of her tunic where her thighs met, "to touch where no other has touched."

Tess gave a little gasp of pleasure. She was so confused. Her mind was awhirl with the pleasure of his caress and confusion of her own willingness. "I . . . I'm afraid, Raven."

He smiled as his fingers found the leather lace that tied the front of her tunic. "Do not be afraid. To touch, to kiss, this is what a woman's body as beautiful as yours was meant for, my fire-haired woman."

Tess didn't know how far she wanted to go with this touching, but she knew she had to feel his hands on her bare breasts. "I just have to tell you to stop, and you'll stop?" she asked.

"A word, a gesture, and this man will stop." Brushing his lips against hers, Raven tugged gently and suddenly her breasts were bare to the hot morning sunshine just beginning to pour through the treetops.

Tess tucked one arm behind her head to watch through half-closed eyelids as he slid his hand beneath the leather. "Oh," she murmured as the rough pads of his fingers moved in a slow circular motion around her nipple. The sensation was even more glorious than she'd imagined.

How could she tell him to stop? How could she tell him to stop when his hand felt so good on her flesh? Why would she tell him to stop?

Tess relaxed on the forest floor, one hand resting on Raven's shoulder, the other guiding his head. His sensual words echoed in her head. His mouth . . . she wanted to feel that splendid mouth on her breasts. "Kiss me," she whispered. "Please . . ."

Raven lowered his head to touch the tip of his tongue to her nipple.

Tess gasped at the sensation of the ripples of pleasure that emanated from the tiny puckered bud. She arched her back, threading her fingers through his thick black hair. "I didn't know," she whispered. "I didn't know it could be like this, Raven."

Squeezing her breast with his hand, he lowered his mouth again, this time taking her nipple between his teeth to tug gently.

"Oh," Tess murmured again and again.

As Raven fondled her breasts, kissing, sucking, stroking, she found herself wanting to touch him. She brushed her fingertips over his broad back, over his corded shoulders exploring his sleek, muscular form. Why had Myron never felt like this beneath her hands? Why had he never made her tremble the way she trembled now? Why had he never made her want to lie with him like she wanted to lie with Raven right now?

Tess lifted her lashes to find Raven staring down at her with those obsidian eyes of his. He still rested one hand on her breast, but he was no longer stroking her in that delicious way.

"Why . . ." She struggled to catch her breath. Reasonable thought was already being restored in her head. "Why did you stop?"

He kissed the tip of her nose and sat up abruptly. He paused before he spoke and when he did speak Tess thought she could hear a tremble in his throat. Could it be possible that she had excited him the way he had excited her?

"This is not right. This man does not take advantage of a woman, not even a white woman."

Tess licked her dry lips, pushing up off the ground to sit beside him. She fumbled with the leather tie of her tunic. A moment ago she had thought nothing of her breasts bared to the hot sun, but suddenly she was self-conscious. "Take advantage of me?" She laughed, an edge to her voice. "I hardly think you could consider it that. I practically threw myself at you."

Now she was embarrassed. She didn't know what she'd done here. Her gaze strayed to the soldier lying sprawled in the dirt only a few feet from them. Yes, she did. She knew exactly what she'd done. She'd killed a man and then she'd let this Indian fondle her in front of a dead man. She'd gone mad, stark-raving mad.

She looked at Raven. He was staring out into the forest. He had found her and she was his captive again. She was his captive and she had let him kiss her. She'd kissed him back. She gave up on the leather tie of her tunic and buried her face in her hands.

A minute of silence between them stretched into two, then ten. It was Raven who finally broke the morning stillness. When she looked at him his black eyes were on her.

"We must return to the village, Tess."

She shook her head. "No," she said softly, getting to her feet. "I have to go home."

"Home, yes, but home with this man."

"I won't." Her voice grew stronger with each word. "I told you. I won't go, Raven."

"You must. It is not your choice."

Tess backed away, trying to hold the front of her tunic together. "You can't do this to me! I have plans. You . . . you can't just keep me. I'm not an object. I'm a person, Raven." She tapped her chest. "A person who can't be owned like a bow or a quiver of arrows."

Raven stood and brushed off the dry leaves that clung to his apron-like loincloth. He was dead calm, which infuriated Tess all the more. "It is your fault my brother is dead."

"That was not my fault!" Tess screamed. "I didn't do it! I didn't pull the trigger!" She picked up a rock, and threw it at him, striking him in the shoulder and leaving a red welt. "Why can't you get that through your thick skull?"

Tess felt rather than saw him move toward her. But this

time she was determined he wouldn't get the best of her. Driven by her anger, she darted around the smoking campfire, her gaze locked on the weapons the brothers had left behind in their hasty retreat. She grabbed the first long rifle her fingers touched. Raven couldn't make her go back with him. She wouldn't let him! She swung the heavy rifle around, aiming it at his middle.

Raven halted, meeting her fierce challenge with a look of amusement. "You would not shoot this man," he scoffed resting his hands low on his hips.

Lifting the loaded long rifle a little higher, she pointed toward the dead man with it. "Killed him, didn't I?"

"But I have not harmed you." His voice was so calm and steady. He didn't think she'd do it! He thought she was bluffing!

Was she?

"Just let me go on my way, Raven, and no one will be hurt. Not me. Not you." She wiped her mouth on her shoulder as if she could wipe away the taste of him on her lips. "I told you, I have to go home to my uncle's."

Raven's eyes narrowed. He still seemed unconcerned by the rifle. "Is there a man whose arms beckon you?"

Was he jealous? "Yes," she answered, holding the rifle steady. "There is. I told you that. I told you I was to wed a man. I'm going to marry Myron. Soon. As soon as I get back."

He held up a finger. "You told me you were to wed. That was not my question." He took a step closer to her.

She tightened her grip on the long rifle.

"My question, Tess, woman of fire, is, does this man's arms beckon you? Can he give you the pleasure these hands could give you?" He opened his palms to her.

Tess took another step back. Her heart was hammering

in her chest. She couldn't help but look at his hands and remember the feel of them on her breasts.

She had to escape. She had to get away, not just from Raven, but from herself. This savage had cast some sort of evil spell over her. Even now as she held the rifle on him, her flesh still tingled from his touch.

"Don't make me do it, Raven."

He signaled with one bronze finger. "Set the rifle aside and come."

She pushed back a stray lock of red hair that the wind had blown across her lips. "Let me go. Let me go or you'll be sorry!"

"I am a patient man, but my patience grows thin, Tess. Set it aside!"

The voice of the gentle lover was gone again, as quickly as it had come. This was the Raven of the Lenape Tess knew. This was the man she could shoot.

"I tell you put the firestick down!" he shouted at her, his accented voice reverberating in the treetops.

Raven took a quick step toward her and Tess leveled the long rifle and pulled the trigger.

Twelve

The long rifle recoiled hitting Tess so hard in the shoulder that it knocked her off-balance, sending her sprawling. The air was filled with the sound of the explosion and the smoke and stench of the black powder.

She scrambled to her feet. Raven was still standing there. She could still see him through the blue-black smoke. Damn, she must have missed him!

Thank God . . .

Now what? Tess knew there was no time to reload. She threw the long rifle as hard as she could at him and turned and ran.

She heard Raven shout in his Lenape tongue. She wondered if the Indians cursed. Surely that had sounded like a curse to her.

Tess raced through the dense underbrush, running blindly. She dared a glance over her shoulder. At first she didn't see him, but then she realized he'd taken the time to retrieve his Brown Bess rifle. *My God, is he going to shoot me?*

Tess turned back, forcing herself to run as hard as she could, harder than she'd ever run in her life. She could hear Raven behind her, chasing her down like a hunted animal.

"Let me go!" she begged desperately. "Just let me go, Raven."

"You are mine!" he bellowed.

She ducked under a low limb. "No! Not yours! Not anyone's! Ever!"

He was gaining on her fast. Each time she lifted a moccasin, he seemed to fill her footstep. Tess pulled back a spruce limb until it groaned and then let it go. It sprang back at just the right instant and she heard him grunt with pain.

Tess scrambled over a log, slipping on the green moss on the bark. She hit the ground hard bruising her buttocks. "Ouch! Damn!" she muttered. But she sprang up just as Raven came over the log behind her.

"You cannot flee the Raven, Tess!" he called to her. "You cannot escape."

"I will! Again and again. You can't do this to me. You can't make me stay!" She felt his hand on her shoulder, his fingers sinking into her soft flesh. She ducked and turned sharply around a tree.

This time he cursed in English.

Around another tree she swung, then through a narrow passageway cut into a greenbriar thicket. In Takooko's moccasins and Dream Woman's tunic she felt like she truly could run with the wind. Greenbriars tore at her hair and the skin of her bare arms and legs, marring them with scratches and blood, but she didn't care. She never felt the prick of the thorns. All that mattered was escape, escape from this red man, escape from what he had done to her deep inside her heart.

"Tess!"

The greenbriar passage was narrowing. He was really angry now. She could hear his moccasins thundering behind her. She could hear him panting with fury. The ground thudded beneath her feet.

Suddenly the passageway through the greenbriars ended and Tess hit a wall of tangled thorns. She cried out in frustration. The briars scratched her hands and face and she wiped at a trickle of blood that stung her eye. There had to be a way out! *Think!* she told herself.

She dropped to her knees. Raven had taken her through one of these in the forest when he'd kidnapped her. When she'd questioned him about the passageway through the seemingly impenetrable greenbriar wall he'd explained that through the years the fox, wild cats, and white-tailed deer had cut these paths and kept them open. There had been a tunnel!

She reached out with both hands. There it was! Tess ducked her head and dove.

This time Raven cursed foully in French. He caught the toe of her moccasin as she pulled herself across the forest floor through the tunnel, but she managed to pull free. The briars were so tangled and thick that sunlight barely penetrated the walls. The forest floor was covered with rotting leaves, prickly thorns, and animal droppings, but Tess pushed on. Another few feet of semi-darkness and the greenbriar thicket suddenly ended. Tess burst into the sunlight of the open forest, bounding to her feet.

Raven had fallen a little behind. Being larger, and carrying his Brown Bess rifle, it was more difficult for him to squeeze through the tangled tunnel.

Tess almost smiled as she ran. She would beat him. She would escape. He wouldn't control her. He wouldn't have her!

Then suddenly she saw him on the path ahead of her. She didn't know how the hell he'd gotten there, but there

he was. He just stood there, sweat on his brow, his face
a mask of fury, and bleeding at the shoulder . . . bleeding
hard.

Tess made a futile attempt to veer left. He grabbed her
by a hank of red hair, nearly jerking her off her feet.

"Enough!" he boomed.

Tess fought like a mad woman. *Last chance,* echoed in
her head. *Last chance to save Abby, last chance to save
yourself!* She screamed in frustrated rage. She punched
and kicked him. She bit his arm. She grabbed a handful
of his midnight hair and yanked as hard as she could,
pulling away with black hair tangled around her fingers.

Raven grunted in pain as she struck his injured shoulder. "Enough!" he shouted between gritted teeth as he
tossed his rifle to the ground. Then, thrusting his leg between hers, he gave her a hard shove. Tess tumbled to the
ground with Raven on top of her.

They fell so hard that he knocked the wind out of her.
"Let me go! Let me go!" she screamed tossing her head
from side to side. Tears ran down her cheeks as he captured her wrists and pinned them to the ground. She
closed her eyes in defeat. He was too big, too brutally
strong. "Let me go," she whispered one last time.

Both of them panted heavily. Raven's weight pressed
against her middle made it hard for her to breath.

"Bastard," she muttered.

"Open your eyes," he ordered coldly.

When she didn't, he lifted her wrists slightly and thrust
them to the ground again. "I said open your eyes!"

Tess opened them. Tears of frustration clouded her vision. His shoulder was bleeding freely. Dried blood stained
his bare arm and chest. His quilled leather vest was dark
with wet blood.

"I hit you," she murmured in shock. "Oh, God, I shot you."

"Thank *Manito* you did not take better aim," he retorted.

She closed her eyes again. She couldn't look at him. She didn't understand how she could hate a man so deeply and still . . . still care for him. . . . Still want to look up at his handsome face. . . . Still want to touch him.

"I'm sorry," she whispered.

"Are you?"

She opened her eyes. "I don't know," she answered honestly.

He shifted his weight, releasing her hands, but still holding her down. He lifted the edge of his vest to get a better look at the wound in his shoulder. "The ball is lodged against the bone. You will have to remove it."

Tess couldn't believe she had shot him. One minute she'd been rolling in the leaves with him, kissing him like a wanton, the next minute she'd tried to kill him. She really had gone mad.

"I didn't want to hurt you," she said, still not trusting her voice. "I just wanted you to let me go. I just wanted to go home."

"To My-Ron."

She turned her head away. "No. Not to Myron. It's more complicated than I can explain. You wouldn't understand."

"Tell this man."

"Get off me!" she threatened through clenched teeth. "Get off!" When she struck him hard in the shoulder with the one hand he had freed, he grunted, slumping a little. She looked up at him.

He was breathing heavily as he pressed the leather of his vest against the musket ball hole in his shoulder. She noticed for the first time that his face was pale. He'd probably lost a lot of blood.

"Get off me," she repeated, softer this time. "Get off me and I'll look at your shoulder."

"Will you run?"

"Just get the hell off me!"

"If you run I will track you. I will hunt you down. You are mine. Your life for my brother's. I will not let you go."

She avoided meeting his gaze. "You don't let me take a look at that and you won't have to let me go. You'll die and I'll walk out of here and leave you to rot in the forest."

Their gazes met, her anger matching his. He hesitated a moment and then got up off her, sliding over to sit on the ground.

Tess wiped her face with the back of her hand, trying to clear her thoughts. What was the sense in running? Even bleeding like he was, Raven was as strong as an ox. Right now she was so winded she probably couldn't run if she wanted to. So she was his captive again.

Tess crawled up on her knees to face him. She jerked back his vest to get a look at the musket ball hole.

He flinched.

She didn't care. Bastard. She wouldn't let him die, but be damned if she had to be gentle. "It's a clean hole. If I can get the ball out and get the bleeding to stop you'll be all right."

"You have removed the musket ball from flesh before?"

"No."

"Can you do it?"

"Guess we'll see, won't we?"

He hesitated for a second before responding. "Do it," he finally said.

Tess bit down on her lower lip. She might be able to

sound cocky, but she was scared. She didn't know how to cut a musketball out of a man's shoulder! What if she hurt him? What if she couldn't stop the bleeding once she removed the lead ball? Of course she wasn't going to let him know she was afraid. "Give me your knife." She pointed to the long blade tucked into a quilled sheath at his waist.

"Not here." He took a deep, ragged breath and rose. "We must go back to the fire. The knife must be cleansed by fire of the evil spirits."

She frowned. "Your mother said you were all Christianized years ago. Evil spirits? That's pagan nonsense." She pointed. "Give me the knife."

He rested his hand on the hilt of his knife. With the other hand he took hers and pulled her to her feet. "Must you argue each step of the way? Let us go." He stopped to retrieve his Brown Bess and turned back toward the soldiers' camp and the place where they'd left the dead man.

Tess walked back at Raven's side in silence. Back at the camp, he knelt and laid his hunting knife on a bed of dying coals in the campfire. From his bag on his waist he pulled out a strip of soft leather bandage just like the bandage he had wrapped around Tess's sore feet that first night after she'd escaped from the Mohawk. He looked at her standing hesitantly near the edge of the dying campfire.

"Do it now. Then we will go home to the village. Tomorrow night Council meets in the Big House. My people will discuss who will become their next War Chief. I will be there."

Tess came around the fire to kneel in front of him. Suddenly she felt guilty. She'd shot him. A few inches lower and to the left and Raven would have been dead. She gritted her teeth. She hated him for holding her prisoner like this, but she knew she didn't want Raven dead. She brushed his hands aside where he was trying to remove his vest. "I'll do it," she said sharply.

He let his hands fall, but there was a smirk on his face.

She jerked his vest off and tossed it to the ground. She touched the area around the musket ball hole, leaning her other hand on his bare chest. This was the place only minutes ago that she had taken pleasure in caressing. "What's so funny?"

"It's good to know that you do not fear hurting this man," he said cynically.

"I want to hurt you." She snatched the knife out of the coals. "I want to hurt you like you've hurt me." She looked up at him, her gaze meeting his for an instant. Then she looked away. "I just don't want to kill you."

"That is why you did not take better aim?"

Tess took a deep breath and plunged the tip of the knife into the musket ball hole. Blood oozed out.

"Exactly. I wanted to torture you like this first. A slow, painful death for my enemy."

She felt the muscles of his chest beneath her hand grow taut as she dug for the musket ball. But he didn't move. Only the sweat that beaded on his forehead and began to drip down his temples indicated that she was hurting him.

Tess finally felt the clink of the musket ball as she touched the tip of the knife to it. "Found it," she said. "Now if I can just—"

She felt his body tremble.

"Almost." She grimaced as she twisted the knife, getting behind the foreign object. She could have sworn she felt the tip of the knife scrape his shoulder bone.

Raven raised his hand to grip her shoulder. He squeezed her arm until it hurt.

"Almost . . ." Suddenly she felt the lead ball pull free. With her other hand she grabbed the leather bandage to staunch the blood that now poured freely from the wound. "Got it!" She held up the musket ball to show him, her hands shaking just a little. "Told you I could do it."

"In the bag." He indicated the leather quilled bag he wore over his shoulder. He was breathing heavily. "A . . . a small pouch of herbs. Crush . . . crush the herbs into the wound and tie the shoulder tightly with the leather strap. The bleeding will stop."

Tess set his knife on the ground and reached for his leather travel bag. Finding the herbs, she followed Raven's instructions. In a few minutes she had him bandaged to her satisfaction. She sat back on her heels and offered him a drink from his water skin. He took a long pull. On impulse Tess reached out to wipe the beads of sweat from his brow.

He stared at her with those obsidian black eyes of his.

She frowned and looked away feeling like a fool. "So are we going or not?"

"Get me my rifle."

"So you can shoot me?" She picked up the Brown Bess and tossed it to him.

He caught it in the air. "No, not today at least." He used the long rifle to get to his feet. "Let us go."

"What about him?" She forced herself to glance over at the man she'd killed.

"Leave him. Take his firesticks and leave him to rot in hell."

Tess hurried to gather the weapons the brothers had left behind in their haste to get away. Suddenly she was anxious to go. Any place seemed better than here, even the Lenape village.

* * *

Myron Ellsworth stood at the dry sink beneath the kitchen window scrubbing his hands with a stiff brush. The smell of freshly baked blackberry tarts hung in the air. Mother had come to visit. Mother always baked something special for her eldest son when she came to visit him.

"You asked me what I thought," Lyla Ellsworth whined. "Then when I tell you, you're short with me."

Myron sighed. "I didn't ask you, Mother. I didn't ask you to come here. I can care for myself."

"Nonsense." She moved around the pine table, setting two places. She was using the good china, china he had bought for Tess for a wedding present. "It's time you got yourself a decent wife. That Negra girl servant don't know how to cook for a strapping man like yourself."

Myron scrubbed his fingernails harder, dipping the brush again and again into the hot sudsy water. "Tess would have made a good wife, Mother. I know you never liked her, but we would have been happy together. She made me laugh."

"She's gone, son. Dead and gone, and there ain't no sense in dwellin' on it."

He shook his head, ashamed by the tears that stung his eyes. "I don't know that," he said stubbornly. "You don't know that and I don't know that."

She dropped a handful of pewter utensils on the table and whipped around. Lyla Ellsworth was over forty, but she was still a sturdy woman. "You're going to make yourself sick dwelling on what can't be fixed, Myron."

He gritted his teeth, scrubbing beneath his nails. "I can't just give up on her. I can't just forget about her.

What if she's still alive? What if, God help her, those
heathens let her live?"

Lyla came across the polished hardwood floor, her cotton petticoats swishing at her feet. "Then may God help
her, because He's the only one who can now!" Lyla
grabbed her son's hands. "Look what you've done. You've
scrubbed so hard your hands are bleedin'!" She grabbed
a cotton towel from the edge of the sink and wrapped his
hands up, cradling them in hers. Her gray eyes met her
son's teary ones. "You got to forget her, Myron," she said
gently. "Else you'll drive yourself mad."

He shook his head, jerking his hands from his mother's.
"I can't forget her. I won't. I've got to know the truth. If
she's out there somewhere, I got to know."

Lyla just stood there, watching her son. "So what are
you gonna do? Search every Indian camp from here to
the Ohio?"

Myron tossed down the cotton towel stained with his
blood and pulled out his chair. "If I have to. Now sit
down, Mother. Dinner's getting cold."

Thirteen

Raven sat cross-legged in the Big House, listening to the opening prayer led by the village shaman, Polished Stone. The old man's chanting was a comfort to Raven. Since the first time he saw a white man when he was a boy, each day his village had changed, each day the world around him had changed. Nothing was as it had been in his grandfather's youth, nothing but the Lenape traditions that were as old as time. This opening prayer was one such tradition. Polished Stone repeated the words that his mother had spoken here in the ceremonial Big House, and her father before her. His long gray braids swung on each side of his face as he pursed his wrinkled lips and sent his voice skyward into the heavens.

Tradition was the one thing that would save the Lenape from the English and the French and any other peoples who would try to destroy the Nation; Raven was certain of it.

The ancient man, Polished Stone, tossed a handful of his magic dust into the communal fire, and the flames fanned out in a puff of bright blue light and smoke, and the village exclaimed with awe . . . just as they had for a thousand years. Raven smiled to himself. It wasn't that his people believed in the magic dust so much as it was the *tradition* to appear to believe.

Raven lifted his gaze. Na-Kee was watching him as Polished Stone continued his chanting prayer. *What lies have you spread about me these last days?* Raven wondered. *Who have you bribed with white-hair baubles and the firewater that is forbidden in this village?*

Raven groaned. How could so many of the others be so blind? How could they actually be considering making Na-Kee their *llau?* Why could they not see through his good looks and charm? Raven knew that Na-Kee would not make a suitable War Chief. Anyone who truly considered the facts would come to the same conclusion. Na-Kee was rash, bloodthirsty, and single-minded. Those were not admirable traits in a War Chief.

Na-Kee grinned smugly. Raven looked away. Polished Stone had completed his prayer and had taken a seat on a soft hide mat beside the chief. Chief She-Who-Swings-From-Stars sat up on her knees. She lit her white clay pipe and took a long pull. Raven watched the smoke rings she blew form over her head in perfect circles. She-Who-Swings was a good woman, but she favored her nephew, Na-Kee. It would be difficult for Raven to convince her that he would make a better War Chief than her dead brother's son.

"Greetings," She-Who-Swings said in Lenape, nodding in the direction of the elders. "Greetings to you all. As you know we have not come here to socialize, but to discuss who we will elect as our next War Chief. Let us get on with the discussion." She looked out into the circle of fifty-odd men and women. "Who will speak first?"

Taande lifted his palm.

Raven smiled to himself. Taande was a good man. He needed to keep that in mind, even when he thought of

Taande's shameless interest in Dream Woman. The man's heart was in the right place.

"This woman calls Taande to speak," She-Who-Swings acknowledged.

Taande raised up on his knees, his gaze moving from one man or woman to the next. "I wish to tell you that you must make the Raven your War Chief. I wish to tell you why." His gaze flickered to Raven. "I have known this man since we were children in our cradleboards. He is a leader if there was ever a leader among us. The Raven will use his good sense, his patience, his uncanny ability to guess the enemy's next move to our advantage. The interest of the village, of the entire Lenape nation will always be his first consideration. The Raven has never done anything that has not been for the welfare of *The People.*"

"He took the white woman, did he not?" Na-Kee questioned.

Taande faced Na-Kee. "As was his right by tribal laws." He spoke slowly to Na-Kee as if he were speaking to a young child. "The white-hairs took the Raven's brother. Raven had a right to take one of theirs." He turned back to the others dismissing Na-Kee's complaint. "The Raven speaks the white-hair tongue well. He knows how they think. He is the man to deal with them."

"And what if we do not want to *deal* with them?" asked Three Pelts, one of Na-Kee's cousins. "The Raven, he always wishes to talk." He opened and closed his hand rapidly. "Talk, talk, talk! What about when the time comes that we must fight? What then?"

Taande's dark eyes narrowed. "Is there a man or woman here who can question the Raven's ability as a warrior?

Is there a man or woman here who would not want the Raven at his or her side in a battle?"

A murmur rose among the villagers.

"It's true. Taande speaks the truth," said a middle-aged woman.

"The Raven, he is a true warrior," agreed a young brave.

"I would enter any forest with him at my side," said another.

"But, that is not to say that Na-Kee is not an equal warrior," She-Who-Swings offered.

Taande sat down realizing his time was up.

"We are not here to say one man is good and another is not. Both men are worthy men else I would not have submitted their names to you," the chief went on. "I ask you, my people, to remember that we are not here to choose sides in a fight. We must all stick together in whomever we choose. We are here—" she raised a withered finger "—to determine who will have our best interest at heart when he speaks with the white-hairs. Who will be the best man to make the decision to fight and then be able to lead our men to victory?"

Raven raised up on his knees. "What about the decision not to fight?" he questioned forcefully.

She-Who-Swings nodded to Raven, giving him permission to go on.

Raven raised his fist into the air. "The position of War Chief is not just to lead men into the fight. It is also making the decision as to whether or not to fight. Na-Kee is a superior warrior, I would not argue that." He paused. "But Na-Kee is also a vengeful man. I fear his desire for revenge will cloud his thinking."

"Vengeful?" Na-Kee laughed. "You say I am vengeful?

Who is it that at this moment holds a white woman captive because her people killed his brother?" Na-Kee addressed the villagers poetically. "To hold an innocent woman prisoner, is that not vengeful my brothers and sisters?"

Again a wave of agreement arose among the villagers.

"Na-Kee speaks the truth. The Raven holds the white woman captive," offered an old man with a carved walking stick.

"He speaks of revenge and yet he is the one who holds a woman against her will," added someone else.

Raven groaned in frustration. This council meeting was not going as he had hoped it would. He lifted his hand and waited for silence. When had Tess become so important an issue to them? Why did they care what he did with a white woman? More of Na-Kee's thrusting a stick down the ant hill, no doubt.

Raven crossed his arms over his chest. "That is not a valid argument because you see . . . you see, I will take the woman you speak of as wife." Raven didn't know what had made him say such a thing. He wasn't even certain that it was his own voice that came from his mouth.

Startled sounds of excitement rose in the ceremonial Big House. Raven saw his mother smile.

"A captive? You will make a captive your wife?" Questioned Sitting Black Bear.

Raven turned to the middle-aged man. "I seem to recall, good friend, that your wife, Kissing Sun, was a captive."

His wife chuckled at her husband's side.

Raven went on. "Is it not true that you carried Kissing Sun on your back from her Shawnee village many days south of here? Did I not understand that they say her protests were heard as far as the Adirondack Mountains?

They say she blackened both your eyes so that on your wedding day you looked more like the brother raccoon than the Lenape warrior."

The villagers laughed. Someone slapped Sitting Black Bear on the shoulder. Kissing Sun looped her arm through her husband's in demonstration of their happiness together now, no matter what the original circumstances were.

"It is true," Sitting Black Bear grumbled. "But that was different. She only fought me out of spite." He pointed accusingly at Raven. "This woman you speak of is white skinned. She is English. The enemy. She is not one of us."

"To join the white with our people, this could be a good thing," Dream Woman offered. "We have discussed this often among the elders, have we not, Sitting Black Bear?"

The chief nodded. "True words, Dream Woman. You have told us you see the future of the Lenape as a blend of red and white. Perhaps it is fitting that your son be the first to wed outside the People?"

"Take her as wife?" Na-Kee scoffed, coming to his feet angrily. "You fool yourself, Raven. How will such a union bring peace to our land if the woman does not wish to marry you? She despises your black scalp. She will not have you!"

The villagers were growing louder as they broke into their own separate conversations. No one had ever expected the Raven to marry. Now suddenly he spoke of marrying a white woman with fire hair, and the chief had practically given her approval. Everyone was abuzz with their own opinion.

"Do you dare challenge the word of the Raven?" Raven demanded above the din, coming to his feet to face Na-Kee. He didn't know how he'd gotten himself in this position, but suddenly he was here. If he said he would marry the white woman, he would marry her. He would do what was best for his people.

The villagers instantly grew silent. Everyone was staring at Raven.

"This man says the white woman Tess will wed me. Do you challenge my word?" Raven repeated directly to Na-Kee.

Na-Kee looked out at the other villagers. Everyone was staring at him. One never questioned another's word in the Big House without strong reason. Here, a man or woman's word was sacred.

Na-Kee frowned sourly, backing down. "My friend here, he changes the subject. He twists the important facts to his own advantage."

"A married man makes a stable man," Speaks Softly, who was breast-feeding her infant, offered. "I tell you, great chief, I would feel better having my husband led by a married man and not a young buck. A man with responsibilities understands the consequences of battle. He does not enter the fight without careful forethought."

"You are going to choose a man by whether he is married or not married?" Na-Kee scoffed.

"I did not say that," corrected Speaks Softly, undaunted. "I only said that would be a consideration."

"Sit down, sit down, both of you," She-Who-Swings ordered Na-Kee and Raven. "This woman believes we have spoken enough on this matter for today. Let us think on the words that have passed among us concerning the man who will become our War Chief. For now we will move on to discuss other matters."

"When will you vote, Aunt?" Na-Kee asked, sounding

much like a spoiled child. "You said we would vote tonight."

The chief glanced sharply at her nephew. "There is no need to hurry this decision. It is too important. Now let us go on to the next matter, *son of my brother.*"

Raven sat cross-legged only half listening to the remainder of the High Council meeting. How could he have told the Council that Tess would marry him. How could he have dug himself such a deep hole so quickly?

If only Na-Kee had not been so smug . . .

Raven sighed, rubbing his temples. There was no need to dwell on what had already taken place. His responsibility was to his people. If the men and women of the village felt he needed a wife to make a suitable War Chief, then he would have a wife. Now all he had to do was convince Tess . . .

Raven stood outside his mother's wigwam beside Taande. The two men passed a pipe between them as they stared up at the sprinkling of stars just beginning to twinkle in the dark sky. The air was warm and humid, and filled with the sounds of night insects. A few men and women still stood outside the Big House discussing the evening's council meeting. Their voices carried on the breeze.

"So what do I do now?" Raven asked softly in his mother's Algonquian tongue.

Taande chuckled. "You are the one who said before all of Council that you were going to marry her, friend. I think your next move would be to ask her."

Raven shook his head. "She will not agree to marry

me. Remember, this is the woman who only yesterday morning shot me with a long rifle."

Taande tried to hide a smile. "Then she is a worthy opponent, is she not?"

Raven brushed his hair back off his forehead. "There is another man she wishes to marry. A white man in the place called 'Napolis."

Taande shrugged. "Then set her free and you marry another. Your cousin Dove's Call would have you. Any single maiden in the village would, perhaps a few who are not."

"You are taking this too lightly, Taande. I am serious when I tell you I do not know what to say to her."

Taande tamped his clay pipe. "Offer her something she wants. All women like gifts if they are brought sincerely."

"She wants her freedom. She wants to be rid of me."

"Then offer her that freedom."

"Marry her and then let her go?" Raven laughed mirthlessly. "Somehow I do not think the elders would approve, my wife living with another man in 'Napolis."

"No." Taande turned toward Raven. "Tell her she must stay with you as wife for a certain amount of time. One full year, maybe two. If she wishes to leave you then, you will absolve her of her responsibility for your brother's death and she may go."

Raven frowned. Tess was his. He had claimed her as his own. He didn't ever have to return her to her people if he didn't want to. It was the price they paid for his brother's death. Why should she be free to roam this earth when Takooko would never walk these forests again?

"It would work," Taande suggested when Raven made no response. "The village will be pleased you are wed. They will make you War Chief. You will charm the red

head on the sleeping mat until she cannot possibly leave
you to return to any white-hair." He lifted an eyebrow
with amusement.

"I would not lie with her," Raven scoffed. "It would
be a marriage only in name."

Taande shrugged. "Tell yourself what you wish."

Raven eyed his friend intently. "Would I be deceiving
the council?"

"Any Lenape woman has a right to divorce her husband. You cannot honestly say that after a passing of the
seasons she will wish to leave your side." He pushed his
elbow into his friend's side. "She is hot for you. Can you
not tell?"

Raven closed his eyes, trying to think clearly. In the
back of his mind he saw Tess. He saw her magical hair,
her dark eyes. He tasted her nipple on the tip of his
tongue. Of course if he married her he would have to take
care not to take advantage of her again. He could not be
so irresponsible as to act on his physical desires. He
would not allow his emotions to cloud his thinking.

Taande slapped Raven on the back. "It will work, trust
me, *n'tschu*. Now go speak with her while the courage of
the great Taande is still in your heart."

Raven looked at the brave. Taande was right, it could
work. If Tess would just be sensible about the matter. He
looked up at Taande. "You could go with me, friend. You
could explain the reasoning."

"Sorry. I cannot." Taande gave him another slap on the
back. "I am busy tonight."

"A woman?" Raven called after him as he walked away.
"I am glad you have found someone to give your attentions to."

Taande waved over his head, disappearing into the shadows of the other wigwams.

For a moment Raven stood there in front of his mother's lodge. He wanted to do the right thing. Only time was running out. Today English soldiers headed for Fort Cumberland had passed very close to the village. The white-hairs were everywhere, closing in on them. The Lenape needed to appoint a War Chief . . . quickly.

Raven tucked his pipe into his leather quilled belt and lifted the doorflap to his mother's wigwam. He nearly collided with Dream Woman who was obviously on her way out.

"N'gaxais."

Dream Woman smiled up at her handsome son. "This woman thought you would pay this lodge a visit tonight," she said, her voice laced with obvious amusement.

Raven glanced over her shoulder at Tess who was seated at the firepit, a cup of tea cradled in her hands. She did not look up at him.

"I . . . I came to speak to Tess," he said in Lenape. "About what I said in Council. You could stay," he added hopefully.

Dream Woman shook her head. Raven could have sworn he detected the scent of flower water in her freshly washed hair. "Many sorries, but I cannot, son."

Raven watched his mother step around him and go out the door. "Take your time, I will be late," she called over her shoulder as she slipped out of the wigwam and into the darkness.

Raven stood for a moment staring at the leather doorway his mother had just left through. Where could she be headed so late in the evening? An old woman's sewing session no doubt. The widows of the village often got together to gossip to pass away the time as they worked.

Raven turned around to face Tess. She was staring at the smothered coals in the firepit. He wiped the sweat that beaded on his brow. "This man wishes to speak with you," he said in English, wishing his words had not come out so formally.

Tess set down the china teacup and hugged her knees to her body. Still she didn't look up at him. "So talk."

He sighed. What had made him think she would make this easy for him? "It is hot in this lodge. Will you walk with me?" He offered her his hand.

It was a moment before Tess looked up at him. She was trying to calm that little trip in her heart. No matter how hard she tried, she just couldn't think of Raven the way she had thought of him before she'd tried to escape . . . before she'd allowed him to touch her the way he had. Nothing was different; she was still his prisoner. Yet everything was different. "Do I have a choice?" she asked softly.

"You do." He gestured with an open palm. "I ask you to walk at my side. The creek is a wonder at night with silver fishes jumping and the moon shining its white light upon the water. I would like you to see it."

Tess got up without the aid of his hand. "I suppose a walk would be all right." She followed him out of the wigwam. He waited for her to catch up and walk beside him.

"How is your shoulder?" she asked begrudgingly.

"It will heal."

"The council meeting?"

"Still no decision is made, but the chief, she says soon. Soon the village will vote."

Tess nodded. The air was cooler outside. A slight breeze

tousled her hair, still damp from the evening swim she'd taken while the others gathered in the Big House. The grass felt soft beneath Tess's moccasins. Her arm brushed Raven's.

Side by side the two walked in silence, down the path toward the creek. Reaching the water, Raven veered left. Well off the path, he took a seat on a rock that jutted up near the edge of flowing water. Tess sat down beside him.

Without speaking Raven drew a flute made of some sort of bone from his belt and began to play. Tess was mesmerized by the sweet notes that rose from the crude instrument. He played a soft lilting song, and then another. In Tess's mind she could almost hear the chant of the Lenape with the music. It was the most haunting sound she had ever heard in her life.

Her first thought was how she would describe the notes to Abby. The sound of the flute was . . . it was like soaring high above the trees, among the leaves that rustled and the wind that blew ever so faintly. Each note of the flute stood alone as a thing of beauty, but blended, they were pure magic.

When Raven finally set aside the flute, Tess looked at him. "I didn't know you could make music like that. It's the most beautiful thing I've ever heard," she breathed.

"There are many things you do not know of me, Tess." He smoothed the bone with his hand. "I am not the animal you think I am."

"I didn't say that."

"I am not a heathen, a hostile, a red-nigger . . ."

"That's not it and you well know it!" she defended herself angrily. "Never, ever have you heard those words from my mouth!"

He nodded. "Your words are true. I have not."

"I don't understand why you just won't let me go." She watched a stick float along with the running water of the creek.

"You care for me." When she said nothing, he went on. "Or at least you feel an attraction to this man."

She whipped around angrily. "What does that have to do with anything? The fact is that I am here against my will! You are holding me responsible for something I had nothing to do with!"

Raven slipped his flute back into his belt. "I will make you an offer, Tess." His voice was as calm as hers was agitated. "The Council would prefer I had a wife. They are upset that I have held you here. Some say it is bad luck. If we go to war with the English it would not be a good thing for any of us."

Tess felt her muscles tense. An offer? What was he talking about, *a wife?*

"I want you to marry this man."

Tess jumped up. "Marry you!"

He grabbed her hand. "Be silent long enough to listen to my words." He went on faster than before. "Wed me. Do not betray me by word or deed, and in one full turn of the seasons I will set you free."

"You're crazy." She jerked her hand from his. "You're a madman. You kidnapped me and you think I'm going to marry you!"

"Just one year and you will have your freedom to return to your man."

"Not one year, not one day," she sputtered, completely taken aback by what he was proposing.

"If our village fights the white-hairs, you may get lucky." He shrugged. "Perhaps I will be killed and then you will be free sooner."

She wrapped her arms around her waist, shaking her head. "The answer is no. No. I won't do it."

He still sat calmly on the tree stump. "So your choice is to remain here the rest of your life."

She drew her hands into fists in frustration. He had her. A lifetime as his prisoner or a year as his wife. "It's not much of a choice, is it?"

"It will give you the freedom you seek. In the passing of the seasons I will return you to your 'Napolis a divorced woman. Among the Lenape a divorced woman is free to marry another." With a hint of sarcasm he added, "Would your My-Ron not wait one year for the woman he loves?"

Tess spun around to face the creek, her back to him. She felt trapped, not just by Raven, but by herself and the feelings she knew she had for this man. "If I did not marry you, you would let me go anyway . . . eventually."

"Tuko."

She looked down at her moccasins. *No.* She had picked up enough of the language to know that word. *No,* he would not let her go. Not ever.

She pushed her damp hair over the crown of her head to let it fall down her back. Did she agree to his proposition and trust him to keep his word? Her chances of escaping were slim, she knew that now. Did she really have a choice? If she was going to make it back to Annapolis, if there was still a chance to bring Abby to the Colonies, this might be it.

Tess turned to the Raven. She could feel herself trembling inside. *This is silly,* she thought. *You're getting yourself all upset for nothing. He's talking about a heathen marriage here. I wouldn't really be married to him. He was talking about a way to get home.*

Tess knew she could do it. She would do it for Abby, no matter what it meant, no matter what she had to do. "I will marry you," she said softly, afraid her own voice would betray her. "But only because I have no other choice." She made herself look at him. "You understand that? It's not because I want you."

Raven's black-eyed gaze locked with hers. "It is not because you want me," he said in a sensual whisper. "This man understands."

Fourteen

"Tonight?" Tess looked up at Dream Woman who stood in the wigwam doorway. "But I only agreed to this last night."

Dream Woman hustled in, her hands in a flurry of activity. "No need to wait." She began to dig through assorted baskets. "Much to do, but no need to wait. The groom, he is anxious, I think."

Tess lowered her gaze making herself busy cleaning up the breakfast dishes. This wasn't the time to turn cowardly. She'd made a bargain with Raven and she would keep it. "It's just that I didn't expect it to happen so soon. I thought I would have some time to . . . well to get used to the idea."

Dream Woman pulled out a tiny white doeskin bag from the bottom of a basket. "Ah hah! This woman knew it was here somewhere."

"What?"

"A surprise." She looked at Tess. "Leave the bowls. I will get them. Today you must rest. I will prepare everything. Already women bake in their hearths for the great feast we will hold tonight in your honor."

"You mean in Raven's honor."

"Yours. For our people this is a bride's day. She must be given gifts. We must dance and sing in her name."

Tess rose to her feet. "Do we have to do it in front of everyone? Can't we . . . you know just let the sha . . . sha—"

"Shaman," Dream Woman offered.

"Shaman," Tess repeated correctly, surprised by how many Lenape words she'd picked up in such a short time. "Couldn't we just let him do what he has to do in private and be done with it?"

Dream Woman cut across the small wigwam and squeezed Tess's hand. "Of course you cannot do that. A wedding is very important to our people. A wedding is proof that the Lenape will live on. Your happiness is our happiness."

Tess groaned. It was going to be hard to pretend this wasn't happening. She lifted her hands in surrender. "All right. Just tell me what to do. I don't want to offend anyone. Raven says there are people in the village who don't think I should be here."

"Ha!" Dream Woman waved her hand. "Old men and women with nothing better to do with their time than complain." She started for the door with the tiny white bag still in her hand. "Rest. Take a sleep. The women will come for you late in the afternoon to prepare you for your night."

Tess nodded, walking to the doorway with Dream Woman. Outside, the village was a flurry of activity. Women hustled about with corn husk baskets full of new vegetables. Young boys carried firewood and buckets of water while the girls kept a close eye on the younger children. Several groups of men were gathered, preparing to go hunting or fishing.

All of this for me, Tess thought. She had to smile. How long had she known Dream Woman? Less than two weeks, and yet the woman was willing to do all of this for her. In the last two weeks Dream Woman had been more of a mother to her than Tess's own mother had ever been.

Tess couldn't help but think back to the days in her uncle's home. No one had ever cared about her there, and those people had been her blood relatives! The day she would wed Myron she expected nothing more than a hasty ceremony performed by the circuit rider in one of her uncle's twin parlors. There would be no dancing, no singing, no wedding guests. Her uncle would never spend his money on Tess, not even for a wedding supper. She would go to Myron without a dowry. And Tess knew full well that the night she wed Myron she would be expected to cook his evening meal in his white clapboard farmhouse on the outskirts of Annapolis.

Tess spent most of the day secluded in Dream Woman's wigwam lost in her thoughts. She half-hoped Raven would come to see her, but he didn't. During the hottest part of the day she took a nap lying with her head on a sleeping mat near the doorway. From there she could feel the afternoon breeze and hear the comforting sound of the Lenape women singing as they worked.

When Tess woke, the afternoon light had shifted. The air was a little cooler and the village had grown quiet. When she peeked out the door she saw that there was almost no one in the open areas of the compound. But Tess knew they were out there. She could feel the air almost bursting with the villagers' excitement. They were going to celebrate a wedding.

Heavens—this was her wedding day.

Of course it wouldn't be a real wedding, she reminded herself. She would just be going through the motions. She wouldn't be his real wife. It was part of the deal she had struck with Raven, she kept telling herself. Yet, she still couldn't help feeling just a little nervous exhilaration. She knew Raven was only marrying her to help his cause, but she also knew he desired her. The thought that a man so virile could find her attractive tantalized her thoughts.

Shortly after she awoke from her nap half a dozen women appeared in the wigwam door. Giggling and chattering among themselves in Lenape, they motioned for her to come with them.

The women took Tess by the arm and led her outside. They crossed the compound, taking her to the far eastern corner. The first woman who reached out to touch Tess's clothing startled her. Tess didn't understand what the young Indian woman was trying to tell her. Surely she didn't want her to take off her clothing here in broad daylight.

"Take-e-of! Take-e-of!" the Lenape woman said, tugging at her own clothing. "Hukee say yes, take-e-of!"

"You want me to take my clothes off?" Tess stared at the Indian woman called Hukee. "I . . . I don't have anything on underneath this. Someone will see me—one of the men."

The woman reached out and gently tugged at the lacing of Tess's short deerskin dress. "No one look at white-skin titties! Take-e-of. Make-e-pretty."

Tess looked at the other women who were all looking at her. They were all waiting for her to strip naked! She didn't want to offend anyone by not following their customs, but she didn't know if she could do this. The family she had been raised in had been very prudish. No one ever saw anyone's body. She glanced around with uncertainty. There were no men in sight.

"Take-e-of!" repeated Hukee in exasperation. She then

signalled to the other women in the group who immediately began to shed their clothes.

Tess stiffened her spine. If this was what the other women did, she would do it, too. It was apparently the custom and obviously custom was very important to these people. She began to slip out of her dress before she lost her nerve. What did she care who saw her naked anyway? The people at home would never know. Uncle Albert and Aunt Faith would never know. Myron would never know. She let the short doeskin dress fall to the dusty ground and someone snatched it up.

The women were all smiling and nodding their heads.

"Inny-side," Hukee told Tess. "Inny-side. Make-e pretty! Make-e pretty bride-e for the Raven."

Tess ducked into the wigwam and was immediately taken back by the moist heat that hit her like a solid wall. She wiped her brow as the other women filed in to sit in a circle.

"Yes, sweat-y, sweat-y good." Hukee nodded, taking Tess's hand and leading her to one of the mats placed in a circle around the wall of the wigwam.

Someone dropped the door on the sweat house and laced it shut. It was dim inside, with only the light coming from the red coals in the center of the wigwam and a small oil lamp that hung from a rafter overhead.

Tess wiped her face with the back of her hand as the sweat ran down her forehead, stinging her eyes. Several rings of flat stones encircled the pile of hot coals in the center of the wigwam. Someone lifted a ladle of water from a bark bucket and poured it onto a stone. The water hissed on the hot rock and immediately turned to steam.

So that's why it's so hot in here, Tess thought. She drew up her knees in the cross-legged position she'd grown accustomed to these last two weeks, wondering how long the women intended to cook her. She looked at the others.

The Lenape women were all staring at her, smiling and sweating profusely.

"Good," Hukee said, rubbing her sweaty arms. "Make-e clean."

Tess nodded in understanding, and Hukee grinned, pleased with herself.

After only a few minutes in the sweat house Tess began to grow lightheaded. She didn't think she'd ever been so hot in all her life. One of the women offered her a water skin and Tess gulped down several mouthfuls. The water was icy cold and sweet. She could taste clover honey in it, but there were other ingredients too that she didn't recognize. She took another drink and then passed it to the Lenape woman seated next to her.

Tess kept wiping her forehead. Her vision was blurry from the sweat that poured down her face into her eyes. Why was everyone watching her? Her body was no different than theirs. In fact, her body wasn't bad at all now that she had all these shapes and sizes to compare herself to.

Tess rubbed her stinging eyes. Why were they all smiling? Wasn't anyone as hot as she was? She wanted to leave. She'd had enough, but she decided that she was as tough as any Lenape woman in this sweat house. If they could stand it, so could she.

Finally, to Tess's relief, Hukee rose and motioned toward the door. Tess stood shakily. "My clothes?" She tapped her bare chest, searching for the right Algonquian word. *"Kah-kon? Kah-kon?"* She knew that was the word Raven used for his leggings. She knew that wasn't exactly the word she wanted, but surely the women understood for what she asked.

Hukee shook her head. The other women laughed, but not in an unfriendly way. She pointed to the doorway. "Sid-e."

Tess glanced at the doorflap one of the women had unlaced. Obviously they were waiting for Tess to leave first. She looked at the door longingly. *Naked?* Could she do it?

Hell yes, she could do it! she thought, a little unsteady on her feet. She'd killed a man to protect herself hadn't she? This would be simple compared to having to do that.

Before she lost her nerve, Tess pushed open the flap and stepped outside into the fading light. The summer breeze hit her like a wave of cool water. "Ah," she sighed actually enjoying the feel of the wind on her nude body.

The Lenape women pushed out of the sweat house behind her. Laughing and talking among themselves they grabbed Tess's hands and led her through the woods at a run.

Where are they taking me? Tess thought wildly. It felt so strange running naked through the empty forest like this. Was this what it felt like to be a wild animal, free to run? she wondered.

Tess knew the heat of the sweat house had affected her thinking. Was she actually running through the forest without any clothes on? Was that herself she heard laugh with the others?

Suddenly the creek appeared ahead of them. The women all gave a shout of excitement and ran straight for the water. Two women still held each of Tess's hands, so she had no choice but to run with them.

The Indian women leapt off the bank into the creek pulling Tess with them. Tess screamed in shock as she hit the water and went under. It was so cold that for a moment everything in her mind went black. Then her feet hit the sandy bottom and she pushed herself up until her head broke the surface.

Everyone was laughing. Some of the women clapped and others waved at her. Tess had passed some sort of rite, though exactly what it was, she didn't know.

Tess smiled back at the women, drawing up her feet and paddling. The creek was very deep here. She wondered if it had been created for this very purpose. One of the women splashed Tess from behind and she turned and splashed her back.

Everyone was splashing and laughing and talking. It didn't matter to Tess that she didn't understand most of what they said. What mattered was that she was being included. They were treating her as if she was one of them.

One of the women brought a fragrant shampoo for Tess's hair. She indicated that she wanted Tess to lay back in the water while she washed her hair. At first Tess was a little hesitant but when the woman ran her fingers through her hair it felt so wonderful to be pampered that she was able to relax in the water and enjoy the special attention.

After half an hour or so an older woman appeared at the bank with rectangles of soft hairless doeskin. She called to the women in the water. Hukee led Tess out of the creek and the older woman wrapped her in the soft doeskin. Someone else wrapped her hair in a smaller piece and piled it high on her head. One by one the other women came out of the water and dried off. Then they headed back toward the village.

The village was so quiet when they entered it that it almost seemed eerie to Tess. The only person she saw was an old man tending the roasting meat at the huge fire that had been built in the center of the village near the Big

House. When the women appeared, he paid no attention to them. He acted as if he had never seen them.

Hukee and two other women led Tess back to Dream Woman's wigwam. The other women waved good-bye. One even kissed her on the cheek. Then they departed to return to their own wigwams.

Tess found Dream Woman in her lodge waiting. She had dressed in a short white skirt and a beautiful sleeveless red tunic that had been embroidered with curling vines, leaves, and flowers. Her hair fell in sleek, shiny waves down her back, tied to one side with a matching red ribbon that was embroidered as well. Seashell earrings dangled from Dream Woman's ears.

"Oh, you're beautiful," Tess murmured. Until this moment she had always wished she'd been born blonde like Jocelyn. Now, suddenly she wanted the same inky black hair as Dream Woman and Raven and all the other Lenape.

Dream Woman clasped her hands, smiling. "This woman thanks you for your kind words, but it is you, the bride, who will be most beautiful tonight." Dream Woman waved her hand toward the other women. *"Paai-aal! Gotschemunk. Paai-aal!"* she ordered. "Go and prepare yourselves. This night I will be her *n'gaxais!"*

Hukee and the other two women nodded.

Tess waved her hand. "Thank you." she called. She turned to Dream Woman. "Please tell them that this woman thanks them."

Dream Woman spoke in Lenape. The women nodded their heads and disappeared through the doorway.

Tess walked across the wigwam to sit on the corner of the sleeping platform. "You didn't tell me they were going to boil me, Dream Woman."

She threw back her head and laughed. "It is to clean the body as well as the soul. You feel good now, no?"

She nodded, having to admit she was right. "I do. I feel great, but I still wish you'd told me."

Dream Woman came toward her with a wide-toothed tortoise comb. "If this woman had told you what would happen, would you have gone?" She pulled the towel off Tess's head.

"No. No I guess I wouldn't have."

Dream Woman sat on the edge of the sleeping platform and patted the mat in front of her. "Sit and I will comb your magic *meelaxk.* The Raven's heart will swell with a man's pride when he sees the maiden he will marry this night."

Tess sat down on the floor and allowed Dream Woman to comb out her thick unruly waves. *This is really happening,* she said to herself over and over again. *I've agreed to marry a savage. I've agreed. Tonight I become the wife of Raven.*

A few minutes later a woman called from outside the wigwam. "Come," Dream Woman beckoned.

It was Dove's Call. She stepped inside the wigwam and lowered her head shyly. "My sorries I could not go to sweat house," she said, addressing Tess. "My grandfather, he take sick."

"Oh, I'm so sorry," Tess answered.

She waved her hand. "He is good now. Only he likes my attention." She smiled, looking up hesitantly. She was holding something out in her hands, a garment of some sort. "This woman, I bring you wedding pre-sent . . . present," she corrected herself. "To wear at your wedding."

Tess rose as Dove's Call unfolded the garment and held it up. "Oh," Tess murmured in awe. "Oh, Dove's Call, it's,

it's the most beautiful dress I've ever seen in my life."
She reached out, unable to resist touching the exquisite
piece. "But I can't take this from you."

The wedding dress was a simply cut sleeveless sheath
made of butter-soft white doeskin. Short and fringed at
the hem, the bodice was fastened with white laces beaded
at the ends. A simple vine pattern was quilled across each
shoulder. The dress was so simple that it was plain, but
simplicity was what made it so striking.

"Please," Dove's Call beseeched. "It was made for my
wedding day. Is it not good enough for the white-skinned
woman?"

Tess could tell by her tone of voice that she had hurt
Dove's Call's feelings. It was her wedding dress. How
could Tess take it? But from the look on the young Lenape
woman's face, Tess knew she had to take it.

"Oh, Dove's Call, if you're certain you want to give it
to me," Tess said holding out her arms, "then this woman
thanks you."

Dove's Call broke into a smile as she carefully laid the
doeskin dress in Tess's arms. "I must go, but I will honor
you tonight." She nodded to Dream Woman and then
backed out of the wigwam.

"Thank you," Tess called after her. "Thank you so
much!"

When Dove's Call was gone, Tess turned back to Dream
Woman.

"You are learning the way of *The People*," the Lenape
woman said, smiling. "This is good. I told the Raven you
were one of us. I told him the color of your skin did not
matter."

"It's her wedding dress," Tess protested, still in shock.

"I didn't want to take her wedding dress but I didn't know what to say. I didn't want to hurt her feelings."

"It was her gift to you. Among our people a gift given freely must always be accepted."

Tess lowered her face to brush her cheek against the doeskin. She looked up at Dream Woman. "Can I put it on now? Is it almost time?"

The faint sound of a drum had just begun to beat.

The Lenape woman nodded. "It is almost time. Let me help you into it and then I will finish your hair."

With Dream Woman's help, Tess slipped the dress carefully over her head. It fit as if it had been made for her. The doeskin was so soft against her skin that it felt like she was covered in a cloud of white. She kept brushing it with her fingertips over and over again and Dream Woman laced up the bodice and smoothed the back.

Dream Woman stepped back and opened her hands. Tears clouded her eyes. "You are as beautiful as my daughter was on her wedding day."

"You have a daughter? I didn't know that." Tess turned around and dropped to her knees so that Dream Woman could finish brushing out her hair. As she worked, Tess slipped on the moccasins that had been Takooko's.

"Kehella. Her name is Walking Tortoise. She lives north with her husband. Soon she will give this old woman her first grandchild."

Tess turned to look over her shoulder. Dream Woman had finished her brushing and was now braiding a few small strands to lay on top of Tess's hair that flowed down her back. "You're not old!"

"Hah, to speak to my son you would think I was ready to walk the death walk."

Tess laughed. "You mean about Taande."

"I do not know what my son knows of Taande and this woman, but I know he does not approve."

"He thinks he's protecting you, that's all."

"I do not want to dishonor my son or embarrass him in front of our people, but the truth is that I care for the young man Taande greatly." She began to gather all the tiny braids she had made in Tess's hair. "And I think he cares for me. He says the seasons between us matter not to him."

Tess reached behind her and laid her hand on Dream Woman's. "Then enjoy your happiness. Raven will have to accept your choice and his friend's, too."

Dream Woman removed something from a pouch at her waist and tied it into Tess's hair. "Now you are ready," she declared. "Let this woman see you. The drum grows louder. It is time."

Tess stood up and turned to Dream Woman. She touched the back of her head and felt a beaded leather hair tie. "Is this for me?"

"Do you wish to see in the looking mirror?"

"Yes."

Dream Woman walked to her sleeping platform and knelt to look under it. From a small basket she removed a silver hand mirror. "It is old," she told Tess as she wiped the surface with her fingers. "A gift from my children's father." She came across the wigwam and handed it to Tess.

"It's a beautiful mirror." Tess held it up and turned her head to see what Dream Woman had put in her hair. It was a long strip of white doeskin that had been beaded in blue and green. She had used the leather to tie back a handful of tiny braids. "Oh, Dream Woman." Tess could feel a lump rising in her throat. It was so beautiful. "You made this for me?"

"Every woman must have a hairpiece on her wedding night."

Tess lowered the mirror. "Thank you."

Dream Woman studied Tess, clasping her hands. "Yes. This is good. You are a woman of beauty and mind to suit my son." She took the mirror from her. "Come my daughter, it is time."

Tess took a deep breath and standing beside Dream Woman, she lifted her chin a notch and stepped out of the wigwam into torchlight that was so bright it was almost blinding. Everyone in the village was there waiting for her. Drums were playing and gourd rattles were shaking. Someone was singing.

Then she saw him. She knew her mouth dropped. There standing a few yards from her was Raven, dressed as no man she had ever seen on his wedding day.

Fifteen

Raven stood before her, his copper-gold skin aglow with the light of the torches. He was dressed in a short-skirted, leather loincloth fringed at the edges. His broad muscle-corded chest was bare, the angry red musketball wound in his shoulder was the only thing that marred the perfection of his form. Beaten copper armbands encircled each of his biceps looking as if at any moment they would spring beneath the might of his strength. Around his neck he wore a necklace of eagle talons and black raven feathers. His hair was pulled back to the crown of his head to fall in a midnight curtain down his bare back. He stared at her with those black eyes of his that Tess knew she was lost to. When he offered her his hand she found she couldn't move she was so mesmerized by his masculine beauty.

"Maata-wischasi," he murmured when his fingertips touched hers.

He must have felt her trembling.

"Do not fear. No harm will come to you as long as this man breathes," he whispered in her ear.

The villagers were falling in behind them, their torches held high as Raven led her toward the communal campfire.

Tess could feel a panic rising in her chest. She couldn't

do this! She couldn't marry this man, not even in a heathen ceremony. She could tell herself that it would mean nothing, but deep inside she knew differently. She feared that if she went through with this she would never be able to escape.

"I changed my mind," she whispered. "I won't do it."

He took his hand from hers; suddenly his gentle touch was gone. *"Matta."* He squeezed her shoulder roughly. "It is too late. A bargain you and I have made," he whispered harshly, his words meant for no ears but her own. "A bargain you will keep."

Tess turned to look at him. His black eyes glinted threateningly. She looked away, giving herself a moment to regain her composure. She would not let this man bully her. She wouldn't allow him to make her feel like a possession. He was right. She had agreed to marry him. And he had agreed to set her free in one year. One year was all she had to endure. For Abby she knew she could do it.

"If you think *this* will make me care for you, you're wrong," Tess whispered. "It will only make me hate you more than I hate you now."

"You will not betray me in word or deed, that is the agreement."

Tess looked out at the villagers. Raven had come to a halt next to the shaman. Everyone was staring at them, their faces solemn with the importance of the ceremony that was about to take place.

Raven released her shoulder and the holy man began to chant. The drum beat slowed to match the rhythm of his words. From somewhere beyond the circle of light came the sound of hollow gourd rattles. The old man, his hair in long white braids, spoke in the Lenape tongue, his voice as haunting as the eerie shadows his silhouette cast against the empty wigwams that surrounded them.

Of course Tess didn't understand anything the shaman was saying. She kept telling herself that his words didn't matter. She wasn't really making any vows. This was a heathen ceremony; she didn't care what Dream Woman said about being Christianized. This was no man of the cloth. The Raven would never be her husband . . . never.

Tess glanced sideways at Raven who was listening intently to the shaman. She saw him move his lips as he repeated a phrase and she couldn't help remembering what those lips had felt like against hers.

Tess didn't understand how she could dislike Raven, no, hate him, for what he was doing to her, and yet still be so attracted to him. As she watched the solemn expression on his face she wondered what it would have been like to have been wooed by this man. Surely he would not have been as dismal a failure as Myron had been.

The shaman offered Raven a wooden cup and he sipped from it. Then Raven passed it to her, his gaze following her.

Tess tipped the vessel, but didn't allow the drink to touch her lips as if it could somehow truly seal the marriage vow.

The shaman took the cup from her and threw the contents into the flames. A great cheer rose among the villagers and Tess realized it was done. She had married a red man.

"Smile," Raven said forcefully beneath his breath. "Act the happy bride."

Tess half-smiled, angry that he would speak to her in that tone of voice. The villagers were crowding around them now, hitting Raven on the back, reaching to take her hand, laughing as they offered their best wishes.

Tess forced herself to smile. She nodded to those who spoke to her, some in English, others in Lenape. She made no attempt to pull away when Raven touched her arm to lead her to the seat of honor.

"Lemattachpi," he said.

Sit, Tess knew that word. She sat on the soft hide mat set out for her and he dropped down beside her. Someone offered them a cup and again she was forced to share it with him. This time she drank deeply. The concoction was strong, but not unpleasant tasting. Heavy wooden trays of food appeared at their feet. A plate heaped with woodland and bay delicacies had been prepared for them to share.

There were smoked clams, raw oysters, baked fish, and squirrel stew. Wooden trays and bowls were piled high with steamed leeks, stewed greens, and fried yellow squash. Raven ate heartily but Tess could barely force a mouthful between her lips. All she could think was that she had married this man beside her.

The music began again, but this time it was more light-hearted. Women chanted while the men danced, stamping out intricate patterns in the dust around the campfire. The Lenape women kept bringing Tess gifts; cooking vessels of clay, baskets made of pine needles, corn husk, twig, and bark buckets, wooden bowls, even two pewter cups and several shiny pewter forks. There were soft sleeping mats, corn husk stuffed pillows, and a red wool blanket. Some women brought her personal items; a pair of knee-high doeskin moccasins quilled at the toes, a skirt, a man's colonial shirt that had been embroidered with woodland flowers, a pair of silver bell earrings, even a pair of snow-shoes.

Tess was overwhelmed by all the well-wishers. No one knew or even guessed that this was merely a business deal between she and Raven. She even felt a little guilty for deceiving them. These people who should have considered her their enemy had welcomed her into their community, and were showering her with gifts. Tess could not even remember the last time someone had given her a gift.

The later in the evening it got, the louder the villagers became. They laughed and drank their heady herbal drink. They danced and sang and made merry. Such simple happiness was difficult for Tess to comprehend. She couldn't help wondering if it would be possible for her to ever be this happy.

After eating more than Tess imagined any man could consume, Raven leaned back on the pile of mats on which they sat and sipped from a wooden cup. He smiled lazily, his humor apparently improved by the food and drink.

"So now we have done it," he said, catching a strand of her hair to twist around his finger.

Tess looked at him. For hours she had been able to avoid speaking directly to him. She'd been so busy accepting the villagers' gifts and well-wishes that it hadn't been difficult. Now it seemed as if they had finally been left to themselves. The villagers had broken into groups of family and friends. A circle of young braves were dancing some dance that had something to do with an eagle. The older women were still serving up trays of food.

"We did it," Tess echoed. "But you and I both know this is not a real marriage." She lifted her chin indicating all those around them. "This is not what they think it is."

"Are you certain, my fire-haired beauty?" He lifted a sleek, dark eyebrow looking intently at her. Tess's heart leaped. Hadn't her grandmother always said Lucifer wouldn't appear with cloven hooves lashing a forked tail, but in the shape of a comely man with eyes as black as midnight and a tongue as sweet as honey?

Tess leaned closer to him, refusing to fear him or be enticed by his handsome looks and sensual words. "Yes, I'm certain," she snapped. "Now tell me what happens when a year from now I pack up and go? What then?"

He still held the lock of her hair and was now rolling it between his fingers. "Perhaps you will not go."

She didn't appreciate his smug attitude. "And perhaps the sun will not rise at dawn."

He chuckled as if he knew something she didn't. "Perhaps."

Tess groaned. "I don't understand," she said to him softly. "Why me? Why is it me you want? Surely I'm not the first white woman you've ever known."

"Not even the first I have kissed." He smiled a devil-may-care smile.

This was not what she wanted to hear. She wasn't interested in his sexual escapades. "Then why me?"

"My mother Hokkuaa Onna, the Woman Who Dreams, tells me she dreamt of you long ago." He brought the strand of red hair to his lips. "She says you are my fate." He looked up at her, his black eyes soft and languid. "She says I am your fate, Tess."

Tess's breath had quickened. She could feel her heart thudding beneath the white doeskin dress. His words were nonsense, all nonsense and yet . . .

His haunting gaze drew her toward him. His lips. . . . She wanted to kiss him; she wanted to be kissed. He knew she wanted to be kissed. Tess let her eyes drift shut.

"We are married," she heard him say.

"I don't want this," she whispered. "It will only confuse matters."

He caressed her cheek with his fingertips. He slipped his fingers into her hair at her temple, guiding her, bringing her mouth inches from his.

"To share pleasure, this is confusing to you, Tess?"

His breath was a caress on her cheek. She shook her head ever so slightly, fighting the waves of excitement that made her tremble. She could feel her stomach tightening, her head grow light in anticipation of his kiss. "I can't do this." *I can't let myself care about you!* His lips brushed hers and then were gone again. "I have responsibilities far from here."

"Tell me, Tess." Again he brushed his lips against hers in the barest caress. "Tell me and perhaps—"

"You can't help." She lowered her head a hair's breath and felt his lips against hers again. "You can't."

Raven tightened his hold on the back of her head and thrust his tongue between her lips. Tess pushed her palm against his bare chest fighting him, fighting herself. His taste was intoxicating . . . the feel of his tongue touching hers. . . . She found herself running her palm over his shoulder gripping it, crushing her mouth to his.

The sound of clapping, footstomping, and hooting caught Tess's attention somewhere in the back of her mind. She pulled her mouth from his, breathless. She looked up to see an ocean of laughing black eyes. They were watching them!

Tess sat up, mortified. Everyone was still laughing and whistling. Men and women alike were calling out to them. Tess didn't understand the words, but she knew the tone well enough to know the comments were of a sexual nature.

Raven pushed up from his reclining position and grinned. "They say they think it's time we retire to our wigwam before our first child is conceived at the communal fire."

Tess was too numb to be shocked by their bawdy words. "I don't want to go," she whispered shakily. "I . . . I'm not ready." The truth was that right now she was afraid to be alone with him. Of course she'd never had any intention of consummating this farce of a wedding, but at this point Raven had her so confused that she didn't know for sure what she might do.

He took her hand and stood, lifting her with him. "Do not be silly," he whispered. "We are man and wife now." He kissed her on the lips again.

There was more laughing and stomping of feet. Tess felt lightheaded. The faces of the villagers were a blur as Raven led her away.

He dropped his arm over her shoulder and squeezed gently. "Do not be offended. My people only offer well-wishes." He smiled and made some comment to the others.

Then Tess felt him stiffen. She followed his gaze. The smile had fallen from his face for a second, and then it was there again, only this time she knew it wasn't genuine.

There, standing in the shadows beyond the fire, were Dream Woman and Taande locked in a lover's embrace, their mouths touching. Dream Woman's arms were wrapped tightly around the young man's bare shoulders, his hand resting possessively on her thigh. They were oblivious to the other men and women around them.

"Let's go," Tess whispered, her own concerns forgotten for the moment. When Raven didn't move she nudged him, fearing he might make a scene. "Your people expect us to go now, *husband.*"

Hand and hand, Tess and Raven left the light of the campfire and the sound of the celebrating. When they were out of view of the others, Tess did not release his hand. "Don't be angry with them."

"If I saw them, others saw them," he answered sharply. "She will make a fool of herself in front of the elders. Taande—"

"Taande is your friend. You said he spoke up for you at High Council."

"He is taking advantage of her. My mother—"

"Taande obviously cares for her. Why else would he risk the friendship he has with you to be with her?" They came to his wigwam, and she stopped. She looked up at Raven. The man who had been laughing lazily only a few moments ago was now angry and solemn. Tess touched a beaten copper armband on his forearm. It was warm from the heat of his body. "They're adults. They have a right to choose their own friends."

He glared at her. "That! That which I saw was *more* than friendship! Taande is my age. This is shameful. It should be stopped before—."

Tess raised the doorflap and ducked inside, pulling Raven after her. "—Raven," she said, gently interrupting him. "Not tonight. This is not the time. No one seems to be upset, but you."

He dropped his hands to his hips, his eyes focusing on his bow on the far wall. "You are right." He ran a hand over his head smoothing his sleek hair. "Tonight is our wedding night. I should not make matters worse by embarrassing Taande or my mother in front of the others. Tomorrow, tomorrow I will speak to them both." His gaze

met hers. "This man says his sorries. Sit, and let me welcome you to my lodge." He gestured to the soft hide mats
that had been laid out on the floor. No fire burned in the
firepit because of the June heat, but an oil lamp hanging
from a rafter bathed the domed wigwam in a glow of
romantic light.

Tess took a seat cross-legged on a mat, her mind going
back to what they had been doing only a few minutes
before. She didn't know what had come over her to be
so brazen. Again she felt her heart trip in her chest. She
licked her lips that were suddenly dry. He was watching
her. She looked up to see him standing there near the
doorway barely clothed, his copper skin glowing in the
light of the oil lamp. *How easy it would be to lose myself
to him right now,* she thought. The worst thing was that
she wasn't even sure that wasn't what she wanted.

"I have a gift for you," he said, walking toward her.

She heard him come up behind her and felt his hands
around her neck. Something cool touched her chest. Tess
looked down to see a necklace made of seashells and
feathers. She remembered the acorn necklace that Na-Kee
had given to her, and that Raven had ripped from her
neck. "Oh, it's beautiful," she whispered. She ran her fingers over the seashells made smooth by the ocean, but
then looked up at him. "I . . . I'm sorry. I don't have
anything for you."

He squatted beside her. "Give me your trust, Tess. That
is all I ask of you."

She averted her eyes, his nearness making her tongue
tied. "How . . . how can I? When I escaped from the
Mohawk, you said you would take me home. You didn't.
You won't."

He rose. "One turn of the seasons. One year and then I will take you to your man myself."

Tess watched Raven as he carefully removed the talon and feather necklace from around his neck, then one by one the glimmering copper armbands. He moved fluidly without wasted motion, like a dancer dancing to a rhythm only he could hear.

"One year," she agreed.

Carefully placing the jewelry in a basket hanging from the rafters, Raven walked across the wigwam to the single sleeping platform. "Come wife, it is late."

When she didn't move, he curled his fingertips. "Come. It has been a long day for us both."

Tess rose and made herself busy removing the leather and bead hairpiece Dream Woman had given her from her head. Raven waited impatiently at the sleeping platform.

I can't do this, Tess thought. I can't sleep with him. Not even if I want to. I have to leave this village no matter how much I may think I'd like to stay. To consummate the relationship would only make the marriage more real. It would make it too hard to leave.

All too soon the hairpiece came free. Raven took it from her, his fingertips brushing hers. Then he reached behind her neck and removed the shell and feather necklace. She lifted her gaze, the tension in the small lodge palatable on her tongue. "Raven, I—"

"You sleep here on the platform. I will make my bed on the floor."

She looked at the bed, then back at him. He didn't mean for them to share it? She breathed a sigh of relief.

He must have known what she was thinking. He took a step back looking away and then back at her again. "A man does not take what is not freely offered from a woman, even his wife." Then he walked away from her, taking care not to touch her.

He blew out the oil lamp leaving them in darkness and then she heard him lay down on the floor near the cold firepit.

Tess climbed onto the sleeping platform, removed her moccasins, and stretched out. She slept, her first night as Raven's wife, in her wedding dress.

Sixteen

Raven sat cross-legged outside his wigwam repairing his bowstring. He could hear Tess inside singing an English song to herself as she ground corn with a stone pestle for their evening meal. Her voice was husky and rich.

He frowned. He didn't have time to think about Tess or the way he knew damp tendrils of hair stuck to her cheek as she worked. He had more important matters on his mind.

The five days since their wedding had passed quickly as Raven prepared himself for the final council meeting tonight, where he hoped he would be appointed War Chief of the village. He purposefully kept a safe distance from Tess, remaining polite but reserved. She seemed content with the arrangement and was making herself busy learning the many tasks a Lenape woman must know.

Not only did Tess cook and work in the garden, but she had taken an interest in herbal healing. She had spent many hours in the last few days at the shaman's side watching him as he went about his duties. Tess had also taken it upon herself to learn to load and fire Raven's Brown Bess with the same skill and timing as he had. Raven had tried to explain to her that as long as she understood the rudimentary elements that was all she need know. It was a man's duty to protect his woman. Tess insisted he teach her anyway. She argued that when she left the village she wanted to be able to protect herself. She said no man, red or white, would ever take her captive again.

Twice in the last few days Raven and Na-Kee had met with the French. The English *manake* General called Braddock intended to begin his march north to Fort Dusquesne within the week and the French still needed Lenape warriors. The Frenchmen said that six hundred men had already arrived at Fort Dusquesne, men of the Delaware, Shawnee, Ottawa, Abenakis, and Mingoe tribes.

Na-Kee wanted to go with the scouts to Dusquesne and he wanted to take men from the village with him. He insisted that the alliance they would make with the French and the white-hairs at Fort Dusquesne would be well-worth their while. Na-Kee looked at this gathering at the fort as a lark, an adventure. He argued that the warriors in the village were growing lazy and soft like women. He said they needed a diversion like this fight with the English to make them men again.

Raven felt that Na-Kee was taking this political move too lightly. The village would be choosing sides. They were surrounded by the English, yet they would be declaring their alliance with the French. This march of Braddock's was insane. The French and the Indians would massacre them on the path to Dusquesne. The English fools would never make it to the fort gates alive.

Raven tightened the torque on his gut bowstring and tested it for flexibility. Behind him he heard Tess appear in the doorway.

"The bucket is empty. Could you fetch me some *m'be?* I'm trying to make those blasted corncakes the way

Dream Woman does." She held the skin water bucket out to him.

Raven looked over his shoulder and frowned. A thin sheen of perspiration dotted her forehead. Her dark red hair was pulled back in a thick braid, but a few twisted tendrils had escaped to stick to her damp skin. Her cheeks were flushed with the heat of the day. "Fetching water is woman's work," he grumbled getting to his feet. He took the bucket from her, taking care not to let his fingertips brush against hers. *"M'be?"*

She nodded. "Pretty good, hmm? Dove's Call says I will be speaking Lenape in no time."

"That is why you spend so much time with her in her lodge? She teaches you our tongue?"

"Of course." A strange look flashed across Tess's face. "What else would I be doing with her?" She turned to go back into the wigwam. "Could you hurry? I want to cook these on the firepit outside. It's too hot in the wigwam for a fire." She stopped in the doorway. "When does Council meet?"

Raven glanced at the water bucket in his hand. This was harder than he had thought it would be, trying to remain at a distance from Tess. He wanted to tell her of his fears if he didn't get the position, and the fears if he did. But of course he couldn't tell her, not and remain impersonal. He couldn't tell her that at night he lay only a few feet from her thinking about her either. He couldn't tell her that despite the circumstances of their marriage, each day he felt more like her husband. Each day he found it harder to resist reaching out to touch her as a husband touches his wife.

Raven ground his moccasin into the dry dust. "We meet tonight, yes. Late."

"They will vote?"

"I am not sure. Perhaps. There is no way to tell. It is She-Who-Swings-From-Stars' decision."

Tess surprised Raven by reaching out to brush her knuckles across his bare arm. "They'll vote for you. Don't worry. Na-Kee is sneaky. Surely everyone realizes that. Why, he even tries to sweet-talk me."

"Time will tell," he responded, walking away. Raven wondered if Tess could feel the sexual tension that arced between them, or if she was too innocent to understand the silent language between a man and a woman. The kisses they had shared that magical morning in the forest had certainly not been innocent. "I will be back with your water. Make my corncakes," he added roughly. "This man is hungry."

Tess smiled as she watched Raven walk away, carrying her water bucket. Such tasks were a woman's place here in the village. So why did he do it for her? she wondered. Dove's Call insisted it was because he was in love with her. Tess only laughed when her friend made such romantic suggestions.

Tess had confided in Dove's Call, explaining the arrangement of the marriage, but the Indian woman had refused to accept Tess's word that she and Raven had not married out of passion. She insisted it would just take some time for them to get used to each other. She said a Lenape man never did anything he didn't truly wish to do.

In the last few days Tess and Dove's Call had spent a great deal of time together. Tess's new-found friend helped keep her mind off Raven and this new relationship they were awkwardly establishing. The two women cooked, worked the communal garden, and cleaned together. Dove's Call was helping Tess with the Lenape language and customs. But more importantly, she was also teaching Tess Indian sign language. When Tess finally was reunited with Abby, she would have so many new words to teach her!

Tess stood in the doorway of the wigwam for a moment, letting the late afternoon breeze cool her prickly skin. She wiped the nape of her neck, thankful for the short doeskin sheath she wore. She wondered how, once she returned to Annapolis, she would ever be able to bring herself to put on those stays and heavy petticoats in the heat of the summer.

Time to get back to work, she chided herself. Tonight Raven would become War Chief of the village. It was an important night and she wanted to make him a decent Lenape meal before he faced the villagers. She was going to try to make honeyed corncakes and fried squash. If it didn't work, she had a back-up plan. She smiled to herself as she ducked back into the wigwam. At this very moment Dove's Call was preparing the very same meal at her grandfather's hearth. If Tess's attempt didn't turn out, Dove's Call would have plenty of extra!

Hours later, sometime near midnight, Tess stood in front of Raven's wigwam listening to the night sounds and waiting. She toyed with the seashell necklace around her neck. High Council was still in session. The sound of a steady drum blended with the sounds of the chirping crickets and the occasional hoot of an owl.

It seemed as if the council meeting was going to go on forever. Tess was so nervous she felt silly. Why did what happened to Raven mean so much to her? She had told herself she would keep an emotional distance between him and herself. It would make things easier when she left next summer. But it was hard, much harder than she'd expected.

Tess suddenly detected the sound of voices and looked up. High Council had let out. Men and woman were beginning to file out of the Big House. She craned her neck to spot Raven, or some sign of the results of the evening. The villagers were talking among themselves, but she didn't see anyone she knew well enough to question. Finally, after several minutes, she spotted Raven. He was crossing the compound, coming toward her.

Tess's heart fell. From the look on his face she knew he'd lost. Na-Kee had become the new War Chief. She watched him as he approached her, his shoulders thrown back proudly.

"Raven?"

He brushed past her ducking into the wigwam. "Get your belongings."

She followed him. "What?"

He picked up a leather traveling bag given to her as a wedding gift. "Take what you will, but take it now." He pulled a small basket down from the rafters and dumped it into the travel bag. Tess's hairpiece Dream Woman had given her tumbled out along with the two stiff slippers that had been Jocelyn's.

"I don't understand," Tess protested. "What are you doing?"

He tossed the bag through the air and she caught it before it hit the floor. "I take you back to 'Napolis. Now. Tonight."

Tess just stood there, staring at him. "I . . . I don't understand. What about our bargain? Raven, what happened in there?"

"I absolve you of my brother's death. I absolve you of our agreement." He was loading his own travel bag now, adding extra black powder and ammunition and a bag of pemmican. "Take a sleeping skin and a weapon. The Mohawk knife is yours, there on the wall."

Tess glanced at the Mohawk skinning knife. It was the one she had stolen from Broken Tooth when she'd dived out of the canoe. Suddenly that seemed like a lifetime ago. Tess looked at Raven. His face was like stone. She didn't know what to say. He said she was free to go home, free to return to Myron and her grand plans. So why was her heart so heavy?

Tess tried to touch Raven's arm but he pulled away from her. "We don't have to go tonight. Tomorrow morning will be soon enough." She let her travel bag slip to the floor. "Raven, tell me what happened at the council meeting."

He took his Brown Bess down from the far wall and propped it near the door. "My village has made their decision. Na-Kee is now War Chief." He turned away to grab his leather bedroll from the end of the sleeping platform. "I have no need of a wife. I will take you back to your family."

"Can't . . . can't we wait until morning." She started stuffing things into her sack, a tortoiseshell comb, a pair of pewter disk earrings, a man's muslin shirt embroidered in the Lenape style. "I want to say goodbye to . . . to your mother, to Dove's Call."

He flung his leather bag over one shoulder, his bedroll ties to the top, and grabbed up his musket. At the doorway he dropped a powder horn and munitions bag over his neck. "Now, Tess."

Tess grabbed a water skin, the Mohawk knife, and her leather bag. As she went out the door she took a red wool blanket off the end of the sleeping platform. "Raven, this is foolish starting out like this tonight." She followed him through the camp, trying to organize her belongings as she ran to catch up. "I can wait until tomorrow morning."

Raven ignored her as he strode through the camp. Someone called to him and he responded briefly in Lenape.

Tess caught up to him, struggling to toss her bag over her shoulder. "Raven, listen to me."

"Silence, woman. I have had enough of your English prattle, enough to last this man a lifetime."

Tess was quiet for a minute, her feelings hurt by his words. They had left the village and were headed toward the creek. Why was he treating her like this? It wasn't her fault Na-Kee had been voted War Chief.

The important question was, why did she care? She was going home. She didn't need this man. He was nothing to her. Or was he?

Tess waded across the creek just behind Raven. In the last few days they had established a comfortable relationship. He had taught her how to shoot his most precious possession, his rifle. She had recited to him all the English nursery rhymes she could remember. They had laughed at her awkward attempts at speaking Lenape and he had recounted his trouble learning the white-hair tongue. They talked about things of little importance, they spoke of the events in their lives that had shaped them. For the first time in her life, Tess had met a man who was willing to sit quietly and listen to her without interrupting, without telling her why she was wrong.

When Tess thought back on the last few days since they'd wed, she realized she'd been happy. Raven had treated her with an air of respect she'd never gained elsewhere. He had made her feel comfortable around him and comfortable with herself. Suddenly she was remembering every innocent touch they had shared, every coaxed smile.

Tess trudged behind Raven, focusing on his snapping turtle shoulder strap, trying to deny the words that flashed through her mind again and again. *Sweet, heaven, I am in love with him . . .*

Tess stopped where she was and let her bag slip to the leafy ground. She was in shock.

Raven walked several feet ahead before he stopped. "Come." He didn't even turn around to look at her.

Tess lowered one hand to rest it on her hip. She couldn't part this way, not knowing what she knew now. She waited for him to look at her.

He spun around angrily. "I said, let us go!"

"You can't be angry with yourself about Na-Kee. You did your best. They made their choice, and whatever happens, it's not your fault, Raven."

He turned away from her and started walking again. She knew he must have thought she would be frightened by the darkness of the woods and run to catch up. Tess stood her ground. He'd forgotten. She'd spent an entire night in the forest alone. She'd killed a man to save herself. This was not the same woman the Mohawk had kidnapped. She wasn't afraid any more, not of anything or anyone.

She listened to his soft footsteps on the forest floor. He must have gone a hundred feet before he finally stopped. There was a pause before he spoke, and then his voice was without emotion. "I do not wish to speak of Na-Kee. I say I will take you back to your home, now come. This is what you wanted, is it not, Tess?"

She could hear the pain in his voice and her heart went out to him. She knew that Raven didn't want the position

of War Chief for the power, as Na-Kee did. She knew he
had wanted it because he thought that was what was best
for the village, for his people. If only they had understood
what was best for them.

"I don't have to go home tonight, Raven. I told you
that. Let's go back to our lodge." . . . *Our lodge.* "We're
both too tired to think tonight." *Both of us are too confused to know what we really want . . .*

He still didn't come back toward her. Tess picked up
her leather bag and ran through the forest. She knew it
didn't make any sense, it would never make any sense.
All she knew was that she couldn't leave Raven with matters unsettled between them like this. Tomorrow would be
soon enough to go back to Annapolis, even the day after.

She caught up to him at a bend in the path. A little
moonlight seeped between the rifted clouds overhead. How
tragically handsome he was with his bare, burnished copper skin and his face as dark and stonelike as the wooden
masks his enemies, the Mohawk, wore.

Tess let her bag drop at his feet. Facing him she
touched his arm. "I'm sorry." There was a husky catch in
her voice. "I wish I could change what happened. I wish
I had had a vote."

He looked down at her with smoldering black eyes, his
brow furrowed. "What will be, will be. I will go home
to my people and I will follow our new War Chief. I will
die at Na-Kee's side if that is what is asked of this man."

He looked so sad. With an awkward impulsiveness, Tess
brushed her lips against his.

When she dared lift her lashes to look at him she found
him staring down at her. "Why did you do that?"

She felt her pulse quicken. The hand she laid on his
broad bare chest trembled. "I . . . I don't know, because

I've wanted to do it since the night we were married. Because you didn't?"

Tess heard Raven's musket fall to the ground as his arm shot out and snaked her waist. His mouth crushed against hers forcing her lips apart. He delved his tongue deep into her mouth taking her breath away.

Tess clung to him, meeting his tongue thrust for thrust. A curious, hot excitement coursed through her veins. She was enveloped by his heady male scent and the feel of his hand on her breast as he caressed her roughly.

Suddenly he pulled away and pushed her from him. "You must go from here," he whispered harshly, his own breath ragged. "There is danger now that Na-Kee rules our warriors."

"I'll go," she answered, coming back to his arms to kiss the point of his chin. She knew what she wanted. Maybe she had known all along. "But not yet, Raven, *not tonight.*"

He twisted his fingers in her loose auburn hair. She knew he knew what she was offering, perhaps even before she had.

"Tess—"

She touched her finger to his lips. She didn't know why she wanted to make love with Raven before she left. She just knew that no other man would ever touch her heart as he had. She knew that no other man's hands would ever excite her as Raven's did.

"It . . ." He kissed the top of her head. "It would be better if we did not . . ."

She looped her arms around his neck, forcing him to look her in the eyes. "You don't want me?" she whispered. "Is it because I'm white? Because I'm English and you side with the French?"

"No, no, you know that does not matter to this man. It is only that—"

"That what?" Tess caught his hand and brought it to her breast, a fierce ache in her chest making it hard for her to breathe. She laid her forehead against his chin, knowing she was doing the right thing, knowing if she didn't do this tonight, she would regret it for the rest of her living days. "I give you myself this night as a gift," she heard herself say, her voice breathy. "A Lenape can never refuse a gift. It would be an insult, would it not?"

For the longest moment Raven just stared at her with those black eyes she had lost herself to the day she escaped the Mohawk. "My heart?" he whispered, still giving her a chance to change her mind and save face. "Do you know what you say to this man? What you offer?"

"I ask will you love me?" Tess begged, threading her fingers through his midnight hair. "Just tonight, Raven? Will you?"

Seventeen

"Let me take you home to our lodge," Raven whispered, his voice warm and sensual in her ear.

Tess was left so lightheaded from his kiss that reasonable thought was nearly impossible. "No. No here, here in the forest where we met. Here, where we can truly be alone." She smoothed his high-boned cheek with her hand. "Please?"

Raven pressed his lips to her forehead as he released her, letting her slide slowly to the ground, every inch of her body brushing his before her moccasins touched the leaves.

Tess stood on shaky legs and watched as he unrolled his sleeping mat and laid it out beneath the canopy of an elm tree. When he offered her his hand, she took it and walked slowly toward him, enchanted by his dark eyes.

"Tess." He murmured her name like a song on the wind. "For many nights I have dreamed of this, since the day I spotted you in the Mohawk canoe." He kissed her temple, the lobe of her ear, the pulse at her throat. "Since this man first laid eyes on you I have imagined making you mine. I have imagined touching you like this."

Tess gasped with pleasure as his hand went down her spine and beneath her short leather skirt to caress her bare buttocks. Only a small leather woman's loincloth separated his hand from her most intimate parts.

She lifted her chin to meet his mouth with her own, curling her fingers around his neck. His hands were everywhere, touching her, teasing her, making her body pulse with desire.

Slowly they sank to their knees on the hide sleeping mat. A tug at her bodice string and he was pushing her dress down over her shoulders, exposing her breasts to the night air. Tess arched her back, moaning with pleasure as he caught one ripe nipple between his lips and sucked hungrily.

"Yes," she whispered. "Touch me, Raven."

"Here?" he asked as he flicked his tongue over one nipple, then massaging it with his calloused thumb.

"Yes . . ."

"Here?" He caught her other nipple between his teeth and tugged, sending a shock of delight through her.

"Oh, yes . . ."

"And what of here, what of this place, sweet Tess?"

She gasped as he drew his hand up between her legs, pulling her leather loinskin tight against her soft folds. What was that throbbing? What was it about his voice that made her hot and flushed?

"Yes . . . yes," she whispered, just a little afraid of the power he held over her.

Raven pulled her down beside him until they were laying side by side, facing each other. "I will not hurt you," he whispered, rubbing her bare arm and then lifting one breast in his broad, warm hand. "Only pleasure."

Tess's eyelids were heavy with passion. What was this spell Raven held over her? How could his mere touch make her tremble like this?

Raven pushed his leg between hers and drew it up until he was pressing against her woman's mound. Instinctively she leaned against him, another moan of pleasure escaping her lips. He was kissing her neck, nibbling, brushing his fingers over the arched fullness of her breasts.

When Raven pulled up her skirt and brought his fingers to that hot, wet place between her thighs, Tess thought she would go mad. Was this what her body craved? He untied the leather ties at her hips and drew away the bit of leather. The first time his fingertips touched the bed of red curls she cried out in shock. Tess was awash in sensation. She had never known it could be like this . . .

Raven stroked her for several minutes, cradling her in his arm, letting her grow used to his touch and the rippling desire he created.

Then he surprised her by taking her hand in his. "Touch me, Tess," he encouraged. "Touch me as I have touched you."

She looked down at the bulge in his loinskin. She was not a complete innocent. She knew what was beneath that leather. Could she bring herself to touch it? But, oh, he was giving her such sweet, wicked pleasure. What would it be to give him the same?

Hesitantly, she laid her hand on his hard flat stomach. His muscles immediately tensed. His breath grew heavier in her ear. She smiled in the dim moonlight. She liked this control over him. Boldly she slid her hand lower until she touched the band of his loincloth and brushed against the bulge.

He groaned.

Gathering her nerve, Tess cupped the soft flesh through the pliant leather, exploring the feel and shape of him. He was kissing her face, her neck, tugging on the lobe of her ear. "Like this?" she whispered. "Do I touch you like this?"

"Yes, sweet Tess, fire and honey, Tess."

She slipped her hand under the leather, empowered by the sound of his husky voice in her ear. "And this?"

"Ki-ti-hi . . ." he breathed as he tugged on the loinskin tie and ripped away the leather.

His organ fell into her hand, warm and semi-rigid. She was amazed by the softness of his skin. Tentatively, she ran her fingers over the loose flesh, testing the feel of him in her hand.

He was moaning, whispering words in her ear she didn't understand.

She liked the feel of him. Just touching him like this made her throb low in her belly. She could feel him hardening in her hand, his shaft growing longer, thicker. She ran her hand along the length of him, again and again, touching the soft tip with her finger, marveling at the sensitivity.

All too soon he pulled her hand away.

Tess pushed up on her elbow. "Did I do something wrong?" she asked softly, afraid she had broken the spell.

He rolled her onto her back until he was on top of her and lowered his head over hers, drawing in her dark eyes. *"Tuko,* no, my sweet thorn."

His hard bulging loins against her bare thigh sent a shiver of pleasure up her leg. It seemed only natural to lift her hips until they pressed against his above her. "Then what?" she asked. "Why did you stop me? I—" she knew she was blushing "—I liked it."

He laughed, his voice rich and husky. "It is only that you rush this man. It will be over before it has begun," he whispered in her ear. "You told me you had not known a man. This is a special gift, to be unwrapped slowly. To savor."

She smiled up at him, appreciating his sincerity. She watched him as he lowered his head until his lips met the peak of one of her breasts. Once again he caught the hard, pink nipple between his teeth and sucked.

Tess moaned, writhing beneath his hard, muscular frame. A fire was building deep inside her, a fire whose flame only the Raven could fan.

He lowered his head, drawing damp circles on her flat belly with the tip of his hot, wet tongue. Every muscle in her body went taut in sweet, agonizing anticipation as she watched him, knowing where his lips would brush next.

Nothing had prepared Tess for the sensation of Raven's mouth on the soft folds of her womanhood. She knew she should feel shame. Surely anything this glorious must be shameful! But this man was her husband . . . her husband! Why should she not enjoy his touch?

"So sweet," Raven murmured, touching her bud with the tip of his tongue. "So full of fire . . ."

Tess threw back her head in unbridled ecstasy, threading her fingers through his inky hair, calling his name. This had to stop, this exquisite torture. If only it could last forever . . .

When Raven lifted his head and stretched out over her, Tess was breathless; her heart was pounding. She was lost to his touch, beyond reasonable thought.

"Now?" he whispered in her ear his breath hot and moist. "Can this man make you mine, now?"

"Yes, yes," she begged, dragging her blunt nails down his broad back.

Tess had long known the anatomical facts of coupling,

but nothing had prepared her for the sensation of Raven deep inside her. He slipped into her with an ease that shocked her. Where was the pain so many women had whispered of? All she felt now was an intense fullness and a yearning inside her that was yet to be satisfied.

Raven gave Tess a few seconds to grow used to the feel of him and then he began to move up and down, sliding in and out with slow, deliberate motions. Tess lowered her hands to his hard, muscular buttocks, lifting her hips again and again in reception of each exquisite thrust. There was a heat building inside her now, white hot and demanding. She moved faster, her own heavy breathing mingling with his. Time lost all meaning. Hours passed, maybe just seconds. Nothing mattered but the feel of this man and the intense pleasure building inside her.

Then, suddenly a shudder went through Tess and she cried out, her fingers tightening on his shoulders. "Raven?"

He thrust again and again.

Half-sobbing, she clung to him as her body convulsed with ultimate pleasure.

Another thrust and Raven moaned, his entire body stiffening before he relaxed. Then, finally his body was still.

Tess let her hands fall to the leather sleeping mat and her entire body relax. It was as if every ounce of energy had been suddenly sapped from her limbs. Now she was just drifting, drifting on a cloud of warm pleasure.

Raven brushed back the damp hair off her forehead and she opened her eyes to look at him. A smile played on her love-bruised lips. "You didn't tell me it would be like this, else I'd have demanded my wifely rights sooner."

He laughed, his voice still husky with passion. He kissed the tip of her nose. "I have made love many times, but never like this, Tess."

She frowned. "I did something wrong? I'm sorry. I told you I didn't know what I was doing."

He laughed again, brushing his lips against hers in a reassuring caress. "No, you did nothing wrong, only right. You and I, Tess, fit together like," he entwined the fingers of one hand with hers, "like we were created as one and then split apart at birth."

She broke into a grin. She could still feel him inside her, warm and semi-hard. "You liked it?"

He kissed the pulse of her throat. "I liked it. Truly this is the most perfect gift anyone has ever given me."

Tess reached up to catch a lock of midnight hair that fell over his shoulder. It was as smooth and sleek as China silk between her fingers. "I . . . I don't understand this." She lowered her lashes so that she didn't have to look directly at him. "I don't understand these feelings I have for you. We're so different, and yet in my heart—"

He pressed his index finger to her lips. "Do not say the words, *ki-ti-hi*. It will only hurt."

She shook her head. "No. I want to. I want to tell you." She lifted her lashes to look up at him. "I want to tell you that I love you, Raven of the Lenape. No matter where I go or what I do the rest of my days, I'll love you. I don't know why. I know it doesn't make sense, but I do."

He lowered his mouth to hers and kissed her. At first it was just a brush of his lips against hers, but then they lingered. He tugged gently at her lower lip with his teeth.

Tess sighed, already feeling warm inside again. She'd said it. She'd told him she loved him and now no matter where she went or what happened to her, she would always have this moment. She would always have this feeling to carry in her heart. It didn't matter that he didn't love her back, all that mattered was that she had been able to give her love to someone.

Raven's kiss grew more insistent and Tess moaned softly. Already her breasts were aching for his touch. To-morrow she would go home to Annapolis, but tonight, tonight belonged to the two of them. Tonight they would share that special love that she knew in her heart would come only once in her lifetime.

Much, much later Tess slept naked in the moonlight, wrapped in Raven's arms.

Myron Ellsworth shifted his weight in the saddle. It was barely dawn; the first streaks of orange light were just beginning to appear in the eastern morning sky. It was already hot. He slapped a mosquito, leaving a dot of red on his bleached muslin shirt. A man in a round felt hat came through the brush and nodded. The knife in his hand was still red with the blood of the Indian sentry.

Myron pointed in the direction of the camp. The other men, mounted on horses, nodded, drawing their muskets. They knew the plan. Myron had paid them well to know the plan. This was the third Indian village they'd visited in the last fortnight.

Surely his Tess would be here . . .

Myron gave a nod, and lifting the reins, he sank his heels into his mount's flanks. The gelding bolted. One of the men behind him gave a hoot as the dozen horsemen descended on the sleeping Delaware Indian village.

The silence of the humid morning was broken by the first explosion of musket fire. Suddenly the quiet village was alive with naked, running savages. Men shouted, babies wailed, and women screamed as they raced from their crude skin and bark huts.

One of his men must have set one of the huts on fire because suddenly there was smoke and more screaming.

"Tess, Tess," Myron cried, riding in a circle near the center of the village. "Tess Morgan!"

A heathen wearing nothing but a cloth across his groin charged at Myron wielding a war axe. His high-pitched cry made Myron shudder. Myron pulled the trigger of his musket, blasting the hostile away at point-blank range. His red-skinned body flew back under the impact of the musket ball, his chest exploding in blood and flesh. Myron reloaded quickly. He hated this killing. He hated it! But what had to be done had to be done—for Tess's sake.

A woman carrying a baby ran by, one bloody arm hanging unnaturally at her side.

"Just find her," Myron screamed to his men. "Leave the females be!" He jerked his horse around and ran down the fleeing woman. "Tess Morgan. White woman! Red hair." He touched his battered cocked hat. "Have you seen her? Is she here?"

The woman only wailed, ducking around a burning hut and into the woods.

"Sweet Jesus," Myron muttered. "Where are you, darling? I know you're alive. I know you're out here somewhere in this Godforsaken wilderness!"

The camp was filled with running redskins now. Women, children, and old folks raced for the cover of the dense forest. The redskin men, on foot, fought the white men on horses. Myron rode through the confusion, darting back and forth as his own men rode in circles hooting and hollering in frenzied excitement. Most of the huts were on fire now. Surely they were all empty.

Myron dismounted, running from one burning structure to the next calling Tess's name, fearing she was tied up inside somewhere. He stepped over a dead man, the side of his head blown away by a musket ball. There were no white women here. None. All he saw everywhere he looked were frightened black eyes and unclothed red flesh.

"She's not here!" Myron hollered above the din. He stood beside a burning hut, rubbing his eyes that stung from the thick black smoke and flying cinders. "She's not here," he murmured, choking down the lump in his throat. "She's not anywhere."

One of his men rode by, and Myron hollered to him. "Get the boys and let's go, Les. She ain't here!"

Les went by swinging a musket with a makeshift bayonet tied on the end. The pointed metal was dark and wet with blood. Myron turned his head away. All this bloodshed made him sick to his stomach. If only the heathen bastards wouldn't fight back. If they'd just tell him where Tess was or where he could find the red bastard who took her. He knew the heathens knew what he was saying. He knew they understood at least a few words of English.

Myron walked back to his horse and mounted. The village was empty now. Everyone had fled into the forest, even the men. He could still hear them running; he could hear their frightened jabbering, and their children crying.

Through the smoke Myron spotted one of his men. He'd dismounted and was holding an Indian woman by a hank of black hair. She was dressed in nothing but an Englishman's red stockless shirt. She was hollering, a string of angry heathen words coming out of her mouth. A wide gash across her eyebrow was bleeding heavily.

"Found one that speaks English," Grisham called to Myron. "Called me a futtering bastard when I rode by.

Caught her passin' out weapons to the men through the back of her hut. Damned thing was on fire and she wouldn't come out!"

Myron reined in his mount. "I'm looking for my fiance. Red hair." He touched his own balding head beneath his cocked hat. "Seen her? She's called Tess."

The woman launched into another tirade, still not speaking a word of English.

"I thought you said she spoke English," Myron complained.

"She does."

"One curse and you think that means she speaks English. She's a woman, for Christ's sake. She can't speak English!" Myron reined around and started off. "Get on your horse and let's get out of here before the men come back," he called over his shoulder. "They regroup and we'll be massacred."

Grisham let the Indian woman go, giving her a rough shove. He turned around to grasp the reins of his horse. Myron saw the glint of the knife in the red woman's hand but there was no time to holler. The bitch sunk the knife between Grisham's shoulder blades and twisted it viciously.

Myron swung around and fired his musket, but he missed. The woman feigned left and disappeared into the smoke.

Swearing beneath his breath, Myron rode back to Grisham. He dismounted and rolled him over onto his back. The shoemaker was dead, his eyes open and sightless. Bile rose in Myron's throat and for a moment he feared he'd vomit. He looked away. There was no way he could lift the body onto his horse. He had no choice but to ride out without him.

Saying a quick prayer, Myron remounted his gelding. Leaving his friend's body behind, he circled the camp calling to his men. Then he rode out. If the bloodthirsty bastards followed him, fine. If not, he'd hire more men in Annapolis.

Flinging curses to doom the balding man with a life of impotence, Dream Woman came out from behind her burning wigwam. She wiped the soot from her eyes and rolled the huge man back over. Stepping on the dead man's back, she retrieved her favorite skinning knife.

All she could think of was thank God her son and daughter-in-law had left the village last night. She knew the white-hairs had come looking for Tess, but no woman deserved to live with animals such as those who had just rode through the village. Not even if she thought she wanted to.

Eighteen

The moment Raven awoke just after dawn, he knew something was wrong. He lay perfectly still with Tess curled in his arm, her cheek against his shoulder. In his head he had heard the sound of Lenape voices crying out in fear, in pain, and yet now that he was fully awake he could hear nothing but the chirp of a sparrow and the hum of a cicada in the elm tree branch overhead . . . that and Tess's soft breathing.

A minute passed and then another as Raven listened, trying not to let the feel of Tess in his arms distract him. She stirred and he smoothed back a lock of her magic red hair. Had he been dreaming? He turned his head suddenly. What was that he smelled on the humid morning air? Smoke? Yes . . . but not a campfire, not a forest fire . . . a different smell.

Raven felt his heart trip. He shook Tess gently. "Tess," he whispered in her ear. "Tess, you must rise."

Suddenly all of his muscles were tense. Something was wrong. Something was out of balance in the forest.

Tess made a soft sound like a waking child. She stretched her long, beautiful legs, brushing them against his.

"Tess, you must wake," he repeated. "Something is not right."

Her eyelids fluttered. "Raven?" she murmured sleepily.

He pulled his arm out from under her and reached for his loinskin thrown carelessly in the grass last night. She stretched on the sleeping mat like a mountain cat.

"Get up, Tess. Put on your clothing."

She squinted in the bright sunlight, his words still not sinking in. "What's wrong?"

"I do not know." He yanked on his moccasins. "Get dressed. Quickly. We must return to the village."

She sat up and reached for her doeskin dress. The sunlight poured through the trees bathing her in bright yellow light. How beautiful her pale skin was, so different from his own, he mused. It was like moonlight.

She stood up and dropped the doeskin over her head, her hands still clumsy with sleep. "What do you mean?" she asked. "You think something is wrong in the village? How do you know that? We must be at least two or three miles from there."

"I do not know how I know, only that I do." He was gathering their packs. He grabbed his musket from where he had left it lying so carelessly last night. In the heat of his passion for this white woman he had been reckless. He was lucky a Mohawk war party had not passed through and scalped them both. How could he have been so foolish? How could he have allowed the sleeping mat to have clouded his thinking like this? Raven checked the load on his Brown Bess.

Her bodice still unlaced, Tess pulled on her moccasins. Raven tossed her her leather pack. "Hurry, Tess."

Her moccasins on, she grabbed the bag. "I'm ready. Let's go." She fell into step behind him.

"Do you have your knife?"

"Here." She tapped the bag she had thrown over her shoulder.

Raven hurried through the forest, veering off the main game path to take a shortcut. "Take it out."

"Tell me what's wrong," she whispered, following his bidding.

"I smell smoke."

"Something's on fire?" She ran to catch up with him. "You think something in the village is on fire?"

Raven reached back suddenly and snatched Tess's arm, pulling her to the ground. He heard the sound of men on horseback. Crouching beside her, he brought his finger to his lips. They were very close, so close he could feel the pound of the horses' hooves on the ground.

Raven looked at Tess. Her face was still smooth and sleepy, but he could tell by the fear in her eyes that she heard the men on horseback. She laid one hand on his arm, in the other, she clutched the Mohawk knife so hard that her knuckles were white.

His heart pounding in his chest, Raven remained perfectly still as the horsemen grew closer. They would pass right by them on the game path he and Tess had turned off only minutes before. Of course they were white men so they would never see him and Tess through the thicket of greenbriars and underbrush. White men were such fools.

Sure enough, seconds later, Raven heard the men come down the game path, their horses' hooves thundering on the hard ground.

Raven glanced at Tess as they listened to the men ride by. She looked frightened. The incident with the white-hair soldiers had obviously affected her more than she let on. Her hand gripped his arm tighter, and he turned his head so that his lips brushed the side of her head. He would protect her. He wanted her to know that. Unto death . . .

She smiled a shaky smile as the men rode by in a blur. Raven could have taken one off his horse with the single musket ball in his rifle, but he saw no point. What was important was that he get back to the village. He had a sick feeling in the pit of his stomach that this was no coincidence, the smell of fire and the passing of these men.

When the horsemen were a safe distance north, Raven rose. Grasping Tess's hand he started to run for the village. She kept up beside him. They raced through the forest, the closer they grew, the stronger the smell of the smoke in the air. In less than a mile he heard the sounds of his people. A woman was wailing. Children cried.

Not soon thereafter, Raven and Tess found the villagers at the creek. There was a great deal of confusion. Women were dipping buckets of water and running for their lodges. Small children sat on the banks wailing while several of the elderly tried to calm them. Men, young and old, ran, searching for family members, calling to friends.

"What has happened?" Raven demanded, leaving Tess behind to wade across the creek alone. The air was thick with smoke and the smell of burning hides. In the distance, where the village lay, he could see a black column of smoke rising through the trees. Even from here he could feel the heat of the flames. "Throws Stones! Tell this man what has happened!" Raven shouted, splashing through the water.

"Thank the heavens you are here!" called the old man in Lenape. "English *manake* come and burn our lodges. Men are dead!"

Raven tossed his bag onto the riverbank and ran for the village, carrying his Brown Bess. Women were running back and forth from the creek with containers of water; pitch baskets, skin bags, wooden bowls, anything they could find. "Where is my mother?" Raven asked one after the other.

The women shook their heads as they passed. No one had seen Dream Woman since the attack. No one knew where she was.

Raven broke through the trees and into the clearing. Two wigwams were still in flames. Several had burned to the ground while all but a few had sustained damage. There was as much confusion here as down by the creek. Men and women and children were running and shouting as they attempted to save what was left of their homes. Young boys were trying to hobble the ponies that had apparently been set free or broken loose. Somewhere a baby screamed for its mother in frenzied bursts.

Raven ran for Dream Woman's lodge on the far side of the village. He heaved a sigh of relief as he spotted her in her red tunic, her feet bare, her hair falling loosely down her back. She was all right; she was safe.

Dream Woman was tending to a woman whose arm had been injured. The woman called Snow held her infant to her breast to nurse as tears ran down her cheek.

"N'gaxais!" Raven hollered.

Dream Woman was squatting beside Snow, bathing her mangled arm. She didn't even look up as Raven approached. "Inside my lodge, son, my medicine bag. Get it."

"Mother, tell this man what has happened!"

"My medicine bag!"

Snow was sobbing now. In exasperation Raven ducked into the smoking wigwam in search of the bag. The entire rear of the lodge was burned so that there were now two doorways. He kicked over two blackened piles that had once been baskets. The sleeping mats on the floor still smouldered. Raven found the beaded medicine bag, miraculously intact, still hanging from a rafter over Dream Woman's sleeping platform. He snatched it off its hook and darted back out of the smoky lodge.

"Tell me, Mother," Raven demanded. "What has happened?"

Dream Woman took the bag and began to dig through it. "Where is your wife?"

"By the creek. Mother—"

"Find her, quickly. She is not safe alone, son of mine."

Raven grasped his mother's shoulders and made her turn to face him. "Tell me!" he demanded. "Tell this man exactly what happened here."

Her eyes narrowed and for the first time he realized that she'd been hurt. A place above her eyebrow was raised and thick with congealed blood. He let go of her.

"They came for her," she whispered harshly.

"They came for who? Who is they?"

"Your wife." Dream Woman spat in the grass. "Filthy dogs. They burned our lodges looking for her. They killed Beaver Tooth and Two Shields. Standing Black Bear is gravely injured. The boy, Turtle Foot, broke his leg trying to get out from under a white man's horse." She went back to tending the injured woman.

Raven looked away, guilt washing over him. So this was his fault. He was the one who had brought the English woman to the village. "They sought Tess, you are certain?"

"I spoke to the man myself. At least he spoke at me. I would not dignify him with an answer. He said Tess Morgan. He said she had red hair. Do you know such a woman other than your wife?"

Raven looked away and out of the smoke he saw Na-Kee appear. Na-Kee spotted Raven and strode toward him.

"Do not listen to his words," Dream Woman whispered

We've got your authors!

If you seek out the latest historical romances by today's bestselling authors, our new reader's service, KENSINGTON CHOICE, is the club for you.

KENSINGTON CHOICE is the only club where you can find authors like Janelle Taylor, Shannon Drake, Rosanne Bittner, Sylvie Sommerfield, Penelope Neri and Phoebe Conn all in one place...

...and the only service that will deliver their romances direct to your home as soon as they are published—even before they reach the bookstores.

KENSINGTON CHOICE is also the only service that will give you a substantial guaranteed discount off the publisher's prices on every one of those romances.

That's right: Every month, the Editors at Zebra and Pinnacle select four of the newest novels by our bestselling authors and rush them straight to you, even *before they reach the bookstores*. The publisher's prices for these romances range from $4.99 to $5.99—but they are always yours for the guaranteed low price of just *$3.95!*

That means you'll always save over $1.00...often as much as *$2.00*...off the publisher's prices on every new novel you get from KENSINGTON CHOICE!

All books are sent on a 10-day free examination basis, and there is no minimum number of books to buy. (A postage and handling charge of $1.50 is added to each shipment.)

As your introduction to the convenience and value of this new service, we invite you to accept

4 BOOKS FREE

The 4 books, worth up to $23.96, are our welcoming gift. You pay only $1 to help cover postage and handling.

To start your subscription to KENSINGTON CHOICE and receive your introductory package of 4 FREE romances, detach and mail the postpaid card at right *today*.

We have 4 FREE BOOKS for you as your introduction to KENSINGTON CHOICE

To get your FREE BOOKS, worth up to $23.96, mail card below.

FREE BOOK CERTIFICATE

As my introduction to your new KENSINGTON CHOICE reader's service, please send me 4 FREE historical romances (worth up to $23.96), billing me just $1 to help cover postage and handling. As a KENSINGTON CHOICE subscriber, I will then receive 4 brand-new romances to preview each month for 10 days FREE. I can return any books I decide not to keep and owe nothing. The publisher's prices for the KENSINGTON CHOICE romances range from $4.99 to $5.99, but as a subscriber I will be entitled to get them for just $3.95 per book. There is no minimum number of books to buy, and I can cancel my subscription at any time. A $1.50 postage and handling charge is added to each shipment.

Name _____

Address _____ Apt. # _____

City _____ State _____ Zip _____

Telephone (____) _____

Signature _____

(If under 18, parent or guardian must sign)

Subscription subject to acceptance

KC 0994

We have
4
FREE
Historical
Romances
for you!

Details inside!

under her breath. "Your marriage to the English *onna* was approved by council. Na-Kee is a fool and a coward. One day the truth will be known to us all."

"Look what you have done to us," Na-Kee shouted, throwing back his shoulders. "You have brought this upon us with your white woman whore."

"Wife," Raven corrected between gritted teeth. This was not the time to pick a fight with Na-Kee. Not over meaningless white men's words.

"They came looking for her you know. If she had been here I would have surrendered her for the sake of our people. Perhaps then there would have been no bloodshed."

"Have you set up perimeter sentries, Na-Kee? They may return."

"Do not tell me what is my place to do!" He rested his hand on the bloody war axe that hung on his belt, speaking with bravado in his voice. "They will not return. They rode away terrified, pissing in their saddles."

Raven strode away, fearful that if he touched Na-Kee he would kill the smirking braggart. "Just the same, you know it is better to be safe for the welfare of *The People*. I will take a first watch. Where is Taande? We will stand guard together."

Na-Kee followed him. "This would not have happened if we had given our allegiance to the French. The English would have been afraid of us, then. The scouts told us it was so."

"And you believe the white-hairs?" Raven stepped into his charred wigwam. The roof had burned, but someone had doused it with water in time to save the main structure. His belongings were wet, but untouched by the fire. He snatched his bow and quiver of arrows off the wall.

"The French *manake* would not dare speak lies and risk the wrath of Na-Kee!" He hit his bare chest with his fist.

Raven chuckled but without any mirth. Na-Kee didn't understand what was happening here. He truly did not understand. He didn't see the building strength of the whites that arrived on their homeland from the great ships by the hundreds each day. He didn't understand that they could no more be stopped than the tide. He didn't see the old Lenape way of life crumbling as Raven did. Perhaps he didn't want to see it.

"The French are not important right now, Na-Kee. What is important is the immediate safety of this village. This man would recommend you bring the old people and children back from the creek. No one should go without escort. You are probably right that they not return, at least not today." He passed Na-Kee in the doorway. "Did you kill any of theirs?"

"Three. I took one with my axe. Taande took another." His mouth twitched with amusement. "Your mother killed one with a cooking knife."

Raven turned back toward Na-Kee. "My mother?"

Na-Kee strode by. *"Kohon.* Perhaps it is she that should have been war chief and not either of us, eh?" He chuckled at his own jest as he walked away.

Raven just stood there in the center of the village for a moment. The air was still thick with smoke and cinders, and he wiped his eyes with the back of his hand. Where was the order of the Lenape he had known as a child? White men burning villages? Middle-aged women being forced to fight like warriors? Why this chaos? Why after thousands of years of peaceful existence was the Lenape way of life changing so rapidly?

The white men of course—the white men and their

wicked greedy ways. How he hated them. But then he thought of Tess. He thought of the gift of her virginity she had given him only last night. He thought of the tightness he felt in his heart for her when he looked at her freckled face—a feeling very close to love. So how could he hate the white-hairs when Tess was one of them?

Raven slung his Brown Bess over his shoulder and started back for the creek. First he would find Tess and put her safely in his mother's care, and then he would locate Taande and together they would walk the perimeter of the camp. No white men would pass through the village on his watch. He would die to protect his people . . . and his white wife.

It was early evening when Tess finally returned to Raven's wigwam. She had spent the entire day cutting and gathering saplings and learning to build a new lodge. Dove's Call and the grandfather she lived with had lost everything. Their wigwam had been left nothing but a smouldering pile of black rubble. Tess had spent most of the day with them. Tonight they would sleep under the open sky with the new framework of a wigwam above them.

All day Tess had kept busy, driving herself. She had ignored the whispers, the accusing glances. No one knew who the English *manake* had been or why they'd come, but they all seemed to feel she was responsible.

Had it been Myron? Was he still looking for her? But that couldn't have possibly been Myron. Myron would never have burned people's homes! He was no killer, nor would he have ever stood for killing.

Tess slumped to the hard ground resting her head in

her hands. She had picked up all of Raven's sleeping mats and hung them outside to dry. In a minute she'd retrieve them. She'd already covered the floor in fresh pine boughs. Of course it would be days before she could repair the hole in the roof. Dove's Call's wigwam was the first priority. And then Sitting Black Bear's wife would need help.

Raven had said he would take her home tomorrow, but she couldn't go home yet. Maybe in a day or two. What would a day or two matter at this point? She'd been gone three weeks.

Tess heard a sound in the doorway and looked up. It was Raven. She felt her cheeks grow warm with embarrassment and she looked away. She'd been so busy all day long that she hadn't had time to think about what had happened last night. But now that Raven was standing there, it all came tumbling back. Just thinking about the way he had touched her last night sent a shiver of pleasure down her spine.

"You look tired," he said softly. "You should not have worked so hard. Dove's Call tells me you built most of a wigwam yourself today."

She got up, brushing back her hair that had come loose from its braid. She was hot and sticky, her entire body covered with a layer of soot. "Tell me the truth, Raven. I know you will. Did this happen because of me? Is it my fault?"

"Go to the creek and bathe. I've just come from there. There is a guard so you will be safe."

"I don't want a bath. I want you to tell me the truth."

"Go. You will feel better. Then we will talk."

Tess wanted to argue, but she didn't have the energy. She pulled her spare doeskin dress out of her travel bag and brushed past Raven in the doorway. "I'll be back in a few minutes. Then I'll see what I can find for us to eat."

Under the watchful eye of a warrior Tess bathed with some of the other women in the creek. Too tired mentally as well as physically for modesty, she stripped off her sooty clothing and threw it on the bank with the other women's. Ignoring the sentry, she waded naked into the creek and washed the grit and grim from her body and hair. Then she sat on the bank with the other women and dried off in the evening air. Dove's Call loaned her a silver comb and she combed out her long thick hair. Finally dressed, she walked back to the wigwam carrying her soiled clothing.

Tess found Raven squatting at the firepit in front of his wigwam. He had a metal frying pan filled with sizzling perch from the creek. The smell was heavenly.

"Cooking?" she asked, a smile tugging at her mouth. "A warrior like yourself doing women's work?"

"A man is not a true Lenape warrior unless he can fry his own fish." He picked up the pan and carried it into the privacy of his wigwam. Tess followed.

Inside he already had a crock of stewed squash and some cold corncakes. The sight of the food made Tess's stomach grumble. She hadn't eaten since yesterday, and suddenly she was famished.

"Sit," he told her. "Eat."

Tess accepted the pewter plate he passed to her piled with stewed squash, a thick fillet of perch, and a sweet corncake. She speared a piece of fish with the two-pronged fork he handed her. "Good." She nodded chewing as she reached for another piece.

Raven sat down across the cold firepit from her and

served himself. The two ate in silence washing their dinner down with a jar of icy creek water. It was not until Tess had gathered the dirty plates that she could bring herself to ask Raven again about the white men.

"Raven—"

He pointed to the place she had been sitting. "Sit down."

"I don't want to sit down. I want you to tell me why those men came." Her voice shook a little. "I want you to tell me why three men are dead and why that little boy has a broken leg. I want you to tell me why Dove's Call and her grandfather have no home tonight." She made herself look him in the eye. "I want you to tell me this isn't my fault."

He got up and came to her, resting a hand on her trembling shoulder. "This is not your fault."

"But they came for me!"

He nodded. "I would not lie to you. They came for you."

"But it's not possible." She shook her head, not wanting to believe him. "My uncle . . . Myron, they wouldn't have done this to innocent people. It couldn't have been them!"

He stroked her cheek. "I do not know who the men were, but my mother says they sought the woman called Tess Morgan. That is you, no?"

Tess squeezed her eyes shut. *Tess Morgan . . . Tess Morgan . . .* The name echoed in her head. That was her. Tess Morgan. And yet it wasn't. She was not the woman who left Annapolis three weeks ago. She couldn't be!

"I'm sorry," she whispered. "I'm so sorry."

He grabbed her shoulders and made her look at him. "This is not your fault, Tess. You did not tell these men to burn. You did not tell them to murder." His dark-eyed gaze met and held hers. "You did not even tell them to come for you, did you?"

She shook her head ever so slightly. Was he asking her to stay. That was what the tone of his voice suggested. She didn't know why he wanted her here, but she knew that was what he was saying. "No," she whispered, wishing he would kiss her, wishing she didn't want to stay. "I didn't tell them to come for me. But I have to go. I . . . I can't stay here."

"You want to go back to a man who kills innocent people?"

She shook her head. She was so confused. How could she make Raven understand when she didn't understand herself. "I have to go back to Annapolis, Raven. I must."

"Because of your sister?"

Tess dropped her hands. "How did you know about Abby?"

"Dove's Call told me."

"Oh." She lowered her head. He had a piece of her hair between his fingers, rubbing it.

"I wonder why you did not tell me. You thought I could not have compassion for your sister who needs you?"

"No," she said softly. His touch was comforting. Just standing here close made her feel safe, but more importantly, it made her feel strong, like she could do anything she had to. "I don't know why I didn't tell you. Maybe because I didn't want to share any part of me I didn't have to share."

"You do not want me to know you?"

She couldn't lie to him. Not after what they had shared last night. "It's like you said last night, Raven." She caught his hand in hers and entwined their fingers. "It will hurt less when I go."

He brushed his cheek against hers and then whispered in her ear. "It is not safe for you to stay here. I cannot be selfish with my lust for you. I fear more white men will come."

"Not if I'm gone," she protested.

He kissed her, smiling sadly. "They will come anyway, my innocent. Only half a dozen today, but a dozen tomorrow, an army next year."

"What do you mean? 'They'll come.' "

"They want our land. They want our bay and our creeks. They want our deer, our fish, our egret, our eagles. They will kill us all for possession of this earth the Lenape call home."

"So why don't you leave? Why don't you go west where there aren't any white people? Make your home somewhere else!"

He draped his arm over her shoulder and led her to his sleeping platform. They sat down side by side. "It is not so easy to leave your home."

"That's true. It was hard for me to leave my mother's cottage, to leave Abby, when I came to the Colonies. But I knew it was the best thing for me and for Abby, so I came."

"My people have lived on this land for more years than you or I can count. Thousands. The storytellers say we came to this place from an Island in the East on the back of a great turtle. Someday that island will rise again and we will climb upon the turtle and return to our ancestral home. Some fear that if we leave this place so near to the great sea," he shrugged, "we will miss the turtle when he comes for us."

Tess got up and swung her leg over his and sat on his lap so that she could face him. "Do you believe that?"

He shrugged. "It does not matter if I believe. It is what the old ones say."

Tess rested her hand on his bare shoulder. She lifted her head, making herself look at him. "I have to go back to Annapolis because I have to find a way to bring my sister to live with me. I guess Dove's Call told you, my sister can't hear, so she doesn't speak. Only with her hands. She needs me."

"Among my people men and women such as your sister are considered blessed by the great Creator, *Manito*."

Tess laughed. "In England, people are afraid of my sister. They call her dumb, sometimes even devil-cursed. They fear what they do not know or understand."

Raven was staring at her as she spoke, watching her with smokey black eyes.

"Tell me something," she said softly.

He took her hand from his shoulder and began to kiss her fingertips, one pad at a time. "Yes?"

"You say that you have absolved me of your brother's death. You say you no longer need me because Na-Kee is War Chief. You say I can go home."

"Yes, all of this is true."

She met his gaze. "Am . . . am I still your wife, then?"

"You are my wife until you declare it is not so."

"What do you mean?"

"Have you placed my moccasins outside our door?"

She giggled. He was sucking on her index finger. It tickled and yet there was a warmth spreading through her, reminding her of the other things he had done with his tongue. "No."

"Have you declared to any others here in the village or at High Council that I am no longer your husband?"

She arched her neck so that he could kiss the pulse of her throat. "No . . ."

"Then you are my wife . . . and entitled to the privileges of a wife . . . if that is what you ask."

Tess threaded her fingers through Raven's thick midnight hair. She was smiling. What could be wrong with prolonging this happiness she felt in her heart for just another day or two? What could be wrong with living this Lenape magic just a little while longer? She brushed her lips against his, touching her tongue to his upper lip. He caught her tongue between his lips and sucked gently.

Tess sighed. She could feel his manhood stiffening against her bare buttocks under her short skirt as she shifted on his lap. He brought his hand up to caress one breast as their kiss deepened.

Tess heard herself moan. All day this had been in the back of her mind, this lust she had for this red man. For Raven. He wasn't just a red man any more. He wasn't even just her captor. He was a man whom in the last few weeks she'd come to respect, to admire . . . to love. It didn't matter that their customs were different, not even their religion. What mattered to her was his kindness and his innate sense of knowing what was honorable and what was not.

Maybe it had been Myron and her Uncle who had attacked the village. As much as it hurt, she knew she had to consider the possibility. Because now that she knew Raven and had a man to compare the other men in her life to, she knew that Myron and her Uncle were not honorable men. She knew that because of their prejudices against the red men and women they called savages, they were capable of these heinous crimes.

Tess pulled her mouth from Raven's breathless, hurting

inside, wanting him to push away the pain of the truth if only for a few minutes. She ran her fingers over his broad shoulders, stroking him.

He squeezed her breasts, nipping at the soft flesh, whispering her name. Somehow Raven sensed the urgency of her sudden need. He had pulled up her skirt and pushed her bodice down until her dress was nothing but wrinkles of soft leather around her waist. He had untied his loincloth and now his male organ had sprung up, soft and hard between her thighs. Tess ground her hips against his, cradling his head as he sucked one taut pink nipple.

"Raven," she whispered. "Raven, I need you . . . now." She went to slide off his lap so that she could lay out on the sleeping platform, but he gripped her around the waist.

"No, stay," he whispered thickly.

Her eyes widened. "Here?"

"Here. Trust me."

He slid his hands down over her hips and then lifted her a little. The tip of his swollen organ brushed against the moist place between her thighs and she shuddered with pleasure. Letting Raven guide her, she raised her hips and let him slip inside her.

Tess moaned, smothering her face in his shoulder and hair. After a moment, she lifted her head to look at him.

Raven's eyes were half-closed, his lips parted slightly.

She kissed him. "What now?" she whispered pushing up with her toes so that she rose ever so slightly before she fell again.

He looked at her through hooded eyes, knowing she was teasing him and seeming to like it. "What do you think?"

She threw her head back and laughed. Pushing on his shoulders she rose up and down, stroking him, pleasuring herself. Was this some Indian love secret? Woman flat on the back, man on top, that was the way God had meant his creatures to do it. Wasn't that what she'd heard the kitchen girls whispering?

Tess rose and fell, again and again, to that ancient rhythm that came to her so naturally. Raven's heavy breathing was exciting her. She could feel him growing harder inside her . . . pulsing.

To this point Tess had been able to control her own rising desire, testing this new position, but suddenly she could no longer control herself. Once she had tasted the forbidden fruit of orgasm, it was what she craved.

Raven was calling her name, showering her breasts with light, tantalizing kisses. Her entire body was quaking with pleasure.

He tightened his grip on her waist and she realized he was close to climaxing. Giving a strangled moan, she lifted and slid down him one last time. Every muscle in her body tightened as she convulsed in ecstasy. At the very same moment, she heard Raven call her name. He wrapped his arms tightly around her waist and she encircled his neck with her arms, hugging him.

Slowly, limbs tangled, they drifted back to reality. Raven stroked her bare back as he panted, trying to catch his breath. Tess felt like laughing; she felt like crying, as she smoothed his midnight hair. All she could think of was why couldn't she have been born a Lenape? Why couldn't she stay here in Raven's arms forever?

Tess slipped off Raven's lap and let her dress fall to the floor. She climbed onto the sleeping platform and stretched out. Raven lay down beside her.

Resting on her back with Raven at her side Tess stared up at the night sky through the hole in the wigwam roof.

After a few minutes of silence, Raven pushed up on one elbow to face her. He drew an invisible line across her breast as he spoke. "Tell this man why you are suddenly so sad."

She smiled a bittersweet smile. "It's just that a part of me wishes I could stay here. I mean I know it could never work—you and I. You know, your brother, the Mohawk, Myron, my sister . . . But—"

"I know that you cannot stay. Because it is not safe, because your sister needs you, but a part of this man," he took her hand in his, "wishes you could stay as well."

"For the lovemaking?"

"Yes." He brought her hand to his mouth and kissed it. "But not just for the touch of your body. For the touch of your mind, Tess. The touch of your heart."

Tess rolled onto her side and rested her head in the hollow of his shoulder. As she drifted off to sleep, her tears fell on his bare chest.

Nineteen

"A week, Tess! One week has passed since the attack and each day you have a new excuse of why you must stay another day." Raven stood on the ground, looking up, shielding his eyes from the bright noon sun.

Tess was on top of their wigwam weaving a cornhusk patch into the existing roof. "The fires did so much damage," she called down, balancing precariously on the sapling framework. "How can I go and leave work unfinished, knowing my uncle or Myron could have done this?"

"Come down from there. There are young boys to do such work. You will fall, break your leg, and then you will not be able to leave until spring."

She stuck her tongue out at him. He was so serious! But, God help her, she felt more like his wife everyday. "I will not fall," she retorted.

"Come down!" He was losing his patience with her.

"No." She threw a loose corn husk down on him. "Come and get me!"

Tess had meant it in jest so when Raven started hoisting himself up the lodge pole that stood near the door of the wigwam, she screamed. Laughing, she started to move away from the center of the dome roof, trying to put as much space between the two of them as possible.

Reaching the roofline, Raven swung easily onto it.

Tess squealed with laughter. The entire roof was shaking, unmeant for the weight of two adults.

A young couple walked by below and pointed up at the two of them and laughed. Tess waved and started crawling for the far side, trying to be careful to keep her weight evenly distributed.

Raven crawled over the roof with agility. "Get down," he ordered. "Pack your bag. We go."

"Not tonight. Tomorrow." Facing him she slid left a little. He was still a good arm's length from her, but she knew that at any moment he would make his move.

"Tonight. Na-Kee has made an agreement with the white-hair scouts. Already the English have left Fort Cumberland headed north. Na-Kee and our men go in the next few days to join the French at Dusquesne."

Raven reached out with one arm and Tess slid right, trying not to laugh. A few weeks ago she'd never have dreamed of climbing atop such a delicate structure, but now it seemed like an adventure. Every day for her in the village was an adventure.

"You going?" Tess asked, snatching up her hand before he caught it. The shell and feather necklace around her neck made a tinkling sound as she moved.

"I do not know. I have volunteered to remain behind with the village. It is Na-Kee's decision."

"So you want to get rid of me in case you march off to war?"

"You have no reason to be here. You must go back to your people where you belong."

She narrowed her eyes. "What makes you think I don't belong here, *neet-il-ose.*" Husband . . . she had called him husband. "Dream Woman says I would make a fine Lenape woman. She says I've got guts and that's what it takes. Taande says I speak better Lenape than you speak English."

Raven dove for Tess, throwing his body flat over the smoke hole in the center of the roof. Tess squealed as he caught her hand. "I said it wasn't true!" she laughed. "He was just teasing!"

He held her hand tightly. "Taande has taken leave of his senses. No one can believe anything that passes his lips. Last night I saw him come from my mother's wigwam. It was very late. He pretended not to hear me when I called to him."

Tess was scooting backward an inch at a time, still not convinced Raven had her. "What do you care where Taande is?"

"I don't. I care only if he is with my mother, a woman old enough to be *his* mother." He tugged on her hand. "Now come and I will help you down."

"You'll do no such thing." Tess heard more laughter from below. Several teenaged boys had gathered near Raven's lodgepole and were laughing at the brave and his wife on top of the roof of their house.

When Raven glanced down, Tess yanked her hand free of his grasp and rolled over, away from him.

He cursed beneath his breath.

"Race you down," Tess dared. "I need another section to finish the roof."

Before he could react, Tess slipped out of his reach and started for the rear of the roof.

Raven hesitated for only a moment and then started back the way he'd come.

Tess crawled across the roof as quickly as was safe. She knew he was angry with her, but she didn't care. He was trying to get rid of her. He wanted to take her back to Annapolis before he cared too much for her, and that made her angry. Why couldn't he just love her for a few days?

Tess hung over the side of the wigwam on her belly. Raven had disappeared from her view, sliding down the lodgepole. She slid down one of the birchbark wall posts. Just as her moccasins touched the hard-packed dirt she felt Raven's hand on her shoulder.

"So you beat me." She laughed. The sun was hot on her face. Why had she never felt so alive among her own people as she did right now?

"Tomorrow Tess. Tomorrow you go."

She dropped the smile, trying to be as serious as he was. She knew he was right; she'd stalled long enough. "All right, Raven. Tomorrow."

He let go of her arm and walked away. She followed him. "Where are you going?"

"Go back to the wigwam and pack your belongings."

She ran to catch up. "Come on. Tell me where you're going."

"Not far from here there is an eagle's nest. I have need of a few feathers."

"Can I go?" She touched his arm. "I've never seen an eagle's nest."

"Go back to your woman's work."

"Oh, Raven. We leave tomorrow. You said it's only a two day walk to Annapolis. In two days you'll never see me again. Let me come." When he didn't answer, she went on. "Besides, how could you send me back to Annapolis having never seen an eagle's nest?"

"You can come, but you cannot talk," he responded gruffly.

She slipped her arm through his. "Thank you."

They were just passing Dream Woman's wigwam when Taande stepped out. As the doorflap fell, Tess caught a glimpse of Dream Woman, naked on her sleeping mat.

Tess looked at Raven's face, hoping he hadn't seen what she had. She felt his arm tense. "Taande!" Raven called.

Tess tightened her grip on Raven's arm. "Raven."

He pushed her away. "Taande! This man speaks to you."

Taande stopped where he was, but hesitated for a moment before turning around. *"Kohon?"*

"Why were you in my mother's lodge?"

"You must ask Dream Woman yourself, friend," Taande responded carefully.

"I ask you."

Taande looked away and then back at the man he had known since he was an infant. "I do no disgrace to your family clan. I am in love with *Hokkuaa Onna*. I will ask her for her hand in marriage."

"Marriage!" Raven scoffed. "She will soon be a grandmother!"

"Raven!" Dream Woman stepped out of her wigwam wearing her red tunic. "You cannot speak to Taande this way. He is a friend to you; he is a friend to me."

"It appears he is more than a friend, Mother."

Dream Woman exhaled slowly, moving beside Taande to loop her arm through his. It was obvious to Tess that there was something more between the two than just sex. Dream Woman was in love with Taande, and he in love with her.

"Son—"

Raven shook his head furiously. "This is wrong, Mother! He takes advantage of you."

Dream Woman laughed. "How do you know I do not take advantage of him?"

"Raven, this man—"

Dream Woman smoothed Taande's arm. "No, he is my son. Let me deal with him." She brushed her lips against Taande's. "Please."

Taande nodded and Dream Woman let go of his hand and took a step toward Raven. "I understand that this is hard for you, my son. Your father was my husband. For many years there was love in our lodge. But your father is gone, and this is the man I choose to love now. It would not matter to me if he was seventeen summers or seventy. This man is my choice. Mine and not yours."

Tess watched the expression on Raven's face as he struggled to understand his mother's needs. Finally he nodded abruptly. "You are the woman who bore me so I must give you my respect. I can accept that Taande is the man you choose, but I do not have to like it." With that, he walked away, passing Taande without looking at him.

Tess ran after Raven. When she caught up to him she fell into step beside him. He returned to his wigwam to retrieve his Brown Bess rifle and his shot bag. From there he circumnavigated the village and walked into the woods in silence.

Twice Tess tried to speak to him in the next hour, but both times he cut her off abruptly. Finally they stopped to drink from a trickling stream.

"I understand how you feel," Tess said quietly.

"I do not *feel* anything. Why must women forever bring *feelings* into every discussion. I am concerned for what is the best for my mother."

"So what makes you think you know what is best for your mother and she doesn't?" Tess jumped over wet mossy rocks, following Raven through a grove of sweet gum trees. Prickly seed pods still littered the ground from the previous fall.

"It just does not seem right," he argued.

"To whom? You? The elders? God?"

"I do not wish to speak on this matter further. She is a grown woman. She is right. She may choose who she pleases to share her sleeping mat."

Tess sighed. She didn't understand this man. He was right. It was time she went back to Annapolis. She didn't belong here.

For a few minutes they walked in silence, until he pointed high in the air above them. Tess moved one way and then the other. "Is it the nest? Where?"

"There." He took her chin and moved her head slightly.

"Oh," she breathed, spotting the huge nest high in a dead tree. "There's an eagle in it!"

Her voice must have startled the female eagle, because suddenly she spread her immense wings and soared straight up and out of the trees.

Tess watched, left speechless by the beauty of the creature.

Raven walked to the tree, leaned his rifle against it, and pulled himself up on the closest branch.

Shading her eyes from the bright afternoon sun, Tess watched as he climbed higher and higher into the tree until it made her dizzy just watching him. She grimaced. "Be careful!" The tree was dead, its lifeless branches brittle and grey. If a branch broke beneath him now, he would surely break an arm or a leg.

Raven reached the top of the tree and she watched him as he plucked several feathers from the giant nest. Then he turned where he stood to look out over the forest. The expression on his face changed as he turned west.

"What is it?" Tess called up. "What do you see?"

"A fire. A cabin, I think." He tucked the feathers into the belt of his loincloth and started down the tree, moving much faster than he had going up.

"Someone's cabin is burning down? There are cabins out here? I didn't know there were any white people so far from the bay."

He reached the ground, plucked one feather from his belt, and slipped it behind her ear. "The eagle feather carries the spirit of good luck," he told her. He reached for his Brown Bess. "Come Tess, we will see the cabin."

Tess smelled the burning cabin before they reached it. High overhead she saw a column of smoke rising and dissipating in the late afternoon breeze. It was hot as they walked and she was quickly covered in sweat, but she kept up with Raven, afraid someone in the cabin might be hurt.

Raven told Tess to stay behind as they reached the cabin's clearing, but she refused. She had her Mohawk knife tucked underneath the fold of the leather skirt she wore under her embroidered muslin man's shirt. She'd be safe enough.

Raven frowned, signalling her to stay behind him as they slowly approached the burning cabin. The sight of the dead man lying in the grass, a feathered arrow protruding from his chest turned Tess's stomach. All she could think of was the soldier she had killed.

Raven turned around quickly, bringing a finger to his lips. He was afraid the killer or killers were still here. Tess swallowed the bile in her throat and went on, taking care to remain behind him.

The next body they found was that of a woman's. She was Indian. She lay facedown in the grass, a bucket still clutched in her fingers. A piece of her scalp had been stripped off leaving a bloody patch in her black hair. Tess thought of Jocelyn and her pretty hair and bit down on her bottom lip until she tasted the metallic taste of her own blood.

Raven glanced back at her. Tess kept her face emotionless. She wasn't a coward.

There was nothing left of the crude one-room cabin but a few blackened smoldering beams, the outline of the crumbled foundation, and the stone fireplace. The barn behind the cabin had been gutted with fire as well. Chickens, pigs, and a milk cow, lay slaughtered on the green grass.

"Who would do this?" Tess finally said when Raven seemed to be confident that those who had done this were gone. "Why?"

"The arrow is Miami. Could be stolen. Could be a loner traveling with others."

"But they killed everything. These people looked too poor to steal from." Tess sat down on a tree stump, trying to regain her composure. "What did they want?"

"Most likely it was a war party. They kill to kill. For the pleasure."

Tess exhaled slowly. This was a crude land, the Colonies, a dangerous land. Perhaps she should never have come here in the first place. Perhaps she belonged home in England with Abby.

"I will look around the clearing once more and then we should go. I do not wish to come upon these men in the dark of the forest, and Na-Kee must know that there are evil men so close to our home."

Tess nodded. "I'll just sit here," she said, shivering despite the warmth of the summer air.

Raven walked away and Tess just sat staring at the smoke still rising from the smouldering cabin and barn. Then a sound caught her attention. . . . Almost a mewing. She turned her head, listening. Was it a cat?

No. She concentrated, filtering out the sounds of the shifting cabin timbers, tree limbs swaying in the breeze, and the cluck of the single spotted hen that had escaped the carnage.

There it was again. Not a cat. . . . Tess leaped up from the stump. A child! That was a child making those sounds!

Tess ran a few feet and then stopped. Where was the sound coming from? Not the trees. That was too far. But the barn and house had burned to the ground. A root cellar maybe? She stood perfectly still, scanning the area around her looking for a hatch in the ground.

There it was again, louder now. A child's voice . . . muffled sobs . . . an echo?

Then Tess spotted the well and took off in a run. The beasts had thrown a child down the well? "Raven!" Tess hollered. "Hurry!"

"Tess?" he called from the woods line.

"Here!" she answered as she reached the well and peered over the side of the stone wall. "Hallo?" she called softly, not wanting to scare the child. "It's all right. They're gone. Are . . . are you there?"

She heard nothing now. Was she losing her mind talking down a well? She leaned over the side to get a better look.

Raven came up behind her. "Tess—"

"Shhhh! There's someone down there. A child, I think." He peered over the well wall.

Tess leaned further over the side of the well, trying to keep her balance. "Hallo," she called again. No answer.

Slowly her eyes adjusted to the darkness, and then she saw him . . . or her, she couldn't tell.

"Oh, God," Tess whispered as her eyes adjusted to the darkness. "It is a child. He . . . he's on a shelf." There, built in the cool darkness of the well, was a crude wooden shelf made for keeping milk and butter from spoiling in the heat of the summer.

Tess put out her hand. "It's all right," she said softly. "I won't hurt you. Give me your hand."

The child made no response but to stare with wide, frightened eyes.

Tess shook her hand a little. "Please," she whispered. "I won't hurt you, I swear it."

The child's cheeks were wet with tears. He turned his head and she spotted a ribbon. It was a girl! A little girl. "Please," Tess said, offering her hand again.

The little girl stared at Tess's hand and then slowly extended her own.

"You hold onto me," she told Raven quietly. "I'll have to pull her up over the wall."

Raven grasped Tess's waist and she heaved the girl into her arms. The child's entire body was trembling with fear.

Tess pulled her out of the dark of the well and into the sunlight. She had black hair, tied back in a red ribbon, and skin as suntanned red as Raven's, but her eyes were as blue as the sky. In her arm she grasped an Indian rag doll with black horsehair.

The minute Tess lowered the little girl's feet to the ground, she took one look at Raven and bolted.

"No, no," Tess called after her. "It's all right."

The child made no response to Tess's voice. Tess looked at Raven. The little girl had only run a few feet and then stopped and turned around. She was staring at them with wide blue eyes.

"We won't hurt you. Do you have a name?"

Still the child made no response.

On an eerie hunch, Tess touched her breast. "Tess. I'm Tess." She pointed to the little girl. "Your name."

The little girl shook her head.

Tess pointed again. Raven just stood back, watching Tess and the child.

The half-breed girl finally touched her own breast and made an indistinguishable, guttural sound.

Tess covered her mouth. "Oh, God, Raven. She can't hear us. She's deaf. I know those sounds. She's deaf just like Abby." Tess pointed at the child again.

This time the little girl pointed to her own breast and then to the sky with sweeping hands.

Tess thought, looking up. God? Clouds? She worked mentally through the possibilities. Then she smiled making the same motion as the little girl. "Sky?" she said.

The girl repeated the motion and again made another guttural sound. This time it resembled *sky*.

Tess turned to Raven. "Her name is Sky. Her mama was Indian. I guess that makes sense doesn't it?"

"Her mother was Shawnee. I could tell by the beadwork on her moccasins."

Tess looked back at Sky who just stood there looking so lost and forlorn. Tess spoke slowly, using her hands. She didn't think the little girl would understand most of what she said, but at least she would understand that Tess was trying to communicate with her.

"Your mama and papa are dead, sweetheart. Why don't you come with us?" She walked slowly toward her. "I'll take you to a place where you'll be safe."

Sky looked at Raven, who remained still. The look of terror in her eyes was obvious.

"No," Tess told her, moving her hands. "He's not bad. He didn't do it. He's mine. Mine. He's a good man." She made an exaggerated smile, nodding. "A good man."

By the time Tess reached Sky, she seemed to have relaxed a little. She let Tess put her arms around her and pick her up. "Oh, what a big girl," Tess said. "You're so big and strong and brave." She smoothed the child's tangled hair as she walked toward Raven. "How did you get down in the well? Did your smart mama put you in there so you'd be safe? Did she?" Tess crooned.

"We will take the child back to the village. Come, Tess," Raven said. "We must not stay here."

"What about the bodies?" Tess followed him, sensing the urgency in his voice.

"Where they have gone, they will not need them."

Tess put Sky on the ground and took her hand, leading her past the charred cabin, avoiding her father and mother's bodies. Just as they walked by, Tess heard the sound of men coming through the woods. Before there was time to react, half a dozen white men dressed in buckskins appeared.

Raven gripped his rifle, putting himself between the men and Tess. "Run," he ordered between clenched teeth.

"I'm not going without you," she snapped back.

The men came slowly toward them, their weapons drawn.

"What the hell happened here?" A man in a red wool hat demanded.

"We . . . we don't know," Tess answered. "We found the cabin burned and the child hiding in the well."

The other men fanned out quickly surveying the property.

The man in the red cap stared hard at Raven with his one good eye. The other was glassy and sightless. He turned to Tess, taking in her scanty Lenape garb. "The name's Boeing. Me and the boys, we be scouts out of Fort Cumberland." His good eye narrowed. "This hostile take you captive, ma'am?"

"N . . . no, no," Tess lied. Well, it really wasn't a lie anymore was it? "He didn't."

Boeing glanced at Raven and then back at her. "He burn this cabin?"

"No!"

"Well looky here, Boeing," one of the other buck-skinned men called, coming back toward them. "Looky what I found."

He held up the arrow that had been in the dead man's chest.

Boeing looked back at Raven who had still said nothing to this point. "I thought you said you didn't do this, you red bastard."

The other men had returned and were closing in on Tess, the child, and Raven. A moment ago Tess had felt relatively safe, now suddenly it seemed that she was sur-rounded by a pack of wild dogs.

"That feathering is Miami," Raven responded in perfect English. "I am Lenape. I could not have shot that arrow."

"Jesus, sweet Christ," Boeing muttered. "Seen one fut-tering injun, you seen 'em all! Take 'em boys!"

Raven moved to raise his Brown Bess barely as one of the men brought the butt of his rifle across the back of Raven's head. Tess heard the sickening crack of his skull and screamed as Raven's body slipped to the ground.

Twenty

Little Sky shrieked in terror as Raven fell to the ground, the back of his head running crimson with blood. Tess tightened her grip on the child's hand knowing that what she did next might mean life or death to them all.

Tess took a step back, pulling Sky with her. The man who had struck Raven rolled him face down on the ground and began to tie his hands together with a bit of leather.

Tess took a deep breath trying to control the panic in her chest. These men meant to take Raven! She had to get back to the village. She had to get help.

"What . . . what are you going to do with him?" Tess asked Boeing, taking another slow step backward.

"Braddock still needs men to cut a path through this blessed forest so's his army can get through. This man's a prisoner. Guess we got us one more axeman."

Braddock's march? Tess was still backing up slowly, keeping Sky close to her. At least Tess would know what to tell Taande when she reached the village. She would know where the men would be able to find Raven.

"Where you think you're goin', missy?" Boeing demanded, staring hard at her with his one good eye.

Tess stopped in her tracks. She had to get away from these men. She had to help Raven. "I . . . I'm going home. I thank you for . . . for rescuing me from the—" the words stuck in her throat "—the savage."

Boeing started walking toward her. "I thought you tole me you weren't no captive." He was looking at her Indian garb, summing her up. "You said you weren't no prisoner of the red bastard."

She gave a little laugh, hoping she sounded convincing. "I couldn't very well tell you the truth with him standing there could I?" She glanced at Raven lying there on the ground, the blood from his head congealing on the sun-withered grass. The men were tying his feet together now. She could see his chest rising and falling. She looked back at Boeing. "I mean, he'd have scalped me if I'd told.''

Boeing looked over his shoulder at his prisoner, then back at Tess.

She still couldn't tell if he believed her or not. "Please," she said. "Just let me go. I can find my way back to my uncle's from here. My . . . my niece and I, we'll just go."

Boeing spat a stream of brown tobacco juice at Tess's feet. "Niece my ass! That little retard's got redskin in her as sure as my name's Portius Boeing."

Tess put her arms protectively around Sky. "Her mother and father are dead. Where's your sense of decency?"

"I don't care what you do with the little half." He squinted his good eye. "But jest who are you? Who's this uncle you're talkin' about?"

"My name is Tess, Tess Morgan. My uncle is Albert MacElby. His plantation is near Annapolis."

"Sweet piss! Annapolis? And you think you're gonna walk? That's two days from here." Boeing pointed a dirty finger at her. "Say, you the one they been looking for? Some smithy out of Annapolis by the name of—" he snapped his fingers "—ah hell, what's his name?"

"Myron," she answered softly. She couldn't believe Myron was still looking for her. But it had to be him. "My fiance's name is Myron Ellsworth."

Boeing pointed. "Yeah, that's him. Offerin' a reward for your whereabouts he is." He clapped. "Hot damn! You'd best come with us, missy." He started west in the direction they'd come.

She shook her head, holding her ground stubbornly. She couldn't go with these men. She had to get back to the Lenape village. She had to get help. "But that's the wrong way. Annapolis is east."

"The major'll know what to do with you. I can't be leavin' any white woman loose in this woods with hostiles all about." He grabbed her arm and gave her a rough push toward the other men. "Now just go on with you and don't be arguing. Yer man's lookin' for you and I got an obligation to see you get back to him." He shook his head mumbling. "Though why in the Christ's sake he'd want you now, I can't tell you."

Tess stumbled in the direction of the other men. She considered just breaking free and running, but she couldn't leave Sky behind, and there was no way the little girl could keep up, nor could Tess carry her. Summing up her situation, Tess realized she'd have to go along with the men, at least until she could figure out how to escape. If worse came to worse, she would join Braddock's march with Raven. Hadn't he just mentioned hours earlier that Na-Kee and the other warriors from the village would be fighting Braddock's soldiers? Surely once the Lenape braves came upon the English army and discovered Raven was a prisoner, they would free him.

Still holding tightly to Sky's hand, Tess walked back toward Raven and the other scouts. Now Boeing was shouting orders. The scouts had cut a pole and were slipping it in through the leather ties of Raven's hands and feet. *By all that's holy,* Tess thought. *They're going to carry him like a slaughtered hog!*

Tess flinched as they lifted the pole, one man on each side. Raven's body hung lifeless above the ground, swaying back and forth.

Sky looked up at Tess, her eyes wide with fright and confusion. Tess smoothed the little girl's hand, making her look her in the eye. Tess nodded slowly. "It'll be all right," she said softly so that Boeing or one of the other men didn't hear her. She knew the little girl couldn't hear her, but the words were as much for her own reassurance as the child's. "I'll take care of you. We'll get ourselves out of this and then I'll take you to the village where you'll be safe." She tried to make the little girl understand with awkward hand motions.

Sky seemed to understand Tess, or at least to trust her. When the scouts started for the woods, one of the men waited on Tess, falling in behind her. Tess glanced over her shoulder at the woodsman. He was a mean-looking man, standing well over six feet tall. By the look on his face it was obvious to her that she was as much these men's prisoner as Raven was.

Tess turned away and followed the men carrying Raven. Sky took one look at Tess and lifted her own small chin with the same determination. Tess had to smile. The little girl was a survivor. If she was strong enough to survive her disability and the murder of her parents, she could certainly bear this. She would make it. They both would.

* * *

The more time that passed, the more concerned Tess grew for Raven. It seemed that he had been unconscious for hours. She didn't know how his body could stand the strain of being hung on that pole. Even from this far behind him, she could see the rings of red around his wrists turn to purple and green, and finally begin to bleed, chaffed by the uncured leather strips. At least his ankles were protected by his moccasins.

Tess tried not to think about Raven, but instead concentrated on the little girl who walked at her side. The child was Tess's responsibility and it was for her best interest that she needed to focus on. Though the scouts who had taken them prisoner were moving quickly through the forest, Sky seemed tireless. The child walked in silence at her side, taking two strides for each of Tess's. Occasionally Tess pointed something out to the little girl, a cardinal, a squirrel, or a flower, and then signed the word to keep the child's mind off their predicament. Sky was quick to pick up the handsignals and repeated them back again and again, pleased with herself.

At one point one of the men carrying Raven asked why the child was talking with her hands. When Tess explained, the man made a quick sign to ward off the devil and turned his back on them.

The buckskinned scouts stopped for a drink in the late afternoon at a stream nestled in a grove of mountain ash trees. The terrain was quickly changing, becoming rolling and rocky. Tess led Sky downstream of them, wanting to keep the little girl as far away from the rough men as possible. Tess drank her fill of the icy water from her cupped hands and then sat down on the bank of the shallow stream beside Sky. The scouts leaned against the trees, smoking their pipes and talking among themselves.

Tess glanced at Raven lying on the ground where the scouts had dropped him. She wanted to take some water to him, thinking that perhaps it would revive him. But she was afraid to. She had told Boeing that Raven had kidnapped her. What woman would take water to the hostile who had captured her? At this point Tess didn't think she could afford to make Boeing or any of the scouts any more suspicious of her than they already were. If they knew the truth, if they knew Tess was Raven's wife, she didn't know what might happen to her or the child. These men obviously hated Indians, and to be considered an Indian lover might mean Tess's life and the life of the child she was trying to protect.

She glanced at Raven again. *Was that eye movement?* Had she seen Raven's facial expression change ever so slightly? She looked away not wanting the scouts to become alerted, then back at him again. Was he awake?

It didn't make any sense. If he was awake, wouldn't he be struggling to get free? Tess had expected that when Raven finally became conscious he would go wild. She expected him to fight, to shout, to become the savage she knew he was capable of becoming.

But then Tess began to think . . . to think like a Lenape. Logic, there was always logic in Raven's choices. How could he fight tied the way he was? If he was conscious he might pretend to be unconscious so that he could sum up his enemy and his options.

A second later Raven made a deliberate movement with his leg. One of the scouts, one the others called Blueball, caught the motion immediately. "Well, looky here. Guess I didn't kill the red bastard after all, eh?" He walked over to Raven and kicked him in the ribs. "You awake you murderin' bastard? You hear me?"

Tess heard Raven exhale sharply as he opened his black eyes and stared venomously at Blueball.

Blueball cackled. "Think you can burn good white folk out and not get caught, eh? Think you can steal our women?" He had just cocked his leg to kick Raven again when Boeing came out of the brush tying up the fly of his leather leggings. "Leave 'im be, Blue! The General needs men who can cut away this bloody forest. A man with broken ribs can't do any cuttin'!"

Boeing glanced at the other scouts leaning against a tree and smoking their clay pipes. "Let's get on with it, boys. We can cover a good four or five miles before she's too dark to travel. Get the redskin on his feet and let's go. The major's waitin' on us."

Tess got up off the ground, pulling Sky up with her. She watched as Blueball and another scout pulled the pole out from between Raven's arms and legs and jerked him to his feet.

Tess had to cover her mouth with her hand to keep from crying out at the harsh handling the men gave Raven. Through the entire ordeal, he never said a word. He only stared with those black eyes of his that were as dark and frightening as the pits of hell.

As they spun Raven around she made eye-contact with him for just an instant. There were so many things she wanted to say, but of course she couldn't. Raven's face remained unchanged. She knew he had seen her and yet he made no indication he had.

The uncertainty of what was going on in Raven's head weighed heavily on Tess's mind for the remainder of the afternoon. Just after sunset Boeing halted his men and ordered them to set up camp. One of the scouts brought her six squirrels and ordered her to skin and cook them for the evening meal. Tess considered refusing. She was no man's servant. But the look Raven gave her out of the corner of his eye made Tess reconsider. Play the game, she thought. That's what he's telling me. Play the game until the time is right and we'll escape. We'll all three get out of here in one piece.

So, keeping Sky close at her side, Tess skinned the squirrels and cut skewers from saplings to roast the meat over the campfire. Everyone sat around the spitting flames to wait on the supper. Tess took a seat just outside the circle of light. Here she knew she and Sky would be less noticeable and the less the scouts noticed them, the better off she knew they'd be. The other advantage was that from here she could watch Raven without the others knowing.

Raven had been tied to a tree on the far side of the campfire. He had been given no water all day and she knew he had to be dehydrating. A man could live without food for weeks, but he had to have water.

When Tess got up to turn the squirrel spit, she left Sky curled sleepily on a mat one of the scouts called Charlie had offered. Charlie had also given Sky a little stick figure made of twisted vine and twigs. The little girl quietly played with the dolly, trusting Tess would come back to her.

Tess turned each squirrel. "Just about done," she commented to Boeing who was seated closest to the fire. Charlie and Blueball and another scout were occupied rolling dice. Tess nodded in Raven's direction. "You want me to give that one some water?" she asked nonchalantly.

"Nah," Boeing said. He was shaving a thick yellow thumbnail with his knife. "Let the red bastard go thirsty."

Tess shrugged. "Makes no matter to me. It's just that you said your General needed him. He dies of thirst and he won't be much good."

"What do you care what happens to the hostile?" Boeing demanded.

She shrugged. "I don't. I told you. He kidnapped me. It's just that I heard you say you were going to use him to cut through the woods. A dead man doesn't cut much."

Boeing scowled, flicking a bit of thumbnail into the campfire. Tess winced as it struck a roasting squirrel carcass. "Reckon you're right. Go ahead, give the heathen a drink of water. Take Blue's skin."

"The hell I want the red nigger drinkin' out of my water skin," Blueball protested from the dice game.

"Shut up, Blue," Boeing called. He nodded to Tess. "Do it."

Tess picked up the water skin and approached Raven slowly, hoping Boeing wasn't paying too close attention. Raven watched her come toward him through slitted dark eyes.

When Tess reached him she glanced over her shoulder. Boeing had turned his attention to the dice game.

She turned back to Raven and squatted in front of him.

"You should have gone when you had the chance," he whispered harshly.

"How about thank-you for the water?" Tess didn't mean to be terse with him, but it just came out that way. She brought the skin to his lips and he drank down several mouthfuls. She pulled the skin away to let him catch his breath.

"If you had not come. If you had gone home to your 'Napolis when I said you should go, you would not be in this situation. I would not be in this situation!"

Tess set her jaw. "They say you're their prisoner. They think you killed those settlers. They mean to use you in the English army. An axeman."

Raven glanced at Sky who was still playing with her little stick doll. "The child?"

"She's fine." Tess smiled proudly. "She's very bright. I already taught her a couple of new words. And she's tough."

He indicated the water skin with his chin and she gave him another sip. "Why didn't you run when they hit me?" He licked a drip of water from his lower lip.

"I couldn't, not with Sky."

He frowned. "This is not good, Tess. They should have let you go."

She looked away, then back at him. "Myron—my fiance, apparently has offered a reward for information on me. Boeing wants the reward. He's going to return me to Myron."

"Then you will be safe. You will go back to your 'Napolis."

She made a face. "I'm not going anywhere without you. I'm not going back until I know you're safe. Don't you understand, these are Englishmen, your enemy."

"You will go when the chance is given."

"Don't talk to me like that." She was trying to keep her voice quiet, but it was difficult. She whipped the cover over the water skin and tied it tightly. "You freed me, remember? You can't tell me what to do any longer, Raven."

He looked at her straight in the eye, his anger obvious. "You should have gone when you had the chance. You should not have remained in the village!"

She stood abruptly. She knew she should see to his wounds, but he had made her so damned angry. He was still trying to possess her! "I guess you're right for once," she snapped. "I should have gone when I had the chance!"

Before Raven could respond, she turned and stomped back toward the fire muttering beneath her breath. Arrogant ass! He was just like any other man, trying to control a woman. What had ever made her think for a second that he was ever any different? What in God's name could she have been thinking when she went to his bed willingly?

She dropped Blueball's water skin at his feet and went back to Sky. She'd been out here in the wilderness too long. She was losing her mind. She'd let Boeing send a message to Myron and she'd go home to Annapolis and take Sky with her. Hell, she'd show Raven. She'd marry Myron. She'd marry him and give him a farmhouse full of children. Then Raven would see who he could order about and whom he couldn't. Then he'd be sorry he hadn't realized what a good catch she had been. Then he'd be sorry he'd ever let her go.

After a quick meal of the squirrel washed down with water, Tess settled Sky down to sleep. The crackle of the fire and hum of the scouts talking became a buzzing in Tess's ears until, exhausted, she drifted off.

Tess threw back her head in laughter as she raced over the hill and through the field of yellow daisies. She could hear Abby's laughter, the one sound her sister made that was unaffected by her lack of hearing. The sun was warm on Tess's face, the grass soft beneath her bare feet. She could feel the weight of her unruly auburn hair on her back as the wind whipped and tugged at the long tresses. She could smell the fragrance of the summer grass and the hint of fresh baked bread coming from her mother's cottage.

Tess turned, taking the shortcut through the woods. Home was only beyond the tree line, just a dip in the path, under the giant oak and back into the sunshine.

Tess reached the oak before she realized something was wrong. Where was Abby? Why didn't she hear her laughter? Still smiling, Tess turned around.

Suddenly Abby was gone . . . gone and the forest had turned black and evil. Something large and shapeless had blackened out the sun.

Tess screamed . . .

The weight of the dark and wicked thing was upon her. She couldn't breathe. It was down her throat. She screamed but no sound came out.

Wake up! Wake up Tess told herself. It's just a nightmare! Wake up! But still the weight of the evil crushed down upon her . . . and then she realized with horror that she was awake.

Twenty-one

Tess began to buck wildly. This thing on top of her, this thing that was suffocating her was a man! It was a man who stank of uncured hides, tobacco spittle, and smoke.

"No!" Tess tried to holler as she opened her eyes. "No!"

It was Blueball. His giant frame was so heavy on top of her that she couldn't get enough air into her lungs to scream loud enough for anyone to hear her. She grabbed a handful of his wiry beard and yanked, trying to kick herself free. In a moment she knew she would faint from lack of air and then she would be powerless to fight off her attacker.

Tess managed one squeak and Blueball clamped his beefy hand on her mouth. "Hush, puss. Ole Blue won't hurt ye. Just gimme a ride," he whispered in her ear, his breath hot and putrid. "I got to be better than that redskin, and if I like ye well enough, I jest might take ye under my wing. Travelin' with an army can be rough business. You'll be in need of a man like myself to protect yer purty red snatch."

"Get off me," Tess managed from under his hand, still struggling beneath him. *Oh God, won't anyone help me,* she thought frantically.

But who would help her? The scouts didn't care what happened to her. Obviously they assumed she'd been soiled by a heathen. And Raven couldn't help her because he couldn't hear her. And even if he could, he was powerless, tied to the tree the way he was.

So outsmart the stinking bastard, Tess told herself. *Don't give in! Don't let him win; don't let him beat you. You've come too far. You've survived too much.*

Knowing she couldn't outfight him, Tess forced herself to let her body go limp beneath the giant of a man. As she relaxed, she heard Blueball chuckle.

"There you go, luv. I knew you'd see it my way." She felt him fumble with his leather leggings. "Give ole Blue a chance and you might just enjoy the ride." He looked down, frustrated with the leather tie of his leggings.

The man's rotting teeth stunk so badly that Tess feared she'd be sick. She turned her head away from his mouth ever so slightly. "You . . . you want me to do that?" she asked, trying to sound like she meant it.

Blueball looked at her. She could see his craggy face by the dim light of the glowing campfire. He broke into a grin. "Yes, indeedy. You and I, we might get along jest fine, puss. Always had me an itch for a redhead."

Tess slid her hand between his chest and hers. He was still lying flat on top of her so that it was still difficult for her to breath. "Can't quite reach," she said softly, feeling the hilt of the Mohawk knife she still carried hidden beneath her linen shirt. "Could . . . could you shift a little?"

"Hehehe," he chuckled. "A wild one, ain't ye, puss?" He gave her breast a hard squeeze as he shifted his weight to one side.

In a single motion, Tess slipped her knife out of its leather sheath and into the soft flesh of his groin.

Blueball bellowed like a enraged bear as Tess scrambled to get out from under him.

"Holy Christ! Holy Christ!" Blueball moaned, rolling on Tess's mat.

The scout sleeping closest to her leaped up from his bedroll, his rifle in his hand.

"Sweet Jesus Christ, she's cut my balls," Blueball shrieked. "Get her!"

By now Sky had somehow sensed the commotion and awoken to find Tess leaping to her feet.

The child screamed in fear.

Tess knew she couldn't run. She knew she couldn't leave Sky behind.

The bloody knife still in her hand, Tess threw out her arms to the child to come to her. Sky came dashing toward her just as the scout brought the barrel of his rifle down on Tess's right shoulder.

Sky screamed. Tess went down on one knee in agony.

"The knife!" Blueball called from where he lay on Tess's sleeping mat clutching his groin. "Get the futterin' knife before you lose your cock, Jesse!"

Tess was numb with pain, but all she could think of was Sky and what would happen to the little girl if these men killed her.

Tess signaled for Sky to go back.

Sky halted, shaking her head, her face still sleepy with innocence.

Tess felt her attacker's hand on her shoulder. She made another frenzied hand motion.

This time, Sky took a step back.

The man behind Tess knocked her face-first onto the grass. Flattening his body over hers, he grabbed her wrist and began to pound it into the ground trying to make her let go of the Mohawk skinning knife.

"No!" Tess screamed. "No!"

The attacker hit the heel of his hand against the back of her head, pushing her face into the grass. Tess squeezed her eyes shut as the pain in her right wrist became so agonizing that it went numb and the knife fell from her hand.

"Got it!" her attacker shouted. "I got the knife!"

"Look out," Blue bellowed back. "The redskin!"

Before Tess could lift her head from the dirt she felt the impact. Someone had leaped onto her attacker's back. Raven? Was it Raven? It couldn't be! He was tied up. But what other redskin could Blue mean?

Tess's attacker was knocked off her back and she scrambled to get free of the fighting. Flipping onto her backside, she scooted backwards.

Sweet God, it was Raven. She didn't know how he'd managed it, but he'd broken free and was now rolling over and over in the dirt, fighting hand to hand with the scout.

Tess wiped at the blood that was running from the corner of her mouth, wondering vaguely where it could have come from. Sky appeared out of nowhere, throwing herself into Tess's arms.

"Get im! Catch the red bastard before he kills Jesse!" Boeing shouted from the far side of the campfire. "Jesus, how did he get loose?"

By now the other scouts were awake and bounding for their weapons.

Raven and Jesse rolled over and over again with first Raven on top, then the scout.

"Shoot him!" Blueball called from where he still lay.

"Christ, no!" Boeing ordered. "You jackasses'll shoot Jesse!"

Clutching Sky, Tess watched in fear as Raven battled her attacker. The scouts were circling the two brawling men, trying to get a hold of Raven so they could pull him off the scout called Jesse.

Tess had to stifle a scream as Jesse rolled Raven into the burning coals of the campfire and red sparks flew. She smelled the scent of singed hair as Raven fought his way out of the flames and certain death.

"Grab 'im! Grab 'im," one of scouts shouted as another man tried to catch Raven's moccasin.

Sky covered her eyes, clutching Tess. Tess wondered if she should run. Maybe she and Sky could get away. But how far could they run? The pain shooting down Tess's right arm made her wonder if Jesse had broken a bone in her shoulder with the rifle barrel. How far would she be able to run with broken bones and a child? How could she run knowing these men might murder Raven at any moment?

A scout finally managed to catch one of Raven's feet. Another scout caught the other.

"Haul 'im off! Haul 'im off," Boeing ordered above the din of the shouting men and Raven and Jesse's grunts of pain.

Slowly the two scouts pulled Raven off Jesse. Raven fought them every inch, but they had the advantage.

Tess leaped up as the men dragged Raven on his back toward the tree he had been tied to.

"How the blasted hell did this happen?" Boeing demanded.

Wincing with pain, Tess slowly made her way toward Boeing. "He . . . he attacked me," she said, knowing her voice wavered. "Blueball, he was going to try to rape me."

Boeing shot an angry glance at Blueball who was now sitting up, staring at the bloody leather at his groin. "That right? You tried to mess with her, Blue?"

"Jesus," Blueball moaned in tears. "I think she cut one of my balls off. Come look, Jinx. I can't. I can't do it."

Boeing strode toward Blueball. "I said did you try to mess with her after I tole you there'd be no futterin' on my patrol?"

Blueball just rocked back and forth clutching his injured parts.

Boeing looked back at Tess, frowning. "All right, so the woman tried to save herself. Serves him right, the stupid bastard."

"Sweet Jesus, Portius," Blueball moaned. "How can you say a man deserves to have his nuts cut off?"

Boeing looked to his other men who were now trying to subdue Raven who was again fighting in earnest. "So how did he get loose? That's what I want to know. The girl do it?"

"No!" Raven shouted. "This man broke free. You will not touch her. No man will touch the *equiwa*."

Boeing glanced at Tess, leaning on the butt of his rifle. He ran one hand through his tangled dark hair. "This red-skin sweet on you or something, woman?"

Tess's breath was coming in short spurts. She was so frightened she could barely think straight. "I don't know. He thinks I'm his," she said, cutting a quick glance in Raven's direction. *Please let him realize I've lied to them,* she thought.

Boeing looked back at Raven. The scouts had him

pinned to the tree and were now wrapping a thick cord of rope around his torso and around the thick tree trunk.

"You want us to kill 'im?" Jesse jerked a musket from another man's hand. "Let me do it. I'll shoot 'im between the eyes and take his scalp back to Braddock. There's men offerin' a hefty price for an Injun scalp!"

"No!" Boeing shouted, grabbing up his weapon to bead in on the scout. "You make one move toward my prisoner and I'll blow you to hell and back, Jesse."

The scout froze immediately.

"Now put it down," Boeing directed. "And back off. I said I was gonna take the red bastard to Braddock and that's what I'll do. He can hang 'im or put 'im to work but it'll be the general's choice."

Tess glanced up into the sky, murmuring a prayer of thanks.

"You got the red bastard tied securely this time?" Boeing went on.

"Think so," one of the scouts responded. "Course Jesse thought he was tied well enough, too."

"Shut your face before I shut it for you, O'Connel!"

"That's enough!" Boeing shouted. "Now back off all of you." He made a quick movement toward O'Connel. "Now!"

Finally the men backed themselves toward the dying campfire.

Tess heard Boeing heave a sigh. "It's going to be daybreak in a few hours. Now you jackasses had best get some sleep because I aim to push onto Braddock come first light." He walked over to Blueball. "Can you walk?"

"I don't know, Portius," he whined. "It's awful bad, awful bad."

"Guess we'll be leavin' you behind then, friend."

"Jesus, Portius. You got no heart."

"Get yourself cleaned up, Blue."

"Hey there, Blue," Jesse called from where he was taking a seat near the fire. "Guess we'll have to start callin' you *No Nuts,* eh?"

The other men burst into guffaws of laughter and Tess breathed a little easier as she walked into the shadows to wait out the darkness. She didn't dare look to Raven, but she knew he was watching her from where the men had left him tied to the tree. She wanted to run to him, to throw her arms around him. She wanted to feel his lips on hers.

"Thank you," Tess whispered beneath her breath, clutching Sky to her side. "Don't pay any attention to what I said, or even what I thought. I love you Raven of the Lenape. And I always will."

Late that afternoon the scouts led Tess, Raven, and Sky into Braddock's camp. Tess was as awestruck by the number of soldiers, wagons, and cannon assembled as she was by the utter disorganization of the army.

As Boeing had explained to her, his voice laced with amusement, General Braddock's forces consisted of thirty-two hundred men, and six hundred baggage horses. They were attempting the formidable task of cutting a twelve foot wide road the distance of one hundred and ten miles to the French-held fort called Dusquesne. Laborers cut down trees, moved boulders, and used block and tackle to get the heavy cannon up steep embankments. Boeing guessed that the army was making about three miles a day, if that.

The moment they entered the encampment, which was

actually moving by the hour, Tess and Raven were separated. Tess watched as Raven was dragged away under heavy guard. Boeing led her and Sky toward a baggage wagon being driven by a short stocky man with a wool hat pulled down over his face. Across the side of the wagon, painted in faded whitewash, was the name of the hauling company the man worked for. Tess noticed part of the word Annapolis scrawled on the rough-hewn planks.

"Yo, Marty!" Boeing shouted, waving his musket.

"Whoa, whoa there," the man called, pulling the horses to a halt. The wagon creaked to a standstill. "That you Boeing?" The man called Marty pushed back his hat and glanced down at the scout. "Thought for sure the Injuns would have your scalp this time, made a tobacco pouch out of yer possibles."

"Nah. Not me. Too fast and too smart for the little red buggers." Then he did an odd thing. Boeing winked at the man. "Say, I want you to do me a favor, Marty?"

"Depends on what it is."

Boeing pointed to Tess. "Picked this woman up in the woods. A redskin had her and I rescued her."

"Well ain't you the hero."

He grinned. "Keep an eye on her. She's got a man illin' to pay for her return and I aim to collect on it jest as soon as I can. I don't want her wanderin' off."

Marty looked down from his wagon seat. "You got a name?" he asked Tess gruffly.

Tess watched Boeing walk off, his musket propped on one shoulder. "Tess, I'm called Tess." She pulled Sky against her. "And this is Sky. She's deaf, so she can't hear what we say."

"This ain't no place fer a lady and child." Marty pulled a long-stemmed clay pipe from inside his fringed leather tunic and reached for a tobacco pouch on the wagon seat. "Is it true? Was you captured by Injuns?"

Tess nodded as she looked up at Marty. There was something strange about him that didn't quite fit. His hair was cut to chin length. He had a broad face with apple red cheeks, but no beard stubble. He was hefty and short. But were those breasts Tess saw beneath his clothing? *Was he a she?* Tess wasn't certain, but she knew one thing, if Marty was a woman, she was the ugliest woman she'd ever seen in her life.

"But the Indians didn't hurt me," Tess explained cautiously. "No one hurt me. It wasn't until the scouts came along that I was really afraid for my life."

Marty tamped a wad of tobacco into the bowl of his pipe. "Portius tells me you got someone lookin' for you."

Tess lowered her gaze. "So he says."

"Ole Portius Boeing, he ain't a bad man. A little rough. But he ain't bad in his heart. Not like some of the others 'round here."

Tess's gaze met Marty's. *She was a woman,* Tess could see a woman's compassion in her nut brown eyes. "He brought me here against my will. I could have gotten home on my own. Now I'm two days farther away than before."

Marty twisted her mouth. "Just like a man, though. Thinks he knows what's best for the womanfolk. Truth is, he don't know a polecat from a piss ant." Marty spat a wad of tobacco over the far side of the baggage wagon and pushed the stem of the pipe between her lips.

Tess had to smile. She'd never met anyone like Marty before, a woman who was more like a man, but she liked her. Instinctively, she knew she could trust her if she could just look beyond her odd ways.

"Glad you can join me 'til they do find your man," Marty went on. "Could use a little company. I got no one to talk to most times but Rosa, and she and me, we just don't see eye to eye on most things." Marty pointed with the stem of her pipe. "You'll meet Rosa after a spell. She's what they call a *washin' woman* 'round here." Marty chuckled over some private joke and then eyed Sky. "The girl child's skinny. Think she could eat a little bean soup? Made it fresh with a hunk of possum."

Tess looked at Sky and handsigned. "Are you hungry?" Sky nodded and signed back.

"She says she is." Tess looked up at Marty who was climbing off the wagon seat. "Bean soup would be good. Sky's been through a lot these last two days. Her mama and papa were murdered, and then Boeing and his men brought us here."

"I ain't much with littl'ins." Marty walked back along the side of the wagon. It was covered crudely with a dome roof and a sail canvas stretched over it. The tailgate was down on the back and a small campfire burned in a large, shallow, metal pan on the end. Above the coals on a spider was a steaming stew pot. "Movin's slow with those men cuttin' a road through this wilderness. But we do move a tad. I like to keep a fire goin' so I can have me a cup of sassafras tea if I take the notion."

Marty picked up a wooden trencher out of a basket just inside the wagon. She ladled a generous portion of bubbling bean soup and added a slice of bread. She handed a wooden spoon and the plate to Sky.

The little girl took the food and nodded, making the sign of thanks.

"She says thank you," Tess interpreted.

Marty watched the little girl eat. "I know what she said. I ain't stupid." She lifted the ladle. "You want some?"

Tess shook her head. "No thanks. But I want you to know I appreciate your being kind to us. Sky needs a place to be safe until I can get her out of here."

"Yeah, well we women got to stick together on this frontier, don't we? I know I ain't much of a woman by the looks of me, but I still got a woman's heart, and I still know what it is to pain over a man's doin's."

Tess stood there beside Sky and Marty as the little girl ate, taking in her surroundings. The wagon was just one of many wagons on the narrow road cut crudely through the forest. Tree stumps, uncut grass and weeds, and rocks cropped up here and there along the mountain ridge they traveled across. There was one wagon to the left, its driver asleep on the wagon seat.

As far as Tess could see in front and behind there were baggage wagons crammed into the tight space. The forest walls were so close that they seemed oppressive in the late afternoon heat. Men in buckskins and soldiers in uniforms wandered everywhere. Horses neighed. Somewhere ahead and around a bend in the crude-cut road Tess heard the sound of a foreman as he commanded men to heave-ho on some heavy object. Tess found it difficult to believe that this was the fierce army Na-Kee and his men intended to fight against at the side of the Frenchmen.

Tess looked at Marty. "Marty?"

"Yeah?"

"The man I came in with . . ."

Marty chewed on the stem of her pipe. "The redskin?"

"His name is Raven."

"He your man?"

When Tess didn't respond, Marty went on. "Look, it

don't matter to me. There's been women in these parts that have settled with 'em, more than most realize. And there's plenty of whites, trappers and such that's took up squaws for wives. I ain't like a lot of 'em. I got no grudge against the red man." Marty brushed her short-cropped hair with her hand. "Long as he leaves my scalp on my head."

"I need to know where they've taken him. What they've done with him. They accused him of burning out Sky's cabin and murdering her parents, only he didn't. I was there, I know it."

Marty shook her head with a gruff laugh. "Too bad these men don't care. The way they look at it, you're a redskin, you're guilty." She eyed Tess. "What kind of Injun is he?"

"Lenape—Delaware."

Marty gave a low whistle. "The Delaware went with the Frenchies. That ain't good news for your man."

"Boeing said he thought they would use him for an axeman. He said the army needed more laborers."

"What they need is Indian scouts and fighters. The Frenchies got hundreds of 'em. Seems some of the officers insulted redskins that meant to come along on this lark of Braddock's. Cherokee and Catawba was suppose to show up. They gave 'em a whole heap of bribe gifts; vermilion paint, scalping knifes, brass kettles, even silver gor-gets, though I can't for the life of me figure what the Indians want with the English trappings."

"But they didn't come?"

"Not yet. And our men are gettin' jumpy about it. They don't want to be comin' on a party of Injuns in these woods here."

"Marty, I have to get Raven out of here. He needs to

be back in his village where he can look after his people. We come upon any Delaware, and they find him among the English, they might torture and murder him. He could be considered a traitor."

"You ain't gonna be able to get him out of here, I can tell you that. It can't be done. But just the same, let old Marty look into what's up with yer man. Ain't a thing that don't happen in this march that I don't know about it." She gave Tess a pat on the arm as she walked away. "You jest don't worry none about it. I'll see what I can do. Meantime, you'd best climb into that there wagon and see what you can find to cover up them long legs of yours. You walk around here lookin' like that in front of these horny soldiers and you'll be defendin' your virtue day and night."

Tess watched Marty weave her way through the congestion of wagons and carts until her hat disappeared in the sea of men, uniforms, cannon, and horses. "So," Tess said to Sky, who was still shoveling the bean soup into her mouth with the zeal only a child could possess. "Let's see what we can do about some clothes, shall we?"

Sky just nodded her head, her black braids swinging, and went on chewing.

Twenty-two

Raven sat with his knees drawn up, the weight of the chains tugging not just at his wrists and ankles, but at his soul. How could he have gotten himself into this situation? Why had he permitted Tess to come along with him to see the eagle's nest when he knew it could be dangerous?

Because he was greedy. Because, despite his anger with her, he had wanted to be with her for as much of the little time they had left before he had to return her to her people. And now he would be punished for his greed. Not only was he now among the enemy, but Tess, his wife until she declared she was not, was out there somewhere with the child, alone and vulnerable.

Raven smiled grimly. Not completely vulnerable. The night before when he had awoken to the sound of Tess's screams, she had already defended herself. She had used her Mohawk knife to cut into what was dear to her attacker. Perhaps the man would think twice before he forced himself upon another woman.

No, Tess was not a woman who simply let things happen to her as did many women. She would not allow herself to be controlled, not by anyone, not even by him, Raven was learning. That was one of her personality traits that had attracted him that first time he had seen her in the Mohawk canoe.

So why was he letting her go? Tess, with her biting tongue, her fiery hair, and her fierce sensuality, was a woman most men searched their entire lives for, but few found. Why had he agreed to send her back to Annapolis to a man who killed innocent people? Raven didn't know. For the first time in his life, he was confused. He wasn't certain what he wanted. And all this emotion was altering his ability to think. Emotion kept a man from thinking clearly, he was certain of it.

Raven heard a sound in the dark camp and looked out over the soldiers. Men lay scattered on their bedrolls for as far as the eye could see, their mouths wide open in sleep. In the distance Raven saw two sentries sharing a bowl of tobacco. The scent of the Roanoke wafted through the thick evening air.

This was insane, this march of the white-hair chief Braddock's. He could not possibly make it to Fort Dusquesne with these inexperienced young soldiers. Raven knew for a fact that the Frenchmen had many Indian allies, not just Lenape. He had heard that the English did as well, but where were they now? Where were the Catawba and Cherokee allies who supposedly numbered in the hundreds? These men of Braddock's who cut their way through the forest foot by foot to drag their cannon and their loaded wagons were like snow geese sitting on the bay. The French and the Lenape, Shawnee, Ottawa, Abenakis, and Mingoe that camped around the fort would wipe them out of the water and eat them for their supper.

Raven heard a sound again, this time from behind. Someone was approaching. The hair rose on the back of his neck. Without a weapon and chained to this tree like some wild beast he could not defend himself.

Two soldiers had been killed today by the French Indians. Raven had heard so, there at the front of the line of wagons where he was forced to cut down trees until sunset. The soldiers had been picked off in plain daylight and scalped. One had even lived a few moments after being found.

Raven squinted in the darkness. Should he call to the sentries who were now busying themselves tossing a pair of dice rather than patrolling as they should have been? Or did he wait to be scalped by one of his own Lenape brothers?

"Raven?"

He heard his name like a whisper on the wind. Had his time come? Was it the spirits of death who beckoned him?

"Raven?" It came again, a caress to his ears.

He gathered the loose chain in his hands so that they would not clink and alarm the sentries. He turned toward the voice. It was not the call for his soul, it was Tess! It was Tess's voice he heard.

Then he saw her coming out of the darkness, moving silently like a shadow dancer. *She has learned much in the short weeks she has lived among the Lenape,* he thought proudly. *She moves like one of us.*

Tess dropped to her knees in front of him. "Raven," she whispered, setting a basket down. She took his cheeks between her palms and peered into his face. "Are you all right?"

She smelled of the pine forest and fiery femininity. He had missed her touch these last two days more than he cared to admit. "You should not be here," he whispered, glad to see her face, glad to see she was safe. "I am a prisoner. You will be punished if they find you here."

"So you want me to take my basket of cold water and freshly baked bread and go?" She touched the basket, raising a feathery eyebrow.

His dark-eyed gaze met hers. "It is only that I am concerned for you," he said softly.

"Not that you don't want to see me?"

He shook his head. "There are sentry guards. See them near the fire?"

"Marty told me." She dug into the basket, pulling out a water skin.

"Mar-ty?"

"She drives one of the wagons. Boeing told her to keep an eye on me so I don't escape. As if I could escape out here in the middle of nowhere." She unwound the piece of leather that held the neck closed on the water skin. "Marty's odd. I never met anyone like her but I've heard about them. Dresses and acts mostly like a man. She's different, but I like her. She tells things the way they are."

Raven accepted a drink from the water skin she held to his lips. The cool, sweet water ran down his parched throat. The work today had been hard even for a man used to hard work. All day long he had dug stumps, cut trees, and hauled wood off the road they forged, all the while dragging his chains. "The English dogs bring their women to fight? That does not sound like the white-hairs."

Tess pulled the skin away so that he could catch his breath. "They're not supposed to. But Marty's father was hired to haul wagon loads of supplies for the army, and I guess no one noticed she was a woman, dressed and acting the way she does." She tore off a piece of warm bread with her fingers from the half-loaf she'd removed from the basket. "There's another one, too. Rosa. I haven't met her yet. Marty says she does wash for the officers."

Raven took a bite of the bread she held to his mouth. He lifted his hand carefully so that the chains wouldn't make too much noise and alarm the guards.

Tess watched him as he struggled with the weight of the chains. "Why did they do this?" she asked, touching the metal.

"So this man does not try to escape."

She slapped a mosquito on his bare shoulder. "Marty says they've made you an axeman."

"I do as they say for now because I fear they will harm you if I do not." He took the bread from her, speaking as he chewed. "Listen to me. You must take the child and run, Tess. Before it is too late. This is an evil place."

"Run? With a child? Run where? I don't know where we are. All I know is that we're days from a settlement and the woods are full of French and English soldiers and Indians all trying to kill each other at once!"

"Listen to me," he insisted. "This man feels the spirits of death about us. Braddock is a fool to think he can cut his way through to the fort. The French know where the English are. It is only a matter of time before they attack, and when they do the blood will run thick down this path Braddock carves."

"But you're on their side. Na-Kee and the others, they've probably reached the French by now. They'll be with them! You said the Lenape were fighting with the French. Surely they wouldn't harm you."

"In the heat of the fight no red man will stop to ask this man of his heritage. Or perhaps they will call me traitor and kill me anyway. They will not care that you are a Lenape wife." He grabbed her shoulders forcing her to look at him, not caring that his chains clanked nosily. *"We will all die, Tess."* But he could not bring himself to tell her what would happen before they died; the blood, the screams, the torture. He did not tell her that he would kill her with his own knife before he would let the French and their Indian allies take her prisoner.

"I'm not going without you," Tess retorted stubbornly.

"You must."

"Would you go without me?"

"It is not the same thing."

"And why not?" she demanded.

"Because I am a man. You are still my wife, Tess."

"And you are my husband, *still!*"

"Shhh." He looked over her shoulder at the guards. One had glanced around but had gone back to his dice. "They will hear you."

"I don't care," she whispered fiercely. "I'm going to find a way to get you unchained. We're going to get out of here together, you, me, and Sky."

The bread gone, he took another drink from the water skin she offered. "You are a crazy *equiwa*. You will die far from your home. The child will have no one."

"I can't leave you, Raven. You've given me too much."

"I have given you nothing. I took you from your people."

"You can go ahead and pretend you don't care about me, but I know you do. I know it." She leaned to brush her lips against his.

Raven couldn't help himself. He let his eyes close at the touch of her mouth to his. Her lips were warm and as sweet as clover honey. When she tried to pull away, he lifted his hand, the chains clinking. Just one more, one more kiss.

He heard her sigh as he pressed his lips to hers again, this time with an insistence born of desperation. The woman was intoxicating. She was a witch and he her bewitched. She said he cared for her. He knew it was true. He cared for her even more than she knew. Perhaps he even loved her, but to admit such seemed a weakness to Raven. This was not the time nor the place to love a woman, a white woman no less. And yet he could not help himself. She was a drug potion he could not wean himself of. He twisted his tongue in her mouth, wanting to possess her even now, chained as he was.

Tess pulled away, breathless. She followed him with her dark eyes. "I have to go," she panted. "Before anyone sees me." She kissed him again, a quick peck on his lips, a wife's kiss. "I'll be back tomorrow night if I can. Take care of yourself."

"If there is an attack, you must run, Tess. Remember what I have told you. If the French attack through the forest as we sit like lame ducks, blood will run freely and we will all die."

"I'll get you out of here, I'll figure out a way."

Tess glanced once more over her shoulder as she ran and then ducked into the cover of the forest. She hurried along the woods line, praying no one saw her. Marty warned that she must be careful. With so many men and too few authority figures, she could easily be attacked and no one come to her aid. An army camp was a dangerous place for a woman.

It was hard for Tess to keep track of where she was as she ran along the side of the road cut out of the forest.

The camp seemed to spread for miles. She knew Marty's wagon was here somewhere, she just had to find it.

Finally she spotted the sailcloth cover. She stepped into the clearing, cutting in front of a supply cart. Marty was at the back of her wagon seated at the campfire. Tess spotted Sky asleep in the rear of the wagon. There was a slender young blonde woman seated on a camp stool near the fire.

"Found yer man all right?"

Your man. Marty's words sounded strange in her ears. But Marty was right. Raven was her man wasn't he? At least for now. "Yes, I found him chained right where you said he would be at the very front of the line. Thank you so much for your help." Tess set the basket on the tailgate of the wagon.

"Yeah, well just so's you don't get caught," Marty answered. "You get caught an I'll say you jest got away from me. I ain't gonna risk my pap's future with the army on you." She pointed to the blonde. "There's Rosa. Rosa—Tess."

Rosa nodded. Rosa was a pretty, petite, but buxom woman around Tess's age. "Marty told me how you got here. I can't believe you got captured by hostiles and lived to tell."

Tess looked at the fire, not knowing what to say. She really didn't want to discuss her situation with this stranger.

Marty, sensing Tess's awkwardness, went on talking. "Rosa here's what you call a washwoman, fer the officers, course far as I know her washtub ain't never seen a speck of water." She slapped her knee with a chuckle.

Rosa laughed, her voice rich and sultry. "Heres to serve

the King's army. A loyal subject like the rest," she answered gaily.

Tess perched herself on the end of the tailgate, smoothing the blue-tick petticoat she wore. She and Marty had sewn a simple seam down the piece of cloth she'd found in the wagon so she could wear it pleated beneath her muslin shirt. It wasn't much of a petticoat. It was a little short and it came untucked easily from her leather belt, but at least her legs were covered decently . . . at least what she once had considered *decently.*

Tess stared at Rosa curious as to just what the two women were chuckling over. What did Marty mean, Rosa's washtub had never been wet? How could a woman wash without water? And why in God's name had the army brought a washwoman along? Couldn't the officers wash their own clothing?

"What made you want to join up with an army?" Tess asked Rosa.

"Not really a choice." She propped her elbows on her knees and leaned on one fist. "Ran away from my family in New Jersey, in love with a soldier, an officer," she said proudly. "But I made the mistake of not getting him to the altar before I went with him. My man left me and went back to England when his time was up. The bastard had a wife and half a dozen sons I heard later." She shrugged. "Nowhere to go. I couldn't go back to my family and shame them. And I wasn't going to stay back at Fort Cumberland with the rest of the women. They don't talk of anything but birthing babies and the pox." She wrinkled her nose. "And I don't intend on having either."

Marty was watching Rosa and chuckling. "Ah, tell her

the truth. The girl's an innocent. You ain't no wash-woman!"

"I most certainly am." Rosa stood. "And I've an appointment with a young Major. Dirty breeches I understand." She winked and sashayed away.

"Yeah, well don't forget yer washtub," Marty called over her shoulder, her hand cupped to her mouth.

"Wouldn't dream of it." As Rosa passed the side of the wagon, Tess saw her pull a small washtub off the side and carry it off. The white pine of the wood tub was sand-washed clean, the brass rings shiny and untarnished.

Tess heard a man whistle as Rosa walked by the wagon next to them.

"Hey, Rosy! How 'bout a little washin' "

"Got the coin, Jake?" Rosa hollered back as she walked by him.

"Not yet."

"Sorry, Jake! You know I love you deeply, but I'm not running a charity service here."

There was an echo of male laughter as Tess watched the young blonde woman until she disappeared in the sea of wagons and horses. In the distance Tess could hear other men whistling as she passed the campfires in the direction of the officers' field tents.

Tess looked at Marty. "She's not a washwoman, is she? She's a whore."

"Now don't be condemin'. Ain't our place, said the good Lord."

Tess looked away, admonished. "I didn't mean that in a bad way. I just wondered." She turned back to study the fire's flames. "I've been with the Indians a few weeks now and they've made me look at things so differently. They're so accepting of each other."

"Too bad us white folk can't be the same, eh?" Marty pulled a knife from her belt and began to carve at a stick she picked up off the ground. "With white folks it seems like if you're a speck different than the rest, you ain't worthy of their company. Me myself, I been thinkin' 'bout takin' up with the redskins. Got a brave south a here, Cherokee, that's taken a fancy to me. He don't care how I dress or if I like my snuff. Says he's lookin' for a huntin' partner much as a bed partner."

Tess turned to her in amazement. "You would consider living with the Indians?"

Marty shrugged. "My pap, he ain't gonna live forever. Drinks too heavy. Once he's gone, I got no one. Why not?"

Why not? Marty's words echoed in Tess's head. Tess had never really considered the idea of staying with Raven. Of course she couldn't live among savages!

But the Lenape weren't savages, she knew that now. So what was stopping her? She'd been happier these last weeks among the Lenape than she'd been her whole life. Raven. He said he wanted her to go back to Annapolis. Abby. Abby was still far across the ocean, waiting, waiting patiently for Tess to send for her.

A lump rose in Tess's throat. Why was life so complicated? Why didn't she know what she wanted any more? Her future had always been so clear to her. Even when the Mohawk had captured her and murdered Jocelyn, she had known she would escape and return to marry Myron. But then she'd met Raven, and he had flipped her world upside down. Everything was jumbled now. Nothing made sense.

Tess's thoughts went back to what Raven had said about the danger of being here among the English. The tone of his voice had frightened her. She knew Raven well enough to know he didn't exaggerate. He was truly afraid for their lives.

So the problem at hand was escape. Tess knew that it was up to her to figure out a way to get Raven, Sky, and herself out of the English camp before they met up with the French and their Indian allies. If what Raven had said was true, it might be their only chance.

Twenty-three

July 8, 1758
The Monongahela River

Tess walked beside Rosa among a sea of red-coated soldiers. She and Rosa had meandered to the very front of the line so that Tess could catch a glimpse of Raven somewhere just ahead, cutting a path through the jungle-like foliage for the soldiers.

Tess glanced over her shoulder searching for Boeing. If he caught her here in the front of the advancing army, there would be hell to pay. She was supposed to be in the rear where no one would notice her.

Tess gave a sigh. She felt as if she'd walked a thousand miles in these last weeks. Moving through dampness and shadow, the army had crossed ravines and gorges, passed waterfalls, and crawled over ridges. Only through the damp leaves and mist of the early morning did they catch glimpses of the surrounding green mountains they passed.

By the eighteenth of June Braddock's army had reached a place called Little Meadows, less than thirty miles from Fort Dusquesne. But fever and dysentery had spread among the men. The movement of Braddock's army had become so slow and cumbersome with the hundreds of baggage horses, many weak or worthless, that Braddock made the decision to separate his men. He had taken fifteen hundred chosen soldiers, a few wagons and tumbrels, a small herd of cattle, his heavy artillery, a train of pack-horses, and pushed ahead. He left the remainder of the army behind under a Colonel Dunbar's command with orders to push to Fort Dusquesne at their own pace.

When the army split, Tess had become distressed to learn that Raven had gone with Braddock to continue cutting through the forest while she'd been forced by Boeing to remain behind with the slow-moving supplies. It had been more than two weeks since Tess had seen Raven—two weeks of not knowing if he was dead or alive.

When Tess discovered that Boeing would be traveling from Dunbar's camp ahead to carry a message to Braddock she'd thrown herself upon her captor's mercy. She told him she was afraid to remain with Dunbar's army without him, even in Marty's care. She said she feared for what still remained of her respectability. She appealed to his sense of masculinity, telling him that she could only feel safe when she was near him. She'd even squeezed out a tear or two for good measure. Boeing had fallen for it.

When Tess told Marty and Rosa she was riding up to the front with Boeing, Rosa had excitedly proclaimed she was going, too. She told Tess that the good money was with Braddock's men, not Dunbar's copper pinchers. Tess didn't know how Rosa had managed to convince Boeing to take her along. All Tess knew was that early this morning when she'd met Boeing, there had been three horses waiting, with Rosa's washtub tied to the back of one of them. When Tess had asked Rosa, in a whisper, how she'd gotten Boeing to allow her to go she'd winked. "Good washing," she'd giggled.

Tess had waved good-bye to Sky, signing to her that

she would be back the following day. Tears had run down Sky's plump cheeks as she signed again and again, *Don't go, don't leave me.* But Tess had held firm, knowing the child would be safer with Marty. *Tomorrow,* she had signed one last time. *I love you, my brave Sky.* And then she had reined the horse around and followed Boeing and Rosa.

Tess quickened her pace beside Rosa. Two soldiers gave a whistle as they passed and Tess wished Boeing had not confiscated her Mohawk skinning knife. Now all she carried tucked into her belt and hidden by her blue-tick petticoat was a paring knife. Still, it was better than nothing.

Tess heard a horseman coming up behind her and she and Rosa moved to the left to let him by. He was a huge man, taller than anyone Tess knew. He was young, not much older than Tess, with a memorable face and an air about him that emanated confidence. Tess pointed as he rode by. "Who's he?"

"Him?" Rosa raised her eyebrows. "That there's Mr. Washington. His Christian name be George, I think. Fine piece, no?"

Tess watched as the man called Washington turned his mount at the head of the line and began to ride back along the column of soldiers.

"A Virginian. Got money, I think. He'd make a fine catch for a husband. So far I haven't been able to interest him in my services, though."

"He's not wearing a uniform. What's he doing here?"

Rosa shrugged. "I don't know. He's one of what are they called? An aide, that's it. You know. Braddock asks him what he thinks, Washington gives his opinion, and Braddock does what he was going to do anyway." Rosa pointed. "Say, look. There's the axemen." She leaned and whispered. "Do you see your man?"

Tess craned her neck, her heart thumping in her chest. *Please let him be all right,* she begged silently. *Please . . .*

Her prayers were instantly answered as she spotted Raven to the right-forward edge of the column of soldiers. Tess's breath caught in her throat. "There," she whispered, not daring to point.

"Where?" Rosa stood on her tiptoes trying to see over a soldier's head.

"He's the only red man among the axemen. How can you miss him?" Tess giggled, giddy with relief.

"Sweet Mary, mother of God," Rosa breathed crossing herself. "I don't believe I've ever seen a body so fine, and I've seen a few."

Tess laughed with Rosa, admiring Raven with her.

Raven was swinging a long-handled axe, his easily defined back and shoulder muscles rippling with each fluid movement. The chains at his feet and hands seemed to be naught but an annoyance as they clanged with each swing. Around his neck was his prized medicine bag that Tess knew held his grandfather's bit of quartz. He was wearing nothing save a pair of tight red soldier's breeches and his own knee-high leather moccasins. His skin, as suntanned red as a potter's clay, was covered in a thin sheen of perspiration. Because he was facing away from her, Tess couldn't see his face, only his shiny black hair pulled back in a thick braid, and the strain of the muscles in his neck as he swung the axe one last time and felled the tree.

"Sweet heaven, were he mine, I believe I'd jump his bones day and night."

Tess felt her cheeks grow warm with a mixture of embarrassment and pride. "I told you, we're not really man and wife."

"And you think that's what it takes to jump a man?" Rosa gave a laugh. "Not hardly."

"Rosa!"

Rosa laughed. "Sweet Mother of God! If you love that man the way I think you do, you'll be getting him free and taking yourselves back to some tepee to make more little redskins."

"He's Delaware. They don't live in tepees," Tess corrected. "And I told you. Once he's free, I'll be returning to Annapolis."

Rosa shook her head making a clicking sound between her teeth. "You're a fool if you let him go. Is he big? You know, his cod." She stared at Raven as he turned around to grab the tree and drag it off the path. "Looks big in those breeches from here."

"Rosa, you're embarrassing me," Tess moaned.

"So how are you going to get to see him? Boeing says we're going back at first light tomorrow before the army crosses the river. Boeing says they're afraid of an ambush at the Narrows so the army's going to cross the Monongahela and then cross it again." Rosa gave a shudder. "Just the thought of Indian attack makes my blood run cold. I intend to have a profitable night, and then I'm high-tailing it back to Dunbar's camp."

Tess watched Raven as he dragged the tree as thick as his calf and as tall as a two-story house out of the way of two men rolling a cannon. He hadn't spotted her, which was just as well. She didn't want him to know she was here, not yet. He would only worry.

Tess looked up at the trees hanging ominously overhead. Despite the breeze, the air was close and foreboding. The army was surrounded on four sides by dense forest and the unknown. Once again she thought about what Raven had said about an ambush. Braddock's army was barely eight miles from Dusquesne and still there had been no attack. Maybe Raven had been wrong. Once Braddock's men made it to the fort, Boeing said the English cannon would splinter the walls in a matter of hours and Fort Dusquesne would fall.

Tess felt a sudden urgent need to be with Raven. She had missed him these last weeks and she was afraid, afraid for him, afraid for herself and Sky. Boeing had sent a message back to Annapolis to Myron, but he had said it was unsafe to send her home right now, even with an escort. The French-allied Indians were picking off Braddock and Dunbar's stragglers and those who wandered from the main body of the armies on a daily basis. Some, they say, were just murdered and scalped; those were the lucky ones. The unlucky were said to be dragged off to endure unspeakable cruelties before being killed.

Tess watched Raven as he lifted his axe and began to cut away the lower branches of an oak tree so that the heavy artillery could pass by. Tonight she would go to Raven. Tonight they would figure out a way to get him free. She shivered despite the overwhelming heat and humidity of the day. She just had to get Raven free before something terrible happened. And something terrible was going to happen, she could feel it in her bones.

It was near midnight when Tess finally heard Boeing's breathy snoring. Only then did she crawl out of her bedroll and out from under the cannon where Boeing had bid her sleep.

Boeing was asleep on his back, fully clothed in his buckskins, his musket cradled in his arms. Beside him, Rosa's bedroll was still empty. Tess looked out over the sleeping army, spotting the shadows of the many sentries. Rosa was out there somewhere, no doubt in one of the officers' tents, entertaining.

Tess took Boeing's waterbag from a pile of belongings at his feet and crept silently away. Tucked in a bag she wore on her waist was a small ration of bread. It was all she'd managed to take without being noticed. With so few soldiers willing to venture far enough into the forest to kill wild game, the army rations had grown sparse.

Tess crouched behind another cannon as a sentry approached. She tried to remember all that Raven had taught her about the forest and about the enemy. She had to believe that she was invisible to the soldier. She stood motionless becoming one with the warm metal, trying to imagine what it must feel like to be made of wood and iron.

The sentry passed not noticing the woman who stood so close she could have touched his hand with hers.

Tess skirted along the camp, avoiding the fires where men remained awake playing at cards or dice, too fearful of the French and their Indians to sleep peacefully. She knew where she would find Raven, at the very head of the column. His guards would have chained him to a tree where the army and forest met.

When Tess spotted Raven she knew that he had heard her approaching. He was staring at her, his black eyes glimmering in the pale moonlight.

"You should not be here," were his first words. "I thought you had remained behind with the packhorses and wagons."

Tess crawled the last few feet toward him. Less than

twenty yards away, hired axemen slept around the dying red coals of a cookfire.

"How long must I be gone before you're glad to see me?" she asked, half teasing, half serious. The sound of his voice made her chest ache. *Heaven above, but she had missed him.*

Raven followed her with his coal eyes as she slipped the water skin from her shoulder and made herself busy with the tie that kept it watertight. "Tell me why you are here, my Tess."

His face was thinner than she had remembered, his high cheekbones more defined with dark shadows beneath his eyes. "I had to see you," she whispered passionately. "Drink this." She pushed the water skin to his mouth. "I had to know you were all right."

He took the water in great gulps. *How often do they give him food and water?* she thought. *Not often enough.*

"You were safer behind," he said, his voice raspy with the strain of the day and the lack of proper hydration. "You should have stayed there."

She brushed her fingers along his jawline, a lump rising in her throat. She hated to see him like this, chained to a tree like a rabid dog. "I told you. I'm fine. But we have to get you loose, Raven. I'm afraid for you." She clasped his gaunt cheeks between her palms.

"I am all right."

"No—And I am truly afraid. It's something I can't explain, just something I feel all of a sudden."

He sighed, softening his tone as he brought her closer to him, taking care not to disturb the chains that bound him to the tree. She rested her cheek on his bare shoulder.

"It is the way of the Lenape to feel the struggle of the

cycle of life and death around us," he told her gently. "Some say it is a blessing, others, a curse."

She lifted her head to stare into his dark eyes, eyes that made her weak in her knees. "It's not just me, then? You feel it, too?"

"For weeks I have known something terrible circles this army of men. A darkness that will swallow them up." He clenched his fists in anger. "And I am powerless, powerless to protect you. I should never have let this happen."

"It's not your fault. Wouldn't Dream Woman say it was just fate . . . in the stars? *Manito's* will?" She smiled at him, at his unfailing bravery. "Now stop worrying about me and let's figure out what we're going to do about you. I told you, I can take care of myself. Last week some soldier thought he'd take liberties with me. I brained him with a cookpot. They say he's still got no vision in one eye, but he's left me alone." She forced herself to smile as she pushed bites of bread into his mouth. Then she grew more serious. "Now tell me how are we going to get you free of these chains, Raven."

"The guard carries the key to the padlocks," he said chewing hungrily. He reached out as he spoke, smoothing a stray lock of hair that had escaped her simple chignon. "There is no way to get his key short of killing him for it."

"I'll do it," Tess whispered, peering out into the darkness. "Tell me which one he is."

Raven laughed. "What a fierce wildcat you have become, my Tess."

Still on her knees she turned back to face him, her face only inches from his. She had missed this closeness to him, this feeling that together the two of them made one. She stroked his cheek, his neck, his shoulder ridged with cuts and scabs. She could have sworn that she detected the marks of a whip on his back, but she said nothing. "Be serious with me," she went on. "Tell me what I can do."

"You can go back to the Dun-bar camp. Better, you can get the man called Boeing to take you home and let your My-Ron pay him for returning you safely."

"Don't say that. I won't abandon you."

"There is no way for me to escape. My hope is that once we reach the fort—if we reach the fort—one of my brothers will see me and set me free before it is too late."

Tess lowered her head, fighting tears that stung at the backs of her eyes. He sounded as if there was little hope. She rested her hands on his bare shoulders to steady herself. "I love you, you know."

"Shhh," he crooned, pushing back the hair that had fallen across her face. His chains clinked as he moved. "The words are not necessary."

She lifted her head, her gaze searching his. "There's no way for you to get loose? You're certain?"

"Not now. Perhaps soon. But you cannot help, Tess. You can only help this man by promising that you will go. If I know that you are safe, I can turn my thoughts to my escape and not worry about you."

What Raven said made sense, she supposed. Braddock had almost reached the fort. Another two days and Raven might possibly come in contact with men from his own village or another Lenape village. Surely someone would recognize him as one of their own and set him free.

Tess looked up into Raven's dark eyes. "All right," she said quietly. "Boeing says we return to Dunbar's camp in the morning. I'll go, but not because I want to." He smiled and his smile warmed her heart. "You really are going to be all right, aren't you?" she asked.

"It is not my time to die, yet, Tess of mine. Now give this man a kiss and go back to your scout who will watch over you. Let him take you to the home you long for, the home this man has kept you from."

Tess felt herself tremble. All this talk of returning to Annapolis had been so easy. Now she realized the reality of returning home. Suddenly she was terrified that she would never see Raven again. She flung her arms around him. "Swear you won't let them kill you. Swear it Raven. Swear it!"

He kissed the curve of her jaw, a soft fleeting kiss. "Not if it is in my power to prevent it. This man promises. He promises in the name of the honor of the Bear Clan of the Lenape." He kissed her again.

Tess could feel her heart pounding in her chest. *I love this man, I love him more than life,* was all she could think. It didn't matter that he had never said he loved her. All that mattered was his voice as he crooned soft words in his native tongue. All that mattered was the touch of his lips on her throat.

Tess ran the palms of her hands over his broad scarred chest, letting her eyes drift shut. There were so many cuts and tears on his perfect sun-kissed flesh. The hard, dangerous work of clearing the forest had taken its toll on his body. Her fingers found the nearly healed scar of the musket wound she'd inflicted and a lump rose in her throat. She climbed into his lap, wrapping her legs around his waist and pressed her lips to the wound.

"No," he whispered, his breath hot in her ear. "We cannot. They will hear us, Tess,"

"I don't care," she flung. She covered his face in fervent kisses. "I don't care. I want you, Raven. I want to remember what it feels like . . ."

Tess heard Raven groan as she settled more squarely on his lap, her arms wrapped around his neck. She could feel his loins swelling, pressing against her woman's mound. Her veins were suddenly running white hot with a desperate desire she had never experienced before.

Tess pressed her mouth to Raven's and their tongues twisted in an urgency born of danger. "I can't go back, Raven," she whispered. He was kissing the pulse of her throat, sending shivers of pleasure through her. Tess's chest rose and fell raggedly as she tore at the opening of her muslin shirt, needing to feel his mouth on her aching breasts.

"You must go," Raven said.

"No." Tess arched her back, guiding his head to one erect nipple, threading her fingers through his thick hair. Somewhere in the back of her mind she heard the clink of his chains and she thought of the guards sleeping so closely to them. But it was too late to care. The want inside her was too strong to stop what she knew she'd begun.

"I'll go back with the army, but not to Annapolis," she whispered in his ear, guiding his hand over her breasts. "My place is with you, my husband."

"Tess, you do not know what you say. It is what you have wanted since the first day. You have wanted to go home. . . . Your sister."

"This is home. You, you are home. I'll find a way to bring Abby to the village, Raven. I'll have you both." She pressed her mouth to his as she fumbled with the tie at his red breeches.

Raven groaned as she wrapped her fingers around his

stiff rod. "Tess, Tess, this too dangerous for us both," he murmured, his voice thick. "And I cannot move with the chains."

"I don't care," she breathed, slipping off his lap. All she cared about was this fierce love she had for Raven and the fear that she would lose him. "Just sit. Let me make love to you like you've made love to me so many times."

Then Tess lowered her head. She heard the chains on Raven's wrists clink as he guided her head. She touched the soft tip of his engorged shaft with her tongue hesitantly and she tasted his saltiness.

Raven gasped.

How many times had he given her the pleasure of his mouth since he had wed her? Tess wondered. She stroked him with her tongue, exploring the length of him. Now she wanted to give him the same pleasure. *Was this what it was to truly love? To want to give entirely of yourself to the other?*

Tess heard Raven groan in passion and felt him shudder. The thought that she could give him a little happiness here in this terrible place empowered her. She wanted to hear his sensuous moans; she wanted to give to him what he had given to her so many times.

Raven's shaft was hard and pulsing in her hand and yet his skin was as soft as new-tanned leather. She took him in her mouth and he groaned, threading his fingers through her hair. He called her name as she stroked him. He crooned in his native tongue. It didn't matter to Tess that she didn't understand much of what he said, what mattered was his voice.

"Ah, Tess, enough," he murmured huskily in her ear.

"Sit here upon me and let this man take you to the stars and back."

She looked up him, her eyes laughing, crying at the same time. She loved him so much that it hurt.

Tess rested her hands on his broad bare shoulders, hiking up her petticoat until it bunched around her waist.

Raven rested his hands on her hips, his clanking chains restricting his movement.

"Shhhh," she whispered in his ear, nipping at the lobe. "The guards will hear you." She pushed down his hands. "Let me."

Resting her hands on his shoulders she raised her hips and then lowered them, guiding him with her hand until he penetrated her. Tess couldn't contain a moan of pleasure. She had wanted this for so long; she had forgotten what it felt like to be possessed by Raven, to possess him as she did now.

Tess looped her arms around his neck and arched her back so that he could take her taut nipple in his mouth. "There has to be a way," she whispered recklessly, her breath coming faster. "There must be a way for us to be together. I love you too much to let you go, Raven. You don't have to love me back. That doesn't matter. I have enough love for both of us. Just need me. Just want me. That's all I would ever ask of you."

"This man wants you," Raven answered, his voice husky with passion. He was rising and falling beneath her, setting the rhythm of their lovemaking. Theirs was a union of urgency, of desperation.

The seriousness of Tess's words were lost to them both in the passion of the moment. All Tess could think of as she rose and fell, her entire body shuddering with each strong thrust, was that this might be the last time she and

Raven would ever make love as husband and wife. Hot tears fell down her cheeks as she drove harder, the need for fulfillment suddenly stronger than the need to live.

At the very same moment that Tess threw back her head in ultimate ecstasy, she felt Raven's body convulse. He spilled into her, calling her name. Tess's entire body shuddered again and again, shivers of delight rippling through her veins.

Raven held Tess in his arms and she laid her cheek on his shoulder. He went to withdraw from her and she shook her head.

"Just a minute longer," she whispered. "I want to feel you inside me just a minute longer."

He kissed her damp temples, first one and then the other. He stroked her back through the bunched muslin of her man's shirt. He kissed the hollow of her shoulder and when he found his voice, he spoke, his words as gentle as the summer breeze that now cooled them.

"What you said of loving me enough for the both of us. It is not true, Tess."

She lifted her head from his shoulder looking into his haunting black eyes. "But it is true. I love you so much that if you'll just have me as your wife, I can make myself content. You and I, and Sky, and Abby. We could be a family. That's what I want, Raven. That's my dream now."

A smiled played at the corners of his mouth. He pressed his finger to her lips to silence her. "What I wanted to tell you was that it is not true that this man does not love you."

Tess's heart leaped in her breast. "What are you saying?" she whispered.

"*K'daholel, ki-ti-hi,* that is what this man is saying. I love you as the heavens love the stars. I love you as the

Creator loves all He has created." He followed her gaze with his, searching for understanding. "It is not until now when I consider I may truly lose you that I know I love you. To admit this kind of love, this weakness, is hard for this man, but I must be true to my heart and to yours."

Fresh tears ran down Tess's cheeks. Raven caught one with his fingertip and brought it to his lips. She threw her arms around him, her chest bursting with joy, her throat constricted with shock. She knew he loved her, she knew it deep in heart, but to have him admit it, made this moment in time perfect . . . perfect forever.

"Tell me the words again," she whispered. "Tell me, Raven."

He took her hand in his and began to kiss her fingertips one pad at a time. *"K'daholel. K'daholel, ki-ti-hi.* I love you, my heart," he said softly.

She smiled, repeating after him. *"K . . . k'daholel, ki-ti-hi.* I love you, my heart."

His hands encircling her waist, Raven gently lifted her, withdrawing from inside her. "Now you must go," he whispered. "Before we are caught."

She pushed down her blue-tick petticoat and pulled up the shoulders of the wrinkled shirt. Then she reached out and grabbing the leather thong that held his medicine pouch around his neck, she twisted it, pulling him toward her. "I'll go back to Dunbar's camp, but I'll wait for you there, Raven. You understand? I won't go to Annapolis with Boeing. *I'll wait for you.*"

"I do not know how long it will take me to escape. It would be better if you—"

"I'll wait," she repeated fiercely.

He sighed. "Go, then," he urged. "Go, Tess, go safely

into the night. Let my love for you protect you as I would protect you with my bare hands were I at your side."

She kissed him hard, wanting him to remember the taste and the feel of her lips on his, and then she ran off into the darkness of the British camp.

Twenty-four

"Wake up, both of you wenches." Boeing pushed Tess with the toe of his boot. "I said get your lazy arses up."

Tess sat up, wiping the sleep from her eyes. It was barely dawn. She had been sleeping so soundly that she hadn't heard the commotion of Braddock's army preparing to march. There was an edge to Boeing's voice that alarmed her. "Are we going back now?" She gave Rosa a push to wake her.

Boeing frowned, squinting his one good eye. "Nope. We got orders to stay put with the army. They say it ain't safe for me to go back to Dunbar's camp right now, 'specially with you two *ladies*. Soldiers spotted some hostiles with ugly painted faces less than a quarter mile from here just before dawn. They don't know how many more there are."

"I don't understand." Tess gave Rosa another push, this time harder. A morning mist hung in the air warm and humid. "Rosa! Get up!" She turned back to Boeing, just a little afraid. "So we're not going back to Dunbar's camp today?"

"Nope. And we can't stay here or the hostiles'll scalp us for sure. Looks like we're headed for Fort Dusquesne with the rest of 'em, like it or not." He picked up his musket and threw it onto his shoulder. "So you two get the horses packed and get yourselves mounted. We'll be crossing the river shortly. We'll cross here then back again about eight miles downstream so's to avoid the place where it would be too easy to ambush us."

"Rosa!" Tess slapped her friend on her bare thigh as Rosa rolled over sleepily. "Get up. We're crossing the river with the army."

Rosa sat up with a groan and pushed a hank of blonde hair out of her face. "What?" She squinted in the bright morning sunlight.

Tess got to her feet. Boeing's talk of scalping made her nervous, but the thought that she would remain with Raven excited her. They wouldn't be separated, that was what was important! She wouldn't think about the danger of remaining with the English army. She wouldn't think about the terrible foreboding feeling both she and Raven shared. "Braddock told Boeing he couldn't go back to Dunbar's camp today, Rosa. It's not safe because of Indians. So we're crossing the river with the army."

Rosa's eyes widened with fear. "I . . . I think I'd rather just go back to Dunbar's camp. I . . . I don't want to stay."

"Didn't you hear what I said?" Tess shook out her bedroll and then dropped to her knees to roll it up. "We can't go back. It's not safe. There're Indians out there. Unfriendly Indians."

Rosa pulled her knees up hugging them to her body. "What . . . what if they attack?"

"It's a possibility," Tess answered frankly. "But what do you think is a better bet? Trying to get back to Dunbar with one man and a musket to protect you, or fifteen hundred soldiers and cannons?"

Rosa swallowed hard. "I guess you're right." She got to her feet, pushing down her stained petticoats. "I'm just scared, Tess. I should have stayed back at Fort Cumberland. I didn't know it would be like this."

"I'm scared, too," Tess said gently.

"Oh, you are not." Rosa began to roll up her bedroll. "You're not afraid of anything. I've never met a woman like you."

With her bedroll tucked under one arm, Tess dropped her other hand on Rosa's shoulder and gave her a gentle squeeze. "It's all right, Rosa. Don't be afraid. Braddock's got fifteen hundred of the finest soldiers in the British army. We're going to be fine." Giving Rosa her best smile, Tess walked off toward the horses to saddle up.

We're going to be fine, echoed in her head. *Going to be fine. . . .* She just hoped her hollow words gave Rosa more comfort than she'd given herself.

Braddock crossed the Monongahela River for the second time near one o'clock in the afternoon. As Tess rode her horse up onto the bank in the midst of a regiment of Virginians, she turned back to observe.

Braddock had sent a strong advance party to the far shore, and once they discovered no enemy troops waiting in ambush, he'd ordered the bulk of his army across the river. They made quite a grand sight with the whistle of their fife and drums, the flying of their banners, and the sea of mounted officers, light cavalry, red-coated regulars, blue-coated Virginians, wagons and tumbrels, cannon, howitzers and coehorns, train of packhorses, and drove of cattle. Tess watched for a long time as the grand procession forded the river and entered the bordering forest. Who would dare attack an army so impressive? she wondered. If the French were going to advance upon them, wouldn't they have done it before now when Braddock was practically at the back door of Fort Dusquesne?

After a brief rest, the army pushed on, advancing on the French fort which lay on a point of land between where the Allegheny and the Monongahela rivers joined to form the Ohio River. Braddock knew the French had to know they were coming, but he was hoping he could get his men to the walls of the fort before they had time to adequately prepare themselves.

Tess rode between Boeing and Rosa trying to fight the uneasiness she had felt in her belly since this morning. Several guides and a handful of Virginian light horsemen led the army down a crude path cut through the woods along steep foothills and parallel to the Monongahela River. The path led to Fort Dusquesne and victory for the British army.

The scouts and light horse rode reconnaissance, followed by three hundred soldiers, a body of axemen to open the road, two cannons with tumbrels and tool wagons, with the rear guard at the end and flanking parties sweeping the woods on either side of the path. The main bulk of the army followed closely behind with the artillery and wagons moving along the road and the troops fanning out through the forest a hundred yards to the left and right. The packhorses, the cattle and their drovers, were left to make their way through the dense thickets with a body of regulars and provincials bringing up the rear.

Tess rode with Boeing and Rosa down the path just behind a column of soldiers. Over her shoulder Tess could see the animal drovers trying to push their herds through the walls of briars that covered the forest floor. The sun shone brightly overhead in cloudless wonder.

Tess shifted in her saddle hoping to catch a glimpse of Raven. She hadn't seen him since last night so he didn't know she had been unable to return to the safety of Dunbar's camp in the rear. She knew he'd be angry when he found out. But there was nothing to be done about it now. And now they would be together when he escaped. Together they would go back for Sky and then head for the Lenape village where they would all be safe.

Tess, on horseback, was approaching a wide and bushy ravine that crossed the path when she heard the first bone-chilling war whoop. There was no warning, only the terrifying sound that broke the stillness of the late afternoon. Boeing immediately pulled up on his mount, turning around and calling out to Tess and Rosa to follow him.

The afternoon air exploded with the sound of musket fire. Ahead, through the dense foliage, Tess could see Braddock's advance column led by Lieutenant-colonel Gage. For a moment she sat frozen on her horse and watched as the soldiers turned deliberately into line and fired at their assailants whom could now be seen all around them.

There were savages, savages everywhere with painted black and red faces and muskets. Feathered arrows rained upon the advance column of soldiers as they spun their cannon around and fired into the cover of the trees.

Tess heard Boeing's voice harsh in her ears as he fought his mount closer to hers and pulled the reins from her hands. The stillness of the forest had broken into a bloody melee of sights and sounds.

Having successfully captured both Tess's horse's reins and Rosa's, Boeing was now attempting to lead them back through the columns of soldiers that had ridden and walked behind them. Any semblance of order vanished as the French Canadians and their Indian allies raced through the forest surrounding Braddock's men on both flanks, hiding behind every tree, every bush, crouching in every gully and ravine.

Tess screamed in terror as musket fire whistled overhead and arrows flew by. The sound of the English and French muskets and the English cannon were deafening in the dense arches of the damp forest.

All Tess could think as she held tightly to her horse's mane was of Raven. Where was he? Somewhere ahead with the axemen, still chained at his hands and feet! Boeing had gotten her horse turned around and was making some headway through the congestion of soldiers, horses, cannon, and herd of cattle that now ran wild through the ranks. She couldn't flee like this. Not without knowing what had become of Raven.

Without thinking, Tess hurled herself off her horse. She hit the ground hard and rolled. Through the whistle of the musket balls, the blast of gunpowder, and the shouts of the men, she heard Boeing curse her. She scrambled through the grass to avoid the sharp hooves of a runaway mount.

The sounds of the men's screams and the ricochet of musket balls off the trees was so frightening that Tess wanted to do nothing but crawl into a hole, cover her ears, and wait for the battle to end. But she couldn't, not when Raven was out there ahead of her somewhere in the midst of the massacre.

Afraid she'd be hit if she ran, Tess started to crawl. Behind her, she heard Rosa's screams. Boeing was shouting for her to go on. She screamed again and again that she couldn't, and then Tess lost the sound of their voices to the roar of a cannon.

As Tess made her way forward she tried to imagine what it would be like to be invisible. She remembered the day she and Raven and Takooko had run from the Mohawk and hidden from them in the brush. She thought that if she believed she was invisible, she would be. If she believed she could reach Raven, unharmed, she would reach him.

Everywhere around her the English soldiers were falling into line to fire volleys into the trees, but their enemies, hidden by every stump, tree trunk, and fallen log, fired from their cover. Death surrounded Tess. It blinded and deafened her. The bitter black powder from their muskets filled her nostrils. She could taste the metallic taste of the fallen soldiers' blood on the tip of her tongue.

Please, Tess prayed again and again. *Please let me see him one last time. Please let him be safe.*

All sense of direction was lost to Tess. She stumbled to her feet and ran blindly. They were going to die; they were all going to die. The French and the Indians had them surrounded. As the English soldiers bunched in the gullied road, their enemies picked them off one by one from the cover of the trees. From a hill above came steady musket fire. English soldiers' bodies littered the ground, some wounded, many dead.

Tess tripped over a man's legs, and fell to her knees beside a faceless soldier, his head nothing but a bloody mass. Someone grabbed her ankle and she screamed, kicking wildly. She scrambled to her feet, running into the smoke.

"Raven," she called, knowing she had to be near where the axemen had been when they'd been ambushed. "Raven, where are you?"

The smoke from all the gunfire stung her eyes and she

wiped at them. No one seemed to notice her as she stood in the middle of the chaos, tears running down her cheeks.

Then she heard a voice. At first she was certain it was only in her head . . . but then it grew more distinct.

"Tess . . . *ki-ti-hi* . . ." *My heart* . . .

"Raven!" she screamed hysterically. "Raven, where are you?"

"Here," he answered, his voice strong. "Here, Tess!"

She found him chained to a maple sapling. Somehow in the midst of the initial confusion of the attack, his guard had thought to chain his feet to the tree so he couldn't escape. Tess laughed until her laughter became a sob as she flung herself at his feet.

"Oh, Raven," she breathed, clasping his face between her palms. "What have they done to you?"

"Why are you here, Tess?" His tone was harsh, but beneath the words, she heard the gentleness she had come to know in him. "You told this man you would go back to safety. I thought you were safe!"

She flung her arms around him knowing they might only have a few seconds before one or both were hit by stray shots. She shook her head. "I tried. They wouldn't go this morning. It was too dangerous!"

"You must run! This will not last long. The English will not live, Tess. The French will kill everything that moves."

She looked around wildly. "Na-Kee, Taande, the others, have you seen them?"

He lifted a hand, his chains clanking, and brushed his bloody fingertips across her dirty cheek. "There are so many, Tess, not just Lenape, but Shawnee, Ottawa, Mingoe. There are hundreds, Tess."

She squatted and began to pull madly on the chain that

bound his feet to the sapling. "There has to be a way to get you free!" she shouted above the din of musket fire and shouting men. All around them was chaos, wounded horses raced down the road, frightened English soldiers were firing on each other in confusion.

Raven grabbed Tess's shoulder, sinking his fingers into her flesh until her arm ached. Slowly he pulled her upright. Grasping both arms he shook her. "Go, Tess!"

"Not without you!" She flung her arms around him again, pressing her lips to his. "I love you too much! I'd rather die here with you."

He smiled and kissed her mouth. "I do not doubt your willingness to die for this man, my brave Tess, but there are others who need you. The child, Sky—your sister," he reminded gently.

She was sobbing now. He was right. She knew he was right. But she couldn't leave him here to die! She couldn't do it! "Where are the keys?" she demanded. "The keys to the padlocks to your chains?"

"It is no use! The guard carried them. He's gone . . . dead."

Behind her Tess heard a voice shouting her name.

Tess peered up into Raven's face. God in heaven, but he was handsome, even with his dirty, sooty face. "It's Boeing," she whispered. "I ran from him."

"Go," Raven ordered. "The scout can get you out if anyone will."

"Not without you," she repeated stubbornly. She scanned the area surrounding them where the bodies were beginning to pile up. She remembered Raven's guard. He had a hooked beak nose. She'd know him if she saw him again. "I'll get the keys," she cried. "If he's dead he's got to be here somewhere!"

Tess pulled away from Raven. Her muslin shirt tore as he tried to hold onto her. "No, Tess! *Matta!*"

But Tess ignored Raven's voice as she climbed over the bodies searching for the man with the hooked nose. Some of the men were merely wounded while others stared up into the sky with lifeless eyes. Behind her she heard Boeing calling her name.

"There, there she is!" she heard Raven shout to Boeing.

Tess turned to see Boeing riding straight for her, a musket in each hand.

"No," Tess screamed. She tried to run, but there were soldiers everywhere. They ran into her. They fell at her feet.

She could hear Boeing's horse gaining on her. "No, Raven," Tess screamed. "I'll find him. I'll find the guard! I'll get the keys. We'll go together!"

Tess tried to feign right as Boeing bore down upon her, but he was too fast for her. He reached down from his horse and grabbed her shoulder with an iron-clad grip. Tess screamed and kicked.

"Enough, bitch!" Boeing shouted. "Can't you see I'm trying to save your lily ass?"

"I don't want to be saved," Tess moaned as he hauled her up and into his lap with one beefy hand. "I don't want to be saved . . ." she whispered desperately as she collapsed over the horse's mane.

As Boeing wheeled his mount around, Tess lifted her head from the horn of the saddle. Her tears blinded her. She pushed back a handful of hair to get one last look at Raven as Boeing carried her away. "Raven!" she called putting her hand out to him.

"Do not give up hope!" he called to her. "Watch for me on a moonless night, *ki-ti-hi!*"

Then he was gone, gone to the mist of the mountain, the smoke of the cannon, and the blur of red uniforms.

Tess dropped her head to her hands where she sat on the saddle pinned by Boeing's body and sobbed. She didn't care if they made it out alive. What did it matter? They would kill him, sooner or later. Raven was dead, dead . . .

Twenty-five

Raven watched as Tess disappeared in the smoke of the cannon and musket fire. A lump rose in his throat and he fought the tears that stung the backs of his eyes. He was a warrior. He had seen death and destruction many times, but nothing was as painful as seeing his Tess vanish, knowing the odds were against him that he would ever see her again.

Raven looked out over the woods' road that had become a battlefield. Musket fire came steadily out of the surrounding forest while the English soldiers still foolishly attempted to line up in the European fashion and fire at the invisible enemy. The scent of death hung heavy in the air. Braddock's men would not escape. The French and their Indian allies would not give up until the last redcoat had fallen.

Out of the corner of his eye, through the thick, black smoke, Raven thought he spotted a familiar face. Was that his guard, still standing? It was.

Raven watched him as he stumbled across the gullied road. Was it possible he could convince the man to release him? A Lenape warrior never begged the enemy; he died an honorable man. But Raven thought of Tess and of the love he now realized they shared. He looked back at the guard who was coming toward him, but moving without purpose. He appeared lost . . . frightened.

Perhaps today was not Raven's day to die after all. The sudden appearance of the hook-nosed axeman couldn't be coincidence. Dream Woman always said there were no co-incidences in life, only the Creator's mighty hand at work.

Raven called out to the guard and the man stopped, squinting. Raven waved him toward him. The guard's thigh was bleeding heavily. "Let this man go," Raven shouted. "Do not leave me to be slaughtered."

Tears ran down the big axeman's cheeks as he limped toward Raven. "Sweet Jesus, we're gonna die. We're all gonna die. They got us surrounded."

"Let this man loose and I will take you from this place. I will lead you to safety."

The guard slumped against the young sapling he had left Raven chained to. He was growing weak from loss of blood. "You . . . you're a prisoner. I ain't supposed to let you go. They . . . they said they'd pay me extra once we reached Dusquesne."

"You will not reach the fort, brother." Raven lifted his chained hands, offering his wrists where the padlock hung. "Unchain this man and you will have a chance to live."

The guard's gaze met Raven's and for a moment the two men considered each other.

"Ah, what the hell," the guard suddenly muttered. "I never believed in it, chainin' a man like a dog. Worst thing that can happen is you kill me. You or another redskin, what difference will it make? I ain't never gonna see the Chesapeake again anyway."

Raven felt his heart pounding in his chest as the man fumbled for the key that hung on a leather thong on his belt. Another moment and Raven would be free!

The guard slipped the key into the padlock and the metal clanked as the lock fell open and the chains dropped to the ground.

Rubbing his raw wrists, Raven took the key from the guard and unlocked his feet. The weight of the chains gone, Raven stood tall, taking in a deep breath. It was not until he was free that he fully realized how heavily the chains of the white-hairs had weighed upon his spirit.

Raven reached for a dead man's musket and the guard shied. "I will not shoot you, friend," Raven said as he grabbed a powder horn and a shot bag. "I must have a way to defend myself." Checking the load on the weapon, Raven leapt over the dead man whose weapon he'd confiscated. "Follow me, friend of mine," he shouted to the guard. "You and I will both see the sun set this day."

At a loss as to what else to do, the guard fell in behind Raven. He ran beside him as best he could, dragging his bad leg. Raven raced around a clump of trees and headed into the forest, directly into the line of fire.

He waved to the guard to catch up to him and crouched behind a fallen hickory tree to wait. "You must stay behind me," he told the guard. "Run when this man says run, drop to the ground when this man says drop."

The guard nodded his head. "I got ye!" He gave him a hesitant smile. "You really are gonna try and get me out a here, ain't ye?"

"Those are my men who shoot from the hill," Raven explained. "If I can reach them before they kill us," he shrugged, "we will make it out."

The guard wiped at the sweat that beaded above his upper lip. "This'll make me a turncoat you know, takin' asylum with the enemy."

Raven stared at the guard. "Have you not seen enough

death for one day?" He brought his fist to his chest. "This man chooses no side. I will not fight for Frenchmen or English. I will go home to my people." *Home to Tess, if I can find her,* he thought.

The guard chewed on his lip, glancing over his shoulder. The English were still falling. "Hell, this ain't never been my battle." He lifted his rifle. "Lead on."

Glancing behind him at a handful of redcoats attempting to load a cannon, Raven ran to the next tree for cover. Musket balls were flying through the air from both sides and he and the guard were caught in the middle. The sound of a cannon boomed and Raven threw himself to the leafy ground, pulling the guard down with him. Cannon shrapnel flew over their heads, striking the tree trunks and branches so that leaves and twigs rained down on them.

Raven lay on the ground for a moment, panting. He knew that only a miracle would see him and the guard who had helped him to the crest of the hill in the distance. He also knew that miracles happened. So, whispering a silent prayer, he moved to the next tree and then to the next. When he heard the crashing of brush and the crunch of leaves beneath booted feet he swung around and fired without hesitation.

The guard dropped flat to the ground. "Sweet Jesus," he cried as he turned around to look at the felled soldier. "I thought you was shootin' on me!"

"Get up," Raven commanded, as he retrieved a lead ball and wadding to reload. He dropped a patch over the barrel and seated the ball as he glanced out of the corner of his eye. Now and then he could catch a glimpse of men in the trees up the embankment. He was certain at least some of them were Lenape. He crammed the ball down the bar-

rel with his rod and dumped a little fine black powder
into the frizzen pan. If he could just get close enough to
call out to his Lenape brothers, if he could just avoid the
English fire another moment or two, he might well escape
in one piece.

Ahead, a clearing stretched between one clump of trees
and the next. The embankment appeared slippery, with flat
rocks and a steep incline. Raven eyed the distance between
himself and the next bit of cover. He could hear his Lenape brothers shouting the war cry.

Raven turned to the guard who lay flat on the ground,
his cheek pressed into the damp earth. "We must make
it to there." He pointed. "Can you run that far?"

The guard made a face. "I don't know. The leg's awful
bad."

"At the top of the hill we will bandage it."

The guard pushed himself up with his musket. "All
righty. I trusted you this far, redskin. Guess I can go a
little further."

Raven glanced over his shoulder at the guard and gave
a nod. With that, the two men picked up their muskets
and darted across the clearing. Musket shot ricocheted
through the trees. The few seconds it took Raven to reach
the cover of the trees stretched into what seemed like
hours.

"*Maata, nuxans!*" Raven shouted. "*Lennape n'hackey!*
I am Lenape! Do not shoot!"

Raven could still hear the shots being fired from below
where the English still scrambled, but the volleys were
becoming erratic. There no longer seemed to be enough
men standing to fight. Ahead, he saw the flash of a red
brother as he leapt from one tree to behind the next.

"*Lennape n'hackey,*" Raven repeated. Another three

steps, another second, and he and his guard friend would make the cover of the trees.

Suddenly a red man, his face blackened with war paint, stepped out from behind a tree, swinging his war club.

"Lennape n'hackey!" Raven shouted, halting to protect the guard. "This man behind me is my friend. Do not shoot us," he insisted in Algonquian.

The painted man slowly lowered his war club. *"Wee-ee-yox-qua?* Is that you, Raven, son of Dream Woman?"

Raven sighed audibly. After all these weeks what a relief it was to hear his native tongue. *"Kehella!"* He threw up one hand to meet the other man's, realizing he recognized him. "Beaver Pelt, is that you, cousin? You have grown fat and ugly since last I laid eyes on you."

Beaver Pelt slapped Raven on the shoulder, laughing as he led him up the mountain to where the French-allied Indians made their stand. Raven signaled for the guard to follow him.

"I thought you were buzzard food, cousin," Beaver Pelt teased. "Taande said you were taken by the English."

"Taande? Taande is here?"

They reached the crest of the hill where hundreds of braves from the Lenape, Shawnee, Ottawa, Abenakis, and Mingoe tribes lay behind trees shooting down into the gully of redcoats.

"Aye, he is here. All of the men of your village are here among us." Beaver Pelt shook his head. "But I have bad news, Raven. Sickness has taken Na-Kee." He tapped his shaven head. "Sickness of the mind."

A familiar feeling of animosity stirred in Raven. Na-Kee had caused him great suffering. Na-Kee had not competed fairly for the position of war chief against him. But if Na-Kee was ill, he would do what he could for him. It was the way among the Algonquian tribes. "Where is Na-Kee?" Raven asked solemnly. "This man would see him now."

"Come."

Raven stopped and turned to the guard. It was obvious the man was petrified to be surrounded by so many red men. Raven pointed to the guard. "This man saved my life. I owe him a life. His injury must be cared for and he must be escorted safely from this battle."

Beaver Pelt glanced at the guard and then called out to a Shawnee brave with a red kerchief tied around his head. "He-Who-Ponders!"

"Ah?"

"See to this man," he said in Algonquian. "Tend to his wounds and see that he escapes safely. He is a friend to my cousin. He saved a Lenape life. His life is now in your hands."

The Shawnee looked doubtfully at the guard.

"Do it, or it will be your scalp on my belt," Beaver Pelt threatened.

Raven looked to the guard who had slumped against a tree for support. "That man will care for you," he said in the English tongue, pointing to the Shawnee in the red kerchief. "He will see you safely from this place of death." Raven offered his hand. "I thank you, you whose name I do not know. This man thanks you for the life you have given him. He will not forget you."

The guard smiled with a nod and waved as Raven walked off at Beaver Pelt's side.

"You will find Na-Kee this way. We have tried to keep him safe from the musket fire. The sounds seem to make him more afraid."

Beaver Pelt led Raven down the far side of the hill to a small hollow beneath the exposed roots of a tree that protruded from the ground. There Na-Kee crouched, his face covered by a square of canvas he held down with his hands.

Every ounce of animosity Raven had ever felt toward Na-Kee fell from him like a shroud. Here was a tormented man that cowered beneath this tree, a man unworthy of hate or jealously.

"How did this happen?" Raven asked.

Beaver Pelt shrugged, answering in Lenape. "Only a Shaman could say for certain. He was his usual strutting self up until the musket fire started. At the first shot of the English cannon, his face suddenly went rigid. He fell to the ground, pissing on himself. He would not get up. He screamed like a mad woman. Then he tried to run unarmed down the hill. My men carried him here."

Raven shook his head in disbelief. "This is not Na-Kee's first battle! He is not a young buck to shy from the first glance at our enemy's faces."

Beaver Pelt opened his hands. "What can I say? I am not a healer. I do not understand the mind."

Raven nodded. Gathering his wits he walked to the tree that Na-Kee huddled beneath. "Na-Kee," he said softly. When he tried to lift the bit of cloth from his head, Na-Kee flinched as if Raven's hand burnt him.

"Maata! Maata!" Na-Kee screamed. "Do not shoot. Do not fire!"

Raven looked up at Beaver Pelt, then back at Na-Kee. He was rocking back and forth on his heels, trying to cover his face again. Raven reached carefully over him and replaced the tattered cloth. "He must be taken back to our village where our shaman can heal him."

Beaver Pelt nodded. "It will not be much longer, this fight. The day is ours."

Raven followed his cousin back up the slope to where the warriors were gathered. There was still musket-fire but the worst of the battle seemed to have passed. "I must find the others from my village. Taande, Crow Talk, and He-Who-Speaks-The-Truth."

"I do not know where they are, cousin, but I will ask."

"No, go back to your men." Raven clamped his hand on Beaver Pelt's shoulder. "This man thanks you for your help. I will find my friends and come back for Na-Kee. We return to our village."

"We return to the fort in victory. You will not go with us, brother Lenape and share in the good fortune?"

"Maata. I cannot say what is right for you and yours, Beaver Pelt, but our place is not here fighting another man's fight. We return to our village."

Beaver Pelt nodded, lifting a hand in farewell. "Then may the winds of the Creator be at your back, friend."

Raven strode away, moving along the ridge in search of Taande and the others. With Na-Kee incapacitated, he would assume the responsibility of war chief. His villagers needed a leader, and in Na-Kee's time of need he would be there for him.

Raven walked along the ridge questioning other Lenape and Shawnee braves he met. A man pointed down toward the road where red men and French were fighting a regiment of redcoats. "A knife," Raven said. "Might I borrow your knife, friend, Shawnee?"

"You go down into that?" It was bloody hand to hand combat on the road below them.

"Kehella. I search for my friends. We were separated."

The Shawnee offered him the knife from his belt and

made a sign of good luck as Raven jogged down the hillside. Raven no longer considered himself a part of this battle. His life had been spared once, he would not tempt fate. He would not kill again, unless it was to defend his own life or that of a loved one's. By the time he reached the road he and the other axemen had walked over only two hours ago, most of the fighting had come to an end. Blood saturated the ground. Bodies, red and white, lay heaped here and there.

"Raven!" a voice called.

Raven looked up to see one of the men from his own village running toward him. He-Who-Speaks-The-Truth was covered from head to foot in blood. "It is a miracle! We took you for dead weeks ago." He slapped Raven hard on the back. "Are you a ghost, brother?"

"I am not. Where are the others?"

He-Who-Speaks-The-Truth caught his breath. "Na-Kee has taken sick."

"I saw him."

The Lenape warrior nodded. "Crow Talk and his brother follow me. Also Corn Man and Sits Straight. Tall-As-The-Sky was killed several days ago while scouting for the French. Wildcat is wounded and waits at the top of the hill."

"Taande?"

He-Who-Speaks-The-Truth shook his head. "I have not seen him since we fought here." He indicated the bodies that were piled on the ground around them.

"I will look for Taande, even if it is only to carry his body back to our village. You gather the other men where Na-Kee waits. I am now War Chief, and I say we return home to our village."

"This man will not argue with you. I have had enough

battle this day to last a lifetime." He shook his head. "This man must be getting old. I do not enjoy the killing of the enemy as I once did." He stared at the ground. "Perhaps because I am no longer certain who the enemy is, Raven."

Raven pointed up the hill. "Go, He-Who-Speaks-The-Truth. This man will find Taande and meet you. We will go home."

With a nod, the Lenape warrior jogged off.

Alone, Raven stood among the bodies, searching for Taande. How senseless this all seemed as he stared at the lifeless bodies, thinking that each man was a father, a husband, a son. What a waste of human life . . .

He glanced up and down the road where the carnage had taken place. The English had retreated now, even Braddock. Raven had heard up on the hill rumor that the white-hair chief had been killed. Raven didn't know; he didn't care. One of his own men was missing.

The thought that Taande might be dead twisted in his heart like a knife. The last time he had spoken to Taande they had fought in front of Dream Woman. They had fought over Taande's attraction to his mother. Raven could not say that he was truly sorry that he had exchanged words over his mother. He was still not certain that he approved of her sleeping with a man so much younger than she. But after all Raven had been through these last weeks, and when he thought about the possibility that he might never see Tess again, he realized that his friendship with Taande was too important to him to let their disagreement get in the way of their friendship.

Raven walked among the bodies, turning men over to see if their faces resembled Taande. There were not many red men among the dead, they were mostly English. Raven called into the woods. Although most of the fighting was over and many Frenchmen and Indians were coming down out of the trees to loot the dead bodies, there was still the sound of occasional musket-fire.

As time passed Raven became more frustrated. He knew his men would be waiting for him up on the hill. He wanted to get out of here before English reinforcements came from Dunbar's camp and the fighting began again. But how could he return to the village without Taande? How could Raven go to Dream Woman without even the body of his friend and her lover?

The shadows were growing longer and soon evening would be upon them. As Raven stood looking again over the carnage of the day he heard his name being called. He turned toward the voice.

"Raven!" Crow Talk came down the hill. "The English may rally again. Let us go. We have all had enough of this bloodshed. We should not have come. You were right. We should not have come with Na-Kee. The Frenchmen can offer us no more than the English. They can give us nothing we truly want; nothing that means anything. But they can take much."

"Taande?" Raven looked for his friend, beginning to feel the weariness of the day. "Have you seen him?"

Crow Talk shook his head. "He was shot down here on the road. I do not know how badly. But I could not reach him. I did not see him again."

Raven turned to look back over the bodies of the fallen men. Crow Talk touched his arm. "Wildcat's injuries must be tended to. Na-Kee must be returned to the Shaman before it is too late. You must lead us back to the village, Raven. You are our leader now, as you should have been from the start."

"I cannot go without knowing what has become of

Taande." Raven caught his medicine bag around his neck and rubbed the piece of quartz inside it. "We have been friends since childhood."

"He is gone," Crow Talk said gently. "If he was not we would have found him by now. We were all to meet at the top of the hill. He would have been there if he could have been."

Crow Talk was right. Raven knew he was right. This was the way of a warrior's life. He had the other men to think about. And the village. With the English taking such a loss today, there was no telling what retaliation there would be. He and his men would have to make it home quickly so that they could defend the village if necessary.

Raven scanned the road one last time where Braddock's army had been ambushed. Then he turned and followed Crow Talk up the hill. He wouldn't think about Taande now. He wouldn't think about Tess or where Boeing had taken her, or if they had escaped alive. Right now his duty was to his people.

He would think about Taande and Tess tomorrow . . . tomorrow when the pain would not be so great.

Twenty-six

"You can't do this to me!" Tess shouted as Boeing yanked the hemp rope that bound her wrists tighter together.

He brought the back of his hand across her face, slapping her. "I told you to keep your voice down else we're dead, the both of us!" He glanced around suspiciously, as if he could see something in the darkness.

Tears of frustration ran down Tess's cheeks. The slap had stung but that was nothing in comparison to the pain that constricted her chest until she could barely breathe. "I have to get the child," she said. "I beg you. Surely she's still with Marty. Dunbar's camp can't be far. Can't we just—"

"There ain't no cash offered for the little half-breed. I told you, she ain't my concern. I took you into this mess, now I'm gettin' you out. You'd be grateful if ye had any sense, woman."

Tess turned her head so that she could wipe the tears that stung her eyes on the shoulder of her torn shirt. Darkness had settled in on the mountain range they were crossing. Gone were the sounds of the fighting army; the musket shots, the thunder of the cannon, the screams of the men. Now there was just silence, the silence of the night and the mist of the mountain.

Tess sniffed, fighting her tears. There was no sense in

arguing with Boeing. In some misguided way he had the idea he was truly doing the right thing in taking her back to Myron. He thought he had saved her life back there on that road to hell. She knew she couldn't possibly make him understand that she had loved Raven, that she had wanted to stay with him, even to die in his arms. Boeing was determined to take her back to Annapolis and to Myron like he'd set out to do before they'd gotten caught up in Braddock's March.

Tess felt dead inside; she wished she was dead. She wished one of those musket balls that had flown over her head had struck her in the chest and killed her. What reason did she have to live? By now Raven was dead and Sky, Sky was left behind with Marty. She would never see either of them again.

"But Sky was my responsibility," Tess whispered, trying one last time. "The child was my responsibility. I told her I'd come back for her."

Boeing went on tightening the girth on the horse's saddle. "Once you get back with yer own kind. Once you have time to look back on all this you'll be glad I done this for you. You won't want no little *half* around to remind you of what the red bastards put you through."

"What you put me through," she mumbled beneath her breath, fearing the bite of his hand again.

Boeing cupped his hands together for Tess to use to step up into the saddle. "Now up with ye."

She held out her bound wrists. They were so tight they were cutting off her circulation. "Couldn't you untie me at least? I can't ride like this."

"And take the chance you'll run off like ye did on me before? I don't think so," he snapped. "Now get up before I put you up."

Tess stepped onto Boeing's broad hands and pulled herself up into the saddle.

"Yer just damned lucky you didn't get caught, that's all I can say," Boeing went on. "Throwin' yourself off that horse like that."

Tess wanted to cover her ears. She knew what was coming. He'd already told her the story twice since he'd carried her from the battle and out of Raven's sight forever.

"It weren't a pretty sight, I'll tell you that. They didn't just shoot Rosy. That wouldn't have been so bad. They scalped 'er and then they started skinnin' her. I'd of shot her myself to put her out of her misery 'cept I was busy fightin' off two Frenchies and a redskin and my musket bein'—"

Tess lowered her forehead to the saddlehorn, squeezing her eyes shut, trying to block out Boeing's words and the pictures he painted in her head. All she could think of was Jocelyn and the screams . . .

Dear God, what has happened to my life? Tess prayed. *What's left for me now?*

Boeing went on talking as he mounted behind her and lifted the reins. They were headed east out of the mountains toward the Maryland Colony . . . east toward the place Tess had once called home.

A week to the day following Braddock's massacre near Turtle Creek, Raven led his men into their village. The women and children swarmed around them, tears flowing as some gave thanks for the return of their loved ones, while others cried for those lost. Raven heard Tall-As-The-Sky's widow give a shriek of pain as her father broke the news of his son-in-law's death. Na-Kee flinched at the sound of the woman and Raven put his arm around the man's shoulders to comfort him.

"It is all right, Na-Kee," Raven soothed, leading him away from the crowd. "Come, let me take you home to your wigwam where you may sleep on your own bedding and drink from your own cup."

Na-Kee mumbled something unintelligible again and again, glancing over his shoulder at the group of villagers as Raven led him away.

Na-Kee was better since they had taken him from the battle, but his head was still not right. Loud sounds turned the once-boastful Lenape brave into a frightened child. Even the musket shot to bring down a white-tailed deer for food paralyzed the man who had once been a warrior to be reckoned with.

As Raven led Na-Kee to his wigwam, where his mother and sister could look after him, Raven couldn't help wondering if this was Na-Kee's punishment for his arrogance and lies, or was it just the Creator's way of preventing him from causing any true harm to his people? It was a question Raven vowed to discuss with their Shaman at a later time. Perhaps the holy man would be able to lead him toward some answers.

After a brief account of what happened to Na-Kee, Raven left him in the care of his sister and slowly crossed the compound toward his own mother's lodge. As Raven walked between the wigwams, he couldn't help remembering the last time he had crossed this path. Tess had walked at his side. He had had her and had been fool enough to think he could let her go. He hadn't known how deeply he cared for her. He hadn't known what it was to truly love.

Now Tess was gone from him, perhaps forever. Taande

was gone, dead for certain. And Raven had to tell his mother.

Dream Woman met Raven at the door of her wigwam. She kissed her son's cheeks, first one then the other. Her tears splashed down to wet his cheek.

Without a word passing between them she took her son's hand and led him into her wigwam. She knew, some-how she knew.

"I will make you tea. Sit, warrior son of mine."

"N'gaxais—"

She lifted a bronze hand to silence him. How pretty she was, Raven thought. How young looking, even in her sadness.

"Let your mother make you tea and then you can tell me what I already know in my heart, what I have seen in the flames of my fire."

Raven took a seat at his mother's cold hearth and stretched out his long legs. The light from a hanging oil lamp illuminated the small lodge in soft yellow light. He could just make out the outline of the wall and roof his Tess had repaired.

Tess . . .

Raven wanted to drop his face into his hands and cry. But of course he couldn't. He was a man, a Lenape war-rior. He was his mother's only protector, and with Na-Kee injured as he was, Raven knew he would soon be War Chief.

A war chief could not cry for the loss of a woman—a white woman. So he cried inside.

Dream Woman pushed a cup of tea into her son's hand. She offered him a trencher of cold fried fish and stewed yellow squash. Raven drank and ate, but not because he was hungry or thirsty, only because he knew it was what his mother wanted of him.

Dream Woman sat on her knees watching her son until he had completed his meal. Not until she had taken away the dirty dish and fork did she finally speak.

"Tell me what has happened, my son," she said finally. "Tell me it all so that I may live it as you have."

"Taande—"

She smiled a bittersweet smile. "Do not speak the name of the dead." She took a deep breath. "From the beginning," she repeated. "Tell me what happened after you and my daughter-in-law left this village. Tell me not just why you did not come home with the man I loved, but why you did not bring the woman who was to save us."

Raven hung his head. He felt as if he had failed his mother. He had failed Taande, his people . . . Tess. "I will start at the beginning," he said softly. "I will tell you all that has happened since I left your side."

So, his idle hands resting in his lap, Raven set out to tell his mother what had happened since last she saw him. He tried to remember every detail, the tastes, the smells, the sounds . . . only his own feelings he left out. Feelings that would do neither of them any good, feelings he knew he could never share, except perhaps with Tess and she was gone.

It was not until midnight that Raven finally finished his tale and sat back, exhausted by the events he had been forced to relive in his mind.

Dream Woman stared at her son from across the cold firepit, her eyes red from her tears, but her face strangely determined. "So you could not bring my lover's body back to me so I could bury him properly?"

"I could not. I made the decision that it was the living I had to attend to."

"And you do not know what happened to the child Tess found in the well?"

"No."

"And it is not within your means to save the mind Na-Kee has lost on the battle field?"

Raven shook his head.

"But what of Tess? What of your wife, son of mine?"

Raven lifted his head to stare at his mother, her eyes as black as his own. "I have a duty to my people, but—"

"But you must find her," Dream Woman finished for him.

"*Kohon.* I know it is wrong. I know it is not our way, but I must leave my people and go." He looked away, fearing his body would betray him, fearing the tears that welled in his eyes would spill. "I promised her."

"You will find her and bring her home."

"I will at least find her body," he said softly.

Dream Woman shook her head. "Ah, where is your hope son? Where is the strength I know you possess inside?"

"You did not see the blood on this road, Mother. You did not see the bodies. No white man . . . or woman could have escaped alive."

"Love is sometimes stronger than war," Dream Woman offered.

Raven gave a mirthless laugh. "Women are so full of the intangibles, are they not?" he mused. "Love, hope—it is no wonder the Creator chose them to carry our sons and daughters."

Dream Woman rose and went to her son. Raven stood,

and she took his large hand in her smaller one. She turned his hand in hers, studying the palm.

"Once this hand was so tiny in mine," she reflected. "Where have my years gone?"

"You are not old, Mother. Not yet."

She smiled a bittersweet smile. "That is what I loved most about *him.* Your friend, whose name I will never speak again, took me back to my youth. His love opened my eyes to that which I was closing them to." She kissed Raven's hand and then let it go, turning away. "I will miss him."

Raven's voice cracked. "I will miss him, too, Mother."

She turned back to him, smiling through her tears. "Go and find her, Raven. Bring the white woman back. You keep yourself so apart from the world ignoring your feelings the way you do. You are missing too much of life. I want you to experience the love your father and I shared and later the other and I shared. I want you to know what it is to cradle your child in your arms."

Raven looked away, his eyes unfocused. "And what is the point, Mother? The more you care, the more you hurt. Duty is not so painful. To die defending your people is not so hard as dying inside like this." He took a breath, trying to calm his beating heart. ". . . Dying without her."

"She is not dead," Dream Woman whispered. "I did not see it in the flames. But you must hurry."

Dream Woman's words tapped his attention. "You have seen her, in a vision?"

"It was not clear. I only know that she escaped one danger to be thrown into another."

He balled his fists at his sides. "I do not know where she is. Where he took her. If he took her or if she is lost in the forest. Captured by others. I do not know where to begin."

"Begin at the beginning."

"What?"

Dream Woman began to make herself a fresh cup of tea. "The beginning. Where did she come from?"

"My brother and I, we found her on the Susquehanna."

"Even before that."

"A place called 'Napolis. That was her home. She lived with an uncle who was cruel to her."

Dream Woman nodded divinely. "That is where I would look for her first."

He lifted his hands in exasperation. "I have never been to the white man's village. I would not know how to find her."

"Lose her life and you lose two," Dream Woman said cryptically. "You must hurry."

"She carries my child?" Raven demanded, not meaning to raise his voice to his mother. "She did not tell me."

"She does not yet know. Bring them home, Raven, son of mine. Quickly, before you cannot."

Raven stood in the doorway of his mother's wigwam for a moment watching her, going over in his mind what she had said. The longer he thought on it, the stronger the sense of urgency to set out after Tess became. These last days he had refused to think about her or his own pain; he had dwelled, instead, on bringing his men home safely. He had concentrated on the pain he knew he would bring home to his mother with the death of Taande.

Now, suddenly he could hear her. Raven could hear Tess's voice on the hot summer wind calling his name. *Watch for me on a moonless night,* he had told her, though why he did not know. A premonition, perhaps? Through the doorway of the wigwam he stared up into the dark sky; a quarter-moon hung low on the horizon . . . a waxing moon. A tightness grew in his chest.

He had barely a week to find her. One week to save Tess and the child who grew inside her.

Twenty-seven

Tess allowed the horse's rhythm to rock her to sleep as she rode in the saddle in front of Boeing. The hours, the days, had slipped by without meaning. She rode listlessly, doing what Boeing told her to do, but without caring. She ate only because he told her to eat. She slept only because he told her to sleep. She didn't think; she didn't feel. The pain in her heart was so great, she had lost so much, that she didn't think she had any emotion left in her.

Boeing talked for hours on end about how women who were captured by the enemy often sympathized with them as a way to survive. Once she was home with her loved ones, he explained, she would forget it all. It would just be a bad dream.

Tess let her head slump forward to rest it on the horse's shaggy mane. *Raven was a bad dream . . . Sky, too. This was best. It was the best thing for her. To return to her own family that was what she wanted, what she needed.* After days of listening to Boeing ramble on, she was beginning to believe him.

"Sit up and make yourself look decent," Tess heard Boeing say in the back of her mind. When she made no attempt to move, he pinched her on the arm.

"Ouch!"

"I said sit up. We're almost there, if the farmer gave

me the right directions. White clapboard farmhouse, just before you get into town, that's what he said."

Tess sat up and pushed back a clump of dirty hair. She'd made no attempt with her appearance since the battle. What was the point? She looked up at the familiar road, one she and Myron had ridden down many times. This was the way to Myron's house. He was waiting for her. He wanted her. He was going to pay Boeing a great deal of money for her return. That was what Boeing had said.

Boeing rode into the yard, the yard Tess had once dreamed of planting a flower garden in.

"This it?" he asked.

She stared sullenly.

He pinched her again.

"Yes."

Boeing smiled. "Told you I'd get us out of that mess. Outsmarted them all, didn't we, Tess? Redskins and the Frenchies."

Boeing rode right up to the house and dismounted, leaving Tess on the horse. She turned her head away, not bothering to watch him walk up the whitewashed steps to the kitchen door. She heard him knock. Hounds began to bay from their kennels.

"Hmph . . ." Boeing came back down the steps after a moment. "No answer. Guess we ought to try round back. He's a gunsmithy, ain't that right?"

Tess made no response. Instead, she watched a starling flutter overhead to land on the porch roof, a bit of grass or weed in its beak.

Boeing caught the horse's reins and led it around back to where there were a cluster of barns and lean-to dependencies. The dogs barked louder. "Hallo? Anyone home? Hallo?"

"Can I help you?" Out of the corner of her eye, Tess caught sight of Myron, Myron and his balding head, Myron who was never quite comfortable in anyone's presence, even hers. "Sweet Jesus, is that you?" she heard him mutter.

She turned her head slowly to look at him. He was the same as she remembered, a little thinner perhaps. She stared without seeing, thinking that he should have evoked some sort of emotion in her. She should have been happy to see him, or even angry that he never came for her. But she should have felt *something*. Instead, she felt nothing, nothing at all.

Myron came running across the yard in his leather gun-smith's apron. "Sweet Jesus, it is you!" He stopped just short of the horse and gaped at her. "I never thought I'd see you again," he whispered in shock. "I thought you were dead. Your uncle said you were dead for sure."

Boeing was grinning ear to ear. "I heard there was a reward for her return. That right?"

Myron couldn't take his eyes off her. "That's right. A reward."

Boeing rubbed his beefy hands together. "I been through hell and high water to get 'er here. I reckon there might even be a bonus in it for me. Reckon there might."

Myron took one of her cold hands in his and rubbed it. "It's . . . it's Myron. Do . . . do you recognize me?"

Tess stared at him with dull eyes. What did he think she was, mind-less? "I remember you, Myron," she said tartly.

Still holding her hand, he glanced over his shoulder. "Where did you find her?" he asked Boeing. "I looked everywhere. I've been to every redskin village within days of here."

Boeing crossed his arms over his chest proudly. "Picked 'er up in the middle of nowhere. Redskin had her. 'Course he's dead now."

"Oh, merciful Father," Myron whispered.

He's dead now. Boeing's words echoed in her head. *Raven's dead.* She looked away fighting the lump that rose in her throat. "Pay him, Myron. Let him be on his way."

Myron released her hand. "Right, I guess you're right." He walked away, then came back to the horse to offer his hand. "Let me help you down."

Ignoring his hand, Tess dismounted on her own.

Myron kept looking over his shoulder at her as he led them both around the house and into the kitchen.

Tess trailed behind the two men for lack of anything else to do. Inside the kitchen she stood near the doorway.

Myron was fiddling in a crock jar above the fireplace, searching for his coin, no doubt. Boeing was boasting of his great accomplishment, bringing Tess home to the loving bosom of her family.

Myron turned back to Boeing, a small bag that clinked with coins in his dirty hands. He waited for Boeing to finish his sentence. "Ah, listen," he stumbled. "No . . . no one knows you're here do they? I mean that when you brought her home no one saw you?"

Boeing glanced at Tess near the doorway then back at Myron. The two men seemed to be communicating without words, but Tess wasn't interested enough to try and figure out what they were saying.

"No, not really, some plow farmer on the road, but he didn't see the girl. I jest asked him where I could find a gunsmith by the name of Ellsworth. I left her—" he hooked his thumb "—back in the woods where she couldn't be seen by no one."

"Good." Myron dropped the bundle of coins into Boeing's waiting hand. "It's all there and then some. Count it if you like."

Boeing weighed the coins in his hand. "I'll trust ye." He glanced over his shoulder at Tess with his one good eye and back at Myron. "She's been through a hell of an ordeal. She ain't quite right in the head jest now, but you never know . . ." he let his voice trail off.

Myron scuffed one boot on the swept pine floor, glancing away awkwardly. "I . . . I'd ask you not speak of this to anyone. There's already been enough . . . gossip. People, they—"

"Christ, just come out and say it," Tess interrupted from the doorway with more emotion than she'd felt in days. "You're ashamed of me. I was kidnapped and now somehow it's my fault."

Myron forced a half smile. "Dear—"

She massaged her temples irritably. It felt good to shout. She knew she couldn't go on feeling like this. She hated this nothingness, this black hole Tess Morgan had once occupied. Even anger was better than nothingness. "I'm sorry," she murmured. "I didn't mean to shout at you, Myron. I know you tried your best."

Myron walked to the door to show Boeing out. The two men exchanged a few whispered words and then Boeing was gone.

Myron closed the kitchen door and then just stood there staring at Tess. She moved to the pine table and sat down, resting her hands in her lap.

There was a long silence before Myron finally spoke. "I . . . I'm glad to see you again."

"Are you?" She glanced up at him, thinking to herself that Myron wasn't a bad man. He had tried to find her. He had even paid to have her returned.

Tess dropped her face to her hands. She wasn't ready to give up living, at least not yet. Perhaps life with Myron wouldn't be so terrible. It might not be all fire and passion, but who had that in a marriage anyway?

She smiled sadly. She had had it hadn't she, if only for a few short weeks. She had shared something with a man that few even dreamed of sharing.

But now Raven was gone and she could either shrivel up and die or she could make peace with herself and do what she could with the long years she had left on this earth.

Tess lifted her head to follow Myron with her gaze as he came toward her. "You really are glad to see me, aren't you?" she asked.

"I am." He stopped an arm's length from her, twisting his hands nervously. "Would . . . would you like something to eat? Bread and cheese? Mother sent an excellent goat cheese over."

She shook her head. "I'm not hungry. I'm not hungry but I would like a bath. Do you think I could have a bath, Myron?"

Seemingly relieved to have something to do, he immediately started for the lean-to pantry off the back of the kitchen. "A bath . . . yes, yes, a bath. You take a bath, and I'll just finish up in the shop. We—" his voice faded as he disappeared through the doorway into the lean-to "—we'll have dinner together, then. After you've bathed and . . . and rested." He reappeared dragging a large round wooden tub. "Would that be all right?"

She made herself smile. She couldn't blame Myron for

any of this. He hadn't killed Raven. He wasn't responsible for her unhappiness. He was trying to do what he could to welcome her back. "I'd like that. But I'll need some clothes." She lifted the dirty, tattered blue-tick petticoat that she and Marty had fashioned weeks ago, weeks that now seemed like years.

"I—"he looked down into the wash barrel to keep from having to meet her gaze "—I bought you a . . . a gown. It . . ." He exhaled sharply, seeming to become exasperated with his nervousness with her. "I was going to give it to you as a wedding gift. I know it wouldn't be appropriate now, but—"

"It's that or I go home to my uncle's stark naked. These will have to be burned." She got up. "Just put the tub there near the hearth and I'll fill it myself."

"I . . . I can do it for you." He lifted his head to look at her with pale gray eyes.

Tess crossed the short space between them and laid her hand on his forearm. "I want to do it myself, Myron." She took down her hand. It just didn't feel right to touch a man that wasn't Raven. She had called their marriage a heathen ritual the night they'd wed, but in her heart it was a true marriage before God. Even with Raven dead, she felt like he was still her husband. She guessed she would just have to get over it. "All right, Myron?" she asked softly.

He set down the tub and went back toward the door. "All . . . all right. There's plenty of fresh rain water in the barrel outside the back stoop. The coals are hot so you ought to be able to heat the water up fine."

"Have you something for dinner?"

"You don't have to—"

"I want to. I need something to do to take my mind

off—" it was her turn to glance away awkwardly "—well, you know."

"There's, there's a nice piece of smoked venison in the lean-to. Green beans, too. I just picked them this morning."

"I'll be fine. Go back to your work. I'll take a bath. We'll have our meal together and then you can take me to my uncle's. All right?"

A strange look crossed his face, but it was gone as quickly as it came. "All . . . all right."

Tess watched him make a hasty retreat out the kitchen door and then she turned to the task of filling the bathtub. What she needed now was something to keep herself busy. These last few days she'd had nothing to do as she rode with Boeing but feel sorry for herself. Once she and Myron were married, once she had a household of her own to run, once she began plans to bring Abby to the Colonies surely life wouldn't look so dismal. It couldn't possibly.

Tess bathed the days of grime from her body, washed her hair, and then dressed in the gown she found in the clothes press in Myron's bedchamber upstairs. It was not a gown Tess would have chosen for her wedding day, but she told herself it was his thoughtfulness that counted, not the dress. It was a gray-striped, floral, day dress with little embellishment. But it was sturdy, a gown suitable for a gunsmith's wife.

Dressing as best she could without proper undergarments or even stockings, she put Takooko's moccasins back on and then went downstairs to cook the evening meal. As she moved about the kitchen, she tried to imagine that this was her kitchen. She tried to imagine that Abby was here and that she and Myron were married. She tried to imagine that she was happy.

The shadows had lengthened into twilight before Myron

finally appeared at the kitchen door, his hands scrubbed clean, his hair wet and slicked back. He knocked on the door hesitantly.

"It's your house, you can certainly come in," she called, trying not to sound irritated. The door swung open. "I was beginning to think I would have to come out looking for you."

He shifted his weight uneasily from one foot to the other. "I just . . . I wanted you to have some time to . . . you know, clean up."

She went toward the fireplace to retrieve fresh-baked squash fritters from a spider over the hot coals. "Heavens, Myron, I could have washed myself and half the colony in that time. I don't know why it is we're so preoccupied with our bodies." She chuckled, shaking her head. He didn't laugh. "Go ahead and sit." She motioned to the sturdy table. "Everything is ready."

After an awkward meal punctuated by small bursts of conversation followed by long pauses of silence, Tess began to clean up the dishes.

Myron rose and took his dirty plate from her hand. "No. No I can do that later. Why don't you . . . we . . . Let's sit in the parlor. I bought a new chair, you know. Ordered it from Philadelphia. I could show it to you."

Tess would have preferred cleaning up the dishes to seeing Myron's new chair, but she followed him into the parlor. It was getting late. It would soon be time he took her home to MacElby's Fate, anyway. Surely her aunt and uncle had a right to know of her return.

Myron lit several oil lamps in the large airy front room. It was sparsely furnished, but the wallpaper was of excellent quality, the few tables and chairs new.

"You see, here it is, Tess. I ordered it from—"

"Myron." She turned to him, laying her hand on his arm. "You and I, we need to talk."

He looked down at the floor then up, his gaze meeting hers. He brushed his hand across her shoulder. "Yes?" He was breathing unevenly. "A . . . ab . . . bout what?"

"We have to talk about what happened to me. I've been gone a long time. There are things you have to know. Things you need to understand if this is going to work between us."

"No, no we don't. We don't have to talk. I . . . I don't want to know about . . . about what they did." He smoothed her sleeve with a jerky motion.

She could tell he was going to try to kiss her. He had that look on his face that said if he could just muster the courage he would do it.

She turned her head slightly in indecision. She didn't want to be kissed by him, but that was what a man and wife did, didn't they? If she was going to marry him, if she was going to take his house, his furniture, his hard-earned money, he had a right to something, didn't he?

Tess closed her eyes. Perhaps if she pretended he was Raven . . .

His mouth touched hers—a little too firmly, his lips tightly compressed. She tried to relax. She couldn't bring herself to kiss him back, but she wouldn't fight him. She'd let him do what he wanted.

To Tess's surprise, Myron pressed his lips harder against hers, at the same time, bringing his hand up beneath her breast. He had never tried to touch her before, not like this.

Tess tried not to think. She tried not to feel anything. There was nothing in his touch or his kiss that excited her, nothing. But it was his right. His right, she told herself.

"Upstairs," she heard him mumble in her ear. He was panting heavily, obviously aroused. "Let me take you upstairs where we can be more comfortable."

Tess pulled back a little. His kisses were wet, a little sloppy. She didn't like his panting breath in her ear. "Myron, Myron we're not married yet."

"Please," he whispered. "I've waited so long for you, Tess. I—"

That nothingness was taking over again inside her. It was like a black void that just spread from the pit of her stomach outward. *What does it matter?* The blackness whispered. *Now? Next week? Once you're wed you'll be his to do as he pleases with anyway. Let him have what he wants . . .*

"All right," Tess heard herself answer in a voice she barely recognized as her own. It wasn't as if she had much of a choice. She had to keep Myron happy. If he didn't marry her, who would? "But then I want you to take me home to my uncle's. I'll stay there until we're properly married. I want no gossip."

He took her hand in his hot clammy one and clambered up the narrow stairway, leading her into the larger of the two upstairs rooms. He closed the paneled door behind them, as if someone was watching.

"I've . . . I've waited so long," he kept saying as he fought to undo his belt and tossed it over a chair. Then he tugged off his boots, hopping on first one foot and then the other. It was so dark in the room that she could barely see him. She and Raven had always enjoyed making love by the light of a lantern so that they could see each other's faces as they shared their pleasure . . . their love.

Tess went to the tick bed and perched herself on the corner. All she could feel was numbness. Maybe it was better that way. "Do you want me to light a candle?" she asked.

He came to her, taking her cheeks between his palms, giving her another sloppy kiss. "No, don't need light, just need—"

He pushed her back on the bed climbing on top of her. Tess just laid there as if it was not her that Myron was slobbering on . . . as if it was not her breasts he was fondling roughly. She kept telling herself that this didn't matter, not any more it didn't, not now that Raven was gone. Myron would soon be her husband. This was his right. He had a right to use her body.

But when he pulled at the tie of his breeches and she saw his member spring into his hands, a lump of bile rose in her throat. Tess gave Myron a push. "No."

He was still kissing her, fumbling with her petticoat. In a second he'd touch her with the thing.

"I said no, Myron," she repeated firmly, giving him a shove at the shoulders.

"What?"

He lifted his weight from her and she slipped out from under him, shoving her petticoat down. Tears ran down her cheeks. "I can't, Myron. We're not wed." She wiped at her eyes with the back of her hand. "I'm not even sure I can marry you."

Myron had gotten to his feet by then. At first he seemed disoriented, but then as he stared at her through the semi-darkness she saw the blank look on his face become a sneer. "Oh, so you'll spread your legs for a redskin, but not for me."

She had never heard him speak so crudely before. "Myron!"

"What have they got that I haven't, huh? Tell me that?"

He stood there in front of her, his erection dangling from the opening in his breeches. Tess was disgusted, by her own behavior, by Myron's.

"I don't have to listen to this," she spat, getting up off the bed.

"The hell you don't!" He came toward her, shoving his now-flaccid member into his breeches. He was between her and the door. "Do you know what everyone's said these last weeks? Do you?" he shouted. "They say poor Myron, poor Myron Ellsworth. His fiance was captured by savages. His fiance was ravished by heathens. Those little red bastards stuck their—"

"Myron!" Tess shouted. "That's enough!"

He brought his hand across her cheek slapping her so hard that she fell against the bed. "Myron . . ." She covered her stinging cheek with her palm. "You had no right to do that," she whispered.

"I paid for you and I want something for my hard-earned coin," he threatened, coming toward her.

The image of the soldier in the forest flashed through Tess's head. She had killed that man to protect herself. Surely it wouldn't come to that again!

Tess slid sideways, trying to maneuver her way around him. "Myron, let me go." She raised her hand. "Just let me go and we'll pretend this never happened. I understand you're distraught."

"Distraught!" he shouted coming at her. "Let me show you what—"

Tess wasn't going to let him hit her again. No man had a right to touch her like that. No man. Instinctively she curled her fingers into a ball and swung her fist, striking him soundly in the jaw.

He stumbled backward under the impact of the blow,

giving her time to run out onto the landing and start down the staircase.

"Come back here!" Myron shouted. "I have a right! I have as much right as those red bastards you spread yourself for!"

He was mad! Myron had gone mad! Tess ran through the parlor toward the kitchen. She would go home to Uncle Albert and tell him what Myron had tried to do. He wouldn't make her marry him then.

Tess had made it halfway through the kitchen when she heard Myron leap off the bottom step and turn the corner to the kitchen. The ominous click of the rifle hammer made her stop dead.

"Myron . . ." she whispered.

"I have a right!" he flung at her. "You ruined everything! I have a right."

Slowly she turned around to face him, fearful that if she moved too quickly he would fire. She held up her hands. "Myron—"

"Don't say it, don't say anything!" he shouted, tears running down his cheeks. "I wanted you! I wanted you more than anyone. I would have married you! I would have loved you."

She shook her head in disbelief. How could she ever have thought she could have lived with this man, married him, given him children? "Tess," she said. "You haven't called me by my name, not once. Say it, Myron." She beat her chest with her fist. "Say my name. Say it!"

His face contorted as a sob escaped his lips. "I had such plans for you and I. I—"

"Myron, there's no reason why we can't—"

"Shut up!" he shouted, shaking the cocked rifle at her.

"Shut up, bitch! You shouldn't have lived! No decent woman would have survived that!"

"I don't understand you," she whispered. "You said you were glad to see me. You . . . you wanted to sleep with me. We were going to marry and now you're going to shoot me because I won't—"

"I wasn't going to marry you," he sneered. "Not after what's happened to you. I couldn't. No decent man could."

As Myron's words sunk in, Tess's fear turned to anger, stark white searing anger. "Oh, so you would have slept with me, but not married me?"

He wiped at his eyes, now streaming with tears. He was shaking from head to foot, but he still held the rifle on her. "I couldn't marry you," he sobbed. "I wanted to. But not now. Not after you've been violated."

"Violated! You don't know what happened to me!" She stood her ground. "You have no idea what went on those weeks I spent in that village! You have no idea what kind of people they were, or how they treated me!"

"Your uncle said so himself," he went on, seeming not to hear her. "No decent man would have you now. He . . . he was glad Jocelyn was dead. You . . . you should have been."

"Well, I'm not," Tess fired back. "So are you going to shoot me or not, because if not, I'm leaving."

When she took a step back, he took a step toward her, his trigger finger trembling. "I . . . can't let you go. It's it's better for all of us if—"

"You're going to kill me because I was kidnapped?"

"V . . . violated. R . . . ruined."

"You son of a bitch!" Tess grabbed the nearest weapon she could reach, a pewter plate off the table, and hurled it at him. She threw herself to the plank floor as his rifle discharged. The plate struck him square in the forehead just below his receding hairline and Myron Ellsworth went down on his knees clutching his bloody head. The rifle skittered across the floor coming to rest against the door.

"I ought to kill you myself," Tess shouted. "But you don't deserve the honor of death by the hands of the enemy. You sorry son of a bitch," she muttered walking to the door. "You ever show your face on my uncle's plantation and I swear by all that's holy I'll put a musket ball through your futtering head. You got it, Myron?"

Myron made no response but to lower his head to the floor and sob.

Tess walked out of the kitchen and into the darkness of the summer night. Raven might be dead. Any happiness she would ever know might be gone, but she hoped to God she would never be as pathetic as that man lying on his kitchen floor—never.

Twenty-eight

It was a long walk to MacElby's Fate from Myron's house on the edge of town, but by now Tess was used to the walking. Actually, she was glad to have the time to herself to think, to decide what she was going to do.

Again and again she glanced over her shoulder, half-expecting to see Myron come riding down the road like a madman. She just couldn't believe what had taken place back there at the farmhouse. Myron, Myron the man she had thought loved her or at least cared for her, had tried to kill her! He had tried to kill her over some misconceived ill-informed notion of what Indians were like.

Tess had always been aware of prejudice. It was everywhere. Landowners were prejudiced against the bondsmen who worked their fields. White men were prejudiced against black, black men against red. But she had never understood how deeply it flowed through a man's veins until she had seen the look on Myron's face when he had spoken of her being ruined. It wasn't that he cared about her virginity, or even her, it was who he thought had violated her! He had never asked what had happened to her. He had simply assumed she'd been raped. He probably wouldn't have believed the truth if she'd told him.

Tess sighed, tucking a stray lock of red hair behind her ear. She was beginning to feel like her old self again. She knew that shadow of a woman she'd been the last few days wasn't the woman Raven had said he loved.

She smiled a bitter-sweet smile. He *had* loved her. He had said so, and the look in his eyes had told her he meant it. He had loved her all along. And now, though he was dead, as long as she could hold onto that love in her heart, she knew he would always still live. That was what Dream Woman had once said. As long as Tak-ooko's loved ones remembered him in their hearts, he would always be alive.

So what to do now? Tess asked herself, trying to focus on the tangible reality of life. What would Raven do if he was in her position? He wouldn't curl up and die the way she had wanted to those first days without him, she knew that.

Raven would find Sky, of course. Tess had made a promise to the child; she had sworn she would take care of her, and now she was out there in the wilderness some-where. How frightened the child had to be, unable to com-municate, lost without anyone who loved her.

Tess questioned now whether or not she should ever have left Sky with Marty in the first place, but she knew she couldn't keep second guessing herself or she'd drive herself mad. What was done was done. She had loved Raven and now he was gone. She had left Sky behind where she thought she'd be safest, and now she had to find her. All that mattered was getting Sky back.

Tess decided that she would go to her uncle and be honest with him—at least partially. She would tell him that the Lenape did not abuse her. She would *not* tell him of Raven or her lost virginity. She would tell him about Sky and would insist her uncle help her find the child.

Tess had to assume Sky was still with Marty. She

prayed she was. She prayed they had managed to escape the massacre. She would just find Marty. The question was, where?

As Tess walked along the dark woods' road, a sliver of a moon lighting her way, she went over in her mind all the things Marty had said that would give some indication of where she was now. She had talked of joining an Indian somewhere south. But she still had her father's wagon. It was only logical that if she had made it out alive, if the remainder of the army had retreated as Boeing had said they would, then she would have returned to her father's home.

But where? Marty had mentioned the Chesapeake Bay, but that was all Tess recalled. She wracked her brain. Marty may have never mentioned a town, or a river.

Then it hit her. When she closed her eyes she could still see the side of Marty's battered wagon.

Abe Wheeler, Hauling, Honest & Cheap, Ann—

Ann— Tess stopped beneath a sumac tree. The rest of the white paint had been worn or washed away by the elements. *Ann* . . . Annapolis. It had to be Annapolis! She and Marty had lived near the same town and never encountered each other. Marty had to be in Annapolis.

Tess started walking again, her strides long and determined. She had reached the edge of the property line to the south of MacElby's Fate. The plantation house wasn't far now. She'd go to her uncle and have him send someone into town to find Abe Wheeler's place. Surely her uncle would be willing to extend his home to an orphan.

As she walked up the elm-lined drive she slowed her pace. The last time she had come down this road she had been in a carriage with Jocelyn. *Jocelyn.* . . . She had never liked her cousin. They hadn't been the best of friends that Tess had dreamed they would be. Jocelyn had never even been particularly nice to her, but the memories hurt Tess. No one should have had to die the way Jocelyn did. Her death was proof that there was prejudice everywhere, among all men. The Mohawk had kidnapped her; they had murdered her because of the color of her skin, because she was different than they were.

As Tess followed the turn in the road on the last leg to the big house, she couldn't help wondering how long it would be before mankind learned to live together in peace on the earth. She wondered if they would ever learn.

The sound of barking dogs signaled Tess's approach to her uncle's home. A black slave called Sleepin' Joe came through the darkness toward Tess, a baying coonhound on a leash, a musket in one hand, and a lantern in the other.

Tess halted. "It's all right, Sleepin' Joe," she called. "It's Tess, Tess Morgan."

"Sweet Jesus, I pray," Sleepin' Joe cried, holding up the lantern to cast a yellow light across her face. "Is you a ghost or is that really you, Miss Tess?"

She smiled, coming toward him. "It's me."

"The masta', he tole us you was dead, Miss Tess. You and Miss Joc'lyn both." He squinted. "You certain you ain't no ghostie?"

She laughed, touching the grey-haired man's arm lightly. "I'm certain. See, it's me, flesh and blood."

He walked beside her toward the house. "I jest can't believe it's you walkin' in here after the months you been gone. I ain't never heard of a woman takin' by Injuns that ever lived to tell it. The masta', he's had us patrollin' the house since you and Miss Jocelyn was taken. He scared to death they's comin' for him."

"Well, I've been with the Indians, Sleepin' Joe, the

Delaware, and when I've the time, I want to tell you the truth of the red men, or the truth the way I know it."

Sleepin' Joe shook his head. "I cain't tell you how good it is to see yer sweet face, Miss Tess. Ain't been no life in this place since you been gone."

They were approaching the front steps of the big white brick house. Candles burned in every window three stories high. "I can't say if I'm glad to be back or not yet," she said softly, "but I can tell you I'm glad to see you, Joe." She squeezed his arm. "You were one of the few people who was ever kind to me here, among the servants or my uncle's family."

Sleepin' Joe raised the lantern to light her way up the front steps. "I'll be seein' you, Miss Tess. Good luck to ya!"

Tess waved, taking the steps two at a time. Without giving herself time to think, she stepped into the airy hallway, and closed the heavy door behind her.

Home . . . not really home, but as close as she could come to it.

The sound of a spinet came down the hallway from Aunt Faith's parlor. Someone was singing slightly off-key. Tess had to smile. It was Aunt Faith.

At that moment Tess heard the sound of footsteps. One of the housemaids, a bond servant by the name of Dory, appeared at the end of the long hallway. Before Tess could speak, the girl gave a shriek. She dropped the tinderbox she carried in her hand, taking a step back in fright. "Sweet Mary," she cried, crossing herself. "She's come back to haunt me!" She waved her hands. "I . . . I didn't mean no harm cutting up your Sunday-best petticoat. It were only a joke, it were."

"It's all right," Tess said, laughing. She'd always wondered which one of the maids had done the rotten deed. "I'm not a ghost. It's me. It's Tess. I've come home. Where's my uncle? With Aunt Faith in the parlor?"

"N . . . no." Dory was still staring at her as if unsure of whether or not to trust her own eyes. She picked up the tinderbox from the floor. "He's out back in the barns with some gentlemen folk. He got a new stallion today and's been showin' him off."

"Dory, could you send someone for him? Better yet, go yourself. I don't want anyone to know I'm here yet. I don't want to appear in front of his guests looking like this. But I need to speak with him right away."

"You want him to come in here to you?"

Tess pointed, answering patiently. "That's right, Dory. I'll wait in his office."

With a nod and a shove of her drooping cap, Dory turned and ran.

Tess stepped into her uncle's dark office. Using a candle from the candlebox on the mantel, she lit several lamps, illuminating the sober paneled room in soft light. As she waited for her uncle, she moved about the room restlessly. She ran her finger down the spines of the leather-bound books in the book press. She fingered the French cut-glass wine decanter. She lifted the lid on the tobacco humidor and took a deep breath of the pungent Roanoke. The smell of the tobacco reminded her of Raven. She let the lid fall, refusing to give in to her emotions. She couldn't cry right now. She needed to concentrate on finding Sky. There would be years left to cry for her husband.

The office door opened and Tess spun around. Her uncle's face was paste white. He closed the door behind him.

"Tess."

"Uncle," she said softly.

"You're alive."

She brushed her hands to her gray petticoats, giving a little laugh. "I'm alive. Someone found me and brought me home." She offered a hesitant smile.

Uncle Albert was not smiling. He wasn't pleased to see her. Shocked, but not pleased. Tess suddenly felt uneasy. She felt trapped.

"Uncle Albert—"

"How is it that you managed to survive and my daughter did not?" he demanded perversely. "What did you do that those heathens spared your life. Did you spread your lily white—"

"Uncle Albert, I—"

"You should not have come here. This is no longer your home. There's no place for a woman of your ilk."

Tess crossed her arms over her chest. For the last two years she had allowed her aunt and uncle, even Jocelyn to bully her, to treat her as if she was something lesser than they because of the humble home she'd come from. She knew she should feel grateful for what they'd done, for paying her passage here. But Tess didn't feel that way any longer. She was as good a person as any MacElby . . . perhaps better. She knew that now. And she knew she could never be beholding to anyone again, no one but the Creator above.

"I didn't come here," she snapped. "I was brought here against my will. Myron paid someone to bring me back. He and his hired men murdered innocent people trying to find me."

Her uncle scowled. "You are a disgrace to this family. If you'd had a wit of sense you'd have died back on that road with my Jocelyn. Any decent woman would have died at the hands of those red bastards rather than live with the shame. Your aunt would have taken her own life before she'd have dragged herself over the MacElby doorstep!"

Tess lowered her gaze, trying to remain levelheaded. She wanted to scream. She wanted to shout, but she needed her uncle's help if she was going to find Sky, if she was going to be reunited with her sister. "Like it or not, I'm here," she said softly. "I'm alive and I'm here. If I'm no longer welcome then I'll ask you for money, money for passage for myself and another. I'll just go home to England, Uncle Albert, home to Abby."

"Abby?"

She lifted her gaze. There was something in the tone of his voice that frightened her. "My sister. Abby. The one I intended to bring here once Myron and I were wed. You remember Abby."

Her uncle's upper lip curled in a strange smile. "I hate to be the one to tell you," he said, obviously enjoying the moment, "but Abigail is deceased."

For a moment Tess thought she might have misheard. Abby, dead? The floor swayed and she caught the corner of the desk for support. "No," she whispered. "Not my Abby." *Not her, too,* she screamed inside. "Not Abby."

"A fever took her. Sometime after Candlemas Eve last. The letter was slow in coming."

Tess lowered her head until her chin touched her chest. If only the room would stop spinning. If only the roaring in her ears would cease, she could think. "I . . . I don't believe you," she said. But she did.

"Believe me or not." Her uncle shrugged. "I imagine your aunt still has the letter from her dear sister."

A sob rose in Tess's throat and she choked it back. All these months, since long before she was kidnapped by the

Mohawk, Abby had been dead. In Tess's mind her sister had been alive, but she'd been dead; dead, and buried.

"Oh, God," she whispered. *Abby was the reason why she'd told Raven she had to go home. Abby was all that had kept her from being content to be his wife.* Tears clouded her eyes. And it was all for nothing . . . nothing.

Tess looked up, realizing her uncle was speaking to her. He had moved to a cherry table and poured himself a drink. She caught bits of sentences as she tried to regain control of her emotions.

"—have to figure out what to do with you—disgrace to the MacElby name—Ellsworth certainly wouldn't have you."

His words brought her back to reality. She started edging toward the door. There was danger in the tone of her uncle's voice. *Trust your instincts,* Raven had taught her. *Go with your gut feeling.* "I . . . I'll just go, then," she said. "If you don't want me here, I'll leave. I'll go—" She didn't know where she'd go once she found Sky. As long as it was away from here, it didn't really matter. "I'll—"

Her uncle stepped between her and the door. "You'll go nowhere," he said with a sneer. "I don't want you seen. You're dead. We told everyone you were dead. We've accepted their condolences. You're dead to us, Tess. Dead to your family. To anyone you ever knew. I drafted the letter to your poor mother myself."

Tess shook her head. She wasn't dead, not even with Raven gone, and Abby, too. She was still alive inside, as alive as she'd been the day she'd leaped out of the Mohawk canoe and into the cold Susquehanna River. There was something inside her, something that told her she must live. "Get out of my way," she warned. "Let me go and you'll never lay eyes on me again."

Still blocking the door, Albert MacElby lifted his glass to his lips and sipped the blood-red wine. "Damned straight I'll never lay eyes on you again."

Tess made a move for the door. If she could duck under his arm, slip past him, she could make it out the front hall. She was halfway through the office doorway when she felt something heavy strike her on the back of the head.

Then she was hurled into blackness.

Twenty-nine

Tess awoke disoriented, groggy as if she'd been drugged. She blinked in the darkness, trying to focus her eyes. She was in some tiny, dank-smelling room. The floor was hard beneath her . . . cold, damp brick. She brushed her hand across the back of her head where there was a dull ache, and felt the warm stickiness of her own blood.

Uncle Albert had hit her, hit her with something heavy. He had tried to kill her. A shiver of fear crept up her spine. Would he be back to finish her off?

Tess fought the panic that rose in her throat threatening to hinder her reason. She drew her legs up under her petticoat and hugged her knees. "Stay calm," she said aloud, hoping to soothe her fears. "You've been kidnapped by Mohawk, nearly massacred by the French. Uncle Albert is just one man. You can beat him," she told herself. "You can do it for Sky. Sky still needs you."

The quiver in her voice echoed off the low ceiling. In the far corner of the cell mice scurried squeaking in fear of the human sounds. She thought of Abby, and the ache in her head moved to her heart. Her sister was dead, dear sweet Abby was gone. First Raven, then Abby. But she still had Sky. She had to believe that. And she had to get out of here for the little deaf girl's sake.

So where was here? She squinted, studying the four

walls barely visible in the pitch darkness. It was so cool that she knew she had to be underground, but where? Directly across from her, she noticed the wall was colored differently than the others. Not trusting herself to stand quite yet, she stretched her feet until her moccasins touched the solid wall. A door—a wooden door.

Tess bounced up, running her hands over the roughly hewn planks. "Ouch!" She brought her hand to her mouth sucking. A splinter. Gingerly she reached out again, this time taking her time. Where was the door handle or knob? She searched from floor to just above her head where the ceiling met the wall. No doorknob. She was locked in with no way out from the inside.

Tess pounded on the door in frustration. "Someone help me! Let me out of here! Help!" Her own voice reverberated off the walls of the brick cell.

My tomb, she thought, slumping to the floor. A tear slipped down her cheek and she dashed it away angrily. There had to be a way out of here. She wasn't going to give up. She wasn't going to let Uncle Albert and Myron win.

"Oh, Raven," she whispered desperately in the darkness. "What now, *ki-ti-hi?* What do I do now?"

Raven slipped through the shadows of the trees that surrounded the estate house on the MacElby's Fate plantation.

Go back to where she started, Dream Woman had told him. Raven had done just that. On the outskirts of the English town called 'Napolis he'd found a cabin where an old Shawnee woman was cutting firewood. He had given her tobacco as a gift and then they had smoked their pipes together. The old woman called Mary Clearwater had heard of a redheaded woman called Tess who had been taken by Indians. She knew where she had once lived, and she sent Raven on the path to the plantation with a blessing and a cloth bag of fresh biscuits.

Raven ran across brittle grass to crouch at the corner of a small building. It smelled of hickory smoke and cured pork. A smokehouse. From here, he spotted the great brick house and let his eyes drift shut, concentrating on thoughts of Tess.

Raven had never been a man of the metaphysical. He believed in his mother's gifts, in the gifts of the shaman and a few others in the village, but he had never thought of himself as possessing any of them. Just the same, he knew that he would be able to feel Tess's presence. At their wedding they had been bound to each other, not just for the life on earth, but everlasting life. He would know if she was here, if only he could concentrate . . . if only he believed.

Raven forced himself to relax, a difficult feat for a man in the midst of his enemy. He made himself listen to his surroundings, to *feel* with his senses.

At first he heard nothing but the chirp of night insects, the neigh of the horses in the stables, the cluck of a stray chick. He smelled only the nearby outhouse and the stench of unwashed bodies. He felt nothing but the cold brick of the great white-hair house that lay before him.

But then, after a time, his senses grew sharper. He smelled the hint of baked apple on the wind. He heard a woman singing her babe to sleep, her voice liquid silk, her tongue of African soil. Then . . . only then did Raven feel how close he was to Tess. He felt her fear, her desperation . . . he tasted her tears on the tip of his tongue. He heard her sob his name.

Raven's eyes flew open. The sensation had been so strong for an instant that his own eyes watered with Tess's tears. She was here; she was alive. She was in grave danger.

Raven strode across the back yard of the great house, one French long rifle flung over his back, another clutched in his hand. On his belt he wore a hunting knife and war club. If necessary he would fight for her. No man would stand between him and Tess, no man who did not wish to be sent straight to hell at the barrel of his rifle.

Raven walked along the side of the house. He would not approach the enemy from the rear. He would meet him face to face and take what was rightfully his.

Up the front steps he went, two at a time. A lantern burned brightly, casting light against the wide door. Raven turned the knob and threw it open. Behind him he heard someone sound an alarm. He heard the words 'under attack' and 'savages,' but he ignored the shouts of men.

Instinctively, Raven turned on the slippery wood floor. He heard a woman shriek from the top of the steps. Lamplight burned from the room to the right. Empowered by the adrenaline that ran through his blood, he gave the heavy wooden door a shove.

A middle-aged white man in a purple robe sprang out of a chair behind a desk, knocking over a glass. Red wine spread across the sheets of paper that lay before him. "Sweet Jesus," he muttered.

Raven raised the rifle. "I have come for my wife. Where is she?"

"Wh . . . what? Who?" Albert MacElby stumbled, his face a pasty gray.

Raven saw his adversary tremble and he nearly smiled.

But of course he could not let his guard down, not even for a moment. This wasn't merely his own life that lay in his palm, but Tess's as well. "Do I not speak the English tongue clearly?" he questioned, his pronunciation impeccable. "I tell you to turn over my wife. Turn her over to this man now or you will forfeit your worthless existence for her precious one."

The gray-haired man grimaced. "Your wife! God's teeth, heathen! I have no wife of yours!"

Raven heard the sound of footsteps in the hallway and came around the desk so that he held the man at point-blank range.

A black man and a white appeared in the doorway with loaded muskets. When they spotted Raven, they came to a halt.

"Do not step foot this way or the man will lose his life." Raven took the chance at assuming this was the uncle Tess spoke of and the master of the household.

The men's eyes grew round with fear.

"Didn't you hear them, you stupid bastards!" MacElby shouted.

Raven heard fear in the man's voice.

"Back off! Get the hell out of here before the red son of a bitch murders me in my own library!"

The two men backed out of the doorway slowly.

"Tell them to close the doors," Raven said, keeping his voice at a threateningly even keel. He raised his rifle a notch for emphasis. "Now."

"You heard him! Out! Out!"

The black and the white man closed the door between them.

Raven nodded. "Good. You do as I say and I give you

my word I will not take your life. Now tell me where she is."

"I swear by all that's holy, when I tell you I don't know who the blast you're talking about." He said the last words with a shudder.

Raven was growing impatient. His finger ached to pull the trigger and blast the twitching frown from the man's face. This was the man who had treated his Tess so cruelly. This man did not deserve to live. "My wife!" Raven shouted. "Tess!"

The verbal blow sent MacElby sprawling. He clutched the chair trying to keep from falling to the floor. "Your wife?" he sneered. "She married you?" His contempt was plain on his face and in his tone.

Raven came toward him, swinging the butt of his rifle, bringing it close to MacElby's head but not striking. MacElby went down on all fours, whimpering like a dog.

Raven was disgusted. He held the rifle over the pathetic white-hair's head. "Do not speak her name again in my presence. You are not worthy of passing her name on your lips. Now tell this man where she is. My patience grows as thin as skim ice."

"The . . . the cellar." MacElby covered his head with his hands, his bare, shaking knees protruding from the silk gown. "T . . . take her. Take the whore!"

Raven struck him on the back of the head hard enough to get his attention, but not render him unconscious.

MacElby made a strangled cry, falling flat on the hardwood floor. Blood stained the walnut butt of Raven's long rifle. "Keep your filthy white-hair words to yourself and take me to her." He prodded him, this time with the barrel. "Someone, anyone moves in a way this man takes to be aggressive and I will kill you." He tipped MacElby's chin with the barrel so that the man was forced to look at him. "I will kill you, but first I will cut off your balls so that I might have a new tobacco pouch."

MacElby dropped his face in his hands. "I'll take you. I'll take you. She's no good to me now. I . . . I'll be glad to have her off my hands."

"Now."

MacElby crawled to his feet and stumbled toward the door. He held his head with one hand and blood seeped between his fingers.

Tess's uncle led him out into the hallway, past the two men with muskets. MacElby held up his hand signalling for them to stand back. "I mean it, you jackasses. I don't want her! He can have her! She isn't worth the trouble."

Down the hallway Raven followed the uncle. In a corner at the end of a hall, he threw open a door and motioned into the darkness. "Down there. I'll need a light."

Raven took a step back and indicated a burning wall sconce with the rifle. "The candle. Take it. Is there an outside entrance?"

"Y . . . yes."

Raven gave a nod, following him down the narrow wooden steps. The cellar was dark and cool. Raven listened carefully as they made there way down a brick passageway and into one large room which led into another. "Tess!" he shouted. "Tess! It is I, the Raven. I have come for you!"

For a moment there was silence, and for that long moment Raven doubted his instincts. Was Tess dead? Had he arrived too late?

"How many days has she been down here?" Raven demanded.

"Only a few."

"How many!" He pressed the open barrel into the man's shoulder.

"Two . . . just three."

Raven cursed beneath his breath. "Tess," he shouted "it is I the Raven. I have come for you."

Raven heard a strangled cry and then the croak of a voice. "Raven? Raven?" The last time, it was a shriek.

"You won't get away with this, coming to our towns. Into our homes," MacElby flung as he reached a squat wooden-planked door. "We'll annihilate you. Men, women, and little red bastard alike. We'll smite you hip and thigh, wipe you off the face of the earth!"

"The door," Raven urged, ignoring the frightened man's tirade. "Tess, this man comes!"

She pounded on the door from the far side. "Raven. Oh, God, you're alive, Raven!"

MacElby lifted the iron latch and swung open the door.

Raven caught sight of Tess in the semi-darkness as she hurled herself out of the little room and into his arms. He had to fight the urge to gather her into his arms and kiss her mouth. "Tess," was all he could say as he held her at arm's length still holding his rifle on the uncle.

"You're alive," she kept repeating over and over again. "How can you be alive?"

"Tess," Raven said softly in her ear, keeping one eye on MacElby. "We must take ourselves from this wicked place. Then there will be time to talk, to hold each other."

She wiped at the tears that ran down her cheeks. She was so pale and drawn, and thinner, thinner than he had remembered her.

"Lead us out," Raven ordered.

MacElby, his back pressed to the brick wall, lifted the candle so that feeble yellow light cast across Tess's face.

"You married this creature?" he spit. "You little whore! You married him and that's why he spared your life?"

"Let's go, Raven," Tess whispered, paying no heed to her uncle's foul words. "Just take me far from here . . . please."

Raven prodded MacElby with the barrel of the long rifle, and MacElby moved along the dark, brick passageway.

They turned a sharp corner and Tess's uncle lifted the candle. "Up the stairs. It leads out. Ask my dear niece, I'm certain she can find her way."

Raven pushed Tess ahead of him. "Go, *ki-ti-hi*."

She scrambled past him, reaching for his hand as she climbed the steep steps.

"Do not come after us, this man warn you. She is mine. She will always be mine."

"Take her," MacElby shouted with disgust, spittle gathering at the corners of his mouth. "Common Indian-loving slut that she is!"

Raven's eyes narrowed. For a long second he contemplated killing the man. Anyone as foul as he had no right to roam this earth. But who was he to decide? Didn't the buzzards have as much right to this land as the Lenape?

Raven backed his way up the steps. Above him he heard the creak of rusty hinges and the bump of the door swinging open. Moonlight streamed down the staircase.

"You won't get away with this!" MacElby shouted. "I know where your village is, you red son of bitch! I'll burn you out, ever last one of you!"

Raven stepped off the top step and dropped the doors down on the man, muffling his voice. Grabbing a stick from the ground, he slipped it between the two handles so that the uncle wouldn't be able to get through the door.

That would give him and Tess a few extra precious moments to escape.

"Raven," Tess cried, throwing herself into his arms.

Raven allowed himself one hug, one kiss, and then he held her at arm's length again. The side yard was empty but he could hear the sounds of dogs barking and the hushed tones of men. There wasn't much time. Soon he and Tess would be hunted like animals.

"Listen to this man," Raven said softly, gently. "We must run from this place. Can you run, my heart?"

She looked into his eyes. Her face was pale and haggard but her eyes, her dark eyes, shined as brightly as the stars overhead. "I can do it. I can run. Take me anywhere, just away from here."

Raven clasped her hand in his, giving it a squeeze, and then, side by side they dashed into the cover of darkness.

Thirty

As dawn's first light streaked across the dark sky, Tess knelt beside Raven on a beach on the Chesapeake Bay and washed her face, letting the droplets of water trickle down her chin to dampen the bodice of the torn gown she wore.

Tess turned and smiled at Raven. She still couldn't believe he was alive. Alive! She brushed her knuckles against his bare arm in a caress. "How could I have ever doubted you? You said you would come for me. How could I have thought you were dead?"

He took her hand, planting a lingering kiss in her palm. "This man is only sorry he did not come sooner. Your uncle would never have brought you water. You could have died, Tess."

She touched his cheek. "But I didn't. You saved me. You did your duty to your people and to your men, and you saved me, too." Tess looked out at the water to see the sun's first rays glimmering off the glassy surface. Seagulls circled overhead, crying mournfully.

Tess felt so dirty, dirty not just from days of being unwashed, but dirty from the touch of Myron and her uncle. Dirty from the touch of English *manake*.

Tess stood up and began yanking at the back buttons of the gray gown Myron had given her.

"What are you doing?"

"What's it look like I'm going to do. I'm going to take a bath." She pulled the shoulders of the gown down and shimmied out of it. Next came the stays.

"Now? You bathe now?"

She laughed feeling freer than she ever had in her lifetime. The air smelled of the salt of the bay and the release of confinement. "I am. Give me a bath and then I'll face the world. I'll fight the whole damned English army if you want me to. But first I'll have a bath." She pulled her shift over her head and ran down the beach naked. "Going to join me?" she called over her shoulder.

In a moment Raven was running beside her, his nude, suntanned body as sleek and muscular as a wild cat's. His shiny black hair rippled down his back, whipping in the salty breeze. Tess threw back her head, running faster. "Catch me!" she dared.

Raven caught her arm, and locked in an embrace they fell into the shallow water. Tess laughed and splashed, spitting and sputtering. She slipped out of his arms and swam out a ways. Standing in waist-deep water, she pulled handfuls of sand off the bay's bottom and scrubbed every inch of her skin until it tingled. As she washed in the Lenape way, she watched Raven.

As his hands glanced over his own flesh Tess began to imagine, to remember, what it was like to touch him. Her heart fluttered and she felt a familiar warmth spread in her loins. Slowly she walked toward him, her eyes only for him.

"Raven," she whispered.

He held his hand out to her. "Tess."

Reaching him, she threw her arms around his neck and he pulled her tight against his hard frame. Their mouths met with such a fierceness that it frightened Tess. It frightened her to think that she loved this man, so different than herself, more than she loved life itself.

"Love me," she whispered huskily in his ear. "Touch me, husband. Take away the pain of our enemy, of our future that's unknown."

"Tess, Tess," he crooned. "Heart of my heart." He covered her face in soft fleeting kisses, caressing her back, her buttocks, her long legs. Bay water splashed against her skin, the cool of the water blending with the heat of his touch.

Tess threw back her head as he kissed the pulse of her throat. His hands, his mouth, they were everywhere, soothing her, tantalizing her.

Tess stroked the thick corded muscles of his shoulders and back. She sucked on one male nipple until it was hard in her mouth and she heard him groan with pleasure.

Raven slipped his knee between her thighs and she rubbed her groin against it, sighing, moaning. He ran his fingers through her wet hair as she covered his chest with fervent kisses.

A seabird soared overhead, calling to its mate, but Tess barely heard the sounds of the gulls or the wash of the tide on the beach. She was lost, lost in the sensation of Raven's touch, lost in the true sense of what it was to love.

"Talk to me," she murmured. "I want to hear your voice."

His laughter was rich and throaty. "I love this place," he whispered, kissing the hollow of her shoulder. "And this place." He closed his mouth over one pert nipple and she arched her back, crying out in delight. "But this place, this place . . ." He ran his finger down her belly to the bed of red curls at the apex of her thighs. "This is the place most sweet to this man."

Tess laughed, running her hands through his wet, thick hair as he knelt in the water to bring his mouth to that secret place she would share with no man but him.

"You'll drown yourself," she teased, tugging at his shoulders. "Let's go up on the beach."

Pressing a kiss to the triangle of wet curls, he stood facing her. Raising both hands to hers, instinctively she clasped them, their fingers entwining. His gaze met hers and held her spellbound. "For all time this man declares his love for this woman," he said, his voice ringing in the still morning air. "I did not take my vow seriously the night our Shaman married us. But I make this commitment here, now, before no one but you and the mighty Creator."

Tears stung Tess's eyes. "I love you," was all she could manage.

Raven swung her into his arms, and she looped her hands around his neck. Their gazes locked, he carried her to the shore and laid her gently on the beach.

Tess put out her arms to him, the need to feel him inside her so strong that she trembled. "Love me," she said, raising her hands to him.

Raven lowered his body over hers and with one gentle motion, he took her. Tess looped her arms around his neck, and letting her eyes drift shut, began to move to the rhythm of the music in her head, the same music she knew Raven heard.

Later, when their desires were fulfilled, their breathing steady once again, Raven sat up. He picked up a clam shell and hurled it into the water. "I wish that this man could stay here with you for many days. It would be good to be alone with you. To fish with you, to hunt, to make love on the beach."

Tess sat up beside him to look out on the bay. The sun was up now, bright and bold in the blue sky. It warmed her heart as well as her face. "But we can't, can we?" she said softly.

He shook his head. "Your uncle vowed to retaliate. He says he knows where the village is. I fear for my people."

"Maybe he's lying," she offered hopefully.

"Perhaps, but you and I know we cannot depend on that. We must return to the village and prepare for battle."

Tess glanced at Raven. "I can't go."

He looked at her. "What do you say?"

She covered his hand with hers. "Sky. I have to find Sky. I'm hoping she's right in Annapolis with Marty. But wherever she is, I have to find her." She looked away. "Raven, I found out that my sister is dead. Abby is dead, and she's been dead for a long time."

"This man is sorry."

Regaining her composure, she went on. "I know I can't bring Abby back. But this makes it even more important that I find Sky and care for her. Your mother says nothing is coincidence. Everything is laid in the stars before we're born. All along I thought I was supposed to be taking care of Abby, but maybe it's Sky that I have to be here for." She took Raven's hand in hers. "So I want you to go on to the village. I'll go back to Annapolis, find Sky, and I'll join you. I can find my way back to the village; I know I can."

Raven pressed a kiss to the pulse at her wrist. "This child is that important to you? You love her in your heart?"

"Yes. Yes."

"Then this man loves her as well. If you want the child to take into our lodge as your own, then I want her as my own. I will be as good a father to her as to the child you carry in your womb."

Tess made a face. "The child I carry in my womb? What are you talking about?"

Raven smiled. "Dream Woman says you carry our first born."

Tess brushed her fingers over her bare, flat stomach. *Could it be true?* She laughed, giddy with the idea. *Raven's child* . . . "But how could Dream Woman know?" she asked suspiciously. "I haven't even missed my courses yet."

"She is the Woman of Dreams. She knows, my Tess."

"A baby," she whispered. "We're going to have a baby?" She lifted her lashes. "And you don't mind?"

"Of course this man does not mind. It is every Lenape man's desire to have a child by the woman he loves. But this means that I must get you safely to our village where our child cannot be harmed." He sprang to his feet offering her his hand. "So let us return to the evil 'Napolis, find the child, and then we warn our Lenape brothers."

Tess squeezed Raven's hand, making the strength of his determination her own strength. "Let us warn *our* Lenape brothers . . ." she echoed.

The following evening Tess, Raven, and Sky rode into the Lenape village on the backs of two fine mares. Tess could not believe their good fortune. After all the bad things that had happened, after all the bad luck and misfortune, it seemed as if suddenly her life was blessed. She and Raven had found Marty's father's cabin on the outskirts of Annapolis. Not only did Marty turn the child over to her safely, but she gave Tess two horses as a gift. Tess and Raven made it back to the village quicker than they could have if they had not taken the time to return for the child.

Marty had wished them Godspeed and urged them to run for their lives. As they spoke, Albert MacElby was already forming a group of men to attack the Lenape village. He had vowed to take revenge on the savages who had kidnapped his dear niece not once, but twice.

At the edge of the village Tess and Raven dismounted. Tess pulled Sky down off the horse; the little girl's face was beaming. "This is our home now," Tess signed. "We are Lenape, you and I."

Sky nodded, slipping her small hand into Tess's.

Side by side, Tess and Raven walked into the village, the villagers gathering around them in excitement.

"We must gather in the Big House," Raven called out. "Summon our great chief and the mighty Shaman. There is danger at our door, brothers and sisters."

Dream Woman met Tess halfway across the compound. She threw her arms around Tess, tears running freely down her cheeks. "My daughter, this old woman feared she would never set sight of your face again!"

Tess hugged her mother-in-law tightly. "I'm so glad to be here, Dream Woman. So glad to be home." She pulled back a little, looking into her eyes. "Raven told me about Taande. I'm so sorry. I know you loved him. And Raven's sorry, too. Raven loved Taande, no matter what he might have said."

"This woman knows, she knows." She smiled sadly. "I miss him, but I must be glad for the time we had together." Dream Woman looped her arm through Tess's.

"Come let me take you to my hearth and give you food while my son speaks to our people in the Big House."

"No." Raven laid his arm on Tess's. "My wife will join me in the Big House. She is one of us now, and she has a right to speak her thoughts, as much right as any of us."

Tess looked up at Raven who stood over her shoulder. "You . . . you want me at the council meeting?"

"Take the child, Mother. Have one of the old ones care for her. She does not hear our words, so you must speak with the handsigns we speak to other tribes with."

Dream Woman took Sky's hand, and with a little encouragement from Tess, Sky went off with Dream Woman.

Less than twenty minutes later, every able-bodied man and woman had gathered in the Big House. After a quick prayer by the Shaman, Polished Stone, the chief, stood. "Friends, we gather here because our war chief, Raven, tells us he has grave news from the white-hair village of 'Napolis." She indicated him with a sweep of her hand. "I will let him speak."

Tess listened as Raven explained in his native tongue how he had found Tess and how her uncle had threatened to attack the village. As his story unfolded, Tess was amazed that not a single villager stood up to express distaste for her because she had brought this upon them. She had passed some rite of fire at an unknown point in the last few weeks, and now suddenly they considered her one of their own.

Several of the men stood up with suggestions as to how to defend the village. Then, hesitantly, Tess lifted her hand.

"Let her speak," She-Who-Swings, recognized Tess. "I will hear the wife of Raven."

Tess stood, a little a nervous, but determined she had

to say what she felt in her heart. She spoke in Lenape, substituting English words when necessary. "This . . . this woman understands why you feel you must defend your village, but . . . but there is another choice." She scanned the crowd of quiet men and women, all their black eyes on her. "Even if we beat these men, they will come again. They are evil; my uncle, and the man I almost married. Tomorrow, next week, next year they will come again. The village is too close to the English villages. I do not truthfully know how you've managed to stay here this long and live peaceably."

"What do you say, then?" asked a young woman with a red feather earring.

"I say, I suggest, that we should consider packing our belongings and going to a place where there are no white men, where no one will ever harm us again."

"Go?" a man called. "Our people have been here for a thousand years. We cannot go."

Dream Woman lifted a finger. "Tess speaks wisely. This is not the first time this has been brought up, brothers and sister of the Lenape. We have talked before of moving as the other Lenape have moved. Perhaps it is time to follow the path of our destiny."

Raven's gaze fixed on Tess. "We can beat them, the English *manake.*"

"I know you can," she answered Raven directly. "But didn't you once tell me that the position of war chief was not just to lead men into battle but to know when to fight and when not to fight?" She shook her head. "This is not the time to fight, husband. If we win today, we cannot win tomorrow. Men will die, women and children will die." She fought tears. "I am afraid for your people's survival, people who have become my people."

Raven was silent for a long moment. The entire village was silent. Raven looked from Tess, to the villagers, to She-Who-Swings-From-The-Stars. "What say you, great chief?"

"What say you, *llua?*"

He turned back to Tess. "I say that my wife is a wise woman. I say that she knows the white-hairs. I say we move north, north into the French Canadas where no one will ever harm our people again."

A murmur of excitement rippled through the crowd.

"What say you, men and women of the Lenape?" She-Who-Swings asked.

"Aye," they called one by one. "Yes. *Kehella.*"

The chief lifted her hands heavenward. "Our people say we go. So lead us, brother Raven. Tell us what we must do to prepare for our enemy's arrival, and we will fly away into the night."

Once the decision to move the village was made, Tess was amazed by how quickly the Lenape men and women moved into action. All through the night they gathered their belongings and built travois to carry them. Foodstuffs were packed into every corn-husk basket and skin bag they owned. Squash and beans were picked from the garden. Strips of dried venison, fish, and clams, were packed into cloth baskets. Lodge poles were dug up and loaded onto travois or burned.

With Dream Woman's help, Tess packed the wedding gifts she and Raven had received. All her household items, stored food, and Raven's weapons were packed, and tied to a skin travois to be pulled by a man or shaggy pony. Of course many things had to be left behind, but after all

Tess had been through, possessions meant nothing to her. For years she had dreamed of living in a big house with clothes and dishes and silver, and now all that mattered was being with Raven and the others she'd come to love.

After most of Raven's wigwam had been emptied Tess found a basket under the sleeping platform. From it, she pulled the pair of hard, dry leather slippers she had brought with her. Jocelyn's slippers . . .

Tess fingered the cracked leather, thinking she should just leave the silly things behind, but then she thought better of it. She would take Jocelyn's slippers with her to the new land to the north, and each time she looked at the slippers she would remember the trials she had had to endure to find the happiness she now possessed. As she dropped the slippers into a small reed basket and handed them to Sky to be loaded onto the travois, she thought to herself that perhaps all the pain, all the sorrow, had been somehow necessary, or else how would she have appreciated her happiness as much as she appreciated it now?

Before dawn, the villagers gathered at the communal firepit to pray to the Creator *Manito* for traveling mercies. After a prayer led by the Shaman, and a brief ceremony, Raven called for the men to light their torches and set fire to the wigwams. By mutual agreement, the Lenape would leave nothing of their village for the English to desecrate.

Tess stood beside Raven and the others as the men lit the homes one by one. And then, with a great cheer, the villagers started out of the village. They would walk west until they were well out of the way of the English settlements and then they would bear north. When Albert MacElby and his henchmen arrived at the village, there would be no one there to attack, there would be nothing left of the Lenape but the smoldering ruins of their homes.

Once the wigwams were set aflame, the Lenape walked out of the village. Small children and the elderly rode on the travois pulled by the young men or by one of the few ponies the village owned. Tess and Raven walked at the rear of the column with Dream Woman and Sky. Warriors, their long rifles primed, flanked the travelers for protection.

Just as Tess lost sight of the burning wigwams she heard a voice calling from behind them. "Have we left someone?" she asked, swinging around to peer into the darkness.

Raven lifted his French musket, brought back from Braddock's massacre. "Who goes there?" he shouted in English.

"Ne nipauwi!" came a male voice. "Wait! Where do you go?"

To Tess's shock, out of the billowing smoke Taande appeared.

Tess heard Dream Woman give a strangled cry as she raced across the forest floor, her arms outstretched. Taande limped toward her, calling her name.

Tears gathered in the corners of Tess's eyes as Taande and Dream Woman embraced, kissing like young lovers. Looping her arm through Raven's she looked up at him. "He's alive," she whispered. "He's alive and somehow he made it back here."

Raven stood beside her for a moment, his face devoid of any emotion. Then, he gently disengaged Tess's arm from his and crossed the woods to his mother and her lover. "Taande," he said softly.

Tess held her breath.

"Taande, this man is glad to see you. We will need a

great warrior such as yourself to get us safely to the Canada mountains we seek."

The two men's gazes met for an instant, and then Raven walked away. "Let us hurry, brother! The *manake* come. This man will explain all that has happened since we last saw your face once we are safe from the danger."

Taande and Dream Woman walked ahead, arm in arm, greeting the other villagers.

Tess fell into step beside Raven at the rear of the group. Suddenly melancholy, she glanced over her shoulder at the village in the distance to see flames shooting into the dark sky, sending columns of smoke heavenward. This was the place she and Raven had fallen in love, the place where she had come to truly know herself, and now she was leaving it all behind.

Raven laid his hand gently on her shoulder. "Do not look back, wife of mine, heart of my heart. Look forward into our future, forward into the future of our children." He threaded his fingers with hers, and kissed her mouth. "Look forward into the future to a day when the red and white men will live under the same sky as one people . . ."

Epilogue

Five years later
The Canadian Mountains

Tess tucked a white rabbit-skin fur over her sleeping infant son and patted the tiny cradle Raven had fashioned from a hollow log. "Sleep well, little warrior," she murmured in Algonquian.

Then she turned to the blazing firepit in the center of the family lodge and set to work on the evening meal. The winter wind howled outside, but the bark and mud outer walls, lined by the tanned skin that made up the inner walls, kept out the frigid cold, wrapping her family in a blanket of cozy warmth.

Tess hummed to herself as she patted out maple corncakes on a baking stone next to the fire. Any moment Raven would return from ice fishing with the girls. Tess smiled. Their girls . . .

Sky had grown into a beautiful young lady, so beautiful that she had already caught the fancy of several of the tribe's young men. Though it would be several years before she and Raven would even consider allowing Sky to wed, it warmed Tess's heart to know that her deafness had no important impact on her life. She had been accepted into the tribe as easily as Tess herself had been accepted.

And then there was little Holly, four years old and full of fire, a redhead with her father's skin tone, and eyes as black as pitch. Just as Dream Woman had predicted, Holly had been born nine months after Braddock's massacre.

Laughter at her doorway brought Tess back to the present. The doorflap rose and Sky and Holly ran inside, followed by their father. All three were laughing and stomping their fur boots, sending powdery snow everywhere.

"Take off your wet things!" Tess called, their laughter infectious.

"Oh, Mama," Holly answered. "Me and Sky, we want to go with Grandma. She and Taande are making maple candy in the snow." The little girl bounced up and down, her red braids swinging from her fuzzy rabbit-skin hat. "Please."

Tess looked to Raven, who was hanging a string of cleaned fish from a hook on the door. "Ask your father. It's very cold out."

"It is not too cold, they can go."

Holly bounced up and down, signing to Sky.

Sky turned to her mother and signed, "Don't worry, I'll watch and make sure she doesn't get too cold."

"Thank you," Tess answered. "Go on with you and don't eat so much candy that you spoil your evening meal."

Raven lifted the leather doorflap to let his daughters out of the lodge and then let it fall. As he shrugged off his heavy bearskin cloak, he looked to Tess who had returned to the firepit. "We're alone, *ki-ti-hi*. Put down your cooking and come to this man."

"The evening meal," Tess objected. "It's already mid-afternoon." But when he put out his hand to her, she left the corncakes to burn and went to him.

Raven wrapped his arms around her and she snuggled against his broad, muscular chest. "You're cold," she protested.

"So warm me . . ."

She laughed, her voice low and sensual in the cozy lodge. "Now? With your son, Takooko, sleeping so soundly."

Raven kissed the pulse at her throat. "How does my son think he got here, but by his sisters sleeping soundly?"

Tess's laugh mingled with Raven's. Life was hard, but good here in the northern mountains. The French left the tribe to themselves and there were other Algonquian villages nearby. Here Raven and Tess's family would be safe, safe from the evils of the English from which they had escaped.

"Come to my sleeping mat, wife of mine, and let me show you something special I have for you," Raven whispered in her ear, already caressing one full breast through the leather of her quilled tunic.

"First tell me you love me. It took you so long to admit it, *neetilose,* that I will never hear it often enough."

"*K'daholel, K'daholel,*" he murmured huskily, kissing her cheeks, the tip of her nose, the cleft of her chin. "Forever and then some, this man will love you. He is only sorry for the years he lived without you."

Tess took Raven's hand and led him toward the sleeping platform they shared at the rear of the lodge. "Come, husband, heart of my heart, let us make up for those lost years . . ."

Please turn the page for an
exciting sneak preview of
Colleen Faulkner's next
Zebra historical romance
O'BRIAN'S BRIDE
to be published in April 1995

Prologue

The Brandywine River
Delaware Colony
July, 1773

The blast of the explosion and the sound of the splintering window glass tore Elizabeth from a deep slumber. For a heart-stopping moment, she was completely disoriented. Chunks of plaster and fine dust from the ceiling fell onto the bed. The bedchamber walls shook with another, smaller explosion and a portrait flew off the wall and clattered across the plank floor.

Elizabeth bolted upright in the bed, bringing her hand to her pounding heart. The entire room was illuminated by the orange light of a blaze outside her window.

With a cry of fright, she threw back her blankets and leaped out of bed. Her bare feet hit the glass and plaster that littered the floor. "Dear God," she murmured as she searched frantically for her silk mules pushed beneath the high bedstead.

Her feet protected, she ran to the window, the broken glass making a sickening crunch beneath her. Carefully, she lifted the heavy wood frame of the shattered window and stuck her head out. The heat of the blaze down the hill from the manor house hit her full in the face and she instinctively pulled back, striking her head on the window frame.

"Ouch," she muttered, running her hand across the crown of her head. The ground below was alive with activity as workmen raced down the dirt lane toward the burning wooden building perched on the edge of the river. A bell clanged and a woman wailed. Somewhere a child was crying. A wagon filled with men with buckets rolled by beneath her. The sounds of shouting men, pounding feet, and the roar of the enormous fire assaulted her ears. The air was filled with the stench of sulfur and smoke and the glowing red cinders of the burning building.

Elizabeth could do nothing but stand there, paralyzed with fear, and stare at the fiery blaze below. Paul had once mentioned the possibility of explosions in the powder mills, but he'd said it was nothing to worry her pretty head over. He said the explosions were rare at his mills. He said he and his men were careful.

Paul. . . . Oh, God, where was Paul?

Elizabeth spun around to stare at their empty bed. Suddenly she couldn't breathe. It had to be well after midnight. Where was her new husband?

One

One Year Later

"I'll not have it!" Elizabeth Lawrence struck her fist on the polished hardwood desk. "How will we ever improve our reputation if we're known as thieves by our own neighbors?"

Jessop leaned against the doorjamb, crossing his arms over his chest. "We're not thieves. The price for the coal was agreed upon by both parties. It's business, dear, plain and simple."

"Robbery, plain and simple." She thrust her quill into the inkwell and added another figure to a column of numbers on the paper. She rubbed her temple absently. She had a headache. Discussing the black powder mill she'd inherited from her deceased husband always gave her a headache. She and Jessop, her fiance, disagreed on basic ethics concerning how business should be conducted. "Give him twenty-five percent more, Jessop."

"Twenty-five percent!" Jessop let his long arms fall to his sides. "Liz, you haven't got much of my brother's money left to throw around. You should see this as an opportunity. Take the money you save and use it to pay one of your creditors in Philadelphia."

She didn't look up. "Do it, Jessop. Twenty-five percent. I still get a good deal and so do they."

"Liz—"

"It's mine to do with as I please, isn't it? *My money,* what little there is of it," she went on, trying not to sound accusatory. Her late husband had led her father to believe that he and his brother were both far better off financially than they actually were. *"My stamp mill and magazine,* which are only half-reconstructed after more than six months of building. *My waterwheel,* on the river that won't turn the blessed grinding stone!" Elizabeth hadn't meant her last words to come so forcefully. She was a lady, and ladies didn't shout at the gentlemen they intended to marry. But, by the King's cod, she'd do what she thought right, and neither Jessop nor any other man was going to change her mind. She intended to get this black powder mill up and running at a profit, something neither of the Lawrence men had been able to accomplish.

Jessop smoothed one prematurely graying temple. He was a handsome man, taller than Paul had been, but with the same clear blue eyes, the same pleasant face. "Liz, you're making a mistake," he said quietly. "I'm not trying to tell you what to do. I—"

"The hell you're not!" Elizabeth dropped her quill into the inkwell and rose from her chair. "Every decision I make, every step I take, you have an opinion!"

"Elizabeth." He was speaking like he was her father now. God, how Elizabeth hated that condescending tone, that *you're a woman and therefore too stupid to know what you're doing* sound in his voice. "I'm just trying to keep you from making any serious mistakes. You lost a great deal in the explosion; supplies, two men killed with twelve injured—"

"I lost my husband," she intoned softly.

"I lost my brother." His gaze met hers and his face softened. "And, as your brother-in-law, as the man who loves you, it's my duty to guide you. I've been in the shipping business many years."

She held up a palm. "I know, I know. And I'm the little lady from Yorkshire with nothing but dancing, teas, and music lessons for experience." She indicated him, then herself with a wave of her hand. "And of course there's the fact that you're a man and I'm a woman."

"Yes, you are, aren't you?" He leaned forward to kiss her mouth, trying to make light of her words, but Elizabeth pulled out of his reach. She was in no mood for pleasures, his or her own.

"I'm serious, Jessop. I don't appreciate your criticizing every decision I make. You agreed that I would run the powder mills, at least until we're wed." She made a tight fist. "I know more about chemistry than anyone on this river. I know that if I can get the right ingredients, the right equipment up and operating, the right foreman to run the whole damned thing, I can make it work. I could make the best black powder these Colonies have ever seen. We go to war, there'll be no more imports. Either we make our own gunpowder or we won't have a chance."

"We?" He lifted an eyebrow. "We? A good English-woman like yourself would dare sell black powder to rebels?"

"I'm not going to discuss politics with you, Jessop. I haven't the time nor the energy. Just increase the payment for the coal and see to the delivery, will you?"

The door to the front office opened and slammed shut, and from her private office in the rear, Elizabeth could hear the nervous scrape of a man's boots. A worker . . .

a worker who had not washed his hands at the washbasin in the front reception area there for that purpose. Something was wrong.

Elizabeth let out a sigh as she strode to the door leading to the front office. What now? It wasn't yet noon and she already had an earful of problems. Her housekeeper was complaining of shiftless housemaids, her shipment of potassium nitrate couldn't be located, and she hadn't made a single plan for the engagement dinner party she and Jessop were having in less than a month.

"Yes. What is it?" Elizabeth looked at the clerk perched on a high stool behind the front desk and then to the worker standing awkwardly near the door, his entire body covered in a fine layer of coal dust. "Can I help you, Johnny?"

Johnny Bennett swept off his battered felt hat anxiously. "Ye . . . ye gotta come quick, mistress. I . . . I'm afraid he's gonna kill 'im!"

"What? Who are you talking about?" Elizabeth followed Johnny out of the office and down the granite steps that would lead them past the manor house to the mills that lay along the riverbed.

"Bad fight, mistress. Him and Samson. I'm afraid he's gonna kill 'im!"

"Who?" Elizabeth quickened her pace. She could hear the sounds of a brawl on the dirt lane below the manor house. Men's shouts mingled with the thuds of fists meeting flesh, one after the other. "You're afraid Samson's going to kill who?"

"Ye got it turned around, ma'am." Johnny stepped out of his mistress's way so that she could see the fight at the bottom of the hill. "It's yer new foreman, ma'am. Look, he's beatin' the tar outta Samson."

"God save us from men," Elizabeth muttered, taking the next set of stone steps down the hill two at a time.

"Elizabeth! Elizabeth!" Jessop hollered from the office door. "Let me handle this. You shouldn't be—"

Her fiance's words were lost to her as she set her attention on the altercation below. Samson, one of her workers, a free black man, and a blond-haired stranger were struggling on the dusty ground. He couldn't possibly be the new foreman she'd been waiting on all these months, could he?

The stranger had managed to climb on top of Samson and was now hammering her worker's face with sturdy fists.

"Enough! Enough!" Elizabeth shouted.

The crowd of mill workers separated, allowing her to walk through the middle of the group that had gathered around the fight.

"Samson!" Elizabeth shouted. "You know we do not permit fighting at Lawrence Mills. She was looking down on Samson who was pinned on his back by the brawny blond. "Mister . . . Mister—" She snapped her thumb and forefinger. *God's teeth, what was the name of the man she'd hired? O'Brian?* "Mister O'Brian, that will be quite enough!"

Somehow Samson managed to flip the new foreman over and roll out of his reach. He stumbled to his feet.

"Now step back," Elizabeth shouted, waving her hand at Samson. "Just step away."

The crowd of dirty-faced men that had gathered had quieted. Everyone was staring at Elizabeth and the men in the center of the road.

Samson's nose was bloody and one eye was already swelling shut. His dirty muslin shirt was torn and he was missing one shoe. The blond got to his feet. Elizabeth still hadn't caught a good look at his face.

"Now tell me what this is all—"

The blond swung his fist, cracking Samson square in the jaw, and the shouting rose again. Samson swung in response and suddenly the men were fighting again as if they'd never heard her or seen her to begin with.

Elizabeth swore beneath her breath. She'd never cursed in her life before she'd come to the Lawrence Mills. But this new land, the harsh realities of being alone in the world, had hardened her in the last twelve months. Hardened her too much she feared.

Elizabeth heard Jessop shout to her from behind, but she ignored him. Men brawling on her property! She wouldn't have it. The both of them could take their wages and go if they liked, but she'd not having fighting among her employed!

"Gentlemen," Elizabeth shouted above the hoots and jeers of the mill workers now crowded around her and the fighting men again. "I will not stand for this!" She grasped Samson's sleeve, sweaty and splattered with blood. "That will be—"

Elizabeth didn't know exactly what happened next. Did she step in front of Samson, or did he step back? All she knew was that suddenly a fist made contact with her cheekbone.

"Oh! Son of a—" The impact of the punch knocked her backward onto the dusty ground.

The mill workers were stunned into momentary silence. The brawl came to an abrupt halt.

"Good God!" Jessop shouted from somewhere behind her, beyond the throng of men. "Let me through! Liz, are you all right? Are you hurt? Let me through!"

Elizabeth scrambled to her feet, resisting the urge to touch her smarting cheekbone.

"God sake, Mistress Law'ence." Samson reached out with one meaty black hand, but Elizabeth was already standing again.

"What is the meaning of this?" she demanded furiously.

"He said somethin' I didn't like—" Samson pointed at the stranger "—and don't no one talk to Samson that way. This man be a free man. I don't take nothin' from no one!"

Elizabeth turned to the stranger. "Well, what have you got to say for yourself?" she panted.

The blond, a tall man with shoulders as broad as a blacksmith's, ground the ball of his boot into the dirt and slowly lifted his head to look at her for the first time.

Elizabeth was immediately taken back by the rugged good looks of the stranger. He didn't look like a mill worker. His face lacked the pinched cheeks, the empty eyes—results of generations of poor living conditions and lack of proper nutrition. It wasn't that he was handsome in the way that Jessop was, but there was an animal-like magnetism that made him frighteningly attractive. He had a broad face covered with short blond whiskers, and green eyes, eyes as green as a summer meadow. His shoulder-length hair hung straight and clean down his back. His mouth, a sensuous mouth, was drawn in an odd smirk.

He was staring at her with more male interest than Elizabeth thought appropriate. Still, she knew she flushed. There was something about the way he looked at her that made her feel overly warm.

"With all respect, ma'am," the virile stranger picked his hat up off the ground and beat it against his knee, "he was the one that started it first, not I."

Proper speech—an educated man? And what accent was that? Elizabeth wondered. O'Brian was an Irish name, but there was a hint of the sound of France in his rich tenor voice. This was not the man she had expected at all . . . in more ways than one.

Elizabeth cleared her throat. "Is that right?" she questioned sharply, hiding her discomfort. "And whom might I ask am I addressing?"

"Patrick O'Brian, ma'am."

"Patrick?" She frowned. "I thought I hired a Michael O'Brian."

"Michael Patrick O'Brian. A Mister E. Lawrence is expecting me."

Jessop appeared at Elizabeth's side. "I told you this wasn't a good idea, bringing him here like this," he said softly in her ear. "He's not been here five minutes and already he's a troublemaker. Dismiss him at once."

Elizabeth ignored Jessop. "E. Lawrence?" she questioned. "You're speaking to him."

O'Brian shifted his gaze to Jessop. "Pleased to meet you, sir. I only apologize for the circumstances. I didn't mean to clip the lady. But she—"

Elizabeth shook her head, crossing her arms over her chest. "No. You misunderstand. *I* am E. Lawrence. I'm the one who hired you, Mister O'Brian."

O'Brian glanced at her suspiciously. "You?"

"Yes. I own these mills. I hired a foreman experienced in the black powder industry, apprenticed in the finest mill in France. Has there been a mistake?"

He was staring at her as if she'd grown a horn in the center of her forehead. Elizabeth would have laughed except that she'd grown tired of this reaction among men when they discovered that E. Lawrence was a woman.

Most men didn't want to do business with her simply because she was a woman, and it made her furious.

O'Brian was looking at Jessop as if for confirmation.

"I'm speaking to you, sir. I said, has there been a mistake? Are you or are you not the Mister O'Brian my solicitor hired to run my mill?" She turned away, giving him a moment to think about his answer. "That will be all," she told the mill workers still crowded around and listening intently. "Samson, I'll see you after supper in my office."

"Yes, ma'am."

The workers began to shuffle off, disappointed that they were being excluded from the conversation between their mistress and the new foreman.

Elizabeth turned her attention back to O'Brian who had returned his hat to his head and was now standing at an easy stance. He didn't look like a man who feared he was about to be released from the job he hadn't yet started. "Well?" she asked. "Are you the man I hired? Do you have the experience you claimed, or was this all a ploy to get to the Colonies on my hard-earned coin?"

"Just dismiss him," Jessop repeated. "Haven't you got enough trouble without hiring the likes of this *Irishman?*"

O'Brian shot Jessop a look that could have carved him into neat equal parts.

"I can handle this, Jessop." She forced herself to smile sweetly. "If you'll just see to the coal shipment, I can deal with Mister O'Brian."

Jessop opened his mouth to say something, but then gave a wave of his hand. "Fine. Be stubborn, Liz. I'm going home to look in on Sister. I'll see you this evening before dinner."

Elizabeth didn't speak again until Jessop was out of

earshot. He'd be angry with her for a few hours, but he'd get over it. Slowly she turned her attention back to the disturbing man before her. "You were about to say?"

He glanced up the hill at the retreating Jessop, then back at Elizabeth. "I'll be honest with you, because it's my way. I didn't agree to work for a female. Had I known, I'd not have taken the position."

Elizabeth touched her cheekbone lightly. "Who says you've got the position? You struck me."

"It was an accident. I apologize, but you stepped in my way. Women have no place in the midst of men fighting."

"Look, the fact of the matter is that I paid good money to get you here. I'm desperate for a decent foreman. If you've got the experience you claim you do, I'll just forget this ever happened and we'll start from a clean slate." She glanced at his face. What was it about this man that was so unsettling? "The truth is I need you. I have the knowledge to make this powder mill run, I just need someone who can see to the implementation."

He crossed his arms over his chest. "What do you mean, you've got the knowledge?"

She glanced at her dusty boots, uncomfortable with the way he continued to appraise her. The other workers didn't dare stare at her like this, like a man looked at a woman. It was as if the others saw her without a gender at all. They didn't treat her like a man, but they certainly didn't treat her like they did their wives and girlfriends either. Not even Jessop looked at her in the way this stranger was looking at her now, as though . . . she felt a heat rise in her cheeks . . . as though he were mentally unclothing her.

"I . . . I studied chemistry in England before I came to the Brandywine." She lifted her shoulders in a graceful shrug. "It always interested me. Odd for a woman I know, some say inappropriate, but a fact none-the-less."

O'Brian gave a sigh, looking away. "I need the job, but I've never worked for a woman."

"My gender should be of no interest to you, Mister O'Brian. This will be a simple business arrangement. You will do the job I lay out for you and in return I will pay you. Get my mill up and running, show me a profit, and I'll pay you handsomely."

Patrick tugged thoughtfully on his whiskers. This wasn't what he'd expected. Maybe he'd made a mistake. Michael hadn't told him his employer was to be a woman. Patrick almost smiled. So the joke was on him. Michael O'Brian had died on board the ship that would have taken him to the Colonies and to his new position as yard foreman in a black powder mill. Only Michael had died, and Patrick had taken his identity, and now it was Patrick stuck working for an uppity Englishwoman. He hadn't thought there would be any harm in him taking a dead man's job, but the idea was already backlashing.

Patrick knew he had the option of just walking away, but that really wasn't an option. He needed a decent job. He'd made a vow to change his life, and here on the Brandywine River seemed like as good a place as any to begin.

Patrick looked up at the Englishwoman with the silky dark hair and tongue that cut to the quick. A feisty little chit, she was. And clever. He had to give her that much. "Perhaps I could give it a try."

He almost heard an audible sigh from her. "Perhaps you could, Mister O'Brian."

"Then you and I have a bargain, Mistress E. Lawrence."

He offered her his hand to seal the agreement. "Might I ask what the E. stands for?"

"Elizabeth."

Her warm hand trembled slightly as they made physical contact.

O'Brian couldn't resist a grin. So she wasn't as cold as she let on after all. He'd always had a way with women. It was interesting to see that the rich ones were no different than the tarts. He let his hand linger over hers for just a second too long before he pulled it away.

Elizabeth cleared her throat, dropping her hand to the folds of her sturdy petticoat. "Let me take you to the house you'll be occupying." She started down the road, obviously expecting him to follow.

Patrick noted with interest that she walked without an entourage. Only a few barking hounds that had come down the hill accompanied her. So she was going to be a hands-on boss. That could be good or bad, depending on whether or not she was as knowledgeable with black powder as she claimed.

"I understand that once you're settled, you'll be sending for your wife and children. Isn't that correct?"

He only hesitated for a moment. "Yes. Yes, that's right." He walked beside her. "Once I'm sure I want to stay, that is."

She looked at him with a sideways glance. They were walking along the road that wound with the river. Granite stone buildings lined the bank. Workmen dotted the landscape.

"I see you've had an explosion recently."

"A year ago." She had lost the aggressive edge to her voice. "Almost to the day."

"How did it happen?"

She shook her head. "I don't know. I'd only been here a few weeks so I didn't know much, but I've talked to men up in the Jersies with their own mills, and from what I've learned it doesn't make any sense. The explosion took place at night. None of the mills were running. Had we been in full operation, I understand we could have lost everything."

Patrick nodded thoughtfully as he scanned the hilly forest that surrounded them. "You've plenty of granite for construction, that's good. I noticed you're rebuilding the magazine. How thick are the walls?"

"Three feet, and I've doubled that in the buildings where there are loose particles in the air."

He chuckled. "So you do know something of the business."

"Powder pressed in the kegs is not the real danger," she said as if she were a student reciting to her master. "It's when the ingredients are airborne that they're the most volatile."

They had turned and were climbing a hill. Ahead lay the workers' housing. He could hear the laughter of children and the hum of women talking as they went about their daily chores. "I'm impressed."

She looked at him again. "I told you I knew what I was doing."

He winked at her. "I know what you said, Mistress. I'm still impressed."

She scowled. "A business arrangement, sir. That's what we've agreed upon. You can keep your antics to yourself."

Patrick gave a nod, a smile playing on his lips. "The gentleman, is he your husband?"

"My husband is dead."

"The explosion?" He stopped.

She kept walking. "Yes. Look, O'Brian, I have a lot of work to attend to. Let me show you to the yard foreman's residence. Settle yourself in and then come up to the office next to the big house." She came to a halt outside the door of a small two-story stone and frame house. "We'll discuss your duties there."

He caught up to her. "I know my duties. I've been a yard foreman before."

She pushed open the front door and stepped aside. "Good. Then it won't take us long will it?"

Before Patrick could respond, Elizabeth had started down the hill again, her stride as long and determined as any man's.

He gave a low whistle. Sweet Mary, mother of Jesus. He'd put his life on the line for the *Cause* when he'd lit the fuse to the powder keg at Dublin Bridge, but something told him this fine-bred English beauty was going to be more dangerous than a hundred kegs of loose black powder in a summer thunderstorm.

About the Author

Colleen Faulkner lives with her family in southern Delaware. She is the author of over ten Zebra historical romances, including *Forever His, Flames of Love* and *Sweet Deception*. Colleen is currently working on her next Zebra historical romance, *O'Brian's Bride,* which will be published in April 1995. Colleen loves hearing from her readers and you may write to her c/o Zebra Books. Please include a self-addressed stamped envelope if you wish a response.

SURRENDER TO THE SPLENDOR OF THE ROMANCES OF F. ROSANNE BITTNER!

CARESS	(3791, $5.99/$6.99)
COMANCHE SUNSET	(3568, $4.99/$5.99)
HEARTS SURRENDER	(2945, $4.50/$5.50)
LAWLESS LOVE	(3877, $4.50/$5.50)
PRAIRIE EMBRACE	(3160, $4.50/$5.50)
RAPTURE'S GOLD	(3879, $4.50/$5.50)
SHAMELESS	(4056, $5.99/$6.99)

WHAT'S LOVE GOT TO DO WITH IT?

Everything . . . Just ask Kathleen Drymon . . . and Zebra Books

CASTAWAY ANGEL	*(3569-1, $4.50/$5.50)*
GENTLE SAVAGE	*(3888-7, $4.50/$5.50)*
MIDNIGHT BRIDE	*(3265-X, $4.50/$5.50)*
VELVET SAVAGE	*(3886-0, $4.50/$5.50)*
TEXAS BLOSSOM	*(3887-9, $4.50/$5.50)*
WARRIOR OF THE SUN	*(3924-7, $4.99/$5.99)*